The Wildcatter

The Wildcatter

DESMOND MEIRING

Secker & Warburg
London

First published in England 1987 by
Martin Secker & Warburg Ltd
54 Poland Street, London W1V 3DF

British Library Cataloguing in Publication Data
Meiring, Desmond
    The wildcatter.
    I. Title
    823'.914 [F]   PR9381.9.M44

ISBN 0-436-27701-8

Photoset in 11/12pt Linotron Sabon by Deltatype, Ellesmere Port
Printed by St Edmundsbury Press
Bury St Edmunds, Suffolk

Contents

PART ONE

1. Wildcats, Wadham, and a Birth of Hatred 1
2. The Shattering of the Line 7
3. Viennese Waltzes 12
4. Dior for Breakfast 20
5. Spudding in a Wildcat 25
6. Leila 38
7. The Judgement of the Board 52
8. Marital Bliss 59
9. A Mark of Cain 68
10. The Kingdom of the Sun 70
11. A Desert Xanadu 81
12. A Night View of the Ships 92

PART TWO

13. Death in the Afternoon 101
14. The View from the Top 118
15. The Ice Maiden Cometh 127
16. An Act of God 135
17. Diary with Sharp Metal Edges 148
18. A House in Millionaires' Row 150
19. A Taste of Victory 155
20. A Fall, and a Breaking on the Rack 167

PART THREE

21. Rebirth to a New Religion 185
22. A Vengeance 202
23. A House on Hydra 206

PART FOUR

24. Reflections of a Southern Baptist   223
25. Pride, and a Fatal Fall   236
26. The Man Who Stood up for His Death   246
27. The Long Arm of Mossad   251
28. A School for Death   274
29. Bombs for Khadaffi   295
30. A Fragile Last Stand   313

PART FIVE

31. The strike from the Sky   319
32. Capping a Gusher   331
33. A Return to Eden   339
34. The Cutting Edge of the Sword   342
35. Other Bolts from the Blue   348
36. Danse Macabre on Dizengoff Street   355

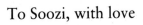

To Soozi, with love

PART ONE

I

Wildcats, Wadham, and a Birth of Hatred

'Anyone would think,' said the Ice Maiden in his chintzy voice with the bitchy steel-tipped curl to it, 'that you were working for the Arabs!'

Kobus van Straten, Chairman of the Board of Eagle Oil International, was the Ice Maiden because he looked like one. He was a slight immaculate man, physically hard as teak, his full silver hair perfectly in place and vertical ridges of muscle bracketing his mouth, puritanical, admitting no margins of error. Kobus was short for Jacobus. His Flemish clan had come to England in the seventeenth century and he now seemed more English than the English, Eton and the Guards, his tone often, as now, arrogant and supercilious. He also had a trick of stillness that could devastate.

'No, for Eagle,' said Philip Blake carefully. 'Sir. But I think that the Arabs may have a case. We, the world, may have underpriced their oil too far for too long. So we might be wise, sir, to bend a little to their demands.'

'*Might?*' mocked the Ice Maiden silkily. 'You're not sure of your facts?'

'Of my calculations, yes,' said Blake. 'Sir. Would you care to look at them?'

'Thank you,' said Kobus van Straten. 'After thirty years in the business, I think I know my oil economics.'

Blake raised his eyebrows slightly, to just this side of outright rudeness. Morgan Sperry, sitting right next to him, saw that clearly. Sperry was a tall and elegantly dressed Virginian of fifty, clean-featured and high-browed, with a full head of iron-grey curls. He was an astute and innately courteous man, with plenty of steel where it was needed. As Blake's sponsor, having experienced it himself, he knew that

Blake never took authority for granted. Blake intrigued Sperry, who saw him as a natural wildcatter. That oil industry beast was the exploration field chief who, whatever the seismic and geological surveys stated, said No, instead we'll drill *here* – and was gloriously right; a magic intuition like a water-diviner's. Blake had something of that, Sperry knew, in his mathematical flair, his near-genius for scanning the thousands of statistics in a trade report and picking out the single fatal error. Sperry had quite often seen him do that with events and men too, though certainly not infallibly. But Blake always worked very conscientiously at it. He had a formidable sense of duty about getting things right. It was as if the world out there was intrinsically due that, at almost any cost, to himself or others. To that extent Blake was not excessively ambitious for himself. That claim simply made him anxious, laid an obligation on him.

As an American, Sperry found Philip Blake very English. The Protestant Ethic could have been written for him. No one ever called him Phil. His father was a Sussex rector from the impoverished English middle class. Blake had fought his way up through Cheltenham and Wadham College Oxford into Eagle International. He seemed from his youth to have seen oil as a natural route to power, a way to apply his considerable energies to helping bring order and progress to a receptive world. Why Eagle? Because, so Blake had once told Sperry over a drink, one Christmas an uncle had given him a rare expensive present – a toy service-station. A toy car set next to its pumps lit their globes up enticingly. The globes said 'Eagle'. On such frivolities do human destinies turn. Blake had evidently sought to improve his by adding a fiancée, miniature-Junoesque, emerald-eyed. Her name was Celia. Sperry knew about her through her father, who was an earl and a major Eagle shareholder. Blake would use Old Boy networks when he could.

In build, Blake was big, blond, blue-eyed, but a silent mover, deceptively bland. Happily, a mordant and irreverent wit masked the true intensity of his drives and passions most of the time. This flippant yet biting black humour was excellent disguise, so effective that it probably hid even from Blake himself, thought Sperry, what he sometimes sensed as some kind of tragic flaw at Blake's dead centre, a tiny racing flywheel, utterly silent, ominously and tenaciously and un-changeably fixated. It was as if Blake were some marvellously sophisticated device of steel and rocket power and electronics which, destined to explore the fabulous infinities of outer space for thousands of years, contained among its many millions of chips just one which *might* conceivably fail. If it did the fall would be cataclysmic, a long chaotic flash across the universe at meteoric murderous speed. Blake showed a flash of that lambent wit now. He seemed to have given his Chair-man's comment due consideration before he replied:

'We may find that a few Arabs know their oil economics pretty well these days too. Sir.'

Van Straten fixed him with his chill grey eye. The Ice Maiden had flicked into his stance of total stillness, so deadly that it was deafening. The other four Managing Directors, including Morgan Sperry, let out their breath slowly, sitting too at the oval table in the opulent Board Room at Eagle's Central Offices at Millbank, overlooking the Thames. Eagle was an independent oil multinational not quite in the Seven Sisters' league. It sold a million barrels of refined products a day in most free-world countries. What it lacked in stature it made up for in sheer ruthless thrust, under the inflexible iron-grey Van Straten.

'Mr Blake,' he said exquisitely, 'this entire question has been discussed and decided at a level, ah, rather above your head. The London Policy Group, led by George Piercy of Exxon and André Bénard of Shell, representing *all* oil companies, will not allow more *and that only as an absolutely last resort*, than a twenty-five per cent rise in crude oil postings to your OPEC Arab, ah, *bosom friends* in Vienna.'

Blake was gently stroking his upper lip with the thumb and index finger of his left hand, from under his nose down and outwards, again and again, a habit of his when really maddened. Morgan Sperry recognized that. Showing great natural voice control, still gazing respectfully at the Ice Maiden, and not moving a muscle of his lips, he said successfully and very quietly out of the corner of his mouth:

'Cool it Philip. Remember the Alamo.'

And Blake grinned marginally to himself, then half-glanced at Sperry in thanks. That light humorous touch had averted a really ugly scene in which he could only lose; he could be nowhere near a match for the Ice Maiden. Not yet. For he had made a stunning discovery. Although this was the first time that he had met the great man in person, neither could doubt that the lines of a mortal struggle had at once been drawn most clearly, etched in bronze. The hatred that had flashed between them was instinctive, total and permanent; chemical, a question of the skin. It was the murderous antipathy between the net hard-won product of his own skills, the intuitive wildcatter, and the orthodox aristocrat and born leader, supremely assured of his own eminence, infallibly consistent as a walking computer, if a little short on human warmth and humour.

For what place Blake had was indeed hard-won. At thirty-six, as Area Co-ordinator, he was assistant to Morgan Sperry, who was Eagle's MD for the Middle East. This Eagle Board Meeting at the start of October 1973 prefaced the OPEC negotiations on crude oil prices which the two were about to attend in Vienna and which were to shake the Western world. You could not lightly touch petroleum, that magic dirty black gold that provided more than half the world's total energy, that many-faceted mineral that served man all the way from jet fuels to petro-chemicals. The world's economy and much of its politics spun on it.

But Blake, glancing round this table, doubted that the men around it had the sense of any such impending catastrophe, except perhaps for Sperry. Edward Poynter, Eagle's MD for Africa, weighed in now, playing follow-my-leader. Poynter was tall and slim with his thick black hair and temples dusted with silver, his cheekbones high and prominent, his lips wide and thin. His black eyes, brisk with malice, and light olive skin came from Armenian ancestors. He looked glossily intelligent and handsome, and sincere as a snake.

'Damned greedy, these Arabs, if you ask me,' he said virtuously. 'Why, even that ceiling seventy-five cents we might give on top of the present three dollars a barrel works out on the free world's fifty million barrels a day oil offtake at thirty eight million dollars more *a day* for the producers! For almost nil production costs! And for doing nothing *extra*! I'd call it sheer ingratitude!'

'I'd go along with that,' said George Paul, MD for Eagle Europe and the UK. 'Pity we ever let them form OPEC. They want something for nothing. It's not as if they have to transport, refine and market the stuff like us!'

But then, Blake felt, George Paul would go along with almost anything the Boss wanted. That explained his progress. Paul was of Blake's height, six foot one, and as strongly built. He had thick reddish hair, very regularly waved; he probably slept with it netted. His very light grey eyes were set close together under a high brow, and his wide lips so thin they were almost invisible. His beaked nose was hatchet-like – aptly so. The Ice Maiden had often set Paul to trim staff numbers, and no one had ever lopped them off with more zeal. The casualties best remembered his smile. Most Eagle men could wield the knife when they had to, but generally deadpan. To smile disarmingly the while was mastery indeed. His small paunch, which he often stroked contentedly, protruded subtly, secure in its superb tailoring. His hands were steepled now under his chin. They were surprisingly long and slim, but with heavy short red hair on the backs. Blake focused on the fingernails; with no trace of dried blood under them, they were as polished as Paul himself.

'Any comments, Sean?' said the Ice Maiden to the last MD at the table. Sean O'Higgins, Eagle's MD for the Americas, was a hoary, oak-like character, the oldest man in the room. He was a renegade Irish Catholic, an old China hand whom the Japanese had taken prisoner as a volunteer Other Ranker in Singapore. He had huge bushy eyebrows, peppered with silver. They were like monstrously overgrown mountain ledges hanging over a heavily seamed cliff. Sean O'Higgins had learnt a hard wisdom in his years on the Thai Railway and in Japanese POW camps. Blake loved him for his humanity. O'Higgins turned his deeply lined face on Van Straten now and opened the palms of his big broad hands towards him.

'Doesn't the assessment of this problem lie most immediately in Morgan Sperry's province? I've every respect for Morgan's professionalism –' O'Higgins glanced a moment at Blake. 'And his team's.'

There was a pregnant silence. In it the other three MDs picked O'Higgins' statement up and looked it over for laughs. They found none. It was not going to advance O'Higgins much in the Ice Maiden's favour either. Van Straten had adopted his indictment posture again. He looked frozen absolutely

5

motionless with anger. This evidently concerned O'Higgins not a jot. He had gone quite as far as he wanted to in his professional life in Eagle, and was profoundly grateful for that. He had seen too many men killed by malnutrition, exhaustion, cruelty and executions to have much time now for merely amateur assassins.

'Let's not build this up into histrionics, now,' said the amateur assassin. 'Anyway, Morgan, as you know, you have really only to observe and report back. It's Piercy of Exxon and Bénard of Shell who'll spearhead the negotiations for all of us.'

'Sure, Kobus,' said Morgan Sperry soothingly. 'We'll do just that.'

'And, after all, they're really only an anarchic bunch of *Levantines*. Semites. We should find it a pushover.'

Yes, but for whom? thought Blake. It may well be the Levantines who are going to slaughter *us*! His researches and his wildcatter's instincts told him in unison that this was how the cards were really stacked. The Western world's oil companies, Eagle, he, were not going to get things right this time. The world had laid a huge obligation on them all, but they were about to get their sums all wrong, and they would bear a heavy guilt for doing so. That seemed true above all for this Eagle Board Meeting. Blake was stroking his upper lip ceaselessly now. Before coming to this opulent oval table he had never expected such crass hostility, such demotion of a grave world problem to brute personal hatreds.

'Well, that's it then, I take it, gentlemen,' said Morgan Sperry, rising to his elegantly dressed height. As Blake limped with him to the door, the Ice Maiden's voice reached out after and curled round them like a whip; imperious, disdainful.

'Remember, Mr Blake, easy on the melodrama now. This isn't just a cheap soap-opera, you know.'

Blake heard Poynter and Paul laugh dutifully behind him.

He spun his head a second and found Van Straten's implacable gaze locked onto him like the twin black eyes of a double-barrelled shotgun.

'Cheap is the very last word I had in mind. Sir,' said Blake.

Some two thousand miles away, another war to the death was starting.

2

The Shattering of the Line

Lieutenant Saad Muhammed felt the fear at his throat. He lay flat on his stomach in his slit-trench, in his commando camouflaged smock and pants and supple parachutist boots, the paratrooper's winged badge proud on his chest. Through his periscope he could see straight across the Suez Canal to the seventeen-metre ramp built along its east bank. Behind it lay the Israelis' Bar Lev Line, heavily fortified and armed, reputedly impregnable.

Well, thought Saad, that remained to be seen. At least one terrifying defence of the Bar Lev Line was already muzzled. At the dead of the night before, tiny parties of Egyptian commandos had gone across in their small rubber boats. Saad Muhammed recalled the utter silence, the terror of breaking it. Even the fragile diamond-prick of the drops from the tip of your lifted paddle upon the sheer mirror-surface of the water sounded each time like a shrieking blasphemy. The commandos had found and securely blocked off the metal pipes that led from the Bar Lev Line to the edge of the canal. They came from huge reservoirs filled with kerosene, probably heavily spiked with gasoline to make it more volatile. At an Arab attack, the Israelis would swiftly pump this lethal fluid onto the canal's surface to flood it, then ignite it to fry the enemy alive.

The Egyptian commandos had known just where to look. Six years before, in the 1967 Six Days War, the Israelis had annihilated the Egyptian, Syrian and Jordanian armed forces, Israeli aircraft wiping out ninety per cent of the Egyptian air force on the ground in the war's first hour. The Egyptian army had footslogged six days back across the desert, under constant air strikes and shelling, the route back marked by their own discarded arms, equipment and boots. The Russians found their clients so pulverized that they afterwards rebuilt their armed forces from top to bottom. They did a particularly thorough job on Egyptian Intelligence, retraining it, and outfitting it with the most advanced intelligence aids, including very powerful listening devices. This reborn Egyptian Intelligence Service achieved several coups. It actually got hold of a copy of Israel's top-secret plan for the defence of the Suez Canal, which included the layout of the kerosene reservoirs and network of pipes to the canal. The revitalized Egyptian Intelligence also got and decoded the Israeli master plan of all place names on their side. Thus Arab attackers in the field, listening in to Israeli fighting commands on the radio, could know exactly and at once what the enemy was doing where, and outwit him. Every Egyptian commander had a map with these coded place names deciphered on it, and their Arabic equivalents. Saad Muhammed had one in his right breast pocket.

Saad Muhammed was well equipped with motivation too. He was twenty-five years old, powerfully built, with black hair and eyes and a heavy black moustache, lush symbol and banner of his manhood, set in an olive skin. Nasser's and Sadat's Egypt had given him everything he had. Originally he was nothing, another mouth among twelve brothers and sisters, his parents *fellahin* in a poor village near Minya, 250 kilometres south of Cairo. So constant was the hunger there that the fact that he reached such a size full-grown seemed a miracle. He was a sincere and pious child, scrupulously attending the village's *kuttab*, religious school, learning the Koran with such verve and accuracy that his father did not have the heart to force him to work in the fields full-time, but allowed him some hours daily to study. While always working hard manually in the village, he progressed through its primary school, then through the secondary school in Minya, from which he graduated with the startling mark of 95%. Here Nasser helped him. After Nasser's 1952 Revolution, he opened Egypt's universities to all, making entry by fair competitive examination, no longer just through social privilege or wealth. Saad Muhammed took Engineering at Cairo University and qualified brilliantly. Then came military service. For the last two years he had trained as a commando.

This time round Sadat was planning his war, the Yom Kippur or 6th of October War, very carefully indeed, using the best men and arms he could, the most meticulous training. And the most brilliantly planned surprise. Saad Muhammed, lying there with his adrenalin pumping, had no shadow of regret or doubt. He knew what the *Shari'a*, the Islamic Law, said about Arab land: if land was stolen from Muslims, and they could get it back but did not, then all were evil. Israel had taken the West Bank and Gaza Strip in 1967. They were undeniably Arab lands. Egypt had the strongest Arab army in the Middle East, with Syria next. They, and a cluster of other Arab nations, must by law try to get back those enemy-occupied lands. At any cost, even that of death, as the Koran decreed.

Saad, like many other young Arabs, felt Israel's repeated military victories over them from 1948 on as a deep humiliation, an unpardonable slight to Arab pride. Sooner or later they would take their revenge. And the Israelis had committed particular insults. Saad had lost one elder brother killed in the barefoot Arab retreat of the Six Days War. Another was captured. He told Saad afterwards that he and other Arab prisoners had been forced to lie face-down in the desert sand under the burning sun and stay there, under the guns of Israeli women soldiers. That was literally dragging Arab male pride in the dirt. *Women* soldiers!

The mere recollection of this sacrilege so enraged Saad Muhammed that he clenched his fists in his slit trench and hardly heard the first wave of Hosni Mubárak's 222 jet attack aircraft, Mirages and MIG 21s, blasting in over his head and deadly low at the Bar Lev Line in front, a murderously effective low-level air strike lasting twenty minutes. He knew that it was now exactly two in the afternoon, the moment the fierce sun would be full in the eyes of the Bar Lev defenders, to blind them. Sadat had not missed that small trick either.

Now, checking with his watch at five past two, Saad Muhammed heard the barrage start from behind him, right on time, from 4,000 guns, mortars, and rocket-launchers; they had told him it would be the heaviest since the British Eighth Army barrage at El Alamein. It and the air strike were to punch enough holes in the Bar Lev Line to let the Egyptian shock troops through. Could they do that?

Saad Muhammed was going to find out.

'*Ta'ali*! Come on, men! We go, *now*!'

9

He dropped with his seven men and their rubber boat, down the long steep sand ramp on their side to the flat edge and the water. They went in very smoothly; their many months of team training were paying off. The noise was fiendish, from the first strike aircraft coming back low, from their own massive barrage on the Bar Lev Line. The Israelis were not sending much back; this attack, on a *Shabat* and the holiest day in their year, had caught them with their pants right down. Saad saw one rubber boat take a direct hit, torsos and torn limbs spinning high apart, but the whole canal seemed crammed and dominated by the hundreds of Egyptian small rubber boats pulling vigorously for the eastern bank, flocks of multi-limbed Michelin men pumping across a wide avenue. What could stop that now?

The shock troops hit the other side, some eight thousand of them, and charged up the seventeen-metre sand ramp. Saad heard the cries all about him: *Allahu Akbar! Allahu Akbar!* God is most great! God is most great! He shouted too; he also was a good Muslim, and God was indeed proving himself Most Great now, his Egyptian disciples victorious at long last. Saad knew that Sadat's *fellah* cunning was helping: that cruelly clogging seventeen-metre soft sand ramp up which they now struggled, for example, would within minutes be cut clean away by high-pressure hoses driven by the very high-powered West German waterpumps that the Egyptians, at Sadat's instigation, had been buying very quietly for years. That would leave naked flat ground. Right behind this stunning shock-troop landing, the Egyptian Engineers would be slinging Russian assault bridges across the canal, and the high-pressure hoses would go into action, quickly to let through Sadat's 1,500 attack tanks and five army divisions and heavy equipment. Saad Muhammed, well briefed, knew too that this was not the only skilled steel thrust at Israel's heart. Simultaneously, Syria would have attacked her north-eastern border at the Golan Heights, with probably equally murderous surprise, and most of the 2,600 tanks she had available. Syria's battle strategy was the mailed fist; an air strike, then a sledgehammer armoured blow launched in depth on a very narrow front. That drive could carry the Arabs that night right through to overhang Lake Tiberias, the Sea of

Galilee and Mishmar Hayarden, poised like a razor-sharp steel scythe at the throat of Israel.

His heart and lungs hammering, Saad Muhammed looked down from the top of the ramp. Ahead was a riot of shattered concrete and snarled twisted metal. One Bar Lev gunbarrel drooped out and down like a failed erection. Saad beckoned to his men and began to run forward. His orders were to do that with his team for four kilometres then to wait in ambush for the Israeli armoured counter-attack that must come. There were still pockets of resistance left in the Bar Lev Line, the flickering jagged white tongues of machinegun and sub-machinegun fire from the black concrete slits pointing at them, eerily soundless under the pandemonium. Saad Muhammed saw two of his men drop. Anguished he still did not stop to help them; his strict orders were to keep going at all costs. At last, he and his remaining men dropped sweating into their positions.

Clouds of sand ahead showed where the enemy armoured thrust was already building up. The Egyptian commandos had a warm welcome waiting for it. This was their Russian-built Sagger anti-tank missiles, fired from the shoulder. They were mobile and lethal.

At the right moment, Saad Muhammed got up and fired his Sagger. He stood steady then, and vulnerable, to wire-guide its flight like a skilled kite-flyer. The first Centurion jerked and blazed and brewed and he saw the bodies cartwheel in the old broken-doll-like gesticulations of agony out of it, their uniforms and flesh burning. Saad Muhammed ducked and reloaded with calm confidence, as he had been trained.

The main gunner in the second Centurion was Yaacov Yaariv. He was twenty-three, a Sabra born in Mishmar Haemek, his parents Polish immigrants, one of whom had survived the Warsaw Ghetto. Just like Saad, Yaariv had a stake in protecting what he saw as his land to the death. He watched his leading tank and its crew die in flames, and he identified their executioner. As that man stood again to fire, Yaariv stitched him neatly across the chest with his machine-gun, exactly on a level with the metal parachutist badge he could just make out glinting in the sun.

3
Viennese Waltzes

'The Arabs have burst clean through the Bar Lev Line,' said Philip Blake next evening in Vienna, 'and deeply penetrated Israel's Golan Heights defences in the north. So Arabs everywhere are jubilant, the world's new overlords. Yet London insists we mustn't let them shift us an inch. Won't that call for some very fancy footwork? Sir?'

He sat with Morgan Sperry in the Yellow Suite of the Imperial Hotel, opposite Vienna's magnificent Opera. Sperry had just introduced him in the lobby to Piercy of Exxon and Bénard of Shell, who led the five-man team from the London Policy Group of twenty-three main world oil companies, dutifully blessed by the anti-trust authorities. The team would start negotiating next morning in OPEC's offices in their bleak modern block with its tomblike entrance. That might be grimly apt, thought Blake.

'We really ought to have the skill to do that,' said Sperry. 'After all, we've the world's most powerful oil companies in the Group, from London, New York, Houston, San Francisco, Pittsburg, Paris, Rome, Hamburg, Brussels, Tokyo.'

'Our line's not really already broken too?' Blake suggested.

Sperry eyed him indulgently. Sperry sat with his Campari-soda in his right hand, his long slim frame moulded gracefully to the deep armchair, automatically getting the best out of it. Sperry did that with people too. He was a very good man-manager. His high brow and rather long hair painted an easygoing academic with a wry wit. But Blake never forgot the steel there.

'How so?' asked Sperry.

'Hasn't it been, really, ever since Colonel Muammar Khadaffi and his passionate young army officer puritans bust King Idris's rule in Libya four years ago, with their Islamic Fundamentalist objectives – social justice, honest public service, the use of oil as a weapon against Israel?'

'Because we were caught on the side of reaction, the Establishment?' said Sperry. 'Yes, I suppose we do tend to have that habit. And Khadaffi used his oil weapon against us too. Against the – what was it? – twenty-odd Western companies drilling there; a twenty per cent jump in the crude oil price of around two dollars a barrel, or I sell to the Russians. Blasphemy. Khadaffi picks on two: Exxon and Armand Hammer's Occidental: forty cents up at once, gents. Or else.'

'That was it, sir,' said Blake. 'So they scream, Oxy particularly. Khadaffi's cunning. He leaves Exxon – they've got alternative crudes all over the world – and really leans on Oxy, whose 700,000 barrels a day Libyan is the only crude they have, their life's blood.'

'I've always envied Hammer that crude,' said Sperry. 'We've always been so goddam crude-starved in Eagle. Having to constantly buy it in has always hurt.'

'Khadaffi was certainly hurting Hammer too,' said Blake. 'Mid 1970 he forces him to shut in 180,000 bd. Hammer flies to New York. Can Exxon help? Well, yes. At the full standard crude price to third parties. Hammer can't breathe on that. So in September he makes a deal with Khadaffi: thirty cents up now, ten cents more over five years, and Libya's tax take of Oxy's profit up at once from fifty to fifty-eight per cent: sacrilege, till then the worldwide holy principle has been government tax take never more than fifty per cent. Then Khadaffi forces a like deal on Oasis. A shareholder – Shell – rejects it. So Khadaffi at once shuts in Shell's 150,000 bd share. Shell's Chairman, Sir David Barran, flies with BP's to Washington. They sit at the State Department with the heads of the five US Sisters – Exxon, Mobil, Texaco, Gulf and Socal. Barran says the same thing London says today: hold the line at all costs, don't give in.

'Within weeks Socal and Texaco do just that. Then all accept Khadaffi's prices and conditions. So domino: Iraq, Iran, Kuwait, Algeria decree a fifty-five per cent tax take at once. In December OPEC makes it general. Domino again: Libya asks another fifty cents, retroactively, plus twenty-five cents for a fancy new tax. Now the rout's really set in.'

'For someone who's only been in his job three months,' said Sperry, 'you sure as hell seem to have done your homework, I have to give you that. But I know all this dismal goddam story. So where are you taking us with it?'

'Before I answer that, sir, could I as a newcomer make a last point? *Why* did it take us so long to talk safety-nets? Hammer talked to Barran end 1970, very cooperative. But *after* the avalanche. You know, the Seven Sisters and Independents all guarantee that if OPEC cuts anyone's crude because he stands firmly against them, the rest provide him pro-rata with what he's lost?'

'I know,' said Sperry curtly. '*Do* help yourself to another Scotch.'

Blake got up from his sofa and walked to the sideboard and poured himself another, stiff, whisky and soda. He was intensely conscious of his limp, the deep throbbing pain in his left knee. It was like the beat of an abscessed tooth, very heavy when the going got rough.

Blake had always had an almost mystic reverence for physical fitness. He had accepted the Cheltenham conventions of his day which saw academic brilliance as somewhat suspect, and made sure that he always came a tolerable fourth or fifth in his class, not the higher places he could have reached. Only that mathematical flair was undisguisable. He had shown himself uninhibitedly in sport, where excellence was socially permitted, gaining his school colours in boxing and rowing. He was a university boxer and rugger Harlequin; a big man very light on his feet. When he shattered his left leg with the Oxford and Cambridge Ski Club in his last winter term, it was as if his God had touched him, saying, see what a fine deformity I've set upon you. Overcoming it, with your talents, and indelible memories of the hunger and poverty in that seedy Sussex rectory, can only project you into gloriously scaling my highest peak, or else all the way down into my colleague's most scalding cauldrons. You will anyway avoid the cotton-wool of anonymity.

Morgan Sperry stared at Blake's broad back as he poured his large whisky and soda. What an intense man this is, thought Sperry. He noticed how he himself had omitted the adjective *young*; automatically, though Blake must, he knew, be only thirty-six or so. Yet it was already hard to see Blake as young. He might have been a man without a past. Obviously, he was deeply concerned, and knowledgeable, about the world oil crisis. But the significant thing was that all his energy seemed *there*, locked into the present and the future. In this, fairly passionate, exchange of ideas, Blake had said not one word about himself. Did he *have* a part? Had he actually *existed* in that key decade of the Sixties? Of course Sperry knew where Blake had been and what Eagle jobs he had done, in Africa and the Far East and Latin America; Eagle's Personnel files containing their annual performance reports were thorough and perceptive. But where many young men and women of Blake's generation had been mesmerized by the Sixties, Blake seemed hardly to have noticed them. He had kept his eyes hard down and looking, on the job all the time. Perhaps that was the secret of his professional success. And what of his *personal* past? Sperry knew no more of that than he had learned when he had had Blake to drinks and dinner that one evening in Sperry's Mayfair flat, a few details about Blake's father, the toy globe-lit service station that had directed Blake uncannily to Eagle. But nothing more about his mother, for example, than that she had died in 1943 as a volunteer nurse in the bombing of London, while he was a six-year-old evacuee with an aunt in Shrewsbury. Blake had put no flesh on these bare facts, no emotion. He was single-mindedly conserving his big guns for his future career, for the epic OPEC–West battle about to be joined, and talking about that, precociously, with all the authority of a Managing Director.

Blake walked back from the sideboard with his whisky and sat.

'That magic benefit of hindsight,' said Sperry. 'We're not all God, you know.'

He can only shoot me, thought Blake.

'Where I'm going, sir,' he said, 'is that perhaps the Arabs and OPEC have been shattering our lines consistently all through the last four years. They've had luck, the time's on their side. The thirty cents Tehran Agreement increase in January 1971 and the Libyan posting and premiums increase of ninety-one cents in April 1972 were within a growing world obsession about a looming oil shortage. Then our OPEC friends try a new one. By what divine right do foreign oil companies own mineral rights in our sovereign lands? These are *our* assets, *our* lands. Isn't that what sovereignty's about? We're independent nations now. And how,' asked Blake, 'have we taken that?'

It was the first time that he had dared open his mind this fully to Sperry. He knew that he had given him little in the dinner Sperry had kindly invited him to. But now the inevitability of the whole historical process they were discussing, and Sperry's evident concentration on it, exhilarated him.

After about ten seconds Sperry smiled.

'How have we taken those new winds of change?' he answered. 'Well, we've bent with them. For the last two and a half years. Since Algeria nationalized fifty-one per cent of French oil in 1971, and Libya all of BP's. Since Iraq nationalized the Consortium last year, hitting all the Seven Sisters and France's CFP, and Yamani got his Agreement in New York to pass twenty-five per cent of all concessions to the five Gulf States' governments now, and fifty-one per cent by 1983. Since Khadaffi nationalized fifty-one per cent of every oil company operating in Libya only last month, including Exxon, Shell, Texaco, Mobil and Socal. And announced he would put Libyan crude up to six dollars, and cut all exports to the US if she went on supporting Israel. So you may have a point, Philip Blake. The winds of change.'

'Hurricanes of change,' said Blake, staring deep into his whisky. It was his third, and he was feeling it. 'So these next weeks could set the shape of the world for the next decade or two.'

'And Eagle's,' said Sperry.

'It's odd how one sees it all from Eagle's viewpoint. Not Britain's, for me, or much less. Perhaps not America's for you?'

Sperry glanced at him.

'It's logical enough, really. Note that it's *we* who're here today, the multinational oil companies, and *not* our governments, to negotiate with the oil-producing *governments* about this absolutely cataclysmic world-scale problem. We, not our governments, shall make history here. Perhaps that's right too; we're much greater than most governments, in our cash turnover and power. We cut right through national barriers. Our loyalties aren't just to a single government, but to Eagle. An Eagle man is that till he dies. In a world often without gods, it gives immense purpose. It's an identity, a life-style. When you're handling the power that drives the Western world, you know that what you're doing really matters. How many people have such a privilege, such a certainty?'

'It can certainly seize your loyalties, and hold them,' said Blake. 'I know now how medieval craftsmen must have felt about their guilds.'

'Medieval guilds,' said Sperry. 'That's good. So what happens next?'

Blake laughed. 'I've risked enough, sir. Last time I talked too much the guildmaster chopped me down to size.'

Sperry glanced at him and smiled.

'Oh, Kobus van Straten? Well, you had your say. Why not?'

'He didn't like it.'

'No. Look, something happens to most people when they become MDs, you know. The power really does go to their heads. They often stop laughing. They deify themselves, disappear assumed upwards into the godhead, abstracting themselves from mere mortality. It's a generic change, irreversible. Like going bald.'

'But it didn't happen to you?'

Sperry smiled and drank the last of his Campari-soda.

'I did a lot of amateur dramatics when I was growing up,' he said. 'It gave me an ear for the absurd.'

'But he'll be there in power for many years yet?'

'Kobus?' Sperry pondered. 'What's he now? Forty-eight? fifty? Short of raping the Archbishop of Canterbury in public he'll hold on for ten or twelve years yet. Yes, I'm afraid you've a problem there, my friend.'

Blake said nothing. So for ten or twelve years that steel-grey ice-cold man would be watching there to murder him.

'Trouble about gods,' Sperry went on, 'and notably Old Testament ones, is that they have whims. They can make or shiver universes on them. You can't ask them why. It's considered bad form. They're inscrutable and they don't change. So watch your back.'

Blake sighed. 'How do *you* see it here, sir?'

'What we have, explosively, in our hands here in Vienna?' Sperry frowned and got up and crossed to his sideboard and gave himself another Campari-soda and added ice. He returned and sank back into his armchair's embrace.

'I'd make five points,' he said. 'First, that trend for the Arabs and other producing countries to becoming fifty-one per cent *owners* of their crude oil is irreversible. As irreversible as our MD's delusions of divinity. That must change the oil business's whole centre of gravity. It shifts to who has best *access* to the crude by long-term contracts with its Arab owners. Against a giant world demand, that's going to put a heavy premium on any sound crude supply contract: a reliable source will be worth its weight in gold. Second, there's an interesting consequence for Eagle, *precisely because we've always been crude-starved*, owning very little, and having to buy in almost everthing. Ironically, we should come out of this whole maelstrom much better than an Exxon, always very long in owning their own crudes. They lose what we never had. While crude nationalizations hit Exxon every which way, we come out smiling, neatly equipped and trained for the new situation.

'Third, it's almost impossible to overstress the really critical world importance of oil today. That adds a dimension of extreme tension to these negotiations. We've rebuilt the whole war-shattered world on oil. Coal met just over half of the US's fuel needs in 1951, the world's biggest economy. The figure's round one fifth this year. What replaced coal? Oil. And that economy's dependence on imported oil is increasing rapidly. The US's oil production *declined* from 1970, when she already imported twenty-eight per cent of her needs. She's acutely vulnerable. So God knows is Europe. And April's *Foreign Affairs* tells us that world oil consumption in the next twelve years will be greater than *total world oil consumption through history to date*. Fourth, the emotional impact of this murderous new Arab-Israeli war can only aggravate the Arabs' already powerful anti-Western drive. I was in the Hotel Intercontinental on Johannesgasse this afternoon where Zaki Yamani's staying, to catch a glimpse of the Saudi mastermind, the OPEC leader; he was as usual dapper-bearded, crisp-eyed, elegant, smiling. Not so his fellow-Arabs. Most pored over newspapers headlining America's generous air-bridge aid to Israel. Their resentment was very ugly – and perhaps prophetic: you could sense that they just might blow up the whole world one day, through their fanatic obsession to annihilate Israel.'

Blake watched Sperry in full flood. This was good hard-etched realistic thinking. He followed Sperry, though perhaps more ruthlessly. For there was still a touch of the academic's pure fascination with the precision of his analysis in Sperry, rather than the power player icily weighing the odds. But perhaps Sperry himself felt that the pair of them were near enough together for that to be why he backed Blake consistently against the Ice Maiden. Sperry had a weakness for intellectual honesty, even when it hurt.

'Fifthly, what does it all add up to? Immediately, the Arabs are going to ask for a very high price increase. Why should this internationally publicized OPEC meeting, led by their best, Yamani and Amouzegar of Iran, settle for anything less than what that gaudy wild man Khadaffi has just decreed noisily – to double the Gulf posting to six dollars a barrel and cut all oil exports to the US if she won't stop aiding Israel? Would they *dare* ask less? These weeks we're going to see the Arabs really learn to use their oil weapon effectively at last. If *we* oil companies once made up an oligopoly, we're going to have two now. I hope the world can take it.'

So did Philip Blake, as he got up to go down to dinner with Morgan Sperry. Well, he thought, at least it wouldn't be dull. He had no shortage of enemies: the Arab adversary out there, and the Old Testament Ice Maiden enemy at home. But Van Straten, certainly, was the Arabs' enemy too. First, the fastidious would-be English aristocrat in Van Straten would tend to see most Arabs anyway as a dirty and chaotic rabble of thieving illiterates. Second, there was that famous story of his civil aircraft forced-landing in the Western Desert in World War Two. The Bedu had accurately selected him as the most entertaining and richest of their hostages, and subjected him to much mockery and some mild torture in front of his companions before they traded the lot in for huge ransoms. Van Straten had never forgotten that.

So perhaps he, Blake, could make some deal with the Arabs. It would be amusing to try, and it might work. After all, the Arabs had that practical proverb: The enemy of my enemy is my friend. And Blake was not just going to stay passive with the huge steel-grey shape of the Ice Maiden looming always there up behind him like some monster silent shark. The name of the game, thought Blake, the born wildcatter, was initiative and action.

4
Dior for Breakfast

But Blake's moment was not yet. For the next three days he relayed facts, questions, recommendations between Sperry in Vienna and the Eagle Board in London, working from his big room in the Imperial next to Sperry's suite. Eagle Austria lent him a senior secretary full time, a tall curvy girl with straight dark hair shoulder-length, wide-set brown eyes, a quick mind. Eva's mother was English, and Eva spoke that and German faultlessly. When Blake first met her he registered her sex profoundly, then put it tidily away. For his work was intense. He sent most of his reports through her in the room, by phone to Eagle Austria's Vienna headquarters, who coded and telexed them to Eagle London, who replied by the same route. The Imperial swore on its mother's grave that its switchboard was secure, but Blake sent his really pivotal messages written, and personally with the girl, to Eagle Vienna by the chauffeured Mercedes-Benz constantly parked for their use at the hotel, and he encouraged Eagle Vienna's President to send him London's hottest messages the same way.

Blake used the Mercedes quite often too, driving through the streets with their massive over-life-size buildings and monuments to meet Sperry at the OPEC office block's hygienic marble entrance for lunch or to get his news. Sperry always came straight back to the Imperial in the evenings. So Blake's coverage was extensive and prompt. It was also alarming. The Arabs had a case for higher crude oil prices, but the rumoured levels of increase they wanted would clearly throw the West and Third World into very grave economic recession for years. Sperry was finding the meetings almost tragically predictable. Yamani had opened as forecast by effectively doubling the Gulf posting from $3 to $6 per barrel. Piercy countered with an increase of twenty-five per cent. Amouzegar saw that as derisory. Yamani fell back to an effective posting of $5. Piercy and Bénard held to their limit of $3.75. Both sides now froze.

Blake also monitored the Arab-Israeli war closely. The Imperial had installed a powerful radio for him. He listened to all the Cairo and Tel Aviv broadcasts he could, and to the BBC's World Service. The first days, the Arabs were euphoric. America's panic-dimensioned support to Israel still maddened them, but seemed too late. They learnt ecstatically that after bursting through the Bar Lev Line on October 6 the Egyptians had gone on dominating the battlefield till October 10. Caught right off guard, the Israelis had thrown in their aircraft, and the Egyptians' Russian Sam missiles on the western bank of the canal had cut such swathes in them that the Israeli Command had forbidden its aircraft further sorties there. And the Israelis had hurled their tanks against the attackers pell-mell, without infantry screens, straight into the jaws of the Egyptian anti-tank defences which included their highly trained missile-carrying commandos. The Israelis had lost wickedly in tanks and crew too. Sadat boasted that the Egyptians had knocked out the entire crack Israeli 190th Armoured Brigade and captured its commander, Assaf Yagouri, in twenty minutes; a world record. Yagouri had looked weeping over his shoulder to see all his following 115 tanks knocked out and burning.

The Arabs' armoured thrust from the Syrian front was even more deadly fast, made by the 2,600 Syrian, Iraqi, Saudi, Kuwaiti and Moroccan tanks, and Jordan's excellent 40th Tank Brigade. These massed forces were also strong in infantry and mechanized troops in trucks and armoured personnel carriers, and with heavy artillery support. Prefaced by a murderous air strike and barrage from 2 pm on Saturday October 6, they had attacked in two spearheads, north and south, again with complete surprise, beautifully coordinated with the Egyptians. Within ten hours the southern spearhead was through the Golan Heights to overlook the Sea of Galilee. For some hours from dawn, only the Israeli air-to-ground counter-attacks held it. The Israelis in the north, stunned and brutally outnumbered, had taken terrible casualties, every one of their tanks having been hit at least once. Blake heard Arab Radio claim that Israeli Defence Minister Moshe Dayan, hero of his country's 1956 Suez campaign and Six Days War, had admitted with tears in his eyes on Israeli TV that Israel was losing the war. Arab radio also claimed the death in one of those suicidal Israeli tank charges of General Abraham Mindler, commandant of Israel's elite armoured corps, and said that it was Mindler's dispatches just before his death that painted the inevitability of Israel's defeat so clearly that Kissinger said to Israeli Prime Minister Golda Meir: 'You've lost the war. Resign yourself to it.'

There was the sour smell of defeat in Vienna too: for the oil companies. On October 10, the third full day of negotiations, Yamani and Amouzegar still insisted that the Gulf posting must go to about $5 per barrel. Piercy and Bénard could not raise their $3.75 ceiling. They cabled their New York and London boards in despair, stating they might still get agreement somewhere below a two-thirds increase, asking for fresh authorities. Sperry, reporting this via Blake to London, was pessimistic. He himself, knowing Blake's calculations, would have leapt for settlement at or near $5. But Eagle and the other independents could only leave the key price decision to the major multinationals. *This* time.

The Arabs were growing daily more exalted and intransigent. Sperry felt it in his meetings and Blake could sense it at once when he dropped in to the Intercontinental to test the waters. By October 10 the Arabs' conviction that they were winning their war with the Israelis gave them a lyrical solidarity they had certainly never had before. *Now* they would teach the Israelis and the West. That day the Arab members of OPEC announced a meeting of their own in Kuwait to determine how to use their oil weapon most effectively. That meant at least a partial or total embargo on Arab oil supplies to the West, two- or three-mile car queues at emptying gas stations in the States, jet aircraft and diesel trains immobilized, thermal power stations and oil-fuelled industry shut. That could stop the world dead in its tracks. The Arabs were learning, thought Blake.

On October 11 Sperry came late at night into Blake's room, with the news of Piercy's and Bénard's post-midnight visit to Yamani in his top suite in the International. They had had their boards' cable replies. Exxon could not budge above their $3.75 offer. Shell saw the economic effects of accepting OPEC's demands as so cataclysmic that the company must first consult with all the consumer governments affected; so could the meeting please be adjourned for two weeks? Yamani shrugged, and booked his flight back to Riyadh.

'So what now, sir?' asked Blake.

'So we've passed the initiative completely to them. From today, our *negotiating* a price with them is probably a thing of the past. Now they *impose* it, tell us what it is. We take it or leave it.'

'I'll get this all off,' said Blake.

'Can you still get your girl at this hour?'

'Oh, yes. Any hour, was the deal. She's on standby at her flat.'

'Spoil the poor kid's sleep.'

'They'll pay her overtime,' said Blake. 'I'll ring her, then send the Mercedes-Benz.'

He did that, then offered Sperry a drink. Sperry took a brandy.

'Might as well get back to London tomorrow,' he said. 'This is no longer where the action is.'

'I'll ring the Hawker-Siddeley pilots at their hotel,' said Blake. 'What time would you like to take off?'

'Oh, ten's fine,' said Sperry. 'And tell London, please. And ask them to tell my wife.'

'Sure,' said Blake. 'May I stay on some days? I just might be on to something.'

Above his golden Courvoisier, Sperry lined his prow-like face up on Blake.

'Meaning?'

'You remember the attractive lady sitting two tables from us at breakfast yesterday? Slim, about twenty-eight, tiny waist, good breasts but conservatively covered, oval face, long black lustrous hair, jet-black eyes also with a shine, fine nose, thinning lips, legs like a model's?'

'I doubt that I could recall all that,' said Sperry. 'But yes, I know the one you mean.'

'Oh, and olive skin,' said Blake. 'She's Arab. Save for that dress sense. That was certainly Dior. And the gold wrist-watch Cartier, the diamond ring about four carat, on white gold.'

'You ought to try copy-writing,' said Sperry.

'I lunched in the main restaurant today,' said Blake, 'because you had that lunch engagement outside. She walked through. Afterwards I went to the bar for an Armagnac. She was there, with an orange juice. When I had got my Armagnac, she walked over to me. The barman, the only other person there, was out of earshot. "Mr Philip Blake of Eagle?" she says. "I'm Leila Jibál, of the Kingdom of the Sun. Do you know us? We're a Gulf State, about half Kuwait's size in oil. My brother's the Minister of Oil. He arrives here in three days' time. We'd like to talk to you."

' "Fancy!" I said brilliantly. "Why us?"

' "Because you're an Independent," she said. "Therefore probably not so locked in to your traditions as the Seven Sisters. OPEC's got you over a barrel and they're going to roast you. Particularly the big Arab producers. You'd get a better deal from us. And more stable; we don't mix politics with business."

' "Where did you get the Oxford accent?" I asked, because it really amazed me. She laughed and said: "A place called Oxford. I came down from Somerville seven years ago. You were at Wadham, weren't you, but eight years earlier?" And off she goes.'

'So they've done their homework,' said Sperry. 'Good for them. They've got an excellent crude, Sun Light, about 34° API and very low sulphur – almost identical to Saudi's Arab Light. That's dead right for our refineries. And they've just national-ized it, so they must be looking for buyers. How did you leave things?'

'I'd check with you and revert tomorrow.'

'Do that,' said Sperry. 'Firm it up. Our supply people must know the Kingdom's Oil Ministry, but why pass up a good personal contact? You think she's authentic?'

'That's the name,' said Blake. 'She showed me her passport. She's down there as a Princess.'

'When could they see us for serious negotiations?' said Sperry. 'And do you know how much they're offering? Their total production's around a million barrels a day.'

'She said about a week or ten days in the Kingdom of the Sun. And she'd rather her brother talked quantities.'

'Fair enough. Well, you really may have something.'

'Another brandy?'

'Thanks,' said Sperry. 'I'm for bed. See you at breakfast, say eight-thirty.'

'I'll be there,' said Blake.

Though he liked Sperry a great deal, Blake was not sorry to see him go. He needed a few minutes to think. So Sperry had left him now to break an opening with the Kingdom of the

Sun's Oil Minister. Good. And the Arabs were rapidly becoming pastmasters in using their oil as a weapon. Blake might be able to leap onto that band-wagon himself. There had to be some way in which he could strike back with that sudden mystically powered Islamic scimitar against his certain and unchanging enemy, the Ice Maiden. Or at least use it as a near perfect protection against him. He just had to have his most sensitive antennae out to catch and retune himself to every subtlest shift in this world-scale war-accelerated power-game, listen very carefully to his intuitions, then decide and stake everything on his action.

5
Spudding in a Wildcat

Though Sperry was gone, Blake's Protestant Ethic, his only legacy from his father, drove him to work quite as hard in the next four days as it had in the previous week. He saw Princess Leila Jibál as agreed at 10 am on Friday October 12 to firm up the first meeting with her brother, the Minister of Oil. Fine, said the Princess over their coffee in the restaurant, Sheikh Abdullah bin Ali bin Jibál would arrive on the evening of October 14. No, regrettably he would not be available for dinner. And he had several important meetings in Vienna already arranged for the first part of Monday October 15. He would, however, be glad to receive Mr Blake at 4 pm in his sister's suite, which happened to be on the same floor as Blake's room in the Imperial. Sheikh Abdullah would be flying back to the Kingdom of the Sun in his Lear jet immediately after that. And Princess Leila was herself lamentably as socially elusive to that date; Mr Blake would understand.

Blake did; carrots and donkeys, he thought, bowing courteously as he left her.

What made Blake's concentration on his work in this next four days of infinite value to him was its focus on the Arab-Israeli war. His intuitions and acute sense of timing told him categorically that somewhere here lay the course of his future career and the rationale of his attack against Van Straten and defence of himself. To his sharpened eye and attuned ear the whole dynamic of this giant conflict was changing fundamentally with a suddenness few others had yet noticed. From his minute and very thorough coverage of Arab and Israeli radio stations, and his frequent visits to the military attachés at the British, French and American Embassies in Vienna, he gained a starkly new picture.

Following the first terrific impact of their heavy surprise attack and penetration of the Bar Lev Line, and their consequent domination of the Suez Canal battle-front for four days, the Egyptian attack army appeared to have gone totally to sleep after October 10. Naturally they had more resounding phrases for it, like operational pause or regrouping. In fact their sudden inertia was typically and endearingly Arab. The Egyptians had done so outstandingly well in their first four-day assault, not only because of the great secrecy and bravery with which they had launched it, but also because they had planned and practised it in such fantastic detail that it had practically become set-piece; commandos like Lieutenant Saad Muhammed had been leaping in and out of and paddling little rubber boats on the Great Bitter Lakes and learning to fire Sagger anti-tank missiles for two full years. An innate modesty and awe of the Israelis had evidently left them so amazed at their own initial success that they did not have the faintest idea what to do in the next phase. Clearly they had prepared no similarly explicit plan for it. So they just sat on their hands for four days. This gave the Israelis the initiative, which they never again lost, just the time they needed to reform themselves as an organic fighting force.

Meanwhile, Blake learnt, the Israelis had already blunted and shattered the Arab attack in the north. It had been touch and go, and the Israeli tank and infantrymen and pilots had been fighting literally all round the clock. Every single Israeli tank there had been hit at least once. Of the 250 knocked out,

Israeli Ordnance Corps men, often under fire, immediately recovered and repaired more than 150, which went straight back into the battle. Recognizing this northern Arab threat as initially gravest, the Israelis, while holding the Egyptian attack in the west, first swung what they could of their military might to the Golan Heights. Of the 2,000-plus Syrian, Iraqi, Saudi, Moroccan, Kuwaiti and Jordanian tanks committed to battle on that front, they knocked out some 1,200, and 130 aircraft, and after the battle recovered nearly 900 Syrian tanks, many still in good working order.

On the Suez Canal front now, the Israelis waited twenty to thirty kilometres east near the Mitla and Gidi passes, in the open ground where they had full mobility and were at their best. When at last the Egyptian armoured columns ground forward on October 14 from under their Sam umbrella, the Israelis, ready with their deployed tanks, anti-tank ground missiles and helicopter-carried air-to-ground missiles, murdered them. This was one of the biggest and most deadly tank battles of all time; in what was to prove a sixteen-day war, a total of more than 3,000 tanks were knocked out – whereas not more than 650 were knocked out on both sides in the full six months of fighting in North Africa between Montgomery and Rommel. After this beating the Egyptians, who were to end losing 1,000 tanks and 265 aircraft, trundled back to their base lines.

Blake got the first flash of the final piece of evidence proving that it was now the Israelis who were setting the pace in the early afternoon of October 15, only an hour before he was to see Sheikh Abdullah of the Kingdom of the Sun. This news was that the Israeli High Command, knowing that Egypt had committed and locked in even her strategic reserves to the main battle east of the canal, so that she had virtually nothing left on the west, had let General Sharon that day counter-attack across the canal at the Deversoir–Abu Sultan gap of thirty to forty almost unguarded kilometres with the spear-head of a full armoured division. What could stop him now from slaughtering the Sam sites on the west bank of the canal or surrounding and annihilating the 3rd Egyptian Army at Suez, or rolling straight into Cairo?

Nevertheless Blake, a fair poker player, was mildness itself when he met Sheikh Abdullah bin Ali bin Jibál in Princess

Leila's suite in the Imperial at 4 pm on October 15. It was an opulent suite, the twin of Sperry's. Blake was quite pleased to see that Leila was evidently taking part in the meeting too. She looked as exquisite as when he had first seen her; slim, fine featured, olive-skinned, with the four-carat diamond in its white gold ring. She wore what he guessed to be a Dior gown, between orange and deep red, a drape from the shoulders, covering them and high-throated, with wide long flowing sleeves. It was cocktail length; he was glad to see her elegant legs and stylish insteps in high-heeled narrow and very dark brown leather shoes.

But Sheikh Abdullah won his most immediate attention. Generosity and sheer vitality looked the key characteristics of this Minister of Oil of the Kingdom of the Sun. He was well dressed, in a dark pearl Lanvin suit, blue and white Armani tie, and dark tan Bally shoes, with a gold Patek watch on his left wrist. These clothes fitted him culturally as well as physically; in them he seemed effortlessly European, in no sense an oriental in expensive disguise. Abdullah was a tall man, perhaps six foot three, lean and brisk, and clean-shaven save for his full black moustache. He had an attractive smile, very white teeth flashing in that dark olive skin. The face itself was hawk-like, the nose thrusting and inquisitive, and the irises of the eyes very black and sharp against the sheer white of the corneas. Blake saw Abdullah's blood relationship with his sister in his lips, for Abdullah's had the same sinuous curvature, at once passionate and ruthlessly disciplined. There were the same hints of humour about them, faint shadows at their corners. This man had tremendous magnetism, huge latent electricity. Blake guessed him about thirty-three, young to be an oil minister. But Abdullah would have earned the job; he looked hard-working and astute.

And a little strained at the moment. Blake thought he knew why. Abdullah, if his sister was anything to go by with her remarkably accurate knowledge about Blake's Oxford college, would be right up to date with his intelligence about the Arab-Israeli war, and about who was now conclusively winning it.

But Abdullah, evidently no mean poker player himself, led off on a completely different tack where he was at least relatively much stronger:

'So the oil conflict goes on, Mr Blake. With OPEC winning, the Arabs setting the pace. You'll know of course that two days ago at their meeting in Kuwait the Arab OPEC members decreed a price rise in the Gulf crude posting from its three dollars per barrel to $5.12, or by seventy per cent. And they did *not* consult the Seven Sisters beforehand.'

Pure Oxbridge like his sister. Blake thought he might as well get that one out of the way. So he said:

'Yes, I did know that. Which college were you at?'

'Oh,' said Abdullah, 'the House. I had Greek and Latin, so I read Greats. I was going up just when you came down.'

Like his sister, Abdullah knew when that was. Well, they were careful and serious people. With style.

'Pity we missed,' said Blake inevitably.

The three sat in the suite's opulent sitting-room, Abdullah and Blake in deep armchairs, Leila more formally on the sofa. She had served them drinks; Blake, who wanted to keep an ice-clear head, had taken Campari-soda, but was glad to see that Abdullah had chosen a strong whisky and water; however genuinely Arab and Muslim, Abdullah evidently did not carry Islam's prohibition of alcohol to excess, but drank it cheerfully in private. He noticed that Leila had, interestingly, poured herself a Campari-soda too.

'What you may not yet know,' Abdullah resumed, 'is that the OPEC Arabs in Kuwait are today also announcing a partial boycott in overall crude supplies to the West. Only *token*, so far. Say of just five per cent.'

'Just to make their point,' said Blake, 'to show the gleaming edge of the scimitar?'

'Just to make the point,' said Abdullah. 'But I'd guess that within a day or two we'll make that boycott *total* to the US and Holland – the US for going on making very heavy supplies of arms and equipment to Israel despite our warnings, and Holland for daring to let the US air-bridge to Israel use their airfields.'

'A *total* boycott of oil to the US and Holland?'

'That's right.'

'My God, that'll hurt the US particularly. They're already importing a third of all their oil needs. This'll make them scream!'

'Good.'

'But hell, *your* side's been getting heavy external support too. What about the hundred battle tanks Tito sent you from Yugoslavia, fully armed and fuelled and even loaded with shells, dead ready to fight?'

Abdullah turned in his chair and lined his dramatic face up on Blake. 'You're well informed,' he said. 'Then we'll make some oil deal with Tito that rewards him adequately. We Arabs have long memories.'

'You really loathe the Jews, don't you?'

'The Jews, no,' said Abdullah. 'Why should we? We're Semites too. We've coexisted with them for hundreds of years. And they are People of the Book, like the Christians and ourselves. The *Zionists*, yes, those we hate, those demented myth-makers like Theodor Hertzl and Jabotinsky who invented a National Home for the Jews in an idealized land conveniently shorn of other inhabitants. Those were completely ignored, invisible, never even mentioned. It was a major and wicked lie. There were hundreds of thousands of local inhabitants existing in Palestine when the first Zionist arrived there. They were called Arabs.'

'And you must get that land back for those Arabs?'

'At the very least those lands which the UN Partition decree clearly deemed Arab and which the Jews robbed from us in the 1967 Six Days War, the West Bank and Gaza Strip. It's not just a question of Arab honour, Mr Blake. Islamic Law obliges us categorically as Muslims to take back occupied Muslim land if we possibly can, by force if necessary.'

'Which was precisely your objective in the present Yom Kippur War?'

'Yes.'

This had brought the conversation round exactly to where Blake wanted it. Abdullah had shed his elegant Oxford ease. The strain was dominant now. In the deep armchair his body was tense as a strung bow. *Now* was the moment to shock, thought Blake; to sink the drilling-bit in deep —

'But, Sheikh Abdullah, Princess Leila, you both of course know that that objective has been totally frustrated. You are highly informed people. The lot has been cast irrevocably against you. You have lost the shooting war —'

Blake heard Leila, to his left, draw in her breath sharply. To his right, Abdullah's face stayed riveted on him, the black eyes

30

blazing, almost jumping from the sheer white corneas.

' – I've had these two copies typed of my best estimate of your total losses to date on both battle-fronts. Here. Tanks destroyed about 2,000. Aircraft, nearly 400. Killed, about 12,000 and wounded double that. The Israeli losses have been less than half yours in tanks, just over a quarter in aircraft, and a quarter in killed and wounded. Agreed, these human losses are severe enough for Israel. The killed represent one in a thousand of their population, proportionately four times as many in this very short war as the US lost killed in its entire long Vietnam disaster. But in exchange the Israelis have shattered and hurled back your northern attack and could walk into Damascus within days. And on the Egyptian front they have locked your divisions in harmlessly on the eastern bank of the canal and blown every bridge except one behind them. And today Israel's General Sharon counter-attacked across the canal with the spearhead of his armoured division. Within days he will have blotted out any Sam site on your western bank that he finds, and can then encircle the 3rd Egyptian Army round Suez and/or roll his tanks unopposed into Cairo. For you have no mobile reserves on the western bank able to stop him.'

'If this is true,' said Abdullah, 'and I have heard some of it, what happens next?' His sinuous carnal lips had whitened.

'It has the ring of truth,' said Leila.

'Next?' said Blake. 'Well, the Russians have been monitoring all these battles with their satellites. I would guess that within days they could be showing Sadat satellite photos of Sharon's advance so terrifying that he will have no option but to sue for peace before total bloody defeat. The world will then know publicly who has won.'

'We know something of the ferocity of the fighting in the north,' said Leila. 'Our Kingdom sent a twenty-tank expeditionary force. Half have been destroyed and almost all their crews killed.'

Abdullah was still gazing fixedly at Blake.

'Taking it that your information is absolutely accurate,' he said, 'why do you relate us this humiliation? Do you think we've not already heard enough such? The Arab defeat in the first 1948 Arab–Israeli War? Dayan's runaway victory over us in the 1956 Suez campaign? The annihilation of the Arab forces in the Six Days War in 1967? And now *this*?'

Blake looked back at him deliberately.

'Because you have now so certainly lost the initiative in the shooting war,' he said, 'I suggest that you will also have lost some of it in your wider war for fairer crude oil prices.'

Abdullah looked at Leila and back at Blake.

'Possibly,' he said. 'And so?'

Blake took a deep breath.

'Suppose that I could give you something with which, despite any such losses of initiative, you could still *quite certainly* get very fair new crude oil prices from the West, and therefore certainly *win* that wider war, what would it be worth to me?'

'Quite certainly?' said Abdullah.

'You can judge from my proofs.'

Abdullah exchanged glances again with his sister. The two had more than that sinuous curvature of the lips in common. They were very close; even, it seemed, in their judgements about people.

'Within reason,' said Abdullah, 'you could name your own price.'

'Good,' said Blake.

'What is that price?'

Blake kept his eyes full on Abdullah.

'In your Kingdom of the Sun you produce a million barrels a day of 34° API Sun Light crude, low sulphur content. I would like to sign Heads of Agreement here with you today, subject to immediate confirmation by the Eagle Board in London, for a supply contract for 500,000 bd Sun Light for Eagle, the term five years, automatically renewable unless one party gives the other three months' prior notice of termination. Payment at sixty days from shipment. Price full OPEC posting. This could give you your first breakthrough of a major long-term contract with the West using your new OPEC-dictated pricing system.'

'Yes, that could be extremely valuable. You have your Heads of Agreement documents there?'

'Yes, I've had them typed in triplicate, one for each of you. Here –'

'You knew that the two of us would be seeing you?'

'I thought it possible to probable. So I had the extra set done.'

Abdullah smiled. 'You're a far-sighted man, Mr Blake. We may be able to go a long way with you.'

'The thought has crossed my mind.'

Abdullah smiled again. 'But this is all contingent on your Eagle Board's approval, Mr Blake. Which means that this Heads of Agreement idea is your initiative. You've come up with that one all on your own. Why?'

Blake looked down, then back at him. What the hell, he thought, why not tell him? You had to trust someone some of the time.

'If it succeeds, it could be a great stroke for me too. I need that. I have a powerful enemy on the Board.'

'Very powerful?'

'The most powerful. The Chairman.'

'At least you have the good taste,' Leila broke in, 'to choose the top as your enemy.'

'But then he could block this?' said Abdullah.

'The rest of the Board would outweigh him,' said Blake. 'That's my hope. A reasonable one, with all the West petrified with fear now of insecurity in their oil supplies. And I can let you know the answer at once, by tomorrow afternoon. I'm booked on the first flight to London tomorrow morning, and I have the advantage of the hour's time difference. I can get Morgan Sperry to call an emergency Board Meeting in the morning. There they'll decide fast.'

'And?' said the Princess.

Blake turned to her. She was elegant and very alert. He raised his eyebrows.

'There's something more, isn't there?' she asked.

'From the papers still in my hands? Yes. I've hand-written the next two, with two clear carbon copies, because I wanted no one else to know of them, including my secretary. Here. This one's a Heads of Agreement identical to the first, but the supply contract's for 50,000 bd of Sun Light, and it's with me in person. The other conditions are the same, term five years renewable, payment at sixty days, and price full OPEC posting.' .

There was a short silence. Abdullah and his sister examined Blake.

'You have that kind of money?' asked Abdullah.

'No,' said Blake, 'but I wouldn't need it. With the West as

paranoiacally convinced as it is that oil supplies are going to be critically short as far forward as one can see, I can easily on-sell that 50,000 bd of an excellent crude for a ten to twelve cents per barrel commission, like a broker. That'll bring me say two million dollars a year. That's the kind of money I think I need to live in the style to which I should love to be accustomed.'

Abdullah laughed. 'A modest enough income,' he said. And Blake knew he meant it.

'The Kingdom of the Sun would lose nothing,' Blake went on. 'You'd still get your full OPEC price on due payment date, I'd guarantee you.'

'And your second hand-written paper, Mr Blake?' asked Leila, missing nothing.

'Of course.' Blake handed them the original and first carbon copy. 'I've just used the word guarantee. This would be a guarantee from you to me, as confidential as your 50,000 bd supply contract with me. And naturally both these undertakings are contingent on my getting your 500,000 bd supply contract with Eagle through the Board satisfactorily tomorrow.'

Abdullah and Leila read Blake's second hand-written document through carefully then looked at each other. Like identical twins, they seemed able to communicate magically, without speaking. Abdullah looked back at Blake.

'All right, Mr Blake. That all looks acceptable so far. Provided you really do have the goods, naturally. So may we now please see your cards?'

Blake looked steadily at Abdullah and Leila, savouring his moment, then smiled and handed them over. They were two pages of very tight calculations and taut economists' phrases, under the Eagle International London letterheads, with dates and signatures, including Blake's. They were the joint work of Eagle International's group of economic whiz-kids and, to a lesser extent, of Blake himself, who had lucidly set them the problem. Blake knew them to be among the best economic think-tanks in the international oil business. They went strictly where the figures led.

Both brother and sister scanned these figures with mounting concentration.

'If these calculations say what I think they do,' said Abdullah when he looked up, 'these two sheets of paper are dynamite.'

'Yes,' said Leila. 'Mr Blake, what are the *sources* of all your energy yields and comparative efficiency factors?'

'We have in all cases taken them from government or independent scientific or engineering institutes' published statistics, *not* oil company figures, however reputable. And we have always erred on the side of taking the most *conservative* findings, notably in the cases of the independent authorities in the West's biggest economies – the US, Japan, Western Germany, France, the UK, Italy, Sweden. I think you'll find that borne out by the many sources listed in, I'm afraid, the rather fine print in the footnotes to the two pages.'

'Yes,' she said, 'I see. It's impressive. And these basic statistics are all recent?'

'As up-to-date as we could get. The sources' exact dates are also in the fine print.'

'Yes, I see. Excellent.'

'Mr Blake,' said Abdullah, 'tell us how you define the main importance of this study.'

'You have to see it in the context of what's just happened in world history,' said Blake. 'The Western oil multinationals, anyway the Seven Sisters, were prepared to increase the Gulf marker crude price of three dollars per barrel by only twenty-five per cent. All hell broke loose and the entire OPEC Vienna negotiations blew up because Yamani dared to ask for an increase to five dollars. The Western oil companies are still yelling their heads off because two days ago the OPEC Arabs in Kuwait went ahead and decreed a new Gulf crude posting of $5·12, or seventy per cent up on the prior price of the deemed standard or marker crude. Yet –'

'Yet, Mr Blake?'

'Yet our Eagle International calculations, which are conservative and I think professional, show absolutely conclusively that, as against the efficiencies and applied costs of all alternative energy sources in the West over the foreseeable future – mainly coal, nuclear, and hydroelectricity – *you could safely quadruple your former Gulf posting of three dollars per barrel and still be competitive!*'

This time the silence was definitely religious.

'Just think of the effect of that,' said Abdullah reverently, for once addressing his sister aloud. 'On Yamani and Amouzegar and on the real Arab OPEC militants and the Shah! And

35

that under the Eagle International letterhead, and signed!'

He turned back to Blake. 'Of course we knew that our crude oil was competitively underpriced, but few of us saw it as that far under. To have its true competitive value set that high that clearly by an executive as senior as you in a Western oil multinational makes you and your calculations worth your weight in gold. Now we know exactly how high we can push it over the next few months. Mr Blake, you've given us photostats of your calculations here. Would you please write "certified true copy" on each and sign it?'

'Sure,' said Blake, and did so.

'One good turn deserves another,' said Abdullah. 'Give me your copies of the two Heads of Agreement and guarantee.'

He signed them as swiftly and returned them to Blake.

'My God!' said Leila. 'If we in fact get the Gulf posting up by nine dollars a barrel, over say the next three months, that on the free world's oil needs of fifty million barrels a day means an extra income to us oil producers of some $165 *billion* a year! That on its own is nearly one and a half times the free world's total trade last year!'

'That extra is what our calculations say you ought to have been getting already,' said Blake levelly.

'But won't an increase that vast simply obliterate the oil companies economically?' asked Leila.

Blake laughed.

'I strongly doubt it. We oil companies survive. We'll just pass that cost increase straight on to the public in our prices. Moreover you'll see, we'll make all-time record profits this and next year.'

'How on earth will you do that?'

'Well, consider that at any one moment the free world, meaning very largely the oil companies, are holding say sixty days' oil stocks. If the price of oil rises by nine dollars a barrel as we're now assuming, that puts 27 *billion* in the stock-holders' pockets as stock profit. That at one stroke is five or six times the UK's entire annual defence budget. No, we oil companies will survive all right!'

Abdullah looked at him fondly. 'Yes,' he said, 'I can see that. It looks as if we're *all* going to gain something.'

Except for the poor bloody public, thought Blake. For this

sharp oil price was sure as hell going to throw the whole of the West and Third World into deep recession. Yet Blake felt no grave compunction about what he was doing. Crude oil simply was viciously underpriced in relation to all alternative energy sources. The Western industrial nations had built and rebuilt themselves on that advantage. They had benefited from it for a very long time. Too long. If Blake's class swore as piously about free competition as they did about motherhood, then let it genuinely be free. The crude oil producers had rights too, even if you hated their guts and deplored their table manners. Those were the facts. Blake had not made them. And with the Western oil companies and OPEC now going for one another's throats these bedrock economic facts were bound to emerge soon anyway. Blake in presenting them first with lucid dramatic impact, was just one jump ahead of the pack. If that happened to serve him personally too, he was anyway going to need some heavy weaponry against an enemy he read as deadly – the Ice Maiden.

'I'm really sorry to have to fly back to the Kingdom this evening,' said Abdullah. 'I'd have liked to give you dinner here. But if you get the deal through your Eagle Board tomorrow, we can have the official signature on the contract out in the Kingdom in a week's time. Then I can show you a little real Arab hospitality.'

'That would be very kind. And quite an occasion. I'm sure my Managing Director Morgan Sperry would like to come out for it too.'

'*Insh' Allah*,' said Abdullah. 'Leila, give our friend here a *real* drink, would you? Now that he's won all his points so far.'

Blake laughed. 'Thank you. A whisky and water then, please.' He turned back to Abdullah. 'But I'll have a tough day tomorrow, with my enemy.'

'Ah, your Board Meeting. What's his name?'

'The Chairman? Jacobus van Straten. Of Flemish ancestry. Now very much of the English aristocracy. He's a powerful and formidable man. They call him the Ice Maiden.'

Abdullah's shining jet-black eyes re-examined Blake. Abdullah said, with enviable total inner certainty:

'Ah, you'll beat him in the end.'

Leila came over to Blake, and he stood up to take his whisky and water. Her smile lit up her face attractively. As she went back to her sofa and sat, she said:

'Abdullah, we don't really have to wait a week to show our new friend the Kingdom's hospitality.'

'No?'

'No. If you agree, I could stand in for you as host tonight. If Mr Blake would care to have dinner with me.'

Blake watched brother and sister commune silently a moment.

'Indeed,' smiled Abdullah. 'Mr Blake?'

Blake smiled.

'Mr Blake would care to have dinner with your sister very much indeed.'

6
Leila

Leila chose the Three Hussars, at 9 pm. So a little before that Blake collected her from her suite in the Imperial and they drove to the restaurant in the constant Mercedes-Benz. He heard the hum in the Three Hussars drop as they went in, and saw the eyes turn to her, men's and women's. She merited that attention. Leila was too wise, and perhaps proud, to try to disguise her fine dark olive skin. Instead she emphasized it. She sat before Blake in a cocktail-length dress of pure white silk, the skirt bouffant, the waist dramatically hourglass. The dress was high-throated, the shoulders and arms covered to the wrists. It achieved its effect by its sheer sobriety against that rich skin. Her breasts were clearly etched in it, high and firm. The only wild touch was in her lustrous jet-black hair, cascading to her shoulders. She wore a silver tiara in it, curved and elegant, and studded with diamonds. It matched the thin silver belt round her slim waist, its small buckle also decorated with diamonds. Diamonds were there again in the platinum band to the Cartier watch, also silver, on her left wrist. A thin platinum bracelet balanced that on her right wrist. She wore nothing on her very slim and feminine hands except the four-carat solitaire diamond in its white gold ring that he had first seen on her. Her shoes were silver too, and high-heeled, slim and light as wings. Blake, who had been a marketer in his time with Eagle, knew a brilliant exhibition of packaging when he saw one. He wondered what she was like within it.

'Now I know,' he said, 'how I'd feel if I walked into a Hollywood restaurant with Marilyn Monroe on my arm.'

'You don't think our colouring's a little different?'

'The beauty's the same.'

'Mostly out of a bottle, a modiste, and a jeweller's shop.'

'I don't believe that. It's visibly intrinsic.'

'Well, thankee kindly, you're not so bad yourself.'

'A bit damaged in transit, though. You can hardly miss the limp.'

'Oh, it gives you rather a distinguished air. War-wound?'

'Ski-wound. I never learnt how to stop.'

'Ah.'

'Would Madame the Princess care for something to drink?' asked the head waiter, superbly dinner-suited, sliding expertly into the small silence on rubber wheels.

'Just orange juice. Right through the dinner, please. Perhaps a jug.'

'And Monsieur?'

'Oh, a dry sherry to start with. Domecq, please.'

'While you think of what you would like to order,' said the head waiter gently, gliding tactfully away.

'Should I call you that?' asked Blake.

'What?'

'Princess.'

'I shouldn't bother. Leila's simpler.'

'Leila, then. I'm Philip. No alcohol in public, I see.'

Her brilliant black eyes, again matching her brother's, steadied on him.

'No, never. Somewhere, eyes are always watching. A Muslim woman learns that.'

'Thank God that you do drink in private, though. Tee-totallers numb me. That abnegation!'

Her right hand, slim as a lily's tongue, took a flat platinum case from her small silver handbag: Balkan Sobranie Virginia. Blake leaned across and flicked his Dunhill gold lighter.

'It's thoughtful,' she said. 'You don't smoke yourself, do you? This doesn't worry you?'

'Not at all.'

'That stems from your rugger-playing and boxing days? *That* indeed must have called for abnegation, hard training, discipline.'

'How on earth do you know all this? And that I came down from Wadham in 1958? Eight years before you did, from Somerville?'

'It wasn't hard,' said Leila. 'One has embassies for things like that. And friends.'

Anyone that beautiful would have friends.

'You'd have read English,' he said, 'since yours is so perfect.'

'No, that was just a string of English governesses. I read PPE. With emphasis on the Politics. You read Mathematics, I recall.'

Christ, thought Blake, there she goes again.

The orange juice and the Domecq arrived.

'You've decided, perhaps?' asked the head waiter, oblique and optimistic.

'A mixed salad to start,' said Leila, 'then a Sole Meunière.'

'That's light,' said Blake. 'I think a Bisque d'Homard. Then a Filet Mignon, well done. And spinach. Again no wine?'

'Thank you,' said Leila, 'no.'

'Then for me a Bordeaux, I think,' said Blake. 'Say your Château Margaux, Premier Grand Cru, 1966. And perhaps I might have it now?'

'A good choice,' said the head waiter, and puttered off to implement it, happy in his client, lyrical in his work.

'Politics because that's what calls the tune in the Middle East?' asked Blake. 'And because you're a patriot?'

He saw her breasts lift slightly, pressing against the trim silk bodice.

'That's what calls the tune anywhere, surely? It's just a little noisier in the Middle East. And bloodier. And yes, I love my country.'

She poured herself another orange juice from her jar. Her mixed salad arrived, his Bisque, then his bottle of Margaux. His Bisque had a rich creamy tang, the bite of lobster beneath. He drank a little water, then tried the Margaux. It had a fine aroma, the taste deep and fruity. It spoke of buried mountain caverns, filled with cobwebbed casks, chests of gold coins, emeralds, rubies, kings' ransoms, silver chalices, diamond-hilted swords.

'We're living key moments in the world's history now, certainly,' he said, 'with this profound shift in political power to the Arabs.'

'Even if, as you tell us, the Israelis are thrashing us soundly?'

'Even then. Your final recognition that you can use your oil as a weapon goes very much wider than that. That puts you right back in the centre of the world stage.'

'It's high time,' she said. 'We've been dead asleep since our medieval peak of power, with our magnificent achievements then in mathematics, medicine, astronomy, philosophy, architecture, geography. Ever since you threw us out of Europe in the fourteenth and fifteenth centuries. We just lapsed into total apathy. As you say the Egyptian armoured columns did after their first four gloriously victorious days in this Yom Kippur War.'

'At least you've had those first four days, shattering the Bar Lev Line. And your deep armoured thrusts in the north penetrated right through to within spitting distance of the Sea of Galilee. You so *nearly* won this war! And by those first great blows you have anyway achieved one major success. You have destroyed the myth of total Israeli military invincibility once and for all.'

'I suppose there is that,' said Leila, attacking her Sole Meunière now as though it were General Sharon. 'We Arabs have a remarkable patience in our hatreds, you know. And there are 150 million of us surrounding these three million Israelis. I'm reminded of something that Chaim Laskow, commander of the élite Israeli armoured corps during Dayan's 1956 Suez Campaign, is supposed to have said after it when he was asked about the quality of our armed forces. "In general, fairly poor," he is alleged to have said, "but one Arab tank crew and one Arab pilot in forty were as good as anything we have. So we must beware. For they have only to wait until they have enough forties, then logically they should win." '

Blake bit into his Filet Mignon. It was succulent, for him cooked exactly right. He took a sip of mineral water, then, feeling duly purified, of his second glass of Château Margaux. The deep fruity taste lingered in his mouth like an afterglow.

'This is the dominant political theme in your Kingdom, of course. You have no other major concerns there?'

Leila's fine eyes looked at him and his question over her sculpted thin nose and lips.

'Certainly we have other major political problems, even threats, in the Kingdom of the Sun. I think virtually every Arab State has them in some measure today. And the gravest of all of them, I believe, is Islamic Fundamentalism.'

'Which you define as what?'

The promptness of Leila's answer told him how much thought she must already have given to the question.

'I would define it as an extraordinarily powerful and intellectually and emotionally seductive movement to return puritanically and with a very high sense of social justice to the basic principles of Islam.'

No oil man is entirely ignorant about the area that holds the world's largest known oil reserves, and when Morgan Sperry had first suggested that he needed a second-in-command, Philip Blake had begun to investigate the Middle East. He knew something of its politics, and a lot about the resources and technology of its major-oil producing countries. But this first long conversation with Leila took Blake that vital first step from keen observer to participant. It began to put real blood into the body of his knowledge. Seeing through the eyes of Princess Leila Jibál would not be like seeing through his wife's. Celia's vision focused most minutely upon her own affairs, and went no further.

Indeed, the contrast between the two women was dramatic, thought Blake. His wife never really waxed passionate about any country or cause. She had her own iridescent universe. Celia had never sought to use the excellent English degree she had taken at Oxford. Fashion was more naturally her bent. That was the world she now inhabited, and which absorbed almost all of her considerable energies. Either as a designer or as a very exclusive model, her success in it was astonishing, hers as if by divine right. The quick, glittering and expensive perfections of the world of Haute Couture sat easily on her, with her strikingly large emerald eyes levelled in their very direct gaze, her high cheekbones, full red lips, slim neck and splendid body. She had that world's exact focus and its lacquer. Perhaps she had always really been like that, and her new brilliant and brittle career had just crystallized out that picture accurately. Perhaps he had shed that reflection on her from his own hard drives and disciplines, and this was her revenge. But he did not feel her very passionate about that either, though they had once known strong sexual passion. That, with the years, and though still practised, was merely faultless, not ecstatic. He could feel no shadowy depths behind it.

If Blake had ever really known his wife, she had put a full stop to that now. This was as far as she would let him go. That exquisite silhouette occupied one flat plane only, even if myriad people were now constantly round her in London, meeting her obsessive need for life, movement, sound always about her. Blake had learned to keep a delicate taut balance with her. But it could be a solitary ballet, so that a sudden meshing of minds and sympathies with a woman like Leila could be exhilarating in the extreme. For she was certainly vibrantly alive. Princess Leila was passionate about the history of her country and her race, and committed to the future of both. If Eagle signed the agreement with the Kingdom of the Sun, then Philip's private agreement would also come into force and Leila's world would start making him a rich man. Could he have a better guide to that world than the woman who was holding his gaze across the table?

She talked about the *Shari'a*, the Islamic Law first set in the Koran and totally holistic, covering every aspect of a Muslim's temporal and spiritual life.

'The *Shari'a* admits no double standards, one for the Sabbath and the other for the working week, one public and one private. Islamic Fundamentalism demands a scrupulous morality, unceasing war against corruption, aid to the poor and under-privileged. It's very nationalistic – Pan-Islamic, rather – and it's passionately committed to the Arab cause in Palestine.'

'You make it sound impressive – dedicated.'

'It's all of that,' said Leila. 'And very jealous of its own identity, suspicious of alien traditions. Communism is anathema; it's godless. Western materialism and consumerism too; an insatiable appetite, and everything for sale.'

'And you see Fundamentalism as a growing movement?'

'I fear most certainly. There's so much to promote it. In Egypt, the poor *fellah* arrives in the metropolis, like peasants all over the world, and he finds worse poverty, starvation, violence. He falls back on his strict Islamic upbringing. But it doesn't stop there. The real drive comes from our best and brightest, intellectuals and young professionals. You've heard of the Muslim Brotherhood?'

'As an organization of fanatics, and a bloody enemy of the British in Egypt.'

Blake had finished his Filet Mignon, and laid down his knife and fork. He was holding his glass of Margaux motionless in his right hand and following Leila raptly. Now his answer raised a rueful smile.

'It's true that the Brotherhood developed a terrorist wing in the early Forties – *El Jihaz es-Sirri*, The Secret Apparatus. It was up against a very ruthless police force. But that was not the key thing about the Brotherhood. *That* was its devoted social work for the downtrodden. If I tell you that its founder was as great a man as any of your Shaftesburys or Wilberforces, you'll have to take it on trust. You won't find the name of Hassan el Banna in many of your Western works of reference. Yet he was a man obsessed with social justice, a practical saint. He founded the Brotherhood in 1928. Twenty years later it had a million followers and thousands of branches all over Egypt, running schools and clinics and welfare centres. Today's Islamic Fundamentalism assumes a great part of that tradition.'

'In your kingdom too?'

'Well, we are a fairly progressive state. Small population, large income. We have no great cities to concentrate tensions, no obvious, massive exploitation, and I think only an ordinary level of corruption. Fundamentalism is strong in Egypt because when Sadat replaced Nasser he had no following – the strong political groups were either Nasserists or Marxists. He built up this third power to back him. Then militant Islam is strong in Northern Syria, and in Iran, in spite of the Shah's Savak secret police. I'd say it's strong in *any* feudal Arab state today, but underground, waiting its moment. Potentially it is the most powerful force in the Arab world. Remember our strength during your Middle Ages? Those are the kinds of energies which are building now.'

Leila noticed the force of her own concentration, reflected in Philip Blake's listening silence.

'You listen too well, Mr Blake. I am beginning to reveal the family secrets.'

'From what you say, they can't stay in the family much longer. You're talking about a great political force. Put that alongside the economic force represented by your region's oil, and the prices it can command according to our Eagle analysts . . . '

He was prompting her back to her argument, and she took the cue.

'Do not leave out the international politics – the Americans and the Russians, backing their own nominees. The Palestinian Arabs: in our Kingdom of the Sun, *Mamlakat es-Shems,* we have a million inhabitants. Only a third are pure *Shemsis*, with full political and property rights. Another third are partly Egyptian professionals and middle managers. There aren't enough jobs for them at home, and Egypt exports its teachers, doctors, engineers, architects, all over the Middle East. But very predominantly our imported middle class are Palestinians. Most of them have the high intellectual standard that the Egyptians also bring, and they do the same generally very responsible jobs. Our economy would collapse completely if this third got up one day and went home. And politically the most dynamic and dangerous in this group are inevitably the Palestinians. The Palestinian Liberation Organization is very strong among them. It taxes them, runs ideological courses for their youth, and – covertly – it trains *fedayeen* fighters for terrorist use against Israel. We shut our eyes to that, and after all we sympathize with their aims. In return the PLO are scrupulously careful to keep out of the Kingdom's internal politics. And by the way, the final third of our population, our hewers of wood and drawers of water, your Bible says: they are mainly Pakistanis and Iranians, who have no rights, but earn ten or twenty times what they would at home.'

Philip could fill in some of the background to what Leila was telling him. He knew about the chronic chaos in Egypt, the

45

most populous of all Arab states, with a swollen bureaucracy and permanent trade and finance deficits. Eagle had people in Cairo, but it rotated its foreign staff there fairly quickly, or they burned out in a spectrum of frustrations. An urgent telex to Eagle's research department in London had also brought him as much as they could learn about the power structure in the Kingdom of the Sun. Its Amir was fairly liberal, and had backed his finance and economy ministers in a series of measures aimed at the welfare of the common citizen – sub-economic housing, clinics, schools, power stations. Entry to hospitals, and to the country's one university, was free to all citizens. Leila's brother was identified as part of the progressive wing of an extensive royal family.

'Why do I get the feeling that you admire the Fundamentalists?' he asked her.

'Your Chairman, Van Straten – I'm sure you admire him, don't you? I don't think you would take on an enemy who was not worth the fighting. Well, the Fundamentalists are dedicated. They are profoundly idealistic in their drive for social justice and against corrupt old systems. They follow in the path of Hassan el Banna, whom I *do* admire.'

'And the catch?'

'The utter ruthlessness. They hold their own lives cheap, beside their cause, and it follows that other people's lives are equally expendable. In looking back towards our Arab past, and in appealing to the peasant masses, it is not culture that they offer, but conquest. It is not art and science and a humane way of life that enthuses such men, but an Islam exercising total control both in public and in private.'

'You make it sound deeply impressive too, if it can mobilize that kind of loyalty.'

He pulled his glass of Margaux towards him and, raising it to her, drank long from it. He could have been toasting the great new creed she described. But Leila did not look overly receptive.

'Think twice about the kind of political philosophy we are facing here. I know that the death of faith has become a cliché lamentation in the West, but we are talking about the Islamic Law which literally applied means stoning the adulterous woman to death, chopping off the hands of recidivist thieves. Do we really want that? In Saudi Arabia, for example, which certainly isn't – yet – Fundamentalist, but applies Islamic Law rigidly and is already rich and equipped with the most modern hospitals, the public executioner no longer lops off the thief's hand in the main square. Instead it's done in the most hygenic conditions by the most modern surgical methods. I find that totally obscene.'

Blake gazed at her intrigued. She was nowhere predictable, but seemed subtle, surprisingly sensitive, as many-layered as the pearls which for long had been her small Arabian Gulf kingdom's main trading asset. Blake had read that the local inhabitants had dived for them in their oyster cases, and for sponges, shoving the sharks out of the way, to earn a taxing and precarious living.

'My brother Abdullah and I see some of the forces acting on the Gulf, including our own kingdom, as inherently unstable, and perhaps lethally perilous. Our long-term plan is to develop the Kingdom into one genuinely unified and finally democratic nation. The key to our success is oil. For such a giant transformation we of course need astronomical sums of money. So anything you or we can do to increase the price of crude oil is vitally important.'

'You've my full commitment that I'll work for that,' he said.

'Yes,' said Leila.

'So you believe absolutely in Islam,' said Blake: as a comment, not as a question.

Her etched neat breasts lifted fractionally again.

'Islam as an essential part of our identity? Our dignity? Yes. As a culture? Yes. As a religion? As puritanism? I pass on that question.'

'But surely a progressive and newly independent country like your Kingdom of the Sun is well past brutish puritanism now?'

She observed him seriously.

'I shouldn't count on it. Why do you suppose I dress always without any décolleté, covering my shoulders and even my arms? Never drink any of that superb wine in public? No, puritanism is still a hell for us. Only a tiny splinter group of my people aren't locked cruelly within it. I could tell you stories about it that would chill your marrow.'

She uncrossed and recrossed her lithe legs. Blake, feeling for her, took another sip of the superb Margaux.

'Then tell me.'

'One incident then, quite recently, from an Austrian friend of mine who is a physiotherapist at our biggest government hospital. The case was of a girl of seventeen from a Palestinian family. They weren't very high on the social scale. The father was a ministry clerk, not very well educated, but very puritanical indeed.'

'So what happened to the girl?'

'She was actually only sixteen when it happened. One afternoon – so she said later – two rich young *Shemsis* in a Cadillac drew up outside her family's house in a southern suburb. They had seen her sitting in what passed for a garden. They enticed her into the Cadillac with sweet words and drove her off into the desert, where both raped her. She was so innocent that she didn't even know what they had done to her. They drove off, leaving her to walk home. Luckily, she got a lift from a lorry at the main road. She told no one what had happened. She knew neither the youths' names nor their car's number.'

'Then after six months or so she began to swell?' asked Blake.

'Yes. Though she bound her stomach tightly at first, to hide it, for by now she realized the truth. So it was not until late in her eighth month that her father learned it. He beat her so savagely with a heavy belt and his fists that the neighbours heard her screams and stormed in. They sent her to hospital where she bore a son, premature, but in fine fettle. The father appeared, apparently heartbroken at his own cruelty. He swore that that was over. They released the girl and her son. Next day the father shot her dead. He kept the son. They gave him four weeks in prison.'

'Christ!' said Blake. 'About what they'd give you in Europe for shoplifting a lollipop.'

'Yes,' she said. 'It shows Arab society's ferocity about girls' sexual morality.'

'I see now why you stick to wearing high-necked and long-sleeved dresses.'

'Yes. The only hope we girls from Arab States can have of any kind of freedom is to get right *outside* our countries. Even then, in any city like this where Arabs gather, puritanical eyes watch you all the time from somewhere, recording everything.'

'You've never married? You'd never marry a *Shemsi*?'

'What, and sink out of sheer boredom into harem lesbianism with my fellow wives? No. Or have my head cut off with a golden sword for taking a local lover? No. I'll keep leaving on my trips to Paris or Rome or New York or –' She glanced at him. '– London, in order to breathe. And meanwhile do everything I can to help pull my country forward, away from these murderous inequities and injustices.'

'Your brother sympathizes with you?'

'Abdullah? About developing the Kingdom of the Sun? Unreservedly. Away from puritanism? Yes, so far as a leader of the ruling class dare do so against the deeply entrenched conservatism of his social level.'

'I admire you both,' said Blake. 'You seem to be striving for a most worthwhile cause. It's impressive. So is what you've told me about Islamic Fundamentalism. Fascinating. A latent but colossally powerful organization. A hugely effective machine –'

'You make it sound like a rather large and highly efficient oil multinational.'

'– Something that could change the face of the world,' Blake went on, only marginally deflected. 'A giant, potentially lethal dynamo.'

'Well, thanks,' said Leila. 'Though I'm not too sure that I'm all that happy at seeing Abdullah and me linked, even if flatteringly, to Islamic Fundamentalism.'

Blake looked at her sharply.

'No. Of course. I see. Then let me offer a toast to you and Abdullah alone. In strawberries. They have imported strawberries on the menu. And perhaps a modest dessert wine? Or a liqueur?'

'Many thanks again, but no alcohol.'

'You think that eyes are watching even here?'

'Drop your napkin and glance half-left behind you when you pick it up. The table in the corner.'

Blake dropped and then retrieved his napkin.

'My God, yes. Dressed very fetchingly Western, but undoubtedly Arab.'

'Yes. In fact from the Kingdom's Oil Ministry too.'

'Still, they can hardly see it as anything more than a part of our business meeting, can they?'

Leila smiled.

'Indeed. What more could it be?'

Blake caught the head waiter on the wing, asking a Benedictine from him as he swooped past their table in a shallow curve.

'One thing still intrigues me, though,' said Blake.

'Well, we can't have that, can we? What is that, pray?'

'I can see why you chose us in Eagle with whom to make your first big supply contract, because we're not one of the Seven Sisters. But why us rather than any of the other fairly big independents?'

Leila, swallowing one of her strawberries unhurriedly, considered him.

'Where we could, we had a look at the senior executives we would probably be dealing with. We liked the cut of Morgan Sperry's jib, your Managing Director for the Middle East. He seemed a gentleman with a sense of humour. As for yourself as his new Area Co-ordinator –'

'As for me? This suspense is cruel.'

'We got what reports we could on your prior overseas postings with Eagle, in Africa, Indochina, Thailand, Venezuela. A mixed bag. Somewhat intense, one might say. Ambition, fierce, and perhaps not all that long on scruples. But quite often original, perhaps out of sheer pig-headedness. One faintly redeeming feature, though: in acute crisis, a tendency impishly to leap outside yourself and mock both yourself and destiny – no doubt simply psychologically to defuse and deflate unbearable situations, but the dramatic effect was sometimes amusing. At least you didn't look dull.'

'Gee, thanks.'

'So the two of you looked to us flexible and unorthodox enough to adapt briskly to new realities. As we think you're doing in the case of this new OPEC supply and price situation. And of course you've made this really vital new contribution to help us. Of your own free choice. We couldn't possibly have expected that from conventional oil men.'

'Oil's far too important, you mean, to leave in the hands of mere orthodox oil men?'

'About that.'

Afterwards the two of them sat quietly with their coffees, and

Blake with his Benedictine, and he said: 'You still feel you've made the right choice?'

She looked at him, frowning, her oval face delicate yet extremely strong, the jet-black eyes direct, the sinuous lips apart slightly in thought.

'Instinctively, yes,' she said. 'And I hope to God we're right.'

'You trust your instincts?'

'After you've checked the facts, what else can you trust?'

'Then we'll come out to your Kingdom of the Sun a week from tomorrow, as Abdullah suggested. That's Monday October 22.'

'Fine,' she said. 'That's contingent, naturally, on your getting the deal through your Board in London tomorrow?'

'Indeed. And, if we do, I'll telex you at once. We could have our private code to mean success. Say: "The wildcat has struck oil."'

'All right,' said Leila. '"The wildcat has struck oil." And telex your firm flight times, and we'll meet you at our airport.'

'I hope we get it through all right tomorrow.'

'You'll get it through.'

'*Insh'Allah*,' said Blake. 'If God so wills.'

Leila smiled.

'You're learning fast,' she said. 'We'll make a good Arab of you yet.'

He took her then in the Mercedes-Benz to a nightclub. She danced well, close to him, her body moving easily with his. If she went by her instincts, this should qualify, for instinctively they seemed to mesh well. He could see no Arab eyes watching in the nightclub's penumbra, nor, from her relaxation in his arms, did she seem to sense any. Back at the Imperial, on their floor, they had to pass his door going to her suite; kismet was on his side. She came into his room without demur. Already he knew her a decided slim lady, strong in natural dignity, not hesitant in what she did.

Leila drank two glasses of his Veuve Clicquot 1955 most cheerfully. When they went to bed together the act was no mere sexual gymnastics. It was an astonishing light brushing, yet deep mixing, of personalities. It had the mellow human warmth of a meeting of lifelong friends, yet also the shock of discovery. They seemed spontaneously already to have a long and valued past, and he, through her, an extraordinarily exciting future. He felt as if he was walking into a new, shadowed, and subtle world, alien yet intriguing, under huge vaulted and reverberating domes, by the slim upwards-surging pencils of minarets, magic and tingling; the whole crisp clean silhouette of Islam, fresh set in eternity. This act of love seemed to Blake the start of a very long contract indeed.

7
The Judgement of the Board

'Getting this 500,000 bd supply contract for Sun Light is probably our greatest trading coup of the year,' said Morgan Sperry.

The four other Managing Directors sitting round the oval mahogany table in Eagle International's twentieth floor Board Room, and Blake beside him, watched Sperry intently, as if concerned that he might get up at any moment and walk off forever with that victory.

'Sun Light's just about identical with Saudi Arabia's Arab Light, the Marker Crude, isn't it?' said Edward Poynter. 'It's 34° API too, I'm told, with very low sulphur content. Which means that it's excellent for our major refineries, designed precisely for Arab Light.'

'I'd suggest we don't allow ourselves to be obfuscated by the, ah, somewhat gaudy *glamour* of this operation,' said the Ice Maiden mincingly, his endemic bitchiness flickering in his voice like a venomous snake's tongue. 'Let's remember that these Heads of Agreement would give us this admittedly admirable crude *only at full OPEC posted price!* By accepting and signing this contract we should automatically be recognizing OPEC's right to *dictate crude oil prices to us*, admitting us no powers to negotiate. Wouldn't that be selling the pass behind the backs of all our colleagues?'

'Quite right!' said George Paul ringingly, tuned in perfectly as usual to His Master's Voice. His thick reddish hair gleamed impeccably on him like a plastic crown, fabulously waved; clearly he had it permed professionally. Under his hatchet nose his almost invisible lips curved lovingly in that exquisitely orgasmic ecstasy just before execution. With any luck he would be lopping off Blake any time now; Paul's antennae were as sensitive to blood slicks and death as the marvellous nostrils on any hammerhead shark; he knew to three points of decimals just how the wind blew from his Lord and Master, Kobus van Straten. Paul massaged his beautifully tailored paunch under the directorial table contentedly, then locked his long slim feminine hands under his chin, the short heavy red hair bristling on the backs of his fingers, and gazed at Blake, like a rather large cannibal at a potted and simmering missionary. 'Creating a precedent,' he intoned. 'After all, we've got to think of the others a bit, haven't we? The good of the industry as a whole, I mean.'

I can see the blood under his fingernails *this* time all right, thought Blake. He wondered who else would fall in behind the Ice Maiden now.

'I suppose there is that element of fair play,' said Edward Poynter, as excessively handsome as a TV doctor going on scene, the perfect sheen of his light olive skin looking as suspect as the rest of him, and half-answering Blake's question for him. 'I can quite see that we've got to maintain some sort of common industry front on an issue as potentially cataclysmic as this.'

'I'm frankly quite astounded, Edward,' said Sean O'Higgins, turning his large frame, spare as the scaffolding round some historic monument, towards Poynter, 'and, I must confess, very moved, to see you so generously giving your attention to the concepts of fair play and overall oil industry welfare. I would suggest that your concern here is misplaced. Since the OPEC negotiations in Vienna broke down on October 11 the oil industry has been in chaotic confusion and it has tended to be every man, or oil company, for himself. Anyway, can any of us round this table seriously pretend that this industry has *ever*, at any time, been anything other, under our veneer of civilized politeness in public meetings and ceremonies, than a world of cut-throat, murderous and merciless competition? Let us, for God's sake, here among ourselves, have the guts and good grace to drop that pious and totally spurious mask under which we pretend primarily to be devoted to public service and to the greater glory of democracy, humanity and whatever. Can't we at least be consistent with ourselves? Our raison d'être, our only genuine premise and objective, is to maximize profit long-term for our shareholders. By that definition we have nothing whatsoever to do with morality, or the oil industry's overall welfare. We are supposed to be buccaneers, highly efficient, operating just within the law, or outside it if we can get away with it. So let's at least not fool ourselves. If we're basically brigands, let's be that frankly. It's cleaner. Texaco, for example, have always been perfectly happy to appear as good tough straightforward businessmen with no spurious haloes.'

O'Higgins turned then and loomed his mountain-ledge silver-peppered bushy eyebrows at George Paul.

'The same comment goes for you, George. I just don't believe in any common industry front here. Now that OPEC, and particularly the Arabs in it, are nationalizing oil concessions right and left, survival in this game is going to depend on who has *secure access* to crude oil long-term. It no longer matters who owns it. We oil companies are going to have to make our living from now on from our *downstream* operations and profits, on how efficiently we run our tankers, refineries, depots, and dealer and service station networks. We've got the jump on the others because we've always been crude-short; we're used to not owning oil concessions or the profits from them. And here – ' O'Higgins went on, opening an arm and a big broad hand generously towards Sperry and Blake, ' – we're being offered what sounds to me like precisely that secure long-term access to an excellent crude that we need, that will give us the whip-hand over our competitors. Let's remember what a tremendous benefit it could be, a 500,000 bd five-year-renewable supply contract for a 34° API low-sulphur crude, ideal for our refinery patterns and market demands. That's enough in one contract to meet *half* our total needs.'

He swung his heavily seamed cliff of a face on Kobus van Straten, who everyone in the room knew now was the real adversary.

'So that I don't think that there can be any doubt whatsoever by any sensible Eagle executive: we should accept and sign this contract at once and very thankfully. And should congratulate and reward Morgan Sperry and Philip Blake for getting it for us.'

Silence, qualified by heavy breathing from George Paul and Edward Poynter, blanketed the room for some ten or fifteen seconds. Van Straten sat at the head of the oval table and looked at the other four men round it. The Ice Maiden had taken up his stance of deadly stillness. He sat immaculate, his silver hair perfectly groomed, the vertical ridges of muscle now bracketing his mouth savagely. His chill grey eye stared at this revolt. When he spoke his voice was still chintzy, but with barbed steel tips in it; incredulous, arrogant, supercilious, contemptuous; an Etonian Guards officer merely irritated at the Tiger tank at the foot of his garden:

'We still, gentlemen, would by accepting this contract be accepting the principle of unilateral OPEC pricing. That would leave us without any say whatsoever in this vital field. How could we live with that? *That* would be selling the pass!'

Morgan Sperry looked up.

'Kobus, we would live with that as we have lived with every other major fiscal or tax change in the business. We should simply pass on to the public, as we always have, any rise in the cost of crude to us. In full. So where is the problem? And we're deluding ourselves if we imagine that by refusing to sign this or any similar contract we shall in any way deflect OPEC from their new unilateral pricing policy. Nonsense. That's irrevocable anyway, until the oil supply-demand balance changes, which could take ten or fifteen years. But now, with world oil demand critically outstripping supply, OPEC and the Arabs are making use of a strength which history and the world's economic development have simply thrust into their hands. They won't stop. It's not only the Arabs. We must watch Iran too. The Shah has been pushing for quick massive new increases. We shouldn't be surprised to see him trying in a month or two to set his Iranian crude price at four or five times its level at the start of this month. So, I suggest, the net effect of our not signing this 500,000 bd Sun Light contract whose finding is very largely Philip Blake's doing, I should stress, will simply be to leave us stripped of a security we could otherwise have had for half our crude stream, and facing the necessity to find a contract or contracts later for that amount anyway, under almost certainly much less favourable conditions. Kobus, we have everything to lose, and nothing to gain, if we do not accept this contract *now*! And I think you know it!'

If he did, the Ice Maiden was keeping it well to himself. He looked at his colleagues with disdain. That, when his grey eye touched Blake, was spiked momentarily with pure hatred.

'I back Morgan Sperry unreservedly in what he says,' said Sean O'Higgins, his voice gravelly with conviction.

The Ice Maiden looked rapidly at Poynter. Van Straten's small hands were on the oval table in front of him. He had not moved them a millimetre.

'Edward? Your view?'

Edward Poynter squirmed visibly, his handsome countenance, even his beautifully smooth olive skin, appearing to pale. His natural instincts were always to back his boss. But here O'Higgins' and Sperry's logic seemed to have floored him.

'On the arguments advanced, and though – well, I feel I have no option, for the good of Eagle, but to accept the Sun Light contract at once.'

For the first time Blake stopped massaging his upper lip, and instead put his left hand down at his side.

'I shan't bother to ask you, George,' said Van Straten, 'since we already have a majority vote in favour of our accepting the Sun Light contract immediately.'

Blake could almost hear George Paul's sigh of relief. The Ice Maiden had kindly let him off the hook.

'Decided, then,' said the Ice Maiden. 'You accept the contract by telex at once, and, Morgan, you go out there for official signature in a week.'

The Ice Maiden turned and started to walk.

'One moment,' said Morgan Sperry.

'Yes?'

'Philip Blake here is mainly responsible for getting this excellent contract. He deserves a reward. He wants nothing material, but only a Board Minute. It would say that in recognition of his initiative in this matter, due consideration be given him when new Managing Director nominations are made in five to seven years.'

The Board Room went into its favourite huddle again, like an American football team before a play.

'That seems to me eminently reasonable and thoroughly deserved,' said Sean O'Higgins, glancing at Sperry and Blake with a slight smile, and lifting and driving his massive eyebrows down on his point like twin hammers.

George Paul glanced at them too, under his faultless reddish permanent wave, his predatory hatchet nose questing instinctively for Blake's jugular, his hangman's smile floating lovingly on his thin lips. 'Why not?' he said silkily. 'The labourer is always worthy of his hire.' Anyway, said that haunting Auschwitz smile, the Van Straten–Paul team should with any luck have lopped Blake clean off the Eagle management tree well before those five or seven years were up.

'Agreed,' said Edward Poynter, his distinguished silver-flecked temples suspect, his light olive skin bland. He went on, a note of considerable satisfaction in his voice, his snapping black eyes slick with intelligence and malice: 'In any event, "Favourable consideration" or "due consideration" carries absolutely no legally binding commitment upon us that I can see actually irrevocably to *appoint* Mr Blake an Eagle Managing Director within five to seven years. Does it?'

'No,' said Morgan Sperry smoothly. 'Of course not.' He went on, showing an enviably deep sense of irony and black humour: 'One would of course leave the actual *nominations* of new MDs to the good judgement and innate fairness of the Board existing at that time.'

The Board existing at this time huddled over that one for a few moments too, darting glances at Sperry. But he, keen amateur actor in his youth, was keeping his face admirably straight. Then Van Straten said:

'All right. You'll write that Minute, Morgan? I'll counter-sign it.'

And he got up crisply, signifying the end of the meeting. Sperry and Blake got up with him and the others, and walked to the door, fractionally more slowly, so that the Ice Maiden could reach it first, as became his Top Dog status. Even if thus moving more quietly, Blake still felt his limp. So, clearly, did the Ice Maiden. As he passed Blake he said:

'Feeling the strain, Blake?'

Gritting his teeth, Blake went on walking.

'Not finding it all a bit too much for you?' the Ice Maiden continued mincingly, and loudly enough for all to hear comfortably. 'You ought to have a doctor look at that thing, you know.'

It was no bad shot at a fast castration on the march. Blake's left hand flew to his upper lip. He heard Poynter and Paul snigger behind him. He also saw Sperry glance warningly at him and half raise his hand. Blake said nothing more. He had got the message. He simply watched Van Straten's thin steel body go out of the door ahead. There was an optimum time for starting any really lethal fight, and his was not yet.

Besides, today's victory, the first small victory in his war to the death with Van Straten, was his. Thanks mainly to Sperry and O'Higgins. He could send that magic message now by urgent telex:

Glad to advise you that the wildcat has struck oil.

And give the details of Sperry's and his flight arrival at the City of the Sun's airport on October 22, in six days. Abdullah and Leila would be waiting for that.

A double small victory, really. For by getting the 500,000 bd Sun Light contract with Eagle through that day, Blake had also got through his own 50,000 bd contract and guarantee. Which would bring him near two million dollars a year and make him a multimillionaire, arming him with all the powers he would need finally to confront and destroy Van Straten. Even if that took a decade. Walking along the twentieth floor in Eagle International's Central offices in Millbank with Morgan Sperry now, he could even manage to beam to himself at it. Blake was becoming more Arab by the minute. He was now finding the prospect of long-term personal vengeance distinctly exhilarating, as good a guiding star for the future as any, and aesthetically most satisfying. There might be other ways than his to really full-blooded zest in life in a generally absurd and impersonal universe, and to occasional deep belly-laughs at it, but Blake could not think of any at the moment.

8
Marital Bliss

'She's a castrator,' said María-Luisa succinctly.

'You don't need a licence for that?' asked Blake.

They stood in a circle of five, the other three of whom Blake knew only vaguely by sight, in this humming cocktail-cum-supper party in the large living-room on the second floor of the Blakes' upstairs flat at 90 Ainger Road, Primrose Hill. Blake rarely knew all his wife's guests. Celia Blake had eclectic tastes, mainly in the realms of fashion, theatre, film, and psychiatry and psychoanalysis. The Hampstead area bulged with these last, with its Tavistock Clinic and Anna Freud's house and institute. Even Ronnie Laing lived only just round the corner. María-Luisa was a member of this club, an analyst from the Tavistock. So was her target, an ineradicably Austrian psychiatrist named Virginia Schacht. María-Luisa, Chilean by birth, turned her magnificent milk-white complexion full up on Blake now like a searchlight, but from rather low down; she was a short lady. Her skin was her best feature and she knew it. Framing or inset in it were standard Spanish beauty equipment, including long luxuriant black hair, full ruby lips, and flashing black eyes. She also had a provocative well-busted body which she never exactly forgot about.

'Why do you mock, Philip? You're frightened of the subject?'

'Ah!' said two of the three faceless people with them, approvingly.

Blake gave a puff of laughter.

'I love it, Maria. Any time we mere laymen keep quiet about your field, then we must be inhibited about it. But if we dare make any irreverent comment, you at once reduce it to proof of our personal fears and phobias! The perfect double-bind!'

María-Luisa's fine bust heaved slightly at him from her fragile décolleté, and she took a long steady draught of her claret, evidently to calm her marksman's nerve and eye. Her gaze dropped then and played pointedly about the area of

59

Blake's genitals, and she said, her tone clinical, and with all the considerable authority of the consultorium:

'Yet we do not invent the fears.'

Her English, by kind permission of Cheltenham Ladies' College, was really perfect. Only the faintest hint of a Chilean accent remained, mostly in the near-lisping r's. Her acolytes in this small group again murmured their supportive 'Ah!'s and levelled their eyes too on Blake's crutch. Such was their combined impact that Blake was powerfully tempted to spring his hands at once in front of him like overlapping fig-leaves. Instead he yielded gracefully; if you can't beat them, join them; and he was after all supposed to be the party's co-host.

'You may have a point there, María-Luisa. I should certainly just hate to lose my pecker.'

The group eyed him with marginally less hostility. He was just another vulnerable human being like them after all. Blake pressed home his advantage at once, fully deflecting their attention.

'And just how and why is friend Virginia Schacht a castrator?'

Now accorded the entire podium without reserve María-Luisa preened herself visibly, snuggling comfortably within her pampered skin. She pushed her empty wine-glass forward through the air. She deserved to be paid court now.

'May I have a little more?'

'Of course. Claret again?'

'Please.'

Blake hurled himself into the tide. There were all of sixty people in this combined living and dining-room which stretched the whole width of the building. All of them seemed to be shouting at one another with great gusto and without cease. Forging ahead, Blake could hardly see a still pair of lips between the lot of them. The din was now tremendous, booming up from the packed multitude at the walls and ceilings and bouncing back at it uninterruptedly, as if in final brilliant breakthrough to a new and heartwarming law of perpetual motion. For this cacophony had now achieved a life of its own, unstoppable. This could have been the thrumming religious roar of some crowded Aztec temple audience at the moment of the blood-sacrifice of the victim on the stone altar. Or the deep-throated and continuing hymn-chant of the many disciples of some modern mystic sect striving desperately to be shriven by its featureless god of the most mortal sin of all, of nonentity. Perhaps, thought Blake, the ritual of this kind of intense and vibrant party, and the catharsis and absolution it could give, or their illusion, made it the nearest modern substitute in a world without God for the earlier orthodox ceremonies of confession and communion. There had been wine in those, and much wine flowed here. There had been hosts in those, and here, in the form of many savouries and foods, were many hosts –

For, as usual, Celia had spared no expense or trouble to provide the best in food and wine. There were Fortnum and Mason pâtés, truffles, cakes, chocolates. Huge plates of smoked salmon and ham, mixed salads with Roquefort and mayonnaise and olive oil and lemon dressings, giant hot bowls of carefully prepared lasagna and quiche and chilli con carne, freshly made pasta, steaks, brochettes, meat balls and Chicken Kiev, were being variously wolfed or nibbled by the guests who adorned the tables and sideboards and chairs and sofas in these two large rooms with their loaded plates balanced perilously on their knees. Blake had ordered the wines from the Travellers Club, the good Club Claret and its Chambertins and White Riojas and Chablis. No one was going to die of thirst or hunger here this night.

As Blake reached the sideboard and the opened wine bottles there he heard the party bare its soul in glittering splinters about him –

'. . . A great big house and garden in Millionaires' Row here for her, my dear, but *not* for his second mistress . . . '

'. . . I suppose fraud if you must be *technical*, but all he really did after all was to *borrow* some of the company's money . . . '

'. . . Gay as Oscar Wilde, my good fellow, and with nothing like the same track record . . . '

'. . . Always trying to climb into her *knickers*, you see, even at the bacon-and-eggs stage at breakfast. So *taxing* . . . '

Blake filled María-Luisa's glass liberally with claret, under the extremely attractive gaze of his wife; this time from the oil painting above the sideboard. There were two other portraits of Celia in the other, the living-room. One was a very striking charcoal; the artist had caught her in harsh and thin black strokes against pure white. The other was an Edward Fox oil, her full body seated against an orchard, her fine emerald eyes hauntingly big, her cheekbones high, the mouth full and warm. Beneath the slim regal neck was that splendid body, curved, feminine, gracious, disciplined. Celia looked straight out on the world, with gravity and courage. And perhaps deep passion, thought Blake now, though he seemed to have been unable ever really to evoke it; how long could you live with someone intimately, in bed and board, and still never really know him, or her?

Blake slid back into the pulsing mass. From the far end of the dining-room music poured through two high-hung speakers. It was a heroic attempt, against the brassy blast of voices in that confined space, climbing inexorably step by step to their communal orgasmic peak. From time to time the music actually succeeded momentarily in piercing this protracted blunt monster's shriek. Blake recognized it. It was Carl Orff's *Carmina Burana* oratorio, that epic setting of medieval church and lay songs and chants, extolling romantic and earthy lusty pagan love, sometimes blasphemous and flirting with black magic and Black Masses, always rich and gloriously many-hued and deep-echoing. Blake found it singularly appropriate to this exotically caparisoned and jewelled, carnal and generally manic assembly, also going its opulent and witty way to hell.

'Mr Blake! May the benign signs of the Zodiac shine upon you!'

That brought him up dead in his tracks, his own Chambertin in the wine-glass in his left hand, María-Luisa's filled glass of claret in his right; Blake the unconquerable chalice-bearer, Blake the undeflectable armoured champion carrying the Holy Grail with undying loyalty to his thirsting female friends.

A small blonde young woman of some thirty-five years or so confronted him amiably. She was chubby-cheeked and a little broadish in the beam and she had a clear direct blue eye. She brimmed over visibly with joy and love. What on earth then was she doing here?

'You don't even remember me, Mr Blake! In a party of Celia's here a year ago! I'm Beth, the children's clown, and magician!'

My God, more magic! Black magic too? No, she was white magic. Very bright gold magic.

'Of course I remember! You showed me photographs of you performing at a children's Christmas party.'

It was as if he had given the secret password releasing the djinn from his magic flask. Beth dived her hands into the narrow-throated prayer shawl bag over her left shoulder and emerged with the photos he had seen the year before, and others. He saw her there facing the camera, the marvelling joyous faces of children scattered about her like shooting-stars. But Beth's face, above her classic big-lapelled clown's jacket, was not joyous, though a clown's big broad-lipped smile was painted on it. Here, against the absurdities of fate, was a distillation of all the sadness in the world. Beth knew tragedy. Beth was at home with tragedy. Beth the compassionate clown.

'It's funny, you haven't changed a bit. Still the most solitary man in the world!'

Blake looked about him and laughed.

'Here? In this dense jagged mass with its sharp cutting edges?'

'Especially here.'

'It's true. I don't see a single other oilman around.'

'So what are you doing here, stranger?'

'What does one ever do anywhere?'

He nodded to her, smiling, and forged punctiliously on with his steady lofted wine-glasses. María-Luisa, locked in her grouplet, was enchanted with her recharged claret.

'So how and why's Virginia a castrator, Maria?'

'My God, you're tenacious! We've got onto God since then. Where's he gone? Even Buddha. But Virginia. Well, because none of us does what he does, is what he is, by accident. We all stumble, slither, back-track, fall about finally into where we fit. Like steel balls into a pin-table game. That's where Virginia fits.'

'Ah, our destiny is pre-struck, etched in our stars, sort of thing?'

'That's near it. Pre-struck in our unconscious, rather, in how we're moulded before we even know about it. In our innate predispositions. And Virginia's inexorable steel pin-table pattern is to dominate.'

They looked across at the dominatrix in question. She was in the living-room holding court to ten or twelve in front of

63

her. Her charisma was undeniable, her magnetic appeal to them evident; when she laughed, they laughed; sighed, they sighed; frowned, they frowned. Virginia was a tall woman, nearly six foot, and broad in proportion. She looked very Saxon, blonde and with very light blue eyes. Her face was striking; a little gaunt, with high cheekbones. Vitality ran through her like an electric current. She exhibited her stature as if by divine right.

'She could be pure Old Testament,' said Blake. 'A ruling priestess.'

'Again that's near it. Certainly she has immense power behind her. Less religious than intuitive, of acute intelligence.'

'But how and why should she need to dominate?'

'Think a little. She's an extraordinarily brave and valuable person. In some of her private and more specialized work she handles only criminals. Consider that any psychiatrist or psychoanalyst treating such – over two-or three-year periods – is presiding over some of the hardest and most intractable human material in the world; they may well be men of great violence, rapists, potential murderers, other deviates. Anyone who can interpret and lead such to sanity needs to have very great moral strength and reserves.'

'And thus castrate? Yes, perhaps she does have a somewhat punitive air about her.'

'Castrate was probably too strong,' said María-Luisa. 'She probably only chops off the really incurably wicked penises. Certainly, she has an excellent reputation in her field. She has helped a great many patients.'

'And in her private life? She carries that same posture over into it?'

'Perhaps a little, inevitably; professional deformation. But she is also known for being an outstandingly loyal friend.'

Well, if we're going to start being *nice* about people now, I'm off, thought Blake, and eased himself imperceptibly out of María-Luisa's grouplet, pointing instead at the living-room, with a vague homing-instinct desire to find his wife. As he moved he noticed that the music had changed. It was now straight rock. In recognition of that people had cleared a space on the far side of the living-room, in which various enthusiasts were dancing. Blake saw Christina, a fashion model of high repute, tall and dark and sinuous, curving lithely to the beat, and more or less accompanied by Reginald Ringland, one of Britain's brightest film actors, who had just achieved notoriety by his lifelike rapier thrusts and hoarse male cries of disdain in an epic about Roundheads and Cavaliers. Reginald, well-built on top, was inclining to the rock somewhat less fluidly. As if to honour some deep principle of equity, Christina's and Reginald's consorts (who got married these days? Who cared?) were also going through rare movements opposite each other, their faces raptly concentrated, like men building up their rhythms to ejaculate. These were Pamela King, in fact very feminine indeed, of curly dark blonde hair and exquisite features, a stage and film actress also of considerable repute; and Benjamin Brace, tall and Canadian, a rising London fashion and news photographer. Watching them from the sidelines were Gloria Black, dark and vivid, star of the West End's leading musical, an East Ender who had reached the top, and Perry Minute, a ruddy-cheeked and white-haired New Zealander who as head of a Booker-Prize winning London publishing house broke tradition by actually making money efficiently from publishing good books and liking doing so; and his wife Rosemary, an elegant and witty columnist in the Mirror Group. Blake also saw scattered through the well-groomed and heeled mass ahead West End and Hampstead fashion designers and boutique owners, a clutch of stock-brokers and lawyers, three playwrights, four authors, several architects, a burst of analysts and Celia's favourite hairdresser.

This technicolour, intellectual, highly talented, and some-what bitchy set of people was some evidence of Celia's monumentally paranoiac social drive. She, either as hostess or guest, needed them constantly about her. She could not do without them in any comfort. They were like a drug. They were her identity – as for Blake was his skirt of power and his shield, his intricate oil-company machinery about him. They were as essential to her as, on María-Luisa's thesis, were her criminal patients to Virginia. But Celia made her fair contri-bution to this élite club. She brought her name, her wit, her money; a certain style. And her beauty, which was ex-ceptional. She made the sight of that available to all, generously; she was never petty. Blake thought that *this* was Celia's main motive for displaying three portraits of herself in these principal two rooms. It was not just narcissism. They were striking works, showing a deep beauty. Why should she not let the world, or at least her select club, see that?

Blake saw her at last then. Celia was in the inside right corner of the living-room, that opposite Virginia's. She stood there like a rather small perfect statue, men in serried ranks around her. That was normal. Her fine emerald eyes looked out tranquilly. She knew their force. Her short blonde hair curled luxuriantly on her head. Her dress was silver lamé, close fitting, cocktail-length, bare-shouldered, bare-armed. Petite and high-heeled narrow silver shoes matched it. For jewelry, she wore a single narrow flat silver band round her throat, nothing else. With that superb body, it was enough. Celia had a great artist's economy in creating effects. She was classical. No childbirth had ever marred that model feminine silhouette. Celia's world was indeed that of high fashion, fast and light, brittle, ruthless, an impersonal shallow wide brass bowl across which glanced legion reflections, mirror-images escorted by dancing tall shadows, chic mannequins sheathed exquisitely, gliding ecstatically across carpeted stages of pure gold. This was her scene, this highly stylized portrayal of female flesh and beauty and grace always a little larger than life, this costly shimmering fairyland. Celia fitted here uncannily, with sweet ease, as if designed for it. In their two years back from Venezuela, she had bought a boutique in Fitzjohn's Avenue just before it met Hampstead High Street, and transformed it into a high temple of Balmain and Ossie Clarke, Lanvin and Zandra Rhodes, Yves Saint-Laurent and Dior, awe-inspiring and diamond-studded with profits. Children had no place here, the awkward protuberances of pregnancy.

Blake, reaching nearer, bowspritted by his outstretched glass of Chambertin, wondered if he had any real place here either. Still, he had a certain strong liking for her iridescent bubble-world. In its complexities and the wide range of its exotic characters, it had great entertainment value. Against it his own world seemed quite a clean and simple jungle. Somehow the two kept a balance. As Blake's relations with his wife were always an intriguing delicate balance. She was always somewhere still an alien. An enemy too, perhaps? But you could learn to love your enemy also. And if all their marriage was really an armed truce, at least it was a truce. You should never after all ask too much. They still made love

66

together very contentedly and physically, even if they found no great heart in it. You could not always have deep passion too, that warm renewing wash of eternity. Perhaps she also felt that hunger, that searing sense of a wind crying across empty moors, waste lands. Perhaps she, as he did, sought out those warming fires in other lovers –

This might be one of them. Chris Morgenthau, a big black-haired man of forty-five in a dark pearl Armani suit, a red polka-dotted dark pearl Armani tie, an accentless Austrian who worked somewhere high in the Agence France Presse. He half-glanced at and saluted the looming Blake:

'The Arabs have blown it again. The Israelis will eat them now.'

'Here's someone who's just been with Arabs,' said Celia. 'In Vienna with OPEC. Hullo, darling. Have the Arabs blown their war?'

'Yes,' said Blake, kissing her cheek, gazing back at her. But she had already broken eye-contact with him, concentrating fully on Morgenthau. Blake had the ugly sensation of one looking by accident through another's bedroom window.

'So you feel that it'll never end, Chris?' said Celia. 'Until the Arabs finally push them into the sea.'

Blake still watched her, separated from him as if by a wall of glass. He had the eerie sense now that there was really no Celia behind that appearance. If you opened that skin, there would be just black nothing within –

The whole orgasmic roar of the party suddenly smote his ears again; another voice of black nothing, of nihilism –

'Or until the Arabs drop a nuclear bomb on them,' said Morgenthau. 'Or something finally binds them into a genuine Pan-Islamic unity.'

'Could anything do that, Chris?' she asked, her soul still bent on him.

'Islam revived could do it. A new crusade that may rock the world.'

Blake thought suddenly of Leila. Somewhere, there was still always that. He could get out to that.

'So that could bring them victory?' asked Celia.

Victory, thought Blake. My God, today's my great day of victory!

But, under the great weight of the blunt monster's roar, that black void, under his sudden sense of the void in Celia, that statement rang false in his own mind. He heard it hollow like a lost cry on the wind, evoking only a conviction of motiveless pain, of limitless sadness. Where was the victory?

9
A Mark of Cain

Beth the sad clown had been near it. She had called Blake the most solitary man in the world. It was not an honour he had chosen. Rather, it was a kind of Mark of Cain. Nor could he decently fob off the responsibility for it onto, say, his father, by claiming that he had inherited it from him. That eternally struggling and threadbare prelate had not been exceptional in anything, not even loneliness. Blake could not hang it on his mother any more credibly. She had died when he was so young that he could hardly remember her.

Blake had discovered this hallmark of his identity, in some agony, at Cheltenham. An English public school's assessment of a particular boy can be subtle and surprisingly incisive. It is popularly supposed to be most merciless against the boy who does not fit into its strict pattern. From the viewpoint of the society it serves, it may be absolutely right to do just that. When Blake grew up, his English world probably still needed more senior managers than Rothschilds, more MPs than Party leaders, more staff officers than Wellingtons. Certainly the system singled Blake out uncannily. Its performance was all the more impressive because he had made such very deliberate efforts to conform scrupulously to its standards, carefully refraining from coming any higher than fourth or fifth in his class examinations, and shining spectacularly at sport, notably rowing and boxing, as was expected and approved. Perhaps here he had pulled out the stops just a little too far, revealing something of the sheer nakedness of his ambitions. For Blake was basically far too serious a man to be a good loser. He had, of course, learnt near-perfect mastery of the usual public school deprecatory and highly stylized argot for victory or defeat on the playing-field. But, unfortunately, Blake's truth glinted through. The system smelt him out, charted the true ferocity of his drives. It did not like what it found. Yeats's 'The best lack all conviction while the worst are full of passionate intensity' might have expressed a very English standard of judgement.

Even Blake's deliberately cultivated bland appearance could not always mask his passion. There was a particular quality to him just before a big race in rowing, or when he sat already gloved before entering the ring. He was utterly still, totally concentrated. He could have been listening to inner voices, or an inner voice. There was almost a glitter to him, to that blond hair, those crisp blue eyes. Certainly human warmth was not conspicuous in him at such moments. He could hardly have had the space for it; he was too stripped for action. Commensurately, he made no really close friend. It was as if he felt that, unencumbered, he could move all the faster. His world, with a fine sense of irony, took him literally. It always gave him respect – his sporting prowess, which made him a house prefect very early, merited that. But it mirrored him, cruelly. It never really let him join the club.

The system had its techniques of punishment too, its own way of making its points. On school holidays during the term, Blake would quite often find that he had not been included in any of the groups of boys crystallized spontaneously for their wild and immensely pleasurable outings. Blake, each time with appalling shock, would suddenly find himself left high and dry on the shelf. It was a bitter, profound, and repeated humiliation, and all the school world knew of it, though no one ever alluded to it to his face. Nor, striving desperately, could he see that there was any remedy at all that he could try. Only his pride restrained him from blasphemy or outright tears. He would stalk off alone, take his paper-packed picnic lunch, and ride off to Tewkesbury or Gloucester or some pub in the Cotswold hills, a solitary cyclist, no warm screen of fellows about him.

These were probably the profoundest agonies of Blake's life. No later threat or defeat could come near them. And there was no way out of it. The system's indictment of him became a self-fulfilling prophecy. It got so used to seeing him as an outcast, however worthy, however muscularly adept, that he became that. He even became a convinced supporter of the theory himself. His final reaction to his spiritual leprosy did him some credit, for there was a practical and positive issue to it. Vaulting tradition, he finally, and quite easily, came first in his sixth form examinations for three terms running, and won his scholarship to Wadham.

But his education cost him scars. He learnt it alone, with no clan members at his elbows. Symptomatically, he learnt sex first the same way, by masturbation, not with a kin of young men in a brothel. But at least those pricey and ineradicable scars taught him something. The deepest pain makes a fine tutor. It taught Blake an intellectual and emotional stature, a focus on infinity. He learnt to hear the echoes to actions, reverberating endlessly. He knew the black roads to nihilism and total despair, the broad roads to hell. As a doomed man, pre-selected inscrutably by God or the Devil, he had his rights in revolt to immortality. Blake had paid up. He had earned his privilege to ask, as he had at Celia's groomed party, where is the victory? Yet he found the silence which answered that question chill. These were cold lands, where he could walk as tragically a clown as Beth. All you could do to keep warm was to find power and exercise it. That made sense. Power was the only solution. Naturally, things being as they were, there was a price-tag on that too. Power might cost you your soul.

IO

The Kingdom of the Sun

'No, in the end Sadat's has proved a hollow victory,' said Sheikh Abdullah bin Ali bin Jibál, Minister of Oil of the

Kingdom of the Sun, calling a spade a spade in the City of the Sun that Monday October 22. 'Four days ago already Kosygin, visiting from Russia, could show Sadat satellite photos confirming without a shadow of a doubt that Sharon had put about a full Israeli armoured division across the canal and annihilated several Russian missile sites. By today Sharon must have drawn a steel noose round the entire Egyptian 3rd Army at Suez and have penetrated to a hundred kilometres or so from an undefended Cairo. Sadat could only sue for peace.'

'Indeed,' said Morgan Sperry. 'And yesterday we heard that the Security Council in New York had unanimously accepted the US and Russian call for an immediate cease-fire. So the war just stops there?'

Abdullah got up restlessly. His *khutra*, head-dress, was pure white. His *ogal*, originally used for hobbling camels, crowned it, drew crisp black lines across it. Abdullah wore it at a slightly rakish angle. The dark olive hawk-like face, the nose thrusting and inquisitive, the irises of the eyes very black above the rich wide black moustache, observed Sperry intently. Abdullah turned suddenly and walked rapidly to the huge window of his spacious fifteenth-floor office. His lean six foot three sinewy body beat crisply against his full-length pure white dishdasha with its high throat and long white sleeves. He stopped, gazed down, turned, and paced back as swiftly to the circle of deep armchairs and sofas.

'Yes. The war just stops there. Until the next time.' The faint lines at the corners of his thin sinuous lips widened. There was a pleasant flash of strong white teeth against the dark olive skin as he smiled. 'But we've another wider war to fight, where possibly we can show ourselves a little more effective.' He looked at Sperry. 'You'll know that since the day before yesterday Saudi has embargoed *all* oil to the US and Holland, and has also cut ten per cent to everyone else just to drive home their point? For we haven't liked America's massive air-bridge aid to Israel, or the landing rights Holland gave for it.'

'Yes,' said Sperry. 'I heard that before we left London yesterday. It's a pity.'

'Yes, I'm sorry. I know you're American. We'll be seeing mile-long car queues at your filling stations soon, fights, pain and tribulation.'

Sperry shrugged.

'Eagle hasn't bought from Saudi so far, so we're not hurt. But presumably the overall five per cent OPEC cut will affect our new contract with you?'

'Inevitably,' said Abdullah. 'Though I can see a way of lightening it.'

'Ah?'

'There's a clause permitting two per cent under- or over-loading of your nominated tankers. We can deliberately overload you that two per cent for the next few months.'

'Excellent!' said Sperry. 'I have the feeling this is going to be a pleasant contract to operate. I've just one other point: price. Can you keep your prices to us fixed for any period? You know that constantly changing them is a nightmare administ-ratively.'

Abdullah looked at the man sitting next to Sperry. 'Kamal,' he said. '*Tafáthal*!'

His Under-Secretary, Kamal Daud, looked at Sperry speculatively. Daud was significantly older than Abdullah, shorter, and more heavily built. Like many ruling Arabs, he loved to stay inscrutable behind dark glasses.

'With pleasure,' said Daud, his English accented but clear. 'Well, I fear I cannot see how we can help. Clearly we cannot deviate from the prices which OPEC decides. For the moment since the OPEC meeting in Kuwait on October 13, it's up to $5·12 per barrel for the marker Arab Light 34° API, low sulphur, with sixty days' credit. Our Sun Light's virtually identical to that, so it's the same price. But to give you that fixed for any significant period? There are still giant pressures, Mr Sperry, to push the prices up well beyond that. And they could take effect in higher prices at any time.'

Daud's been reading my calculations, thought Philip Blake, sitting on Sperry's right. Or he's been making some pretty shrewd ones of his own, which come out something like the same . . .

'So no guarantee of that firm for six or say even three months?' asked Sperry winningly.

The third Arab in the room gave a short surprising bark of laughter. He in turn sat on Under-Secretary Daud's right and, scrupulously, just perceptibly back from him in the circle line of armchairs. No one, not even a professional courtier at Louis XIV's palace, could ever be as needle sharp as an Arab on the finer points of protocol. Abdullah had presented this third man as Ibrahim Sabri, the ministry's chief petroleum economist. Ibrahim Sabri was a short squat Arab in his forties with a paunch and a complexion like the face of the moon. Like Daud, he clung to the aloofness accorded him by his dark tinted glasses – worn it seemed, as faithfully within buildings as out under the harsh sun. Unlike Daud and Abdullah, however, Sabri wore no flowing and graceful dishdasha, but instead affected a pedestrian European-style shirt and slacks. Blake learned later that he called himself a Jordanian and prided himself on his economics degree at Amman University. Blake guessed him really Palestinian. Now Ibrahim Sabri followed his startling short bark by eyeing Sperry sceptically and sucking air in audibly through his teeth. He could have been nerving himself to spring physically to the attack.

'I don't think, *ya Sheikh* Abdullah, that we can in any way qualify what *El Wakil* Kamal Daud has so soundly said,' intoned Ibrahim Sabri gutturally. 'The Kingdom's oil ministry *cannot* sensibly give Eagle International a fixed crude price for any significant period, not even one month, let alone three or six. That would be transgressing our OPEC agreement with our sister states. And the market is *very* volatile.'

Pompous little bugger, thought Blake. Though the man was of course quite right. Here was where Daud had got his calculations. Or his interpretation of Blake's.

'Well, that's still quite a hell of a price rise as it is,' said Sperry spiritedly. 'Up from three dollars. That's more than seventy per cent up all in one go! Will the Seven Sisters ever really pay that? They came nowhere near to agreeing it in Vienna.'

Abdullah glanced at him a trifle impatiently, got up lithely, and beat his way to his huge window again. The starchy thrashing of his long lean hard body against his full-length white dishdasha made its tart conversational comment. He swung and stared at them. He was tall and taut and dominating.

'The Seven Sisters can always walk away from it,' he said, 'but they won't get much oil. And we'll find buyers all right.' His voice hardened, and he faced more deliberately towards Sperry and Blake. 'Look, we're not totally uninformed. We know what the Majors are saying about us, that we're imposing economic blackmail. Well, we also know business morality when we see it. We're negotiating a very fair 200,000 bd supply contract with a Sister, to recognize that it was *they* who discovered oil in our Kingdom and opened up the oil industry here. We've sometimes seen a different business morality from your side. By what morality did you in the industrialized West, and notably the international oil Majors, sacrifice us oil-producing countries by *imposing* on us for the sixty years till 1973 artificially low prices for our crude oil, often our only export earner? Proof of how you rigged that price is that when we at last freed ourselves from your iron hand by these recent OPEC moves we could within weeks charge you *two-and-a-half times* what we'd got before – there used to be a two dollar crude, remember?

'Yes,' said Morgan Sperry, 'I remember.' He looked back at Abdullah and he smiled infectiously. 'I didn't do it personally, you know.'

'Maybe not,' said Abdullah, still in full flood. 'But we have been forced, compelled at the cost of long misery, to subsidize virtually your entire industrial and economic development. Your international Majors, Seven Sisters? What true competitive play of free market forces did they really allow here? Didn't they run the whole worldwide show, in the most massive, sustained, and successful of all their conspiracies, explicit or tacit? So isn't it only fair that we should have our turn now?'

'I don't think it was ever a fully explicit conspiracy at all,' said Sperry, doing his best for the Seven Sisters. 'That's melodramatizing in hindsight. I don't think we've ever seen it quite as you've put it.'

'Try looking at it from my seat,' said Abdullah. 'Then you might.'

'Frivolously, criminally low prices,' chanted Kamal Daud, like a loyal echo.

'For our primary commodity,' contributed Ibrahim Sabri lyrically, as if intoning from his economic bible, 'which was at the same time the world's most important source of energy.' He sucked air violently in through his teeth to underline this indictment.

'Perhaps so,' said Sperry equably. 'But anyway we in Eagle were never in the alleged Seven Sisters cartel which you say carved up the oil world between them.'

74

'Which is the main reason why we're dealing with you,' said Abdullah.

Sperry smiled. 'All right. So when do we start?'

'Lifting?' asked Abdullah. 'Daud?'

Kamal Daud turned heavily to Sperry and that oddly sinister mask of eternal black glasses (perhaps their frame was fused now with Daud's bones, thought Blake) addressed him.

'You'll have seen our standard operational contract, of course, Mr Sperry. That gives all our tanker-loading procedures in some detail. It's all pretty routine. We'll need to give our loading terminals about a week's prior operational details of the vessels you'll be sending us, of course.'

'I can get that detail telexed you from London tomorrow,' said Sperry. 'So why don't we target to make our first lifting in ten days, on November 1? That leaves it all nice and neat.'

'No problem,' said Daud. 'I guess you'll be putting in mainly Very Large Crude Carriers?'

'Yes, almost entirely VLCCs. And Mr Blake here can sort out any final questions with you. He's staying on tomorrow. I must leave for London, unfortunately. But Mr Blake has full power of attorney for Eagle, including supply contracts.'

'Ours should be ready for your signature at any moment now,' said Abdullah. 'Our head lawyer, Ahmed Feisal, should be here already with that work of art, in duplicate, so that you can take yours back fully signed and valid with you early tomorrow, Mr Sperry.'

'Fine,' said Sperry. 'That way I can present it to our Board in double-quick time as an exemplary achievement for both sides.'

'Until Feisal arrives,' said Abdullah. 'Come and have a glance at the Arab world with which you are now casting in your lot.'

Sperry and Blake got up and walked over to join him. They looked vertically down the sheer drop of fifteen floors. The effect shocked, producing vertigo, hypnosis. For down there in the sun-soaked inferno a wide six-lane highway spun past the Oil Ministry building. Along it in either direction massed columns of cars shot like shells, Cadillacs, Buicks, Chryslers, Chevrolets, Fords, a Rolls-Royce or two, and a plethora of lesser Japanese and European makes. No hint of that cacophony, or the superheated air outside, reached into

Abdullah's big office. The vast windows were hermetically sealed, the temperature within scrupulously kept at a comfortable level by ubiquitous air-conditioners.

'The wide avenue is *Sharia el Quds*, Jerusalem Road,' said Abdullah. He glanced at Sperry and Blake. 'Yes, from the latest news we're finding it a long road to travel. But one day we shall achieve it.'

He gestured beyond the pulsing highway, lined with its tall neon signs of Rolex and Canon and Chanel and Coca-Cola and IBM and Motorola, and its Ford and Nissan and Toyota showrooms.

'And we carry much of our past still with us. That's the old quarter of the City of the Sun. Part of our spiritual inheritance –'

Indeed, the city's character changed abruptly there. The high gleaming and impersonal towers of modernity ended this side of the avenue. Beyond it were sand-coloured one-storeyed buildings like sheds, and a few stone-walled Arab houses. Blake saw many mosques, the curves of their domes generously warm and feminine, the minarets lifting in aching slim jets of stone up into the cloudless pale blue sky, the walls crenellated, in the eternal etched profile of Islam.

Blake's gaze followed where Abdullah pointed now, half and far left.

'See there? The multitudes crowding through those twisting alleys, throttled lanes? That's the City of the Sun's main souk. There you'll find bric-a-brac from all the world; pocket computers, transistors, cameras, any make and size of television set from Japan. Vivid silks and cottons from India, bright floral prints from Zanzibar, gold bracelets of all kinds from many lands, superb rugs, carpets, prayer-mats from Bokhara and Isfahan, *kilims* from our own Bedu, the carcasses of whole camels and sheep, fish of all kinds and fancy spices, and a whole range of cheap restaurants, many simply kiosks on wheels. You'll find many of our helots wandering there, manual labourers, porters, messengers, rubbish collectors. You'll see more affluent visitors there too, Saudis and Kuwaitis and Iraqis and Egyptians and Palestinians and American and European tourists – sometimes even a *Shemsi* or two. To know us, you should walk there a little –'

'And why the swarm of ships?' asked Blake. He was looking

to where the sea began, two kilometres off, after wide white silk bands of sand. The water was still and opaque, rather ominous.

'Ah, the merchantmen hanging three kilometres out from the land, all anchored and lying identically in the current, like iron filings held by a far magnet? Well, we three hundred thousand *Shemsis* have grown wealthy since World War Two, Mr Blake. Even if one of the Seven Sisters owned and produced all our crude oil as a concessionaire, we still got our fifty per cent royalties from their gross profits. So, like spoilt children, we've bought just about everything we've wanted. But our eyes have been a good deal bigger than our port facilities. So each ship carrying our new treasures to us, our luxury cars and TV sets and refrigerators and fine furniture and china and crystal, may have to wait three months out there before unloading, locked in that tepid sea patrolled by the legions of sharks that the ships' refuse attracts so swiftly –'

'Your oil port doesn't suffer from the same bottlenecks?' asked Sperry.

'No, as you'll see this afternoon. We finished our first phase of modernizing it this year. We can now load three VLCCs of 400,000 tonnes each simultaneously.'

'That's very good,' said Sperry.

It was as they were walking back to their armchairs that what appeared to be an interplanetary intercommunications machine behind Abdullah's large and efficiently clear walnut desk gave a long bleep and started to flash a white bulb imperiously. Abdullah crossed to it and flicked a lever. The white bulb stopped obediently and the voice of Abdullah's secretary came on:

'*Wasala es-Said Feisal, ya Effendim.*'

'*Tamaam,*' said Abdullah. '*Ta'al, ya Ahmed!*'

The door opened.

'This is Doctor Ahmed Feisal,' said Abdullah, 'the head of our legal department.'

The newcomer walked across to the ring of armchairs. He held foolscap-sized papers in his hands; the contract and duplicate. Blake, half facing the door, got a preview of him before he and Morgan Sperry stood to greet him. Blake was glad of that extra time.

For he saw Ahmed Feisal as a man at once worthy of the

fullest attention. He was dressed in European style, in white drill jacket, open-necked, and very light, immaculate white cotton slacks and neat brown sandals, and wore a chromium-cased Rolex watch on his left wrist. Yet he was no European. Blake was immediately certain that he was Palestinian. Yet Feisal evidently felt no need to mask himself from the world with dark glasses, like Ibrahim Sabri, or for that matter Kamal Daud. He presented himself with what looked like absolute openness, without even the traditional Arab male banner of a moustache. It was an extremely intriguing face, the features so regular and clean-cut that he might have been the model for a newly minted coin. At the same time there was humour, intelligence, and just possibly compassion, about that full-lipped and strongly defined mouth; these qualities were like shadows lurking at its corners. Feisal's eyes held the same dichotomy of passion and discipline, humanity and dedication. They were wide-set, light grey in colour – an indication that he might somewhere have Turkish blood. So powerful and mesmeric a statement did this face make that Blake found it hard at first to put any age to it. It could have been anywhere between thirty-five and fifty. Blake glanced instinctively from him to Abdullah. The two were of like stature as personalities, he felt, and indeed not far different in physical stature: Feisal must have been six foot one to Abdullah's exceptional six foot three, and both had that lean and highly trained air to them, of whipcord muscles, of not carrying an ounce of excess fat, of extraordinary vitality and endurance. Both, immediately, at first sight, had the charisma of natural leaders. Blake wondered which of the two would be the greater. Feisal seemed to carry himself and his powers the more easily, with a professional's economy and nonchalance.

'It all looks fine to me,' said Feisal, seating himself gracefully in the empty armchair left for him on Abdullah's left, and smiling. 'I shall probably go down as the only lawyer in history who *didn't* ask for a single change in a contract.'

His English was perfect, quite accentless; in some way so perfect that it seemed to warn subtly, give the faintest hint of a note of alarm, like some virginal snow-slope covering lethal crevasses. His smile revealed remarkably regular teeth, small and very white.

'Eagle would like the effective date to be November 1,' said

Abdullah. 'That's when they think they can get their first VLCC in for loading.'

'Excellent,' said Feisal. 'I'll write that in and initial it in the original and duplicate.'

He did so, then passed the papers to his right to Abdullah. 'For your signature, *ya Wazir*. And initials at the foot of each page, please.'

Abdullah leant forward to the low table in front and wrote busily, swiftly flicking over each page. Then he passed the original to Sperry, and went on with the duplicate. Within minutes both sets were fully signed. During this small ritual Blake watched Feisal quietly. He was conscious that Feisal was acutely aware of that regard. However sophisticated, and he was certainly that, Feisal seemed still to have kept all his native animal instincts and other powers intact, at their full primitive jungle or desert pitch. That made him a formidable character.

Suddenly he looked straight at Blake. The impact was tangible. Blake's hand tightened automatically on the arms of his chair. Having made his effect, Feisal promptly and generously cushioned it.

'Not that the finer points of the actual texts of contracts like this are necessarily the most important part,' he said.

'No?'

'No. You know that, Mr Blake. What really matters is the spirit and intentions of the two contracting parties. A question more of good will and trust, wouldn't you say?'

'Yes,' said Blake, 'I'll buy that, Dr Feisal. There must be achievements and aims in life greater than that of always being perfectly correct legally.'

And what are yours? he wondered.

'No, there's not much to mere legal perfection on its own,' echoed Feisal. 'Mere dull exact legal texts.'

'Go on like this much longer,' said Abdullah, 'and you'll have talked yourself out of a job.'

All in that ring of armchairs laughed dutifully, but Blake detected deep down another somewhat suspect note, one of faint warning. Abdullah and Feisal might greatly respect each other professionally, but there was no love lost between them.

'So, there, that's the last page done!' said Sperry, looking up pleasantly.

'Excellent!' said Abdullah. 'Then, if we've a deal, let's have a cup of Arab coffee on it!'

He sprang up and strode decidedly to his desk, his dishdasha thrashing tautly like a close-hauled mainsail. He bent over his intercom again.

'*Hoda?*'

'*Na'am, Effendim?*'

'*Kahwa arabía, tafathali. Sita.*'

'*Hather, Effendim.*'

Abdullah sailed himself skilfully back to his armchair.

'As arranged, then, for this afternoon,' he said, glancing at Sperry and Blake, 'Sabri here will pick you up at four, after you've had your lunch and a decent siesta. He'll drive you to Mina es-Salaam, so you can see our refinery there. Oh, and satisfy yourself on the spot about the oil loading rates at our new jetties.'

'We'll appreciate that.' said Sperry. 'It's thoughtful of you.'

The door had opened again, and the Arab coffee-man was among them. He carried his toucan-beaked copper coffee-pot with a true professional's pride, clicking two of his small handle-less cups together in his right hand. He filled his cups and handed them round, refilling each cup as it emptied. The liquid was hot and bitter, and Blake found two cups enough. Ahmed Feisal saw that at once.

'Wave your cup from side to side when it's empty and he next comes round,' he said. 'That's if you've had enough. It gets you off the hook.'

I must remember to stay off yours, thought Blake. Aloud he said: 'Many thanks. It's a little bitter for a newcomer.'

'You'll get used to Arab ways,' smiled Feisal. 'They'll grow to be yours.'

'Why not?' said Blake, also smiling.

Abdullah accompanied them to the lift.

'After your afternoon visit and a rest, my driver will pick you up at your hotel at eight tonight for dinner at my house.'

'It's most generous,' said Sperry.

'Please,' said Abdullah. 'All guests are sacred in Islam. You and Mr Blake are particularly welcome.'

A Desert Xanadu

Abdullah's vast black Mercedes, the bloom of bank vaults on it, was waiting for them at precisely 8 pm at the entrance to the glass and concrete monolith of the City of the Sun's Supercontinental Hotel. The Mercedes was longer than usual; a bright young German entrepreneur had made himself a small fortune by inserting extra sections into Mercedes-Benzes for *Shemsi* potentates. Consequently this opulent machine carried a collapsible extra seat for three facing forward, a television set, a telephone and a bar.

'It only lacks its own swimming-pool,' said Blake.

Sperry laughed.

'If it has all these facilities,' he said, 'why don't we use them? A vodka-tonic would fit the moment nicely.'

'Sure,' said Blake, and mixed him one, complete with ice and a twist of lemon, then one for himself.

Now they moved north, the same route as they had taken that afternoon to see the Kingdom's 200,000 bd refinery and its new tanker-loading jetties.

'That was a murderously hot afternoon,' said Blake. 'It must have been all of 45°C, well over 110° Fahrenheit.'

'Yes. Thank God it's cooler now.'

'Indeed,' said Blake. 'Though they seem to do all they can to please. They encase you in a cool air-conditioned bubble almost all the time. You move from air-conditioned office to air-conditioned car to air-conditioned hotel. Even the refinery and installation managers this afternoon lived in their bubbles. It was leaving them for the refinery and jetties outside that was so killing.'

'This car's fine,' said Sperry. 'I expect Abdullah's house will be too.'

They were passing now from an old quarter of low sand-yellow sheds and dignified Arab houses with thick stone walls into a slick modern suburb. It was gaudy with neon signs and glittering high new apartment blocks and wide glass-fronted shops of chromium and concrete. The highway was four-lane now. The elongated black Mercedes ran in an august company of Rolls-Royces and Cadillacs and Buicks and other Mercedes, either chauffeured or driven by olive-skinned young *Shemsis*, clearly sons of rich fathers, electric in pure white *khutras* and dishdashas and disdain, wearing strong black moustaches, and gold at their throats and wrists. All these gleaming vehicles, and clusters of smaller European and Japanese cars tailing them like obsequious camp-followers, shot from one set of traffic signals to the next, stopping at each red light like a film breaking down.

Then abruptly they were in the desert. It was as if the City of the Sun had suddenly run out of steam, its soaring new buildings and wide new avenues rubbed out by an atomic sponge. Now there was just the desert, the eternal flat sand, with, looming through the dusk eight or nine kilometres to the left or west, the Kingdom of the Sun's stark mountain-range. Blake knew that the sea must lie two or three kilometres to his right; an ominously still and ageless sea, unchanged there from its birth in primeval slime, with poisonous water-snakes still swimming on it, their heads wickedly raised and questing, and with huge and voracious hammerhead sharks ranging silent and unsleeping. This was the oldest waste land, a void, the end of the earth, or its beginning in evil –

With no perceptible slackening in speed, the black Mercedes leapt off the last of the paved road and onto the desert. Yet they did not sink horribly from sight in soft sand. They simply bounded on into the unknown at the same pace. Evidently they were on stony ground here. Two or three kilometres on into this apparently trackless desert bereft of any human life they came across Abdullah's avenue. The driver was doubtless a Bedu, with a camel's sense of direction, for he had taken them infallibly to exactly where Abdullah's avenue enigmatically started or petered out. The driver mounted it and turned to the right. The avenue could have taken four lanes easily. The black Mercedes nosed solitary along it, as eerily as the first man walking on the moon.

'My God, look at that!' exclaimed Sperry reverently.

Ahead of them reared a weird and lofty phallic symbol, sudden and superb in the sand. It was all of fifteen metres high, with a light burning at the top, pulsing away at a regular beat, like the beam from a lighthouse. Perhaps it had indeed been set there to reassure the lonely passer-by; whatever happened, it would always be operating there. As the Mercedes reached this tall slim tower, the avenue curved to the right and narrowed, walls rising up on each side of it. They were in a driveway, a giant S. The avenue curved now fully to the left, in a semi circle perhaps seventy metres in diameter.

Abdullah's residence burst on them across a vast courtyard. House, as Abdullah had termed it, was the understatement of the day. The building was concrete and epic, of three storeys, with separate wings, several balconies, and floods of steps which cascaded down like waterfalls. A Rolls-Royce and two Mercedes-Benzes stood parked before it.

'It's like the Xanadu built by Citizen Kane at the end of the film,' remarked Blake.

'Careful!' said Sperry. 'Our host!'

Sheikh Abdullah bin Ali bin Jibál was waiting for them at the main entrance, by a fine brass-studded teak door made for some other splendid Arab dwelling hundreds of years before. Abdullah, or a servant, must have been watching out for them.

'*Ehlen wa Sehlen*! *Wa Barakát*! Welcome and Blessings!'

He had changed into a gold-coloured and gold-brocaded dishdasha and gold-coloured *khutra* with a gold *ogal* round it. His lean lithe body inclined and embraced them one by one, arms round their shoulders, cheeks upon their cheeks.

'Come in, please!'

Blake got an idea of the building's huge size from the hall. It was full of stairways, and corridors long as cricket pitches, rooms opening off them, sumptuously carpeted, with poufs and divans and brocaded cushions against the walls. He saw no portraits. Abdullah could be following the strict early Islamic tradition which forbade the reproduction of Allah's image, even of man's. But Blake could judge and admire the quality of the rugs; Bokhara, Isfahan, Turkestan, Kashmir.

'Here's our room. There's someone here you've met before, Mr Blake.'

Blake's heart leapt.

It was a great quiet room to his left. Again he saw no portraits, but exquisite carpets. Again he saw divans and poufs and brocaded cushions against the walls, and delicate mother-of-pearl side-tables between them. Two stained-glass windows, set quite high, faced the world outside. Their vivid reds and blues and golds tugged at the heart. Leila, on a deep red divan, was also in gold. She wore gold lamé, satin-lined, tight to her slim waist and fine breasts and down her arms. A top layer, in the form of a hooded poncho flowed from her shoulders like gold foam. Her model's legs were crossed, her arched feet in high stiletto-heeled gold shoes. There was gold too at her wrists and throat. Her black lustrous hair fell in heavy waves, visible through the golden gauze of her hood. Blake was delighted that her brother was not so set on Islamic convention that he required her to sheathe that wealth of hair from their sight; Arabs, he had read, found a good deal more dynamic a sexual charge in women's hair than did Caucasians.

Leila's jet-black eyes and her sculptured lips smiled at him in warm welcome, and she lifted her right hand to him. He saw the four-carat diamond still on it, set in its pure white gold. Blake, uncertain of Arab customs on this point, was bending to kiss her hand, but she pulled it back a fraction. Obediently, he turned his movement into a bow.

'Princess.'

'Mr Blake. How good to see you again after Vienna.'

'This is Morgan Sperry, our Managing Director for the Middle East. Perhaps you saw him at the Imperial in Vienna? We were together.'

'Of course. A pleasure, Mr Sperry. And I hope all went well with your meetings today?'

It was a pretty conceit. All the others from that morning's meeting in Abdullah's office were in this great quiet room too; Kamal Daud, squat and still visored in his dark glasses, dressed now in a more formal grey-white dishdasha; Ibrahim Sabri with his pocked, ravaged complexion, masked like Daud, still dressed European and further dignified now by a lightweight jacket; and the extraordinarily handsome and magnetic Ahmed Feisal, elegantly at ease in what looked like a very light suit of white Shantung silk. Blake could not believe that this assembly had not been discussing precisely that meeting, with Leila or in her presence.

'Certainly,' said Morgan Sperry gravely. 'I found it a very illuminating day indeed. And I think very positive – I hope for both sides.'

'It's certainly been positive,' said Abdullah. 'And what will it be? Whisky? Vodka? Gin? Campari?'

Blake saw that all the Arab men in the room had glasses in their hands. All held the pale liquid gold of what looked like whisky. This was one Islamic prohibition, then, that the kingdom's élite did not take too seriously, in private anyway.

'I'll stick to vodka-tonic, if I may,' said Sperry. 'I started off the good work by having one from the bar on your Mercedes.'

'Good. That's what it's there for. Mr Blake?'

'I'll follow that, please. For the same reason.'

'Good again. And how did your visit to our refinery go? And to the tanker-loading terminal? Do you approve?'

This again was ballet, thought Blake; Sabri would have contacted Abdullah, probably here, the moment after Sabri had dropped his Eagle guests back at the Supercontinental at 6·30 pm, and told Abdullah their reactions to the last minor comment.

'Very much,' said Sperry. 'You have one of the most modern and efficient loading terminals I've seen. It was Bechtel, wasn't it?'

'Thank you. Well, they're good engineers. Yes, it was Bechtel.'

'Then the whole thing should prove a very smooth operation,' said Sperry. 'I'm very glad your sister contacted us in Vienna.'

Blake's eyes met hers an instant, and locked. So by God am I, he thought. He wondered if she would dare to see him alone here in the Kingdom, even if it were only just this once, to celebrate this pact. He had to leave that decision to her. Blake guessed she was a good political judge. He noticed that, while the Arab men now all drank hard liquor, she did not even test the ground. Instead she sat demurely, her tall tumbler of orange juice and ice before her. What happened to Westerners who fell in love with Arab princesses? With one called Leila, say? Leila meant night. *Elf Leila wa Leila* was A Thousand and One Nights. Leila had that saga's magic. She was as astute, as brave as Sheherezade in outwitting the King –

'Yes, I'm very glad we've got this contract squared away,' said Abdullah. 'It's the first, or among the first done in the context of the OPEC pricing policies just decided. That wider conflict's all the more vital to us as of today. And particularly for us Arabs.'

'Oh?' said Sperry.

'I had a phone call just as I was coming to meet you at the entrance,' said Abdullah. 'It follows on from what I was saying this morning –'

All in the room fixed their eyes on him.

'Sadat has today signed a cease-fire with the Israelis at Km 101 on the Suez-Cairo desert road. The war is officially over. And we have not won it.'

There was a terrible silence. Then Kamal Daud took off his glasses for the first time and blew his nose loudly. '*Ya khassára!*' he said sadly. 'What a loss!'

Blake saw that Ibrahim Sabri had shed his dark glasses too. Perhaps this was symbolically a final valiant confrontation with reality. It was certainly brave, for his desolate complexion, naked now, looked stricken indeed, a cornfield ripped to pieces by hail. 'Perhaps it's too early yet for us to take them on directly in open war,' he said gloomily. 'Perhaps we should stick still to sapping their life-blood with our *fedayeen*. That way, though it must take longer, may more certainly destroy them.'

Instinctively Blake turned now to Ahmed Feisal. And saw, astounded, with great shock, that it was as if the other had suddenly been pole-axed by heart attacks. Feisal had gone white to his lips. His very light grey eyes, earlier so sardonic, easily in control, stared straight ahead, almost bulging from his head, and his hands on his chair's arms had bunched into tight hard balls.

'For long it can only be the *fedayeen* now,' he said. 'Those who sacrifice themselves, the martyrs with submachineguns and grenades. Operating from all sides. Wherever they operate from. We can only keep tightening that pressure without cease. Until we have cut every Israeli throat, driven every Israeli into the sea –'

'Until then,' said Abdullah crisply, looking straight at Feisal, 'we shall of course scrupulously observe the laws of this Kingdom and use our oil weapon exclusively, and *not* guns and explosives, to defend our legitimate interests and to carve out our own place in the sun.'

Feisal's almost rain-coloured eyes fixed unwaveringly on him.

'"Ourselves" there meaning *all* Arabs, of course? *Effendim?*'

Blake heard, deep down, the mocking twist of irony to that title. He glanced swiftly at Abdullah. He had no doubt that Abdullah had heard it too.

'"Ourselves" meaning *all* Arabs, of course. Dr Feisal.'

'Including Palestinian Arabs, *Effendim?*' said Feisal, but with a most charming smile, turning the whole thing now into really quite a light-hearted joke.

'Including our brothers the Palestinian Arabs, of course,' replied Abdullah, smiling back quite as smoothly. 'How else?'

With what innate grace, thought Blake, did these two born leaders feint and lunge instinctively for each other's jugulars, like rival leopards circling and striking lightning-fast.

In that lethal silence Morgan Sperry, ever the elder states-man turned gently to Abdullah and asked: 'Sheikh, I wonder if you would be so kind as to satisfy my curiosity on one point? Though I realize my question may be indiscreet —'

'Please feel free to ask what you wish, Mr Sperry.'

'It's this, then, Sheikh. Even if your present OPEC-decreed crude price of $5.12 per barrel goes no higher — though everyone seems to believe that it will — you're still getting $3.12 more per barrel than for the two dollar crude you mentioned this morning, and which was the norm until recently. And at no extra production cost. So on your million barrels a day production that's more than an extra $1,100 million a year. Where's it to go, Sheikh? Or, better, take the whole picture. You now get $5.12 per barrel. I'd put your total operating costs including depreciation for your drilling and production at not more than those twelve cents per barrel — you sit here on one or two huge lakes of oil just under the surface; push your finger into the sand and out it spurts. So your Kingdom makes a net profit of five million dollars a day or 1.83 *billion* a year. You have 300,000 pure *Shemsis* here, forgetting the other inhabitants. That makes $36,500 per annum per family. Do they get it?'

'Good question,' said Abdullah. 'Yes, they do. Most of it. Or they will. First, every inhabitant gets free medical attention for *everything*. We have two excellently equipped and staffed new hospitals, and anything they can't handle we fly abroad. Everyone gets that, including the Egyptians, Palestinians, Pakistanis and Iranians — plus free primary and secondary schooling.'

'You're forgetting the university, Abdullah,' said Leila, making her first contribution to the discussion.

'Of course,' said her brother. 'Yes, and from last year *any* inhabitant of the Kingdom of the Sun can get university education virtually free too. He has simply to pay for his books. Entrance is strictly by competitive examination through the secondary schools.'

'We've just had the first year of it,' said Leila, 'and it's going very well.'

'It's from here on that the pure-blooded *Shemsi* scores most,' Abdullah went on. 'First, he's virtually guaranteed a job in some government ministry or department when he leaves school or university, if he doesn't want to strike out in business on his own. Second, the government will give him interest-free loans for more or less worthy causes – any *Shemsi* male of eighteen can get a loan up to $200,000 to erect a building, repayable interest-free over twenty years. He can also get 1,000 square metres of land as a grant. Many build small blocks of flats or offices and sell them at huge profit to speculators. Third, the Kingdom of the Sun invests its surpluses regularly overseas on its *Shemsi* citizens' behalf, mainly in the US, European and Japanese stock markets. At last count we had five billion dollars out there, earning $550 million a year. That'll come back too, compounded, to the *Shemsi* citizen one day.'

'It sounds a great nationality to be born into,' said Sperry.

Abdullah laughed.

'It's like being born white in South Africa before there's any black revolt. Unless you're a cretin or a convicted criminal, you can hardly go wrong economically.'

'And the management of your country's affairs is evidently very astute,' said Sperry.

'It ought to be,' said Abdullah. 'Those of us here who have started off with wealth, social position and higher education have a very clear duty to turn this country into an élite. The Israelis have done that, with nothing like our material resources. Why should we do any worse? We've an enlightened Amir and Crown Prince and a technically excellent Finance Minister.'

'And no bad Oil Minister either, from the look of it,' said Sperry.

Abdullah shrugged, and his glance crossed Feisal's. There's one who doesn't share Sperry's view, thought Blake.

'Just one last point,' said Abdullah. 'Talking about the fifty thousand *Shemsi* families' share of our wealth, Mr Sperry, you said "forgetting the other inhabitants". Yours was just a manner of speaking, I know, but in fact that's exactly what we *can't* do, forget them.'

'No?'

'No,' said Abdullah, his glance brushing again lightly over Feisal. 'We've got to do better by our non- *Shemsi* inhabitants. So far they have no political or property rights here. They can't vote for our National Assembly and they can't own property. Those must come, of course, to any who intend to stay here permanently, make this their home. Meanwhile we've got to improve their material conditions as far as we can. That's a main aim of our new development plan, which both our Amir and Crown Prince are backing, and which our new oil revenues will finance. It involves intensive development of sub-economic housing in new townships designed by the best architects we can find in the States and Europe, plus everything that goes with them – new shopping-centres, schools, clinics and a third hospital, power-stations, sporting facilities, new road systems –'

'The Princess was telling me about it in Vienna,' said Blake. 'It sounds most impressive. Once implemented, it should have a powerfully stabilizing political effect.'

'That's the idea,' said Abdullah.

'What happens if you *don't* push that through?' asked Blake.

'If we don't move towards *some* kind of democracy, however slowly but at least clearly? If we don't make some decisive and visible march away from traditional feudalism? And not just this kingdom; almost *every* traditionalist Arab state today?'

'What then?' said Blake.

Abdullah looked at him steadily.

'Then blood and destruction. So I fear. A savage return to first principles. A bloody re-start. A sword-wielding puritanism chopping out the corrupt, but unfortunately the moderates with them.'

'That revolution fuelled simply by a fierce desire for social justice?'

'Fuelled strongly, certainly, by that drive for social justice beloved by the Koran. But also I think fuelled by a fanatic Pan-Arabism, itself dangerously susceptible to real or imagined slights to its dignity. A Pan-Islamic movement certainly directly towards a *jihád* with Israel, to the liberation of Palestine, for the rebirth of Arab pride. It would be Islam Militant, with a vengeance. Islamic Fundamentalism –'

Without conscious design, Blake was resting his eyes on Ahmed Feisal as Abdullah spoke. Feisal met that regard blandly, his strikingly handsome face relaxed, his smile ready and seductive. Feisal looked down then at his right hand, curled its fingers, and surveyed their manicured nails with detached interest.

'All the more power to your development schemes, then,' said Morgan Sperry.

Abdullah smiled and looked at his gold Rolex watch.

'Gentlemen, it's time for your Arab dinner.'

'A sheep roasted whole?' asked Sperry.

Abdullah smiled again.

'Yes, complete with his eyes. But we won't subject you to the supposed Arab test of newcomers, and make you eat an eye whole. We seldom do that in fact, you know; we're quite a considerate people.' He stood up.

'So goodnight to you all,' said Leila, rising also.

'You're not joining us, Princess?' asked Blake, his heart missing a beat.

She smiled. 'You don't know our Arab culture yet, Mr Blake. Arab entertainment tends to be very male. No, I'm off to my flat. We Arab women have to know our place.'

There was quite a bite to that.

'It's our loss,' said Blake.

'We'll see each other again,' she said lightly. 'Perhaps here, perhaps in London. And goodbye, Mr Sperry. A good trip back tomorrow.'

Abdullah led them left through a long corridor, then left again into a patio well lit by lights from the walls and open to the glittering stars. At this hour the temperature outside was quite pleasant. Dinner was indeed a roasted sheep served whole, cooked so well that the meat came off in the hand. The sheep lay in an enormous earthen bowl like a boat in port, on a sea of saffron rice spiced with nuts and raisins. Cooked vegetables were passed round in earthen jugs, the diners pouring portions onto the rice in front of them. Abdullah showed his Christian guests how to eat with their right hands, the left being used in Arab lands for other purposes. The trick was to tamp the food down in the hollowed palm with the thumb into manageable size for the mouth. Here, by custom, the drink was water only. From time to time Abdullah tore off particularly succulent pieces of meat and passed them to Sperry or Blake, in their honour. Abdullah was a long way from Christ Church's High Table in Oxford now, thought Blake. Seated cross-legged in his formal gold dishdasha and *khutra*, crowned by his gold *ogal*, he looked very regal, a desert lord.

As if to confirm that impression, to underline that role, Abdullah began to talk to them now about falconry. He went fairly regularly into the desert to hunt. Blake, watching that long lean olive face, electric with energy, with its snapping black eyes and thrusting beak-like nose, felt that Abdullah had chosen his hobby aptly. Falconry's fierce silent ritual of killing, with its sudden vertical strokes from the heights, seemed consistent enough with his character. Blake, between luscious mouthfuls of mutton, glanced automatically half to his left to Ahmed Feisal. You did not see the steely curved talons so clearly, but they would be there too all right, sheathed perhaps a little more silkily under that appearance of affable easy sophistication, that perfectly modelled face. Finally, Blake watched Abdullah mark the end of the dinner formally by getting up and going to a corner basin to wash his hands. They followed him there, one by one, then went back to the first room within, where they sat and drank Arab coffee; *masboot*, medium, half-bitter, half-sweet, that drunk by men of moderate tastes. If this was modern Islam, Blake liked it. For him the only lack was Leila.

A Night View of the Ships

Back at the Supercontinental, Blake did not see the note until he had bidden Sperry goodnight and gone on to his room. The note was propped neatly by the phone on the side-table next to his bed. He lifted the envelope; there was weight to it. Blake tore it open: a single Yale-type key. The note said, in crisp copperplate:

> If you'd care for a drink after dinner, and to see how poor downtrodden Arab females live, an inconspicuous black Toyota saloon will be waiting for you in the main avenue just to the right as you emerge from the Supercontinental. The key is for my building's entrance. My flat is 38, on the fourth floor. The Toyota's number is 331273 and its driver, Tarek, is trustworthy. Should you be too tired, or not wish to come — and your free choice is absolute — then please give the key back to the hotel desk, sealed in another envelope and marked for Tarek, and he will pick it up at 2 am. Perhaps then we can meet in London. My love.

It was not signed. It did not need to be.

Blake raced for the lift. Outside he easily found the black Toyota and Tarek, and sat in the front with him. They drove north, out of the oil money's chrome and concrete and wide fashionable shops, through a belt of low drab shed-like buildings, then again into a realm of high luxurious buildings, expensive shops, and restaurants of Lebanese and Syrian and Palestinian and French and Italian cuisine — a rich residential suburb. Suddenly the black sea was by them, immediately to their right across sheer white sand. They drove into a huge courtyard packed with cars, next to a great eight-storeyed building a hundred and fifty metres long by a hundred wide, which faced straight onto the sea. The whole ground level was taken by shops: fashion, jewelry, a bakery, a butcher's shop, a supermarket, laundry, tailor, hairdresser, bank and post office; this was a world in itself.

Tarek pointed and said: 'The entrance. I wait here,' in

tolerable English. Blake smiled and shut the car door behind him and walked quickly to the high glass doors at the sea end. The key fitted, the front door opened; no one in Reception. He took the right-hand lift and pressed the button for the fourth floor.

Flat 38 was to his right. He glanced at his watch: 11.30 pm.

Leila opened the door quickly. He saw her with great joy. She was wearing a light blue *jelabíah* down to her feet, which were shod in silver sandals. At her throat, round the wrists of the long wide sleeves, vertically down the front, then round her waist, was a fine spiralling design in silver thread, as intricate yet geometrically balanced and satisfying as the patterns on the walls of a mosque. Her rich black hair fell freely down over her shoulders. She wore many slim silver bracelets on her wrists, and a heavy silver anklet on her left ankle; Blake was to learn from her in bed, where it dealt him a shrewd blow in her passion, that it was from the production of Siwa Oasis on the Egyptian-Libyan border, famed throughout the Arab world, for slave girls to princesses.

'I'm more glad than I can say that you invited me,' said Blake.

'Fine,' said Leila, casting swift glances left and right. 'But rather say that inside.' And she closed and double-locked the door behind him.

The flat was large; downtrodden Arab females lived well here. Marble steps led down from the hallway to two great rooms, both fronting the sea. The entire sea-side walls were sliding glass doors that opened onto balconies.

'Come and look at the view,' she said. 'It's my best asset.'

They walked together onto the right-hand balcony. Straight below was a half-Olympic-sized open-air swimming pool, its springboards and high-diving towers to the right. Beyond them was a marina, with many cabin-cruisers drawn up on the ramp. The sea began behind the pool, beyond a last wall. It was still and black, opaque and menacing. It showed no healthy pulsing beat of waves. The poisonous sea-snakes, thought Blake, could be executing ballets in it, in this flat stillness, in this silence. He saw the fifty ships hanging far out on these dark waters, identically, as if marshalled on parade, their lights blazing. They might have been magic citadels, flung out there as a last desperate defence against the black forces of evil, the great swift silent sharks, their eyes obscenely mounted on the outer edges of their hammer wings, their constant ravenous guardians. Blake turned away. They went back into the flat.

He saw that Leila, unlike her brother, with his formidable official role and duty to entertain, had not allowed Islam to inhibit the paintings on her walls. They were everywhere alive with beautifully framed prints of Gauguin, Matisse, Cézanne, Van Gogh, Manet, Monet, Caravaggio, Ribera, El Greco, Velasquez and, in a place of honour, an original Miró. Then in the large room to their right her paintings reached another peak. All seemed Arab, and originals; dhows with their decks sprung like archers' bows, the ragged blacks of Bedu tents in the desert, poor Arab villages, the walls of the houses tawny-earth, stoically suffering, the shutters closed in self-defence against the shimmering heat and iron hand of the sun. There were some exquisite mosques and soaring minarets, El Azhar in Cairo, and the horizontally striped Qaitbai Mausoleum in its Northern Cemetery. A very deep-brown L-shaped sofa fitted into the master-corner of this room. Three elegant deep-brown armchairs echoed it. They were grouped round a jet-black wooden table two metres square and forty centimetres high. Bokhara rugs rich in reds and hessian curtains in pure orange, injected vitality into this room like cocaine.

'What's that behind?'

'The kitchen.'

He looked in; it was modern, gleaming, huge.

'I can't see a bedroom, though.'

'What a practical mind you do have! There are two, upstairs. With two showers. It's a duplex, see.'

'Could I indeed please see, Princess?'

'Leila, please.'

'Leila.'

She took his hand. She had a small warm dry palm.

'The bedrooms, see? In fact there are three; I use that back one as a box-room. Here's the main shower and bathroom –'

It too was impressive, larger on its own than the average London bed-sitter.

'So here's where you keep it, Leila! I'm sticky as hell from the heat. I knew I was looking for something!'

'You want a shower? Go ahead, why not? I'll wait downstairs.'

'No! No! It wouldn't be the same!'

'You mean me too?'

'My God, what marvellous ideas you do have!'

She burst out laughing.

'A man after my own heart! A born brigand! Putting decisions like that into the mouths of infants!'

She ripped the *jelabíah* off over her head in one swift fluid movement. The impact took his breath away. She had nothing at all on underneath. She was as stripped and beautiful as a hurricane-swept sapling. And as full of sap. She got into the bath and turned on the shower taps. Under the fanning lick of the water her deep olive skin, even in tone all over, took on an even stronger and brighter sheen, as if just burnished. Blake took off his clothes and joined her. They stood together under the cascade.

'Christ, you like it hot!'

'Very hot,' said Leila, 'or as cold as I can bear.'

'I can't fault that.'

'You were limping a little at Abdullah's this evening. Is that old break still worrying you?'

'It's nothing,' said Blake. He felt no shame or embarrassment that she had commented on this deficiency. Her question was from friendship. She wanted to help. The two stood companionably.

'Shall I soap you?'

'Why not?' she said. 'It's what I'd be doing if I were on my own.'

So he soaped her high firm breasts, and felt her nipples stiffen like small prehensile fingers, and his penis rise in harmony. She was sheer and brown and gleaming now as a seal, a lissom physical perfection. It was awe-inspiring. If there is a God, Blake thought, I shall never come closer to him. He soaped her body. When he slid his hand between her legs her sex was open, at blood heat, like warm silk. She breathed suddenly more swiftly. Her body shuddered and she held him.

'Philip!'

He, much the taller, lifted her and set her on him. She wrapped her legs, snake-like, round him. The water poured steaming over them. He began his rhythm. They came exactly together. She screamed high cries, like wild birds in a storm. Afterwards he still held her. The curtain of water washed endlessly over them, shutting out other sound and time. She stood down, turned off the shower.

'Come and rest.'

They lay on her bed. Through her wide window, through the great dark, they could see the far white-lit city of the ships. They made love again once, quite gently.

Soon after, he got up and dressed.

'Yes, it's better,' she said. 'You could stay, but why tempt the fates? They've been good to us so far.'

'And it's dangerous here?'

'So dangerous that we shouldn't ever make love here again. London, anywhere else. But tonight was special.'

'I'll see Abdullah again tomorrow,' said Blake. 'I've got to give him the final details about our first tanker liftings on November 1. And pick up my own contract and guarantee. Then I'll leave for London in the evening by the commercial flight. Sperry's taking the company's Hawker-Siddeley tomorrow morning. But that's right, what you said about London? You'll be visiting?'

'In two weeks,' said Leila. 'I've a flat there.' She gave him an address in Bryanston Square, and a telephone number. 'I'll ring you when I get in, in the early afternoon.'

Blake gave her a card.

'That's the Eagle International number, and my extension. The second's my direct line at Eagle; you don't go through the switchboard. The last's my home address in Hampstead, and phone number.'

'But you have your wife there?'

'Yes, when she's not busy running her boutique. Or running with or being run by her high-fashion friends.'

'I'll avoid ringing there, then. I avoid natural hazards.'

'Yes, she does kind of come with the package, I'm afraid.'

'Never mind. I'll use your personal number at Eagle.'

'Fine.'

'I like direct lines,' said Leila. 'I prefer special contacts anyway.'

Leila gazed out at the floating citadels of light in the far black shark-ridden sea. She thought of the departed Philip Blake, his blond look and blue eyes perhaps as deceptive as those still waters. She recalled the big yet surprisingly lithe body. Seen naked, the badly scarred and broken left leg brought it sharply down to the level of humanity. Leila liked that touch; she mistrusted perfection. Though he had proved a good enough lover, if more ardent than subtle. The act of love told you something of the drives in a man, and his weaknesses. She had felt the considerable ambition in him, as she had when they had first met and dined in Vienna. Well, that was no fault. It was not her style to be linked to someone so modest and restrained as hardly to be visible. She was less sure about his weaknesses. His whole approach to Abdullah and herself in offering Eagle's inner calculations in return for the half million barrels a day crude oil contract and guarantee had been very astute and forceful indeed. But she still sensed an innocence in him somewhere, and innocence, as all the world knew, could be a two-edged weapon. The far-out and romantic might still sway him.

It so happened that at this particular stage in her life Leila was not entirely averse to such vulnerabilities. For a young woman filled with vitality and born into the royalty of an Arab Gulf state, life offered no easy choices, if she had any pretensions to the kind of rights to identity and personal freedom that a Western girl would expect. Oxford and the more liberated of Leila's English governesses had given her such pretensions. Yet the only kind of bed she was likely to get in fact would be one shared symbolically with three other official wives and countless concubines, and which allowed her precious little identity save as a reflection of her Arab (and, in view of her rank, necessarily of the royal house) husband, and no personal freedom except that which she could assume precariously by skulking off alone or with trusted girl-friends to the sybaritic capitals of the Western world. In such a marriage, Leila knew, she would probably be even more desperately alone than she was at times as she had lived to date, officially in celibacy. Nor did she by temperament have much time for the idea of planned periodic and furtive escapes from her arranged lawful Arab husband.

Loving Blake was simpler. Or being in love with him. She was there already, in decision if hardly yet totally and permanently in feeling. That would come with practice. They

97

fitted. Blake was right for her because when they were together their chemistry filled and vibrated the universe. There would, thus, just not be the space to be bored or alone. So they would always stay lovers. Leila knew that she might seem outrageously over-confident about that. In compensation her expectations were not excessive. She was not notably concerned that they might never marry, though she would have liked him to father her children. He was anyway an improvement on her prior lovers. Leila had lost her maidenhead experimentally at Oxford to an entranced philosophy don in a punt on the Cherwell one summer month, at a time when she knew she could not possibly be fertile. She had liked the experience, and terminated it bloodlessly a month later. Back in the Kingdom of the Sun, she had then had what had been at least for her a profound affair. This had been with the French Military Attaché. They had pursued it in Paris after his re-posting home, but his compulsive trawling among his receptive fellow countrywomen (he was a tall and singularly charming man) at the same time brought it to an end which she had found both humiliating and painful.

Leila had really loved no other man deeply in her life save for her brother Abdullah. He was the only man of her race who had ever both loved her profoundly in return, and treated her automatically as his intellectual and moral equal. She loved Philip Blake because she felt that he did that too, without effort, and doubtless because it would never have struck him to do anything else. She was at ease with him as a fellow, as she sensed he was with her. He was treating her exactly in focus, in the sense that he was not using her for anything else; he already had his oil supply contract and guarantee. Also she knew him to be as much a loner as she. He was already important to her country too, and she guessed that he would somehow and somewhere play a pivotal role in its future. Leila loved her Kingdom of the Sun.

There was the small change of love too, the tiny things so vital, his errors of identity; his trick of stroking his upper lip when annoyed, as if he had a moustache there; the tone and curl of his voice; the exact contour of his mouth, set suddenly in the profoundest depths of her unconscious like some etched primal truth, or so discovered there; copyrighted nuances in mind and blue eye; the precise and unrepeatable warp and warmth and flavour of his skin; what went to make up Blake. He offered her another major attraction. He could make her laugh for hours inside. He had that black sense of humour and that mad sense of timing. As their act of love that night in the shower had shown. In due time they could have done that in her present bed, and far more comfortably, as they later demonstrated. Instead they had performed that rampantly naked exhibition under a boiling cascade. Still, in its own weird way that act of love there and then had been mathematically right, a magic milestone registering the progress of their destinies, a riotous manic burst of life and light and laughter in the absurd, a work of wild genius. For people could be geniuses in absurdity too.

PART TWO

13
Death in the Afternoon

'She said the bomb would go off in exactly half an hour,' said
Kayyali. 'At 1.30.'

'She just talked direct to the telephone operator?' Blake
inquired. 'Didn't ask for anyone?'

'No,' said Kayyali, across Blake's desk, squat and moust-
ached and olive-skinned, a Palestine refugee for twenty-eight
years. With him that day of March 1976 in Eagle Egypt's
eight-storey HQ by the National Bank in Cairo's Qasr-en-Nil
were two others. First was the Ice Maiden, out lightning-like to
see how Blake was doing after two years as Eagle President
here. He sat carved still as granite, his chill grey eyes steady, the
bars of muscle at the corners of his mouth vertical, as Blake
talked of this threat of death. Kobus van Straten had been next
door with Blake's Executive Vice-President, Jimmy Byrd,
when Blake had called Byrd at Kayyali's message. Byrd was a
fair big-framed Scot with a blond arrowhead of hair and a
lantern jaw, in it a wide thin rat-trap of a mouth which masked
a very straight character and a generous heart.

'She identify her organization?' Blake asked Kayyali. 'Or
say why they'd picked on us?'

'*Junood Illah*,' said Kayyali. 'The Soldiers of Allah. Why us?
No. Just: "Eagle's Head Office? We've planted a bomb of high
explosive power. It will explode at exactly 1.30. We advise you
to evacuate."'

'You've told the police?'

'I told the operator to, while I called you on the internal.'

'First class. Please check she's done so. Then get your
messengers to search every floor thoroughly for parcels.
Watch the lavatories, they love those, men's and women's.
Then meet us back here in five minutes. We'll check the lobby.
People always leave parcels there. Jimmy, let's go.'

'What about me?' asked the Ice Maiden.

'I'm sorry,' said Blake. 'Perhaps you should go back to the Nile Hilton, sir. I'll get your car called –'

'Not I!' said Van Straten. 'I'm Eagle too, remember? I'll wait here.'

'Fine,' said Blake. Bastard or not, he thought, he had his nerve.

'One point,' said the Ice Maiden. 'Isn't it odd that a *girl* terrorist should call?'

'Not really,' said Blake. 'I hear that the Islamic Fundamentalists give them more and more equality of opportunity. A girl attacker's element of surprise is better. So Women's Lib should love the Fundamentalists.'

The lift was packed, most going down to Sub-Basement 1. Eagle had three main dining-rooms there, taking four hundred people. Some five hundred worked in the building, half Eagle and half in sub-let offices, Eagle providing the messenger, cleaning, and lunch services. Byrd and Blake got off at the ground floor. Blake told the Head Porter the score. Tall and white-haired, he was an ex-police sergeant. He had seen bombs before.

'Anyone bring in a parcel over the last hour or so?'

'Only people I know. A few typists left their shopping.'

'Let's look,' said Blake. 'Behind the counter, where people can't see us.'

Hidden there, they split the nine parcels, opening them as decently as they could: the small change of humanity – groceries, toothpaste, paperback novels, cigarettes, Tampax local variety.

'Let's get back,' said Blake.

There was only the operator in the lift. Blake said: 'What would you do, Jimmy?'

'I don't know,' said Byrd. 'Look, most of the five hundred people in this building are in the basement now. They wouldn't stand a chance.'

Byrd was big and he had that spade-like jaw. You knew what he meant.

In Blake's office Kayyali waited, already a little ill-at-ease with the Ice Maiden.

'Well?'

'We've checked all floors. The lavatories. The basement

car-parks. So far, nothing. The police say they're coming.'

'What did they advise?'

'Nothing beyond what we've already done, *Effendim. Mafish.*'

' *Mafish* is a big help.' Blake turned to Van Straten. 'Here's the problem, sir,' he said. 'What do we do? Fling the five hundred employees in this building out for an hour or two onto one of Cairo's very busiest avenues and block the traffic and look like idiots if nothing happens? That's great for morale too, nearly as bad as the bomb itself. A great advertisement for our confident free-enterprise society!'

'I suppose you could say,' said the Ice Maiden evenly, 'that they would at least still be around to take part in it. There could be a bomb?'

'Yes.'

The Ice Maiden examined his well-manicured fingernails deliberately. It was a mannerism Blake always mistrusted.

'Then it's your decision,' said Van Straten. 'I'd not have the temerity to advise you. Or the lack of form. You know that Eagle's policy is to leave the absolute maximum of autonomy to our Chief Executives in the field. I'm here simply as a visitor. So it's really over to you.'

Then live with it, thought Blake. Or die with it. He turned to Kayyali.

'Are the other directors here?'

'Dr Wahid el Bakr and Mr Wiggan are down in the Directors' Mess. The others went out for lunch.'

'We'll go down too. I'll ring you from there, in your office.'

'*Effendim.*'

Van Straten looked up at Blake.

'You're taking us down to the *basement?*'

'Yes, that's where we're going. It would be an honour to have you there as our guest.'

Van Straten's grey eyes went on examining him icily. Then he shrugged and got up.

Down in the Directors' Mess, El Bakr and Wiggan sat in armchairs drinking aperitifs. They got up when they saw Van Straten, El Bakr with alacrity. Blake glanced at the clock on the far wall.

'We've had a bomb threat. To blow in just fifteen minutes, at 1.30.'

'God!' said El Bakr, reseated, but now bolt upright. 'By phone? Via Kayyali?'

'Yes. We've five minutes in which to decide. With the alarm, we can clear the building in ten.'

'Kayyali should at once have told me, as Admin Director!' cried El Bakr, at the phone.

'Leave it, Wahid. He only got me first because I was still in my office. We've searched and found nothing. The police are coming. Now we just have to decide.'

There was a heavy ten-second silence.

'What would you do, Wahid?'

That was playing it rough. Dr Wahid el Bakr was Egyptian and a fine geologist. He was also very conscientious and tense. He took decisions as if he were building a cathedral. He had gone white.

'I don't know, Philip. I'm not sure.'

The place was full of geologists, not all the rest as cautious as Wahid el Bakr. Jimmy Byrd had started off as a geologist too, but Eagle were trying him out now in General Management. That complexion of staff was logical, since Eagle Egypt was an Exploration and Production company, not an oil marketer; Egypt had nationalized those in 1970. Eagle Egypt had joint E&P ventures with other searchers for crude oil like Emenex, BP, Shell, Amoco, Agip and Exxon in the Gulf of Suez and the Western Desert. Eagle and her consorts had found a small oilfield whose viability still had to be proved in each area; Blake had just helicoptered Van Straten to both. What was Blake, demonstrably not a geologist, doing heading an E&P company? Managing it, Eagle would have said, their doctrine being that a good manager could handle anything from producing peanuts to selling laser beams. Blake now addressed the only other of the twenty expatriots he had on his staff who was not an E&P specialist. 'Derek?'

Derek Wiggan, Blake's Finance and Economics Director, a short and deliberate man with a mordant wit, was as slow to reply as El Bakr.

'It's not easy,' he said finally, automatically addressing the Ice Maiden. 'There's been this ground-swell of anti-Western-ism recently, in tune with the upsurge of Islamic Fundamental-ism since that assault by the Islamic Liberation Organization in broad daylight just under two years ago on the Technical

Military Academy in north-east Cairo. Sadat ordered a witch-hunt of its members afterwards. So the Fundamentalists not only hate Sadat as an opponent, but see him and his wife Jihan as going so pro-Western so fast that they betray Islam. Companies like Eagle get the backlash from Sadat's Pierre Cardin suits and Jihan's love for Dior. We're Western, thus an enemy too. A bomb makes its point. And we've most of the building down here with us now, including hundreds of women. It's a nice choice.'

'Jimmy?'

Byrd, having helped Van Straten to a dry sherry, was pouring himself a gin and tonic. 'Derek's just said it,' he said. 'We've some four hundred folk at risk here with us. Our searchers might just have missed the bomb. Look, Philip –'

'I'm looking.'

'It's really your decision. Just yours.'

'Thanks.'

'In the end you're the boss. This is what they pay you for.'

'I'll take it, then.'

Blake felt the eight eyes set on him like gunsights.

'All right. We stay.'

He saw Van Straten's eyes glitter as he looked away. But Van Straten said nothing.

'Cheers!' said Jimmy Byrd, downed his gin and tonic, and poured himself another.

Blake limped to the phone. 'Kayyali? Anything new? A police patrol-car is on its way. About time. Kayyali, I don't think there's a bomb. We've taken all reasonable precautions to find it. So we're not leaving. Yes, you can get me here.'

'Have a drink, Philip,' said Byrd.

'Yes, I think I will.' Blake turned to the waiter, just come in. 'Suleiman, make it a whisky and water.'

'That's the first time I've seen you take spirits at lunch here in two years,' said Byrd.

'I don't much like feeling bombed early in the afternoon,' Blake answered, and then heard what he had just said. 'Hell, sorry. Why don't we sit? Mr Van Straten – what's on the menu, Suleiman?'

'*Saumon fumé* to start with, *Effendim*. Or *champignons* on toast or avocado. As a main course Wiener Schnitzel or Spaghetti Bolonese or *Poule à la Mystère* or *Chateaubriand*.

Mixed salads. Spinach or *petits pois* as vegetables. Potatoes roast or *frites*. *Effendim*.'

The heavy French touch on the menu, Blake knew, came from Eagle Egypt's passionate Francophile pride in its kitchen, an abiding relic of Napoleon's invasion of Egypt in 1798 and his considerable injection into it of *La Présence Française* before Nelson ejected him by destroying his fleet in the Battle of the Nile and by making louder and more convincing noises. *The Poule à la Mystère* was probably an equally masterly stroke in pure confection. The only true mystery would have been which village road it had been knocked down on by a passing car.

'Mr Van Straten?'

'I'd like your smoked salmon, chicken, and mixed salad.'

'Jimmy?'

'I'll go for the smoked salmon, chateaubriand, and peas. The steak medium-rare, please.'

Blake's eye was on the clock. It said 1.20. It ticked away inexorably in his mind.

'And the others, Kayyali?'

'They've ordered already, *Effendim*.'

'Good. I'll have the same as Mr Byrd here. And, Kayyali –'

'*Effendim*?'

'Two bottles of really chilled Giannaclis Villages.' He turned to the Ice Maiden. 'It's a dry white, I think the only really good wine that Egypt produces, in the Giannaclis vineyards about Alexandria. I find the reds a disaster. But a dry white should suit what you chose.'

'Indeed, so it should. You meat-eaters don't mind drinking a white?'

'We're all hardened to it, if it's Giannaclis.'

'None in the fridge here,' said Suleiman. 'I fetch.'

And he sped away, red tarboosh bobbing, and a red cummerbund bisecting his white jelabíah – Shepheard's Hotel under the British occupation to the life.

'Splendid!' said Blake, doing his best to sound hearty.

Blake was well placed to be either genial host or death's head at this feast. He had the Ice Maiden on his right, Jimmy Byrd on his left, and the clock conveniently ahead on the far wall. The windows to his right faced onto a basement courtyard that partly roofed the underground car-park and service station, whose tanks were always kept nearly full of gasoline. That was handy too. The clock said 1.25. 'Christ, four hundred souls,' said Blake, half to himself, 'so why do they pick on us?'

Wahid el Bakr, second down on his left, stared back at him as if addressed personally. Blake blenched. El Bakr was an excellent fellow, but not exuberant. He was dark for an Egyptian, with black hair and a thick and lustrous black moustache. Cairo, with its crushing heat, was fairly informal about dress; short-sleeved shirts, slacks and sandals were permitted in most offices in all seasons except the brief winter. But El Bakr always dressed conservatively in a grey-and-white-lined drill tunic, smartly pressed pants of the same material, and highly-polished dark tan shoes. He was not thought to own more than two, identical models of this ensemble, and was known to own only two ties, both also grey, for really serious occasions such as marriages and funerals. Funerals were indeed what El Bakr always made Blake think of, whether he wore his grey tie or not. That might make him just the right man to have around this day.

'They chose us because we're a Western-based multi-national,' said El Bakr sepulchrally. 'I fear few would weep to see us destroyed.'

'I find that logic odd,' said Van Straten tartly. 'We have explored for and found crude oil for Egypt. By marketing chemicals here we make profits, much of which goes to Egypt as tax. And ninety-five per cent of Eagle Egypt's employees, including some of its directors, like you, El Bakr, are Egyptians. We help to integrate you in the modern technological world. We support Egypt's economy.'

Christ, thought Blake, in two minutes we're due to be integrated into the street. It was now 1.28.

'Which needs all the support it can get,' said Derek Wiggan. 'Egypt's in a grim economic state, the faults deeply structural. Food subsidies alone are some two billion dollars annually, a quarter of the national budget. It's in permanent balance of payments deficit of one or two billion a year. Its five main hard currency earners – which are oil, remittances from the two million Egyptians working abroad, tourism, Suez Canal dues and cotton – just don't bring in enough. Egypt has spent so much on a twenty-eight year war with Israel that its internal infrastructure's shot – road, sewers, electricity, phones. And a population of thirty-seven million expanding at three and a half per cent a year for the sake of *machismo* and the *fellah's* wish for old-age life insurance. That's 25,000 new Egyptians a *week*! How do you feed them? Egypt already imports more than half its food. Only four per cent of the land is arable. You need aid, Wahid. Or the whole place blows up.'

Normally Blake would have cut short Wiggan's characteristic battery of statistics. Now he welcomed them. They helped fill the time.

Near 1.29. The whole place could blow up at any moment now.

'I know,' said Wahid el Bakr. 'Yet our Fundamentalists still scream passionately against any input of Western influence which might threaten Islamic values. Sadat's *Infitah* Open Door economic policy is supposed to have unleashed consumerism and godless materialism. We Arabs, you know, can not only cut off our noses to spite our faces but also sing fervent patriotic hymns while we do so.'

'True,' said Philip Blake. 'And anyway nobody, but nobody, seems to love your friendly old international oil company these days. But anywhere.'

Perhaps stung at that flippancy, Van Straten said, with the steel back in his voice: 'Well, shouldn't you do something about that? Seek to change our image by intensive Trade Relations programmes, university scholarships, whatever? I stressed earlier that we gave our Chief Executives in the field great autonomy. We expect a great deal from them too. Even in highly critical situations.'

Which meant, thought Blake, that the Ice Maiden, who hated his guts anyway, also did *not* like the way he, Blake, was handling this bomb scare. As for getting the Islamic Fundamentalists to love Eagle, Blake would first have to get the rest of the Sinai back for Egypt and free the West Bank and Gaza Strip from colonizing Israelis. Until that day, while Eagle was his small empire, he was going to run it as he judged best. Even if he exploded it.

The door opened: Suleiman, with a huge tray holding many plates and two bottles of Giannaclis Villages. On Blake's left Jimmy Byrd said: 'My God, Suleiman, you're fast today!'

Every eye turned with his to the clock: 1.30. Would Suleiman's plates ever reach the table?

Two down on Blake's left, El Bakr said sadly: 'I wonder what went wrong?'

'Went wrong, Wahid?' asked Jimmy Byrd.

'With today's youth. So many have gone Fundamentalist. They're our enemy. Or they see us as theirs.'

'Suleiman,' Blake broke in, 'open the two wines, would you? I'll sign. Wahid, would you please pour? Or pass one to Jimmy.'

He was trying to deflect El Bakr from that theme of youth. It was a region of agony for El Bakr. But then Blake heard Jimmy Byrd go straight on in, tactful as a bulldozer.

'Any news of your son, Wahid?'

Blake watched El Bakr pour the dry white wine into the five glasses, then put the bottle down very carefully, and pass the first four glasses round slowly. He saw El Bakr put his right hand round the stem of his own glass. It had a very tiny shake, like a high-speed engine vibrating. By a miracle, no wine spilt.

El Bakr said: 'You all know what happened. Not yourself, naturally, Mr Van Straten. My son jumped from home and Cairo University a month ago. Disappeared. He'll have joined one of the Militant groups, the Islamic Liberation Organization or the Soldiers of God. You know they work in activist cells of say six or eight, swearing their oaths of loyalty and secrecy on a dagger or pistol, totally committed to creating a purely Islamic State, ready to give their lives for that cause, passionately anti-corruption, anti-Zionist, anti-Western materialism and sexual permissiveness? It's a return to the murderous and merciless first purities of perfectionism, and they are most highly indoctrinated and trained in all the techniques of terror to achieve it.'

'Wahid,' said Blake urgently, 'he'll come back all right. You'll see.' He kept his gaze on El Bakr, but out of the corner of his eye he could see that the clock said 1.32. They were already living on borrowed time. El Bakr's face had gone an odd taut grey. He swung it round onto Blake like a radar-screen. 'How, Philip? Feet first? Another shot while escaping? Or fallen accidentally out of an eighth-floor window during questioning?'

Blake knew now with total certainty that if he could keep

this conversation going, at whatever cost, the bomb would get up and go away. He did not think he needed to be too impressed by the fact that the clock already showed past 1.30. How pin-point accurate was the timing device on a modern bomb anyway?

'So they're fashioned into first-flight terrorists,' said Blake. 'Highly motivated and trained, eager to die for the cause. Then to do what? Hit us, Eagle?'

'To destroy,' said Jimmy Byrd curtly.

'Just that,' said El Bakr. 'The whole fabric of society's rotten. So rip the lot out. Why us? Because, through us they hit Sadat.'

'Total destruction?' said Blake.

It was now 1.34.

'Yes,' said El Bakr. 'It's like what that Tupamaro leader said whom they took in Uruguay: it wasn't his group's job to build the just society. That was the next generation's worry. This one's full-time task was to annihilate the present social structure, shatter its law and order. It's intelligent division of labour. And these aren't workmen or workmen's sons, any more than they were in Uruguay or Argentina. They're intellectuals, mostly doctors, architects, lawyers, lecturers, journalists, university students.'

'They sound like just a bunch of spoilt rich kids to me,' said Van Straten. 'Can't you control them more strictly?'

'Say by shooting the lot, sir?' said El Bakr, suddenly valiant, and staring straight at the Ice Maiden. 'Including my son?'

'I'm sorry about your son,' said Van Straten, his voice steady. He was evidently not going back on what he thought, whoever's son was involved. El Bakr returned to his Chateaubriand. His knife screamed suddenly on his plate, and he retrieved his piece of meat from the table. Cooked rare, it had left a streak of blood. We may see more of that, thought Blake. If the bomb blew, it would probably bring all eight floors of the building down round their ears.

1.38.

'There's still some good dry white wine here,' he said. 'Pity to leave it.'

Derek Wiggan turned to him with the ghost of a smile.

'Yes, so it would be.'

He filled the Ice Maiden's glass on his left, his own, then

pushed the second bottle of Giannaclis across. Jimmy Byrd took it. There was just enough for the remaining three glasses.

'Cheers!' said Derek Wiggan, toasting the table, ending at Blake.

'It'd be quick, anyway, Philip.'

'Yes, I expect it would.'

What would Blake leave? Not much, he thought. Leila. And Celia, of course. She would survive. Looked at objectively, indeed, she might find it quite a neat solution.

Blake had tried to leave her the day before, not very hard. The meeting had been rather like one between foreign ministers, highly stylized. But not to start with.

'You mean you want to leave me for a *woman*?' Celia had said in cold fury, in cold contempt, her emerald eyes daggers of ice. 'Who is it?'

'You've never met her.'

'It's as well. I'd have taken her eyes out.'

Celia sat magnificent as a miniature statue on the sofa opposite him, the Vee of her décolleté revealing the rich inner curve of her breasts, her heavy jet-black hair emphatic. The house in Maadi was huge, full of teak, mahogany, silver, fine china, paintings and good carpets. It sat in its gardens of sixty metres by sixty. Not far from the Nile, its few flower-beds even had irrigation. The gardens held a fifteen-metre swimming pool, like a rare outsize jewel. Here, at Eagle's expense, and for Eagle's and their greater glory and advancement, they had most memorably dined many a minister and business magnate, general of army and police, newspaper editor and owner, president of powerful state company, radio and television tycoon. For all this worthy and sustained effort, the Blakes had, in due course, received just and wide acclaim. Who could possibly have wanted anything more?

Blake could.

'And you expect me to let you go just like that?' asked Celia, with ferocity.

'I'd be most grateful if you would. It would be very civilized.'

'*Civilized*, the man says!'

At that almost vertical take-off in her tone, Chunt raised his square-jawed head with alacrity and lined it up on her most attentively, his brow deeply furrowed in case he had committed some awful social gaffe. Chunt was a squat, brindled and pig-eyed Staffordshire bull-terrier, two and a half years old and thus theoretically mature. But Chunt was a slow developer. He was powerfully chested and muscled like a cut down wrestler, but his intellect lagged behind. Chunt was a dog of sudden manic interests, perhaps insights. He could sit motionless as the Ice Maiden and watch a beetle for hours. Though not too fast on the uptake, he lacked nothing in loyalty or the desire to serve. Put him to guard a door, and he would sit stock-still there until he fell over sideways dead from hunger. He was naturally amiable. It was his formidable aspect, compact and lethal as an artillery shell's, that repelled burglars, not his pugnacity. Chunt would have made friends with anyone. In a country flecked with rabies, behind their hermetic fence and gates, Celia watched over him as over the child he partly substituted. He lay now by accorded privilege on a towel on the sofa by her, diplomatically neutral in this conflict. Blake hoped he would stay that way. He had enough on his hands.

'Well,' he said. 'I thought we were supposed to discuss our problems.'

'This kind you can keep to yourself,' said Celia. 'When did you last see her?'

'That last month's leave that ended three weeks ago. You know, when we agreed to divide. You wanted London, and I went to Formentera, by Ibiza.'

'And she was with you there?'

'Yes.'

'My God! I see. You've done this before?'

'Well, yes.'

'When, Philip?'

'That month a year ago, when I went to Greece.'

'Christ, you're a devious bastard! And now of course you want to marry her?'

'I don't know about that,' said Blake, 'but it's messy like this. Divorce would be cleaner. I'm not in love with you any more, Celia.'

'Were you ever?' she said. '*Love? Divorce?* Now that I've got you so well launched? Without me you'd still be nothing. And I can still probably break you. I should try very hard!'

Blake did not doubt it. He had helped get the Sun Light contract, but he knew the sweep of her family's power, and the Earl was a very major shareholder in Eagle.

Well, Blake had some slight defence now, the millions in his numbered bank account in Lausanne, there for long-term investment, bringing in their steady eight to eleven per cent annually, mainly in the safe and sure Eurobonds. Celia knew nothing of that. But Blake wanted more than a pile of money. That was mere security, a tool for survival in reasonable comfort. Blake wanted ends of a totally different order: power, the exercise of real power in the world, a position of top command.

'And to think of the really *monumental* work I've put in for you in Eagle. Your eternal hostess, unpaid housekeeper! These last sixteen years, nearly seventeen. In *everything*!'

'Well, at least it's left you pretty fit.'

'Don't give me any lip, my lad! Again, if our marriage is finished, so is your career. I *promise*!'

At that stridency Chunt, who had relaxed, looked directly up at her again, then put his ears back in extreme guilt. He got sadly down off the sofa, and sloped off with a doomed gait to the stairs which led up to the bedrooms, a convicted recidivist assassin, only now seeing the whole hideous error of his ways.

'What on earth can there be in it for you now?' asked Blake.

'I don't like divorce,' said Celia. 'Divorce wouldn't suit me.'

And that was that.

'What can she offer that I haven't got?' said Celia.

Human warmth, thought Blake. He noticed that her tone was much more composed now.

'I know you've had your little affairs here and there,' she went on. 'But pretty few, really. Always discreet; no social embarrassment. And you've always come back –'

He said nothing.

'So keep on your liaison with her if you absolutely must. But out of sight, please. I don't want to know about it. Or have anyone in London know about it.'

'So no divorce?'

'No, no divorce.'

Again he was silent.

'Come!' she said. 'Is our present relationship really so awful?

Am I really so frightful in bed? I've always thought that our sex was pretty good.'

'No, no,' said Blake. 'You're an extremely beautiful woman, Celia. You know that. And sexually very attractive indeed.'

He sounded to himself like a trainer consoling a boxer who had just lost on points. She must have felt something of that hearty tone, for she said: 'I see. Athletically competent.' But it was clear that his comment had warmed her.

'So it's your choice,' she went on.

Blake knew that. In the last analysis, was anyone worth an empire? Even Leila. And Blake would be nothing without an empire. Blake needed power, the range between heaven and hell. Moreover, as the cards were stacked now, he could still keep Leila anyway, as a lover. If under cover . . .

'All right,' he said, 'I accept.'

Celia said nothing. She was never small in victory.

'What about you?' asked Blake. 'Do you expect the same secret freedom?'

'I suppose I should, shouldn't I?'

'I don't think I'd like that.'

'Male chauvinist pig! Where's your sense of equity?'

'I don't think,' said Blake, 'that I was ever burdened with one of those.'

'No,' said Celia, 'I hadn't noticed any sign of one.'

'But you've had them, haven't you?'

'What?'

'Such liaisons.'

'Have I, now?'

'For example,' said Blake, 'that outsize black-haired Austrian from your parties, the one who works in Agence France Presse and just loves his Armani suits.'

'Oh, Chris Morgenthau, you mean. What about Chris?'

'Are you lovers? Or have you been?'

Celia's clear emerald eyes glinted at him.

'You'll never know that, will you?'

The phone rang suddenly in the Directors' Mess. Wahid el Bakr, who had finished his steak and lit himself a cigarette with a hand that still blurred marginally, raised his eyebrows at Blake. But Blake was already on his feet.

'Kayyali? The police have arrived: At 1.45? It does them

credit. They want me? Just to look around? Let them feel free. You know where to find me.'

Blake went back to his place.

'Your police are brisk for a supposed 1.30 bomb explosion,' said the Ice Maiden critically. He was still looking a shade tense.

'They must have plenty on their plates as it is,' said Blake. 'There's a hell of a lot of pressure building up around and amongst us these days.'

'Such as?'

Blake looked at Van Straten.

'Such as the vicious civil war that broke out in the Lebanon a year ago.'

He knew Van Straten must be very fully briefed on this by his excellent London staff and by Eagle's GM in the Lebanon. The slaughter was between the Christian Phalangist militia, and Palestinian Rejectionist Front units with guerrillas from the Syrian-backed *Saiqa*, or Lightning. Fatah had kept its 12,000 heavily armed men out of that fight and on the southern border with Israel, officially their main enemy. But the right wing Lebanese Christians forced Fatah into the Beirut act by razing a Palestinian refugee camp and overcrowded Muslim *bidonville* there that January.

'So the poor bloody Palestinian Arab Resistance still has no real place to go since Hussein's crack Bedu troops flung them out of Jordan in 1971, killing thousands,' said Blake, half to himself.

'Still quite sympathetic to the Palestinian Arabs, I see,' observed the Ice Maiden snidely.

Blake shrugged. 'They're today's underdogs. They can't even trust Assad and the Syrians too far.'

Van Straten must know that too. Assad wanted to get on stage as the big Middle East arbitrator, with Russia four-square behind him. He would put in regular Syrian occupation troops, taking Lebanese–Christian right-wing Phalangists and Chamounists as allies if he had to. And the US said no negotiations with the PLO until it recognized Israel's right to exist and Security Council Resolutions 242 and 338 – which the PLO wouldn't, since 242 called the Palestinians refugees only; in other words, without innate right to their national home. So the Palestinian Arab Resistance was having it hard.

Perhaps one shouldn't be too surprised, thought Blake, if they and their sympathizers tossed a few bombs around –

One of which might still go off here at any moment now. It was 1.48.

'And what's causing your pressure to build up so dangerously in Egypt itself?'

The Ice Maiden really loved to needle him, thought Blake. Van Straten already knew most of the answers here too.

'The continuing economic mess and poverty I described in my last visit to you in London this January,' Blake answered. 'That never stops. The worst aggravating event is still last September 1's announcement of Sinai II, by which the Israelis make their second major troop withdrawal, and Egypt lifts the blockade on cargoes for Israel through the Suez Canal. The Fundamentalists particularly saw Sadat here as leaning too damned close to the Israelis – who still have given no guarantee that they will get out of the West Bank and Gaza Strip, *ever*.'

1.50. Surely they *must* be safe by now –

'So you can never feel or be really safe,' said Wahid el Bakr lugubriously, putting his knife and fork down reverently next to his massacred steak. 'This may be a new shape of the world. The new world of the idealist guerrilla. Everywhere. In Latin America. Europe. North America. The Middle East. Try to stamp them out, and they grow back tenfold. They're young and brilliant and totally dedicated. Perhaps co-existing with them is the new style for living, the new fashion. With this new underground and faceless élite of terror.'

'A splendid phrase,' said Van Straten.

It was nice to see him trying to cut down somebody else for a change, thought Blake. You could see how this puritanical primate Van Straten really hated anything even mildly histrionic.

'Underground because you never even know they exist before they strike,' said El Bakr. 'Elite because they're generally among the best your culture produces. Terror because that's their chosen language. Faceless because they could be everyone or no one. A total stranger, the common face of the crowd. Or your own son –'

There was a long and painful silence. I think Wahid won that one, thought Blake, ravished at the idea.

1.53.

'For God's sake,' said Blake, 'enough is enough! Where the hell are those police? Have they actually *found* something?'

El Bakr went promptly to the phone. With swift prescience, it rang before he reached it. He began to echo the speaker's words, in his stolid way. ' . . . Searched and gone? . . . might easily have been genuine . . . congratulated for searching and not panicking, or spreading panic. Well, thanks!'

El Bakr walked back to the table very seriously. Evidently unaware of his playback habit, he sat and intoned: 'Kayyali says the police have searched, found nothing, and gone. The threat could have been perfectly genuine. We're to be congratulated for –'

By now the laughter of all the other men but one had become Homeric. El Bakr watched them, startled. Then slowly he joined in with that laughter too.

Blake knew why Van Straten had not laughed. He was furious that Blake had not found a way elegantly to exclude him from this primitive test of *machismo*. It was not that Van Straten was in any way a coward. A man completely consistent with his own extraordinarily exigent standards, he had unshakeable nerves. Blake had committed a sin grave far beyond any mere question of courage or cowardice. He had put Eagle's single most valuable piece of property – Van Straten himself – seriously at risk when it was not utterly indispensable to do so. This was misusing assets. This was economic blasphemy, sacrilege and high treason, thought Blake, politely seeing the Ice Maiden off in his car to the Nile Hilton Hotel.

Blake met Derek Wiggan in the lift on his way back to his office. 'Well,' said Wiggan, 'a small victory there, I think, over friend Wahid's subterranean and murderous forces of the terrorist élite. Well done, Philip. What the Eagle textbooks on management would call using your initiative.'

'And what would they have called it had I got it all wrong and blown us all up, killing hundreds?'

'Ah!' said Derek Wiggan. 'Then that would have been totally exceeding your authority, of course. An act of lunacy.'

14

The View from the Top

Philip Blake looked down from the window of his top-floor suite in the Hypercontinental Hotel in East Beirut at 11 that night in mid-June 1977. The city below him across to the overhanging mountains hummed with light and movement. Yet he knew the menace in it. Beirut's signature was already cheap death in bulk. A year before, the right-wing Chamounist and Phalangist Christian militias had stormed the remaining Muslim enclaves in this Christian half of the city, the Shia Nabaa and the Palestinian Arab refugee camps of Jisr el Basha and Tel ez-Zaatar. In the last they then slaughtered in cold blood many hundreds of defenders, old men, women and children indiscriminately, often with knives or bayonets. Just before that the pro-Syrian Elias Sarkis, supported by Camille Chamoun, had been elected Lebanese President, and Syria had packed fresh regular troops into Northern Lebanon and the Bekaa Valley, to join the thousands who had already intervened, ostensibly to stop partition by Kamal Junblatt, the Druse mountain chieftain who headed the left-wing coalition called the Lebanese National Movement.

Now there was open bloody warfare between the Syrians, increasingly allied with the Chamounists and Phalangists, and the Joint Forces, composed of Junblatt's LNM, the PLO and the Lebanese Arab Army, who were Muslims defected from the regular army with its heavily Christian officers. In June 1976 the Joint Forces had stopped the Syrians before Beirut and Sidon, knocking out some twenty tanks. That September the Syrians had dislodged the Joint Forces from the key sector in the Upper Metn mountains, starting at the town of Bhamdoun, but the following month the Palestinians and left-wing Muslim Lebanese had decisively smashed the Syrian armoured thrust on Bhamdoun itself. Only then could Arafat appeal to Crown Prince Fahd of Saudi Arabia for the Arab Summit that stopped the civil war in Lebanon that had run for eighteen murderous months.

But Blake knew that the conflict was not truly over. It festered still between the Syrians and right-wing Christian militias on the one hand, and the left-wing Muslims and PLO on the other. Only three months before, in March 1977, a hidden hand that was surely Syrian had assassinated Junblatt in his mountain fastnesses, and provoked the erosion of his once powerful leftist coalition. And the greatest tragedy, as Blake saw it, was that this most bitter and cruel fighting was between Arab and Arab. Against that harsh reality the PLO's ringing statement at the thirteenth session of the Palestinian National Council in Cairo three months before in March 1977, that their objective was now to create an independent sovereign Arab state on any liberated areas of Palestine, sounded simply like a pitiful cry of defeat on a desert wind. In fact Israel was now grown mightier militarily than ever, its armed forces reorganized and heavily rearmed, while politically it was pushing its settlements on the West Bank ahead at maximum speed; soon there would be no Arab land left to liberate. And the month before, Menachem Begin had been elected Israel's Prime Minister. He and his Likud alliance were mortal enemies of the PLO which, banished for six years from its secure position in Jordan, could exist now only precariously on the treacherous quicksands of Lebanon. If the PLO tried to strike now against its true enemy, Israel under Begin would retaliate overwhelmingly and without mercy. There was no joy to being vulnerable.

This external Arab infighting was so complex and chaotic, so evidently hell-bent on self-destruction, locked in a giant death-wish by its eternal aggressions, shifting alliances, betrayals, treacheries, brutal cruelties and windy histrionics, that Blake could hardly be surprised that a westerner as mathematical and intellectually fastidious as Van Straten should find Arabs and their behaviour a total disaster. Blake, after working three years among them, and beginning to get some slight idea of the extraordinary intricacies of their traditions, sensitivities and loyalties, now no longer found their posturings, their abrupt political about-faces, so in-scrutably and contemptibly odd. He was starting to feel *with* them, from the inside, *on* the inside. By empathy, he now sensed their true vulnerabilities, feeling with them above all when he knew them doomed.

And Jimmy Byrd, thought Blake now sadly, was now most

truly vulnerable too. For Jimmy Byrd had been Eagle Lebanon's General Manager for just three months now, and his neck was already at risk. Blake had a vested interest in its survival. He was partly responsible for Eagle Lebanon's welfare. And he liked Byrd.

Eight months before, Blake had left his job as GM Eagle Egypt and taken two months' leave. Part of this he spent with Leila in Crete (but only part; with Celia a now vigilant wife, it did not pay to exaggerate). On his return to London, he had been named Regional Co-ordinator Middle East. That put him only one step down from the gods, the MDs, and therefore into a state of exhilaration; he had moved one step nearer to his lifelong ambition. The only catch was that the MD who had taken the Middle East as his Region since 1977, and to whom Blake consequently reported, was Kobus van Straten. When Jimmy Byrd's name had come up for the GM Lebanon slot, Blake had backed it unreservedly.

He had just dined with the Byrds, not too comfortably though they had done their best to seem at ease. One other thing had helped. By a prodigious effort, Blake had got his telex to London away before he left the Eagle Beirut office. It meant that he had not reached the Byrd's house in the smart residential quarter in the foothills until 8.30 pm. Blake had sat at dinner with the uncoded copies of his telex still in the inside pocket of his light jacket.

Now, as they warmed up in their talk of old times in Cairo, it was as if nothing had changed. Jimmy Byrd's Scottish jaw still stuck out like a small spade, echoing the shallow snatch of stiff blond hair that jutted out in front of him like an arrowhead, apparently immune to the stiffest brush or any brand of hair oil. His frame was still big and angular, but he was not quite filling it now. He still had his beak nose and his wide thin rat-trap of a mouth, and no doubt he was still as straight as that himself. Blake's worry was whether that was getting him anywhere positive. Blake's antennae could not pick up the same worrying hints of shock and uncertainty in Nancy Byrd. He knew her less well. She was silver-blonde and small, and looked more balanced and resilient than her husband, and more obviously Highland. After the *khummus* and *tchina* and *pita* starters, and as the filet mignon and mixed salad was being served, Blake turned from their anodyne reminiscences to the theme that really dominated all their thoughts. He said abruptly:

'Jimmy, I kept your secretary, and I got my telex off –'

Neither Byrd spoke. The Arab waiter came in with a richly creamed mayonnaise sauce, and set it on the table. He glanced at them seated round the table, assessed their tension at once, and departed hurriedly.

'It doesn't fault you at all,' said Blake. 'I think it clears you completely.'

He might just have granted each of them a million pounds sterling, tax free. Jimmy Byrd was actually filling his frame again. He even beamed. For a moment.

'Will the Ice Maiden see it like that?' he said, suddenly shrunken once more.

'Surely he *has* to see it like that!' said Blake. 'Jimmy, you weren't at fault. How could you have been after only three months?'

Jimmy Byrd stared back at him, clearly unconvinced. Blake could sense the fluttering again. He could understand Byrd's fear. The axe now meant that the Byrds' two sons could not finish at Westminster. The Byrds would also probably lose their house in Surrey. Far the worst, Jimmy Byrd would lose his pride. That would embitter him for life, and not even Nancy would be able to do anything about it. Byrd was straight-run material. If Eagle judged against him, he would accept it. He was totally loyal to Eagle, a real medieval guild man. He and the eighteen hard-fought years of his career would be a total loss.

'Jimmy,' said Blake, 'read it for yourself. It's as objective as I could make it.'

He pulled out the telexes from his inner jacket pocket and gave one to Byrd. 'I've a spare one for Nancy, if you'd like her to read it too.'

Byrd glanced up.

'Of course.'

The three bent forward over their telexes on the table, like diners saying grace. Blake read his own work again:

GETIM VAN STRATEN EAGLE LONDON.

FALCON AVIATION LIMITED. HAVE EXAMINED THE BACK-GROUND TO OUR LOSS OF THIS BUSINESS TO TULSA OIL THREE DAYS AGO. THE FACTS APPEAR:

AAA:FALCON AVIATION IS INCORPORATED IN BEIRUT, ITS SHAREHOLDING BEING 51% LEBANESE 26% NORTH AMERICAN 23% BRITISH. IT OWNS 21 BOEING 727S OF WHICH 7 ARE STILL BEING PAID OFF OVER 5 YEARS AND FLIES MOST MAJOR ROUTES TO WESTERN EUROPEAN COUNTRIES PLUS MIDDLE AND FAR EAST CAPITALS AND TORONTO, NEW YORK, BOSTON, CHICAGO, ATLANTA AND MIAMI ON THE NORTH AMERICAN CONTINENT. THE AIRLINE IS ECONOMICALLY VIABLE, JUST BREAKING EVEN LAST YEAR WHEN THE GOVERNMENT SUBSIDY WAS ELIMINATED FOR THE FIRST TIME.

BBB: EAGLE HAVE FOR 16 YEARS HELD FALCON AVIATION'S OIL BUSINESS EXCLUSIVELY WORLDWIDE FOR BOTH AVIATION TURBINE FUEL AND AVIATION LUBRICANTS AND PROVIDED INTO-AIRCRAFT FUELLING SERVICE AT ALL AIRPORTS BY BOWSERS OR HYDRANT SYSTEMS. TOTAL EAGLE BILLING TO FALCON AVIATION IN 1976 WAS US$100 MILLION.

CCC: EAGLE'S INITIAL CONTRACT WITH FALCON AVIATION WAS FOR 3 YEARS, AUTOMATICALLY RENEWABLE ANNUALLY, UNLESS ON ANY JUNE 15 EITHER PARTY GAVE THE OTHER ONE MONTH'S NOTICE OF TERMINATION. FALCON AVIATION GAVE EAGLE LEBANON THAT NOTICE BY REGISTERED TELEGRAM THIS JUNE 15.

DDD: EAGLE LEBANON EVIDENTLY HAD ABSOLUTELY NO PRIOR HINT OF THIS SUDDEN MOVE. THEY HAD GIVEN ALL REASONABLE SERVICE AND TECHNICAL SUPPORT TO FALCON AVIATION WORLDWIDE. THEIR QUALITY CONTROL OF THE EAGLE AVIATION TURBINE FUEL THEY HAVE DELIVERED INTO FALCON'S AIRCRAFT, ALWAYS THROUGH MICROFILTERS, HAD NEVER BEEN FAULTED, AND CLEARLY THIS SECURITY AGAINST ACCIDENTS WHICH WOULD ALMOST CERTAINLY BE FATAL HAS BEEN OF INESTIMABLE VALUE TO FALCON. AT FALCON'S BASE AIRPORT, BEIRUT, EAGLE'S AVIATION FUELLING CREWS HAVE PROVIDED EXEMPLARY SAMPLE TESTING OF EVERY DELIVERY 24 HOURS A DAY, AND THEIR RECORDS DEMONSTRATE THIS. THE EAGLE AVIATION SALES MANAGER, VON LÜBECK, HAS VISITED FALCON'S OPERATIONS MANAGER IN BEIRUT MONTHLY FOR THE LAST SIX MONTHS AND THE NEW EAGLE GM, BYRD, HAS VISITED THEIR GM TWICE IN HIS FIRST THREE MONTHS HERE AND HAD HIM AND HIS SALES MANAGER AND THEIR WIVES TO DINE TWICE AT HIS HOUSE DESPITE HIS OTHER HEAVY COMMITMENTS.

EEE: ANWAR MUGHRABI, FALCON'S GM, TOLD ME THIS MORNING THAT HE HAD THE HIGHEST REGARD FOR EAGLE'S PRODUCTS AND ABOVE ALL FOR THEIR QUALITY CONTROL IN DELIVERING THEM, AND FOR THE ATTENTION SHOWN FALCON BY EAGLE'S NEW TOP MANAGEMENT HERE. HOWEVER, HE ADDED THAT:

1. FALCON AVIATION WOULD NOT REVERSE ITS DECISION TO SWITCH TO TULSA. THAT WAS IRREVOCABLE. THE TULSA CONTRACT WAS EXCLUSIVE WORLDWIDE FOR ALL AVIATION FUELS AND LUBRICANTS FOR 3 YEARS FROM JULY 15 AND FALCON WOULD BREAK IT ONLY IF TULSA'S PRODUCTS OR SERVICE FAILED.

2. FALCON AVIATION HAD BEEN VERY HAPPY WITH EAGLE'S PRODUCTS AND SERVICE, MOST NOTABLY OUR QUALITY CONTROL, BUT FELT THAT OUR 16-YEAR MONOPOLY OF THEIR BUSINESS SHOULD END, GIVING OTHERS A CHANCE; LEBANON HAD ALWAYS PRIDED ITSELF ON ITS ECONOMY OF FREE COMPETITION. TULSA DESERVED THEIR REWARD. THEY HAD NEGOTIATED 5 YEARS FOR THIS CONTRACT. WE HAD NOT PICKED THIS UP LOCALLY BECAUSE TULSA HAD WISELY MADE THEIR MAIN CONTACTS THROUGH NEW YORK AND HOUSTON.

3. TULSA HAD QUOTED FALCON AVIATION PRICES AVERAGING 10% BELOW OURS, SUGGESTING THAT TULSA WERE EITHER MARKEDLY MORE EFFICIENT THAN EAGLE OR CONTENT WITH FAR SLIMMER PROFITS. ETHICALLY FALCON COULD ONLY ACCEPT THIS US$10 MILLION ANNUAL SAVING AND PASS IT ON TO ITS SHAREHOLDERS. (IF FALCON IS RIGHT IN IMPLYING THAT WE MIGHT HAVE BEEN SOMEWHAT AMBITIOUS IN OUR PRICING POLICIES OVER THE LAST FEW YEARS, WE CAN PERHAPS HARDLY HOLD THE PRESENT EAGLE MANAGEMENT IN BEIRUT RESPONSIBLE FOR THAT.)

4. MUGHRABI SAID FINALLY, WITHOUT ELABORATING, THAT TULSA WERE ALSO GIVING 'OTHER SIGNIFICANT AID' WHICH WE HAD NEVER OFFERED. (PROBABLY EXTENDED CREDIT.) WE SHOULD, OF COURSE, BE GIVEN EVERY OPPORTUNITY TO COMPETE WITH TULSA'S PRICES AND CONDITIONS IN 3 YEARS' TIME.

FFF: BYRD EVEN MANAGED TO GET AN INTERVIEW THIS AFTERNOON WITH HIS EXCELLENCY THE NEW PRESIDENT OF LEBANON ELIAS SARKIS, ABOUT WHICH BYRD WILL DOUBTLESS INFORM YOU FULLY SEPARATELY. H.E. HAD EVIDENTLY BEEN

WELL BRIEFED. HIS REACTIONS WERE IDENTICAL TO MUGHRABI'S. LEBANON BELIEVED IN AND PRACTISED FREE COMPETITION. HE WOULD THUS CERTAINLY NOT STOP IT NOW. SURELY WE OURSELVES ALWAYS EXTOLLED THIS PRINCIPLE? WE HAD GIVEN EXCELLENT SERVICE TO FALCON FOR 16 YEARS BUT SEEMED NOW TO HAVE BEEN BEATEN IN FAIR COMPETITION. SHOULD WE NOT THEREFORE ACCEPT THAT, AND CONCENTRATE ON SHARPENING OUR PENCILS APPROPRIATELY IN 3 YEARS?

I AWAIT YOUR COMMENTS. BLAKE.

These comments, as Blake reflected now, might well be caustic in the extreme. Falcon was among the biggest single pieces of aviation oil business in the Middle East. Losing it after sixteen years to Tulsa like this could make Eagle, and Van Straten the laughing-stock of the oil industry. Van Straten, wouldn't even be able to go into the Travellers without provoking hoots of derision from all the old leather armchairs. He wouldn't like that. And the Ice Maiden, Blake knew, had pretty rigid views about accountability. He would want a head for this.

Still, at least Blake's telex was having a rejuvenating effect on Jimmy Byrd across the table. Byrd looked up now over the tail end of his filet mignon. 'My God!' he said. 'You've really gone out on a limb for me on this one. You've practically pinned it on the Ice Maiden herself for being too greedy with her prices!'

Byrd looked cheered at the thought. He leaned over and poured Blake some more red wine. It was Château Musar's Cabernet Sauvignon, from Lebanon's small but rich and high-quality wine production at Ksara; as a seasoned expatriate, Byrd always gave pride of place to local goods where he reasonably could.

'Well, I'm damned if I can see how anyone could pin a thing on you,' said Blake.

'I like your tailpiece too,' said Jimmy Byrd. 'Where you instruct London to be good sports and shut up till the next time round. Van Straten'll love that one!'

Jimmy Byrd beamed under his craggy blond brows. He seemed to have got a lot of his old bounce back.

'I'd not meant to make it sound quite that categoric,' said Blake, 'but at least we have the President of Lebanon behind us too.'

'Jimmy and I are just lucky that we have you as Regional Co-ordinator,' said Nancy Byrd, to Blake's left at the head of the table. 'Jimmy's worked very hard, you know. This is his first big chance, an independent command in the field. I don't think he could have worked any harder.'

'Christ, Nancy!' said Byrd. 'Lay off it, will you? You'll have my pants off me next, in front of him.'

'Aye, and that's a shock he could take too,' said Nancy, unperturbed. 'You're just born lucky, Jimmy.'

'I set out the facts as I saw them,' said Blake. 'Hell, it would be *cockeyed* to try to pin the blame for this one on him!'

'Aye, and it's a rough enough area for an oil man to work in as it is,' said Nancy. 'What with this murderous bloody infighting and the political and economic instability, almost every other oil company has pulled out now. You know Shell and BP sold out to their local staff?'

'Indeed,' said Blake. 'They were marketing jointly as part of their old Consolidated set-up, weren't they? And when they sold out the Shell half became Coral Oil and the BP Speed Petroleum.'

'Leaving just us from the multinationals,' said Jimmy Byrd. 'And Tulsa, but as an Aviation Service at Beirut Airport only. *Christ!*' he added suddenly. '*That* should have tipped me off!'

'What?' said Blake.

'The fact that they were still keeping on their Aviation Service even after they'd pulled out from their Mogas and industrial products marketing and bunkering and everything else. *That* should have told me that they were still gunning for Falcon Aviation!'

'Stop crucifying yourself, Jimmy,' said Blake. 'What more could you have done? You couldn't have stopped it. It goes too far back.'

'Still,' said Byrd, 'it happened, didn't it? And I was the Joe in charge of the shop at the time.'

'And what were you supposed to do?' asked Blake. 'Pick up the facts by ouija board? Look, maybe you can kick *others* for not having had their ears nearer to the ground. But not you. Hell, you'd only *been* here five minutes!'

'Like who?' said Jimmy Byrd.

'Like Von Lübeck. Like your tame Prussian sergeant major. He's the Aviation Sales Manager isn't he? So isn't a major client like Falcon Aviation one of his direct goddamned responsibilities?'

'Well, yes —'

'And how long's he been here?'

'Who, Johann? Three years.'

'*Three* years? Christ, by now his market intelligence ought to be so good that he knows the instant that the Falcon Aviation GM trots off to have a pee. No, the instant that the GM first *thinks* that maybe he wants a pee. By sheer intuition. So why don't we pick on him? It's dead logical. We're probably morally right too. Why don't we pin dear Johann?'

'He's been very quiet these last few days,' said Nancy. 'He and his wife. I hardly even noticed him at that Ministry of Industry and Commerce cocktail party yesterday. So subdued. He's keeping a very low profile.'

'I'll bet,' said Blake.

'I don't think you can blame Johann,' said Byrd. 'The whole thing was done at too high a level.'

'Keep talking like that, Jimmy,' said Blake, 'and it'll be *your* head that falls!'

'Listen to the man, Jimmy,' said Nancy. 'Look, he's a friend, remember?'

'Yes, sure,' said Byrd, glancing at her absently, then looking back at Blake. 'But, well, I was the Joe in charge, wasn't I?'

Blake suddenly felt very sick. Jimmy Byrd was practically willing this fate on himself, almost approving of it. Blake could have been watching a soul destroy itself, a whole identity, a very straight and decent human being. It was life or death, it could go either way, but Blake would not have betted now on a favourable outcome. It was as if Jimmy Byrd's pride were already shot in advance. Clearly he was still a very worried man. He had fallen right back from the buoyancy that reading Blake's telex had injected into him. He had shrunk again. One way and another, he was certainly moving around a hell of a lot inside the scaffolding of that big Scottish frame. And if he destroyed himself, Nancy Byrd would destroy herself too; she was a good loyal Scottish wife. What hell of a system did this to people?

'I've done what I could,' said Blake, really to himself.

The two turned uniformly onto him, like sad blank white

masked faces in a mime. 'Yes, yes!' they chorused. 'We know that, Philip.'

So, early after that dinner, he had got the chauffeured limousine that Jimmy Byrd had provided for him to drive him straight back to the Hypercontinental, and he had gone up to his top-floor suite to sit in the dark by a window and gaze down at the lights and the movements and think. He could find no sense at all of guilt down there, in that slick lit concrete jungle that had seen and would still see so much bestial slaughter. There was only somewhere that certainty of threat, pulsing and permanent in the darkness between the lights, that mindless pact, eternal promise of pain.

15
The Ice Maiden Cometh

The Ice Maiden's telex reply, crisp and quick and not even coded, was waiting for Blake and Byrd when they got to Eagle's Beirut office first thing the next morning. It made its point simply but with impact:

GETOP. FOR BLAKE. YOUR TODAY'S GETIM. ARRIVING TO-MORROW 19/6 AT 2100 BY FALCON FLIGHT FC 123. PLEASE ADVISE BYRD AND ASK HIM RESERVE ME SUITE HYPER-CONTINENTAL TWO NIGHTS. VAN STRATEN.

The Ice Maiden had wasted no time. Blake had got his telex away at 8 the evening before, or 7 pm London. Eagle London would have got and decoded it by 8.30, then delivered it to an alerted Van Straten; Getim meant you had to get the message to its target at once, wherever and in however ceremonial or intimate a situation he might be. Van Straten must have decided as promptly to take the earliest Falcon flight out, remembering even under that stress to fly only by his client's airline, even if that client had just rudely jilted him. The very real physical dangers of being shot or bombed by Beirut's multiple and often scarcely distinguishable militia would not have deterred Van Straten one whit. He was a hardy man, at base so puritanical and austere that he was totally contempt-uous of physical discomfort, or indeed mortal peril, if he felt it his duty to endure them. He was also clearly not taking Eagle's loss of this prestigious account at all lightly. Blake could see Byrd working that out too from his copy of Van Straten's Getop reply. Byrd's face had gone very white. He looked up and across at Blake.

'That's it then, Philip.'

'*Nonsense*, Jimmy! You've got no skeletons in the cup-board, nothing to hide! What can Van Straten find out that's not already known? There's nothing to discredit you. So take it easy. The man just wants to come out and see for himself. That's very laudable, surely. The Field Marshal who really goes to the front line and tries to put his troops fully in the picture and allay their worries. You can't kick him for that, Jimmy. Van Straten just has a very high sense of his own responsibilities.'

'Christ, I'll say!' said Byrd.

'Well,' said Blake, 'so stop painting yourself guilty. You *aren't*! Don't talk yourself into it!'

'No,' said Byrd absently. 'Okay, we must make that Hypercontinental reservation for him!'

Byrd got his secretary on the phone and did that. Then he sat back in his chair and looked at Blake.

'What time does FC 123 get in?' asked Blake. 'In fact, I mean? I know his telex said 9 pm.'

'It's generally dead on time. I'll keep checking nearer the hour, of course. But I'd say we ought to leave the centre at 8.25 to 8.30. We'll lay on the double-VIP treatment for him, of course –'

Byrd broke away again and Blake heard him telling his PRO on the phone to pull out all the stops for Van Straten. Then Byrd looked back at Blake.

'If we've still got all day to plan,' he said, 'who will he want to see?'

'Falcon's GM Mughrabi, certainly. First thing tomorrow, if I know Van Straten.'

Byrd phoned through personally and fixed that at once.

God Almighty, Blake was thinking to himself. And what hotel do I have to book myself in? The Hypercontinental, that Home of Romance, the Ice Maiden's very own favourite. Aloud he said: 'Also Von Lübeck.'

'You really think he ought to see Von Lübeck?'

'I sure as hell do, Jimmy. Of course he ought to see Von Lübeck. And if I'm right he's the one Van Straten ought also to screw most heartily too.'

'Well, all right, if you insist. And what about the President?'

'Excellent idea. If you can set it up. It won't change anything, we know that. But the more people tell Van Straten that, the better.'

'In that case, the British Ambassador too?'

'I'd put that one to Van Straten when he arrives; I'm not so sure he'd want to bother. But I'd set up preliminary arrangements for Sarkis right away. That's the head of the snake around here, isn't it?'

'Sure.'

'And you, Jimmy, of course. He's got to get the fullest possible picture from you. Which I'll support wherever I can. And I'd lay on two or three quality-control staff, including your Aviation Service Airfield Supervisor, to show the very high level of service you've been giving Falcon. Make sure they have their technical records handy. And let's have exact dates and details of your and Von Lübeck's visits to their management, what you discussed and so on. And of the dinners Nancy and you gave for Mughrabi and his Sales Manager. You know the sort of thing. It'll all help.'

'You think even down to that degree of detail?' asked Byrd.

'Down to any degree of detail,' said Blake. 'Let's use everything we can get.'

Eagle Lebanon might lose a $100 million-a-year aviation service contract here and there, but no one could fault their double VIP treatment. Falcon Flight FC 123 had hardly ground to a halt on the Beirut Airport parking-apron and switched off its jets before the kid-glove handling started. The front passenger hatch opened to display that small taut internationally known figure – anyway inside the oil industry – with its neat and striking head of pure white hair. Within instants under the floodlights deferential uniformed officials had whisked him out and into the first of two waiting and gleaming limousines. Practically no passenger-ladder seemed to have been needed; the gloved hand of one of those groomed officials might simply have reached up with marvellous efficiency to the side of the aircraft and lifted him reverently away the moment he appeared. It was like some exquisitely conducted kidnapping – a slick and criminal pastime already commonplace in this riven and violent city.

Blake and Byrd were waiting for the Ice Maiden at the entrance to the reception building, which was the nearest to the aircraft they could get under the sudden excruciating severity of Beirut Airport's spasmodic security arrangements. Here the limousines delivered him. The officials bowed, murmured as Byrd pressed notes into their willing palms, and withdrew.

'Good evening, Mr Van Straten.'

'Evening, Blake.'

'James Byrd, sir.'

'Yes. I know.'

'Welcome to Beirut, sir.'

Van Straten made no comment. The muscles at the corners of his mouth had built their little vertical iron ridges.

They led Van Straten through to the double-VIP room, which they had to themselves. He sat. Byrd said: 'Could we have your passport, please?'

Van Straten gave it to him. 'How long will *that* take?' he asked.

'Three minutes, sir. Not more than three minutes.'

'My return ticket's in it. You might as well confirm that. And my luggage-tag's there.'

'Certainly, sir. For when is the flight back?'

Van Straten glanced up. 'Day after tomorrow. '10.30 pm. Falcon.'

That was the exact weight he gave it, then, thought Blake. Two full working days. Three, if you counted the 5½-hour 2,500-mile flight each way. That added up to a bomb of money in an MD's time.

Byrd's PRO, an old Middle East hand, had gone off like

lightning with the Ice Maiden's passport and ticket, exploiting all his contacts to the hilt. 'We don't have to wait for your luggage,' said Byrd. 'It can come on in a second car.'

'Good,' said Van Straten. 'I've my pyjamas and toilet kit in here.' He patted his briefcase. Blake wondered what else he had in there, what assessments of Byrd, what scenarios on his life, or professional death.

'A drink, sir? A whisky, perhaps?'

Van Straten glanced at Byrd again. 'A lemon squash would do.'

Byrd got it for him from the bar.

'How was the flight, sir?'

Again that glance. 'Long and somewhat turbulent,' said Van Straten. Was he measuring Byrd for accountability for that too?

'Could we interest you in some dinner?'

'Thank you, I had dinner on the plane.'

Always that probing look. By now he must know Byrd's weight to the nearest pound and all his past sins. The Ice Maiden sized you up all the time, Blake knew. Well, you could find a mathematical equation for anything. Van Straten simply dug for yours. He was naturally a very careful man. He did not make mistakes. Nor did he waste energy. He put himself into position and did exactly what was needed from there, no more. Van Straten did not muck about. He never waved his hands around, used them to light cigarettes for others or himself, or even ran them through his hair. His economy was that of genius. It also terrified. Compassion was just not relevant. Van Straten was an extraordinarily honest man, utterly consistent to himself. His silver-white hair was like a badge of precision. It was brushed straight back and never out of place. There was no black in it and no parting. It was, like him, all of one piece. That flawlessness chilled. It lacked the scars and blemishes of humanity.

'And what arrangements have you made?' he asked.

Byrd told him.

'Good,' said Van Straten. 'Yes. Mr Anwar Mughrabi tomorrow morning at ten. And please go ahead and firm up that appointment with His Excellency the President in the afternoon. And, indeed, I must talk to the members of the staff you suggest. Good.'

The atmosphere had lightened. It was as if they were suddenly all back on the same team again. Encouraged, Jimmy Byrd then said brightly: 'And perhaps you'd care to see the British Ambassador too?'

The Ice Maiden gave him another probing scalpel look.

'I don't really think so, you know,' he said. 'We're a bit of a third-rate power these days, aren't we? Besides, no ambassador of any nation really has all that much clout today, does he? Certainly nothing like the autonomy and weight we give to our GMs in the field, for example. So let's discard that idea. I don't think that we should really talk to anyone except the top.'

It was really impressive, thought Blake, with what surgical wizardry Van Straten could deflate anyone, just those few deft strokes. He watched the craggy Byrd blush, a remarkable sight in itself, and turn away. The gong saved him; the old Middle Eastern hand was back.

'Your passport, sir. Your return ticket, confirmed. I'll bring your suitcase to your hotel in my car.'

'Yes. Thank you.'

In the Daimler, Blake sat in front with the Lebanese driver, Byrd in the back with Van Straten; this was still, perhaps just, Byrd's bailiwick. They passed shattered buildings, outer walls sheared clean off, the tangled metal rods and piping and floor tiling hanging out of the brickwork like the stuffing out of sandwiches. Militiamen were everywhere: perhaps some of them had been trained at the secret bases Leila had mentioned, in the Kingdom of the Sun. They came in all guises and disguises, many bearded, some so young that their automatic rifles looked bigger than themselves. Not all were uniformed. How, wondered Blake, did each sect know itself from any other, to prevent suicide instead of patriotic and worthy slaughter of its official enemies? Or perhaps that did not matter too much. If killing were the operative word, the fashionable imperative? Perhaps this was the final mindless face of Armageddon –

'The political situation?' said Van Straten.

'A powerless central government,' said Byrd. 'Sarkis is nothing without Syria's support. Or Camille Chamoun's hard right wing – which, just, got him elected. You have regular Syrian troops dominating the Bekaa Valley and Northern

Lebanon – Syria's political objective, as ever since modern Lebanon was first invented, is to hold it as a vassal state. Ironically, their allies are the right-wing Christian Lebanese militias, their overt enemies the PLO and left-wing Muslim fighters. Meanwhile the real and most lethal enemy remains Israel, who truly rule that part of Lebanon south of their Red Line, either by their own paratrooper or commando incursions, or more usually through Major Haddad's Israeli-trained and equipped South Lebanese Army. Israel will call the next shots; the Syrian occupying forces have not dared to confront them –'

'Israel will invade,' said the Ice Maiden, 'just when it suits her. And when the PLO are foolish enough to give her a good internationally saleable pretext. Here is your final conflict, between a Fatah-dominated PLO and Israel. In the end, one must destroy the other.'

Blake found an interesting note of satisfaction in Van Straten's voice. He was talking mathematical equations again, not human beings. He was making a forecast that was probably bitterly accurate. As a natural Manichean, this might in a sense be what he wanted too. But he filtered out the screams. They were not his concern. For him it was business as usual.

After that there was total silence in the Daimler for some minutes. Van Straten simply gazed out of his window at the lights and militiamen and astonishingly nonchalant townspeople and at the sudden gutted hulks of buildings, stripped there by the gale force of shells and shrapnel, like the bony carcasses of shipwrecks hurled onto the hidden razor reefs of a shore of plenty; for often trim and elegant high-rise blocks soared unruffled beside them. Van Straten looked equally unmoved by this selective obliteration. He seemed quite at home in it, at ease. He was a man who made his desires known by understatement. You sprang automatically and at once to satisfy them. Similarly, if evidently he felt that no conversation was called for, as now, there was none. Blake watched Jimmy Byrd break that tacit rule, but not for long –

'Sir,' said Jimmy Byrd, about halfway on the car trip, and still clearly bursting to do the right thing, 'would you like me to lay on a small dinner-party or cocktail in my house in your honour tomorrow? It's not often we have the Chairman of the Board here as our guest –'

With the back of his neck, Blake could feel the Ice Maiden turn his head and measure Byrd again with his eyes in the dark:

'Thank you, Byrd, but I doubt if it's quite the most opportune moment for parties, don't you?'

'No, sir, I suppose not,' said Jimmy Byrd wretchedly, and shut up.

And that was that. It was, thought Blake, a little like having a white-haired leopard with you in the car on a leash, very balanced and controlled, indeed with trim lean muscles and classy lines, very still and tranquil for the moment, but still a leopard; and one which, as Blake knew with total certainty, while hunting other prey for the time being, hated him, Blake, most cordially, instinctively, and with every fibre of its sleek precise being. Then why on earth had Van Straten approved Blake as his Regional Co-ordinator Middle East? He could easily have found another; competition was myriad and ferocious at that level in Eagle. Had it been just to set him up? That was not to be excluded out of hand.

At the Hypercontinental Hotel Van Straten booked in quickly, then turned to them.

'Don't bother to wait. I'm going to bed. I'm sure my suitcase will arrive safely.'

It was not a courtesy, but an instruction.

'Sir,' said Byrd.

'I expect you two must be wanting your dinner,' said Van Straten, most genially, examining them. He had very clear light grey eyes. The two men looked at each other appropriately.

'Oh, and I'll be wanting to see those people tomorrow on my own,' said Van Straten, eliminating that frivolous touch of humanity. 'Mughrabi of Falcon and President Elias Sarkis. I want no one with me.'

'Sir,' said Byrd again. Blake inclined his head.

'Then I'll see you and your staff and Mr Blake here again the day after tomorrow, before I leave.'

Blake saw Byrd pale slightly. That would be when the verdict was delivered.

'Car ready here at eight in the morning?' said Van Straten. 'Then I can touch base with you in your office at eight-thirty.'

'Of course,' said Jimmy Byrd, and glanced at Blake. The Ice Maiden picked that up at once.

'Mr Blake can come in with me, of course,' he said. 'There's no point to using two cars. We don't want to waste money, do we?'

He had no need, thought Blake, to add 'Particularly now.' Falcon Aviation had after all been a cool hundred million US dollars a year.

'No, sir,' said Jimmy Byrd, admonished in advance, dropping his gaze guiltily.

'Oh, and sleep well,' Van Straten added, without discernible irony.

16

An Act of God

That second day of the Ice Maiden's visit, June 21, Blake was not required to see him before 4 pm. He therefore prevailed on the luckless Von Lübeck to take him out to visit a few worthwhile Eagle customers, once Von Lübeck was free from Van Straten's ministrations at 10 am. After that Van Straten would be interviewing Eagle Beirut's aviation quality-control staff, their Beirut Airport Aviation Supervisor, and Jimmy Byrd. It was anyone's guess how much blood there would already be on the floor when the Ice Maiden saw Blake.

Von Lübeck took him to see two textile factories, an electronics manufacturer, a plastic toy works, a shipyard specializing in repairs, and a car-hire firm which operated its own Eagle service station; the oil industry played a catholic role in the modern world. Von Lübeck took him to a small but good Lebanese restaurant where the wine was again the excellent and vigorous dry red Château Musar Cabernet Sauvignon. That wine was the day's high point in stimulation so far. Blake did not find his guide brilliant company. Von

Lübeck was a squat Bavarian of about thirty-five, gifted with no great imagination or vivacity. The Ice Maiden's majesty had moreover stunned him. He could not say from his interview whether Van Straten blamed him at all for the loss of Falcon Aviation, but he was clearly not a happy man. Nancy Byrd had said that Von Lübeck had been keeping a very low profile since the disaster. Blake now found it so diminished that he could hardly see the man at all. The Ice Maiden had that effect on people.

However, Van Straten could be very explicit indeed about what he thought when he wanted. Blake had had that etched out in fire for him the evening before. It had been almost by accident. Wanting a quiet night, he had declined Jimmy Byrd's hospitality and gone back to the Hypercontinental, reaching the hotel's dining-room early, about eight. He was already well into the room when he saw the Ice Maiden. Van Straten was on his own, and beckoned to him. Blake could not refuse that royal command. He smiled, and sat.

Van Straten was drinking a Mouton Rothschild 1967. He poured Blake a liberal glass and they toasted each other. The wine was awe-inspiringly rich, but Blake found the going rough. His left knee throbbed diligently with pain. He saw no point to mentioning Van Straten's two interviews that day, for he knew from Byrd how they had gone – about as Byrd and he had predicted. Anwar Mughrabi of Falcon had apparently said to Van Straten just what he had said to Blake, and been as adamant against changing Falcon's decision to switch to Tulsa, while His Excellency President Elias Sarkis had been as categoric as he had been to Byrd against intervening with Falcon on Eagle's behalf: free competition was the Lebanon's first principle in business, as surely it was Eagle's.

So the conversation at Blake's obligatory dinner with the Ice Maiden had been desultory, at least until the marital incident. That had occurred quite anarchically. A couple sat at the next table. They were recognizably British at a hundred yards, Oxbridge, but not in the top drawer of success. He could have been a fairly senior business executive or civil servant or a doctor, either working locally or perhaps visiting on holiday. They were obviously upper-middle-aged and heavily married.

'But it was precisely *because* Hermione's dress was pink!' shrieked the lady suddenly. 'Can't you *see*?' She wept at once and totally, like a tap turned on full, leapt to her feet, flung down her napkin and marched loudly out of the room. She was a big blonde woman with heavy shoulders and ample breasts. That cloudburst of tears had ravaged her cosmetic cheeks like shotgun wounds. But she had gone off at certainly her best dramatic moment, leaving her riddle still quite unscrambled, probably permanently. She would continue to intrigue all in that large dining-room for days, perhaps years. Probably except for her husband. He had gone on dining phlegmatically. He could have been putting up with this sort of thing forever.

'Classical!' said Van Straten, with such intensity that Blake looked at him curiously.

'You don't think much of women, sir?'

Van Straten calibrated him with his piercing light grey eyes.

'Of these congenital liars?' he said icily. 'These *cheats*, these histrionic melodramatists? No, I do *not* think much of them. Indeed, *anything* of them!'

'Of *any* of them?'

'Of *any* of them. That's true, to one degree or another. Seriously, how can any man in his right mind think anything favourable about these cheap cowards, these shallow thieves, these pathological egocentrics?'

'Agreed, that was a remarkable performance.'

'And almost always that recourse to moisture, you see. The ready tears, the constant extremely shrewd use of them as a weapon. As if they had an endless source of it, a bottomless well, an unhealing wound!'

'Yes. I wonder what this was all about, though?'

'The details wouldn't really matter. It's always some form of emotional blackmail.'

Blake glanced at him, made bold by the fascination of the theme, and by the excellent Mouton Rothschild.

'But I thought you were married?'

Van Straten smiled at him. It was a fairly spectral performance.

'I *am* married. And have three good sons. All well launched now, thank God. In banking. In medicine. In teaching.'

'Well, then?' asked Blake, uncertainly.

'Oh, that at least women can do,' said Van Straten. 'Breed. It's about all they're any good at. Standing on their heads.

Lying on their backs, rather. They don't even have to think. It's just as well. They're not equipped for it.'

'But you're not divorced?'

'No,' said Van Straten. 'I wouldn't give her that satisfaction. But I've not lived with her now for many years.'

'I see,' said Blake, who did not.

After a few moments of silence Van Straten said: 'You asked me if I felt like that about *all* of them. Well, perhaps one shouldn't generalize totally. Your wife, for example, just might be different. The one exception.'

'I certainly hope so,' said Blake.

'Celia, isn't it?' said Van Straten. 'One's got to try to be fair, of course.'

'Yes,' said Blake. 'It's Celia.'

He wondered why Van Straten should have mentioned Celia. Blake had not even realized that he knew her name. Of course they would have been introduced at the usual senior staff parties but Van Straten must have glanced off hundreds of Eagle wives that way. He had never met her anywhere else as far as Blake knew. So why should he cite Celia as the one possible exception to his annihilation of her sex? An olive branch to Blake? What other reason could there be? He looked again curiously at Van Straten, who seemed almost to be on guard for that.

'Have a touch of Mouton Rothschild?' he said.

'Many thanks,' said Blake.

'Thank God I never had any daughters,' said Van Straten.

Thank God, indeed, thought Blake, as he knocked exactly at four on the afternoon of that second and final day of Van Straten's visit on the door of Jimmy Byrd's office and went in. For he guessed that Van Straten was already quite irritated enough, even without domestic causes. He was sitting behind Byrd's desk. There was no sign of Jimmy Byrd himself; Van Straten was taking his place in more senses than one. There was a window just behind the Ice Maiden. Carved out there now, immobile in judgement, he had become his nickname. There was the same frozen passion about him, the same keen murderous edge, as there had been the evening before.

'Sit down,' said Van Straten. 'Let's talk about your telex.'

Blake saw that Van Straten had a copy in front of him, heavily annotated.

'You have your copy?' asked Van Straten.

'Yes.'

'Your "A". I've no quarrel with your presentation of Falcon Aviation, its shareholding, type and size of fleet, outstanding debt on aircraft, major air routes flown, and overall economic viability. Or of the great length and high value of our supply contract with them as given in your "B". That all looks factually correct.'

'Thank you.'

'Your "C" goes to the core of the matter: the *terms* of that contract, initially three years exclusive worldwide, then automatically renewable annually unless one party gave the other one month's notice of termination any June 15 –'

'Yes.'

'Doesn't that strike you as an intrinsically *weak* form of contract?'

'No. Why? The terms were presumably the best they could negotiate at the time, sixteen years ago.'

'Wouldn't it have been better to go for renewable terms of three years each, consistent with the original period? And why on earth not have insisted on periods of notice of at least three and preferably six months? The present notice period of just one month simply gives us no time to argue and defend ourselves! Why not at least have started to *work* on such improvements? There's nothing in any bible or anywhere else that forbids you to strengthen the terms of a contract by agreement while it's still running in its original form, is there? Why just leave this contract as it was? Wasn't that just *asking* for trouble? Just intellectual laziness? *Criminal* laziness?'

The little vertical bars at the corners of Van Straten's mouth had gone quite rigid.

'Imagine our losing a contract the size of this and value when we've held it for practically an eternity!' said Van Straten. 'This will make us the fools of the international oil world!'

'Tulsa worked on it for all of five years, according to Mughrabi,' said Blake. 'And mainly in New York and Houston. Could we have known that?'

'If we'd secured our Falcon Aviation really long-term in the ways I've suggested we wouldn't have *needed* to know that! But, vulnerable as we were, if it wasn't Tulsa it would have been some other enemy, Exxon, Shell, Mobil, BP, Texaco, Gulf, Chevron, what's it matter? And tell me –'

'Yes?'

'You've been at the Regional Middle East desk for six months now?'

'Yes, six months.'

'That's quite a time, isn't it? And you've made two long visits out to the Region, I believe?'

'Yes, one for three weeks in my second month, and another of about the same length six weeks ago.'

'And you came here?'

'Yes, on my second visit. Very shortly after Byrd had arrived.'

'You saw the Falcon Aviation contract?'

Blake could feel the sweat building up under his armpits now, across his back, across his stomach. It was like being probed by a delicately focused blowlamp.

'I glanced through our copy in London before I left. I visited Mughrabi briefly here, with Byrd. I must confess that I read no hint at all from Mughrabi's manner of what would happen.'

'Well, it was only your second time round, your first here. And you've a tricky, explosive Region –'

Blake said nothing.

'Still, you did read that contract.'

'Yes,' said Blake.

'That's what I can't get over. Couldn't you *see* its innate fragility?'

'I didn't. Sir.'

'That we were totally vulnerable *every single June 15 that came round*?'

'No, sir. Though in fact it was renewed every year for thirteen years.'

'That was our good luck, not our good judgement. We live or die on our *judgement* in this business, Blake. Not our luck. Luck's the sort of thing *women* count on.'

'Sir.'

'One can't forget that *your* judgement failed in this too. One must take that properly into account somewhere, recognize it adequately. And as for the management here, *quite certainly*, without any slightest shadow of doubt, *someone* here should have seen our vulnerability and acted on it!'

Blake stayed silent.

'Another point,' said the Ice Maiden. 'How *dare* you imply that we were at fault in London by the greed of our pricing policies?'

Blake's stomach fell from him. He looked quickly at his telex.

'I was simply quoting Mughrabi, sir. In my "E" 3.'

'That is a lie, Blake, deliberate or not. You were doing a good deal more than reporting Mughrabi. I quote your bracketed passage. This is *your* comment, not Mughrabi's: "If Falcon is right in implying that we might have been somewhat ambitious in our pricing policies over the last few years, we can perhaps hardly hold the present Eagle management in Beirut responsible for that." I suggest, Blake, that your meaning here is clearly that we in London *were* guilty of greed in our pricing, and that Eagle Beirut's management, particularly *top* management, were not at all to blame for our losing Falcon Aviation.'

Blake looked back at him in silence for fifteen seconds. His left knee was pulsing with pain like an acute toothache, and he could feel his heart pumping heavily. It was almost jumping out of his ears.

'I do not believe that Eagle Lebanon's present top management is significantly to blame for our losing Falcon Aviation. Sir.'

'Let that alone for a moment, Blake. We must look again at your pricing point. Even if we in London *had* pitched our prices too high, *then it was the clear responsibility of Eagle Beirut's top management to have told us so*! *They* were the men on the spot, at Falcon's headquarters, not we! *They* were the ones to know exactly what the situation was in the field, not we. Mind you, we might not have listened to them. In fact we almost certainly would have. You know how great a stature we give to our top executives in the field, and how closely we consider what they tell us.'

'Yes.'

'*But no one here picked up that pricing fact either*! As no one in Beirut noticed that Tulsa had been cutting our throats slowly for the last five years. That argues a *huge* fault. For which ultimately top management here must answer.'

'But surely not the *present* management, sir? Byrd's hardly been in the place three months!'

The sharp light grey eyes across the desk observed him caustically. 'I'm aware of your deep friendship for Byrd since Cairo,' said the Ice Maiden. 'Good for you. Loyalty to a friend is an admirable quality. I put it second only to loyalty to a company or a cause. And *why* not Byrd, pray?'

'Look at his record since he's been here. In three months he's visited Mughrabi in Falcon's headquarters twice and had him and his Sales Manager and their wives to dine twice. He has personally inspected all the quality control equipment and procedures at Beirut Airport several times; you'll have heard Eagle's Aviation Service men speak of him. He *could not* have done more than he had in his short time here!'

'Yet he missed the essential fact,' said Van Straten. After a while he went on: 'And, if not Byrd, who?'

'The prior GM, who was here a full four years. Or Von Lübeck. He's been here three years. As Aviation Sales Manager, who was more responsible for Falcon than he?'

'Forget Von Lübeck!' said Van Straten immediately and with contempt. 'I can find nothing at all to say about Von Lübeck. He is anyway going nowhere.'

It was as crisp and final an elimination of a personality as Blake had ever heard. And it was as if this minor massacre had crystallized Van Straten all at once. In that split second he had made his decision. It would be quite irrevocable. Blake saw him suddenly, as if for the first time, against that window. He could have projected himself there in this instant dead on cue, like a priest at the temple's altar precisely ready for sacrifice. Van Straten was utterly still. Even his voice was absolutely uninflected.

'Blake, I find you critically, even dangerously, lacking in proper concepts of accountability. You may of course take my comments just as you will. But morally I cannot, *will* not, forget your part in this. And I may have to act on that.'

'Sir,' said Blake, 'you'll follow your own judgement, of course.'

'Remember that mistakes don't just happen in a void. They run, inevitably, through people. Just as even the most powerful electric currents must pass through conductors. And, tell me, Blake, what do we normally do if we judge the conductors to be flawed?'

'We change them,' said Blake uneasily. It was as if he were

being pulled in personally now to take part in this judgement.

'We *change* them!' repeated Van Straten enthusiastically, delighted at this apt pupil. 'If there's a fault found in the house, it must be rooted out. That's a very old wisdom!'

Blake gazed at this silhouette, motionless as a god. Its pure white hair held him like a flag. The sharp light grey eyes nailed him, the ridged bars of muscle at the corners of the mouth bracketed him. The decision was made, and Blake knew what it was. The hairs pricked eerily at the nape of his neck. In some way that decision covered him too. No one had to tell Blake now that the meeting was over. He got up spontaneously.

'Just tell Byrd to come in, would you?' said the Ice Maiden. 'He's waiting in Von Lübeck's office.'

'Yes,' said Blake. 'I'll tell Byrd to come in.'

He found Byrd alone, and told him that Van Straten would see him now. He could not reply when Byrd asked him how the ground looked. Blake stood at Von Lübeck's window most of the time. He saw the townspeople and the militiamen mixing, the slick smart cars and the armed jeeps. Perhaps murder was never very far from the surface anywhere, and you just had the privilege of seeing that with more clarity here. Byrd was back within fifteen minutes. It had been a pretty swift execution. He was smiling, but under that he was ashen. He was putting the best face he could on disaster. Jimmy Byrd had always had a lot of class. 'Come back to my office and have a drink,' he said. 'Well, what *was* my office.'

'He's gone?'

'Yes,' said Byrd. 'By car to the Hypercontinental, to get his suitcase and to write up his last few notes there. He said. Then he's going to the airport in his own good time. He'll look after himself for dinner. He didn't want either of us to accompany him.'

'*Elkhamdulillah!*' said Blake. 'Praise be to God!'

Back in Byrd's office, Blake saw that Byrd had got his GM's bar in the corner open already. Sensibly, he was making the most of it while he could. He poured them two stiff whiskies, and added water and ice. They walked over to the four comfortable armchairs in the opposite corner, where Byrd usually received his visitors. 'By the way,' said Blake. 'Where did he sit when he saw you? Over here?'

'Not on your Nelly,' said Byrd. 'He sat in *my* chair, and he had me across the desk.'

'That's the Ice Maiden all right,' said Blake. 'He never misses a trick. Like a doctor receiving his patient, he'll always take the position of authority.'

'He showed that all right,' said Byrd.

'What happened, Jimmy?'

Jimmy Byrd had stopped smiling. He took a strong pull of his whisky, then looked straight at Blake. Byrd's lantern jaw and arrowhead of flat blond hair addressed him. 'First of all, Philip,' he said earnestly, 'I want to thank you very much for all you did and tried to do. You were a real friend. You went out on a limb for me.'

Blake could have wept. A real friend? he thought. What the hell good have I done here?

'Jimmy, it just wasn't enough. It hasn't saved you, has it? That's the test: how has it changed the facts? Though I did it all quite honestly you know. I didn't even have to cheat. I still can't see that he can blame or punish you fairly for this loss.'

Byrd looked away, and down at the floor. 'I don't know,' he said. 'I don't know.' He looked back at Blake. 'He had this colossal *majesty*, you see; you can't deny that. He's absolutely honest in himself, he never lies, not even by a millimetre. How can you stand against the judgement of someone like that?'

'That's all true; you *can* get rare people like that. But they can be bastards too. What did this bastard say?'

Jimmy Byrd glanced back at him.

'That it was through a grave fault in this company that we lost Falcon Aviation. I was the man in command. As such, I had to bear the full and final responsibility.'

'Shit!'

'He went a bit Old Testament then. If there was a flaw in your house, you had to find it and root it out. The worst dishonesty was just to ignore it, to let it slide.'

'Yes, he sang me the same song.'

'Therefore he saw it as his duty to relieve me of my post immediately. I was to be out of here within a week, with my family. I should hand things over to a deputy until London could fly out a new GM.' Byrd shook his head painfully. 'My Aviation Sales Manager would do. Von Lübeck would do.'

Blake looked at him and felt sick.

'He said that his decision was irrevocable, though I could of course appeal it if I wished.' Byrd turned to him again. 'What do you think, Philip?'

Blake thought a moment, then said carefully: 'I doubt that it would help, Jimmy. He's Chairman of the Board, remember. Two of the five MDs will vote with him almost automatically.'

'Yes, I suppose it'd be useless,' said Byrd. He looked away suddenly again. 'Christ, how do I tell Nancy?'

'Has he thrown you *right* out, Jimmy?' asked Blake quickly, to get Byrd's mind off the agony of having to tell Nancy. 'All the way? What do you plan to do?'

Byrd looked back at him and smiled again, wretchedly, doing his best. 'Maybe I've exaggerated it,' he said hopefully. 'No, it's not *right* out. Because of my eighteen years' good service up to this – cataclysm – Van Straten wouldn't recommend my dismissal from Eagle. They'd find me something in London. I mustn't expect it to be *this* level again, of course. I suppose in the end that's not really so bad, is it?' Jimmy Byrd was asking for absolution, for a rebirth of faith, for his pride back.

'No,' said Blake. 'That's not so bad, Jimmy.'

That *was* so bad, Jimmy. *Very* bad. It would have been much cleaner had Van Straten flung him out completely. That way if Byrd could get back up onto his feet at all it would at least be with hatred, thus with full-blooded pride. Van Straten's present way would castrate him. What Blake had seen in these last four days, these last four minutes, was the sudden fatal swing in a man's life, like a definitive flick of a coin, from being fully stretched in a shining and beautifully upwards-arcing trajectory, to being always hobbled and hooded in a known and accepted defeat – to a life lived always at second-best, and always known to be that. The world of Eagle, those hundred thousand devoted acolytes flung out across the globe, murderously competitive under the club smiles, would never let Byrd forget that. He would become a new constant in Eagle's mythology, his epic fall to humility an eternally quotable illustration of the need for that quality. Eagle would keep him, thus, set in useful abjection, and never really give him, humiliated, a second chance. So Eagle disciples would point him out in bars, or talk about him in them the world over. But if Jimmy Byrd did not himself see this as his worst defeat, Blake was not going to point out that truth.

'At least this way we can still keep the boys at Westminster,' said Byrd valiantly.

'Yes, there's that,' said Blake.

'And the house in Surrey.' Jimmy Byrd laughed. In that room it was a very sad sound. 'So this way at least we'll all still eat!' he said.

'Yes,' said Blake, watching this man break up before his eyes into the shivered waste pattern that he would carry for all the rest of his life. 'At least you'll still do that.'

There was a sad and viciously savage coda to this incident, the full details of which Blake only learned about some six months later, when events brought him into close contact with the Tulsa MD who dealt with the Middle East. Harvey Green was a Texan, a qualified mining engineer who had come up the hard way in Tulsa, starting off as an oil-rig driller in the steamy and seamy backlands of Lake Maracaibo in Venezuela. He was a tall, lean, sunburnt man with whipcord muscles and a quiet, biting wit. He was also the MD who had masterminded Tulsa's five-year steal of Falcon Aviation's oil business from Eagle.

Van Straten had by no means taken Eagle's loss of Falcon lying down. Arriving back in London at 3 am local time, he had at once got his Eagle minions to book him on the next day's Concorde to Washington, then on the next flight to Houston, Tulsa's centre. Because Houston's time was seven hours earlier than London's, he got there that afternoon. Tulsa's Chairman and two MDs received him at once. That much Blake learnt in London. Green told him the rest. The locale was the top floor of Tulsa's soaring Louis Kahn skyscraper in Houston. There were computer-screens everywhere against the walls. From here Tulsa's Board monitored its activities scientifically worldwide. The atmosphere was of cool precision, harmony, the triumph of reason. Tulsa's Board members reflected that. They were a calm élite. If Beirut seemed the anarchy of Armageddon, the mutual murder of faceless men heavily armed, each sworn to sacrifice his life virtuously for a contradictory cause, then these were the sons of light, men of a rarified sunny atmosphere high above street level, the last lords of moderation and logic. They were almost always engineers, geologists, technicians, in contrast to Eagle's, who like Shell's or BP's could be anything – lawyers, graduates in the humanities, even failed Oxbridge philosophers. Blake, on his future visits, was to get to know these measured tranquil rooms well.

Van Straten, Green said, burst into them like a high-explosive shell. He beat his fist on tables and shouted. In one usually so totally controlled, it was like seeing Buddha turn suddenly into a shrieking fishwife. Falcon Aviation, he ranted, was a traditional Eagle customer. Tulsa's robbery of this business was primitive and criminal. They must give it up, or Eagle would unleash similar raids on Tulsa clients worldwide, and price wars to ruin Tulsa.

The Americans heard out Van Straten's braying menaces to the end. Then their Chairman observed blandly that Mr Van Straten would of course know that Tulsa believed deeply in the virtues of free competition, as he understood did Eagle. Tulsa also delegated maximum authority to their top field executives as a principle – as, they thought, did Eagle. Tulsa's GM in Beirut had initiated this action to take Falcon, and from then the Tulsa Board, and notably Mr Green, had just given him the usual support. The Tulsa Chairman could hardly reverse events now, without disrupting Tulsa's entire structure and philosophy, so like Eagle's own that he could not believe Eagle would seriously want him to do that. Would Mr Van Straten care for a little light refreshment? Some English tea, perhaps? Tulsa had Earl Grey on the premises.

The thefts of Tulsa clients and ruinous price wars never materialized. Whatever the relative merits of humanists or technocrats on oil multinational boards, there seemed no doubt about who won this encounter. This fact was unlikely to induce the Ice Maiden to love Byrd, or indeed Blake, any the more. Or they him, in reply.

But someone loved Van Straten.

17
Diary with Sharp Metal Edges

I love K with all my heart, she had written. Is it with her heart that a woman truly loves? Or with all her being, all her body? Just as she feels and expresses her sensual love through far more than a mere single physical organ like a man. For a woman's breasts and nipples are powerful sexual organs too, sources of what splendid pulsing and almost endless waves of ecstasy, diffused through all of her, subtle and almost endless. In subtlety, think too of the sheer smooth grace of her loins, housing a clitoris tucked usually clean away out of sight, secretive, immensely sensitive, sentinel to a vagina that reaches up flexibly to her vaulted womb, safe cavern for infinite future generations. So graceful a design for life and love! How much more satisfactory aesthetically and perhaps morally seems this curved integration than the knobbly profile presented by man, his sexual organs hung on him like some awkward after-thought!

Yet what am I without him? A nothing; K and K alone has brought me this magic awareness, carried his flame across how many bleak continents of arid land, to lick with it all the sad tinders of my unlit fires, and give me that blessed and enduring warmth I have never before known. Without him I should probably have gone to my grave knowing nothing, as I have known nothing before he came, of the true and generous joy of my body, this magnificent procreative instrument, or of my spirit, blossomed to fulness under his touch. I have been dead leaves until he came. My life has only two phases, before K and after K. With the other I have had nothing of worth, though now we have fair wealth, and he some power, and we have travelled exotic lands, and he has brought me my due gifts, in gold and rubies. With the other it has been a grim charade, softened only by many physical comforts, the anaesthetics of habit, a weary sense of form and humour. Even the act of love has been only athletic. I have never burned with the other, fused with him, known any god with him. I have never wanted a child by him – the thought causes me revulsion, so we have had no child; a point which he, locked wholly in his drives and ambitions, seems scarcely to have noticed. We are all blind in our own manner, I too, to all these barren truths, until K brought me light.

But with K I shall use all these rich springs for creation. I have time, just time. I shall bear him a son, and soon. I shall carry K with me, create him within me. How could there be any finer fulfilment? That son will be my eternity. Perhaps we should seed him tonight. For K comes here this evening, to our flat which looks down on Kensington Square. It will not, sadly, be for very long. But one of these days P will leave again to tour his beloved Region, then K and I can meet more freely, in heaven's own blessed time. Until then, my diary, my companion —

She shut it and gazed down reflectively at it. It had dark blue leather covers, three inches across and about double that deep, with gold metal edges protecting its corners. She kept it carefully up to date these days, meticulously chronicling her passion. The diary fitted neatly into her handbag. She loved to carry it with her and when alone, to refer to passages in it. It was a reassuring verbal mirror, a twin and more faithful memory. Sometimes she deliberately left it locked up at home, as if zestfully testing out her gods, revelling in the sense of danger it gave her. She sighed, packed the diary away, and got up and went to the polished mahogany sideboard. Opening it, she poured herself a vodka and tonic, then pulled out the Campari bottle to have it ready for him. Kobus was a predictably abstemious man in his drinking habits. Celia glanced down at her Patek wrist-watch. 6 pm. He would be here at any minute now.

18
A House in Millionaires' Row

'I suggest that we eat in the patio this evening,' said Celia, 'if you approve. Very informal, after your seven-hour flight.'

'Of course,' said Blake. 'Let's do that.'

He thought she was looking at her most charming. She was wearing a very light and frothy cashmere sweater, patterns of light grey and light brown across it, and quite tight-fitting and beautifully tailored black Lanvin slacks. The sweater made sense, he thought; though it was early summer, the English nights still had an edge of chill in them. It moreover showed her off brilliantly, etching her fine breasts, her slim waist. There was a horizontal slash of silver at her throat, a touch of it in the tiny Patek watch on her left wrist, and silver sandals on her feet. Celia almost always went instinctively for simplicities, even if they were generally highly costly ones. The band round her neck was flat and elegant and unadorned. It was also of platinum. Only her belt was elborate. Silver in harmony, in balls and oblongs and strange symmetrical patterns, it was from Sri Lanka. It sang of temples and high ceremonies; a Hindu goddess or Thai dancer might first have worn it.

Celia's face seemed as exquisitely balanced, her wide emerald eyes clear and chaste and formal, her rich black hair tumbling and exuberant. This beauty had its own laws. How could you not love it? Blake, back from his wars, his heart bruised by Jimmy Byrd's castration, opened it now to her. They were old lovers, or at least old companions; they had after all been married now for eighteen years.

The chauffeured Eagle Daimler had picked Blake up at Heathrow Airport an hour before and brought him here, and they had driven in to this by now familiar driveway off The Bishops Avenue in Hampstead, called Millionaires' Row because that was what it was. Blake had bought this house three years before, to Celia's delight; Celia spent money generously, her own or others'. Blake qualified for the Row now. His numbered account in the Banque Indosuez in

Lausanne stood now at the multimillion level; Blake's personal Sun Light contract had served him well; he had been able easily to on-sell that 50,000 bd at ten to fifteen cents a barrel, to a world still obsessed with the fear that oil would always be short, and glad to ask no awkward questions. The house stood in half an acre of lawns and gardens. It was two-storeyed and huge, richly furnished and carpeted. Its dining-table was mahogany and seated fourteen. Its china was Wedgwood and Delft, its silver Georgian, and its paintings two Canalettos, then one each of Modigliani, Gauguin, Braque and Miró. Celia had had them framed, hung, and lit in such a way that not even the most casual visitor could easily miss them.

Blake was very happy in his fortune, and he had not noticed that Celia registered any marked objection to it. He had explained his sudden affluence to her as the result of Eagle's definite selection of him as a future star, and his consequent elevation on Eagle's salary scales. The fact that she knew that his strongest single remaining ambition was indeed to reach the Olympian heights of Eagle's Board no doubt made his interpretation seem authentic. For, knockabout though it might be, she clearly accepted it; probably because it mattered much less to her where his money came from than that it should in fact be *there*, readily available, and in bulk. In reality Blake spent little more than his entire salary. To do Celia justice, she came some part of the way to matching Blake's contributions. Her boutique in Fitzjohn's Avenue, where she usually spent two or three hours a day, was doing extremely well, so much so that she had already bought premises for a branch in Camden Town, to be distinctly more trendy. Thus, between Blake and herself, Celia almost always had to hand whatever funds she needed to satisfy any whim to buy, which she usually did fast, and always with impeccable taste.

So it looked as though Blake had a happy wife. He had never so far been too concerned about what she did with her truly private life. That had not been part of their initial implicit pact. On the surface (and how deep down did one have to look?) their marriage, their alliance, went very well. His earlier fears of her fashion and intellectual crowd had disappeared. His increase in personal financial power, his sense of surging constantly upwards to Eagle's peaks, had lent him great confidence. He took her friends now quite easily. Love might cast out fear, and so might hatred, but the certainty of owning solid financial resources might be even more effective. Their bedroom life seemed perfectly satisfactory too. They still shared the same large double bed. Two or three times a month they still made love vigorously and with all normal signs of satisfaction, or so Blake thought. Each could look at the other with clear eyes afterwards, without hypocrisy. For there was none, within that strict frame.

Outside it was another matter, at least as concerned Blake. His three-and-a-half year relationship with Leila had never faltered. Both had obvious interests in keeping it discreet. But he had met her on every one of his annual or bi-annual leaves. They had gone together for a week or two to Spain or Italy or Greece, avoiding the most fashionable centres. Blake had always explained these brief absences to Celia as resulting from his occasional need to be alone and think. After he told her in Cairo that he had a lover, this might remain little more than a polite fiction. But Celia never queried him. Probably she did not think what he really did important. He was after all breaking no formal social images. Moreover she always had her immense creative interest in her fashion business to engage her. Or Blake met and made love to Leila when he was in London on business, combining his visit with hers. After the first few times they never met in her central and expensive flat in Bryanston Square; it was too well known as hers, and there was always the fear of a spy from the non-moderate political sections in the Kingdom of the Sun. So Blake found and leased a flat off Queensway behind Bayswater tube station. It was unprepossessing without, but he furnished it handsomely within. Blake had among his times of greatest happiness there.

Blake had not lost contact with Abdullah either, or with Eagle's business links with the Kingdom, while he had been GM in Egypt. He had followed developments closely, through Abdullah and others. He had heard from Abdullah, well before it became public knowledge, about the extension that they had discovered to their northern oilfield, and got from him first option for Eagle for the additional production. This, peaking after two years' development at 200,000 bd, was picked up by a grateful Eagle Board in the first months of Blake's return to London, so that the Kingdom of the Sun's contract with Eagle was now for 700,000 bd – seventy per cent of Eagle's total crude supply needs. Surely only the most petty minds could cavil at Eagle putting so many of its supply eggs in one basket, for wasn't Sun Light unquestionably an excellent crude? Van Straten might have long toes and a long memory, but so did Blake. Blake was nothing if not a thinking man.

He had been thinking deeply enough, indeed, as the Eagle Daimler had brought him into his driveway early that evening and he had seen, mildly pleased, that Celia was probably in; their two cars were in the garage, whose electrically operated doors had not yet been closed on the metallic-grey Rolls Royce Silver Spirit and the red four-door Aston Martin Lagonda which she preferred. The whole sad saga of Jimmy Byrd still weighed very heavily on Blake. Showered and changed into a light blue Club de France sports shirt and a white open-necked Armani sweater and grey slacks, he told Celia the whole story as they sat in their ample Modigliani and Canaletto-bedecked sitting room, she with a Cinzano-soda and he with a vodka and tonic. Celia listened very attentively. As they went out to the patio and sat, she said quietly:

'It's tragic, Philip. And the Byrds were always such good and loyal friends to us in Cairo. But perhaps your Van Straten is right.'

He glanced at her, startled. There were three tall candles lit on the glass-topped patio table with its whorled and white-painted Spanish iron legs. That light put her face magnificently into relief, brushing in shadows dramatically under the high cheekbones, making her hair a dark dense cloud. Her scent reached him subtly; Joy, of Patou. Celia, it struck him, was intensely attractive sexually. She almost glowed with it. She was a highly desirable property. But siding with the enemy?

'What makes you say that?'

Celia raised her eyes too his question, then dropped them to her wine-glass, and raised that to her lips. They were drinking a fine dry white Graves with the avocado and shrimp starters, a 1971 Château La Mission-Haut-Brion. For Marta, a Catalan from Barcelona, had already served their first course. There was a second live-in maid, Asunción, a Basque from San Sebastián; it was a big house, and the patio table's legs were not the only Spanish thing about it.

'He's arguing on principles of accountability, isn't he?' said

Celia. 'Very strict principles, admittedly. But in his position don't you have to have those? I can understand that.'

'Christ,' said Blake, 'but Jimmy had only been there about five minutes!'

'Still, Philip, I can see that concept that responsibility runs through *people* like an electric current. I think it's a very apt simile. So it's logical that your Chief Executive in the field should be the one finally accountable, isn't it? I mean, you've got to put it *somewhere*, haven't you? *Someone's* got to carry it!'

'It sounds to me like the doctrine of original sin,' said Blake. 'There's a lot of cruelty and mindless evil around in the world. You want to explain it, so you look for a home for it, a cause, a scapegoat. Then why not park it on old Joe Soak, the human being? He's probably too good-natured and scared to answer back. Like Jimmy Byrd.'

'You're being too hard on Van Straten.'

Marta seemed to think that too. She had removed the avocado plate and brought in the beautifully grilled Dover Soles and the big wooden bowl of mixed salad. Evidently picking up Celia's tone, she shot a critical look at Blake, supporting her mistress to the death. Marta was very Spanish, with jet-black hair, fine light olive skin and sharp and vivid black eyes, like Abdullah's. Nobody listens to me around here, thought Blake morbidly. But would Abdullah, for example, have damned Byrd? Abdullah would be too generous to do so. Still, at least Marta had brought the wine that Blake had selected. It was a 1971 Chablis Grand Cru, from the Vaudésir domaine, green-gold and dry and richly flavoured; a little masterpiece.

'No,' he answered Celia. 'It's Van Straten who's being too hard. How can he hold Jimmy Byrd responsible? Responsible means answerable for. How can you be answerable for something you haven't been given enough time to learn?'

Celia shrugged her slim shoulders delicately.

'He even seems to hold me partly responsible,' Blake went on. 'Because I didn't pick up what he sees as the weak point in that contract. We must have some twenty or thirty contracts like that in this Region!'

'So what will he do to you?'

'I don't know. Nothing predictable.'

'Probably nothing at all.'

'I wouldn't bet on that,' said Blake.

As if in sympathy with him, a tremendous low and heart-breaking wail suffused the patio, rattling the glasses on its table. It was Chunt, their brindled Staffordshire bull-terrier, now a mature and well-travelled dog, locked away briefly in his kennel because he had developed the ungracious habit of begging at meals. Blake had an ally after all.

'I think him a great man,' said Celia, over her chilled Chablis, 'a man of regal stature. He seems to me totally honest. And as hard, with those very high standards, on himself as on others.'

'That's true enough.'

'And I would, for that matter, think Kobus extremely fair. Decent.'

'Mathematically fair,' said Blake, 'but chilly.'

Kobus? he thought. Kobus, is it now, indeed?

He looked back at her curiously.

19
A Taste of Victory

Blake did not see Van Straten again until lunch the day after next. The Ice Maiden had, he knew, made a lightning trip to Tulsa, Houston and back but no one in Eagle London was saying a word about the loss of Falcon Aviation. The wound was too deep, down to the bone. Above all, no one was confronting Van Straten with it. There was no point to provoking thunderbolts.

Blake left his opulent Regional Co-ordinator's office just on one. It was on the eighteenth floor of Eagle International's Central Offices in Millbank, and had a magnificent view down over the Thames. It also had thick wall-to-wall carpeting, and in one corner an attractive set of four teak-backed armchairs and a sofa, set about a round low glass and chrome table, suitable for cosy chats with his fellow Regional Co-ordinators or, if he was feeling munificent, with someone his junior in Eagle's minutely categorized hierarchy. Blake had mounted one framed print only in this office. It was six feet wide, on the long inner wall, of Frans Hals's *Civil Guard*. The symbolism seemed clear. These sturdy gentlemen, stalwart protagonists of a thriving mercantile society, Princes of the Protestant Ethic, were undeniably powerfully individualistic, yet they would always join fully and generously in a corporate effort for the common good. In the Eagle context, this meant the greater economic advancement of Eagle's shareholders and, conse-quently, of her Managing Directors. The painting could serve as a fair image of the Eagle myth, save that the burghers needed to be portrayed armed not with rapiers but with petrol pumps. Blake thus saw this painting as useful Public Relations for his office. But that was all. He personally had no time at all for its message. If he ever *gained* an empire, everyone would know its hallmark as Philip Blake. He would never merely merge into the background and run it by committee. Blake gambled his soul, but he wanted his name on the chips.

He caught the lift to the Midshipmen's Mess on the twentieth floor, which had almost exactly the same epic view of the river as Blake's office. It also had a very well-stocked sideboard. Blake went straight to it. He mixed himself a vodka and tonic, then turned to the man nearest him. A convinced gin drinker.

'Beefeater or Gordon's, Cope?'

'Beefeater, I think, thanks. And a tonic and a slice of lemon.'

Copeland – he was always Cope, even to his juniors – was a man as fastidious in his work and manner as he was in choosing a drink. He was a slim gentleman of fifty-seven, of medium height, dressed in a pepper-and-salt suit with a waistcoat, and rimless glasses. His matching pepper-and-salt hair was militarily trimmed. Copeland was Regional Co-ordinator The Americas, which put him on the same august level as Philip Blake. He was quite an amiable man unless he believed his personal interests threatened, when he could react like a barrow-boy. This put him in good company in Eagle.

There were some thirty other Copelands in the Midshipmen's Mess that day, Regional and Functional Co-ordinators, and down to one level below them. They were from the top hundred men in Eagle, a predatory élite. Sometimes a Managing Director would drop in for lunch in this mess, under the endearing illusion that he was boosting the morale of the lads, and thereby rubbing shoulders with reality. It was a reality that wore no badges or rank, but everyone in it knew the correct pecking order to two places of decimals, and no one better than Copeland.

Another man moved over towards them, from one of the windows overlooking the river, searching for truth, searching for gin.

'Morning, Nel,' said Blake.

'Good day to you,' said Nel de Jonge. 'Hullo, Cope.'

'Hello,' said Copeland. 'You're looking very serious today, Nel. Even more Jesuitical than usual. More Mephistophelean, even.'

'Jesuitical will do,' said De Jonge. 'Remember that my father was a *predikant* in the Orange Free State. Why am I so serious? Because I have had the slightest hint that my lord and master may be gracing us here today with his presence. An unusual enough event, though of course certainly not unknown, to merit serious conjecture.'

'Meaning Kobus van Straten?' said Blake. 'And the conjecture, Nel?'

'Meaning Kobus van Straten,' said De Jonge. 'The conjecture? That he's braving something out. You'd know about what, Philip. The old wise policy; the best defence is to attack.'

De Jonge enunciated everything very painstakingly. He had a precise, old-maidish way of speaking. It was not just measured. Its effects were calculated to decimal points of millimetres. This meticulous elocution partly reflected his acutely puritanical upbringing, and partly the fact that English was not his home language. The De Jonges were tenth-generation settlers in South Africa. They had travelled on the Great Trek away from the pernicious English liberal influences of the Cape Colony, they had helped found the two Boer republics of the Transvaal and the Orange Free State, and they had farmed in the latter ever since. Nel's father had indeed been a pastor of the Dutch Reformed Church, of which all the family were fervent members, except Nel.

From his tenderest years Nel had shown a terrifying gift for logic. By the age of four he had earned the nickname of *Jamaar*, short for *Ja maar* – or Yes, but . . . With this short phrase he cut a swathe through his schools and Pretoria University, then joining the Native Administration. He confounded his superiors after his first field mission by advising them he could find no real difference in innate capacities between black and white. Shocked, they could only kick him upstairs. The process repeated itself. Within years he had reached such dizzy political heights that there was little left for him to conquer, save perhaps the State Presidency. He resigned out of sheer boredom, then sold himself to the highest bidder on the open market. This was Eagle South Africa. Awed by their bargain, but dismayed at what it would do to them locally, they shipped him off promptly to their London Central Offices.

Here Nel found his slot by empathy, and with surprising speed. He became the Ice Maiden's *éminence grise* in all matters of company structure and organization. It was a happy marriage of minds. De Jonge had very real gifts for this highly specialized watch-repairer's craft. Fortunately he retained a wicked black sense of humour and a human touch. He was a real professional at it. He eclipsed George Paul, the Eagle MD with the short red fuzz of hair on the backs of his fingers and the sweet lethal smile. George Paul had often seemed to lop heads just because he liked decapitation. De Jonge was analytic and scientific, making huge increases in efficiency and manpower savings, but also creating new staff positions where they were needed. Next to him George Paul was just a bouncer dressed by Jermyn Street. Nel could have eaten two George Pauls before breakfast. He had after all single-handed taken on the entire right wing of the Afrikaner Establishment, including the *Broederbond* and the *Ossewa Brandwag*, and emerged with his head and testicles still attached. Copeland's snide remark about his looking like Mephistopheles had similarly simply slid off Nel's carapace. For he had that scaly quality, in a benign way. De Jonge was thin and wizened, behind thin rimless glasses, with an emaciated brown face and a deliberate neck, and his bite, when he bit, was as tenacious as a tortoise's.

'Looks as if you're right as usual, Nel,' said Copeland, sounding as if he was taking that as a personal insult. 'Let every head bow, men, and every knee bend!'

Indeed, thought Blake, one's instinctive reaction was to do exactly that. For Kobus van Straten had just come in through the door to the longish corridor leading to the Mess's ante-room and its well-charged sideboard. Inside, he stood stock-still. A seasoned campaigner, he was taking a lightning fix of his bearings before proceeding into potentially hostile seas. Yet there was no real question about his confidence; there never was. He stood slim and whipcord, the iron-ridged mouth set, his clear light-grey eyes locked on their targets, accurate and incisive as first-class camera lenses.

'Looking dead pleased with himself too!' said Copeland waspishly.

That was true. There was the faintest shadow of a smile on those austere lips. And there was something electric to Van Straten's whole posture. It was a little eerie.

'That air,' said Nel de Jonge, half aside, and mainly to Blake, 'that iron elation, that grim ecstasy, means that he has just faced a very difficult decision. Probably with the Board. Which he has of course pushed through.'

Van Straten walked on to them.

'Morning, Cope. Blake. Nel.'

Blake noticed that in the replies, only De Jonge used Van Straten's Christian name.

'Have a drink, sir?' said Copeland. 'A gin and tonic?'

'Thanks. Perhaps we could go straight in to table. I'm a little pressed.'

At the Ice Maiden's arrival a ripple had run through the men drinking their aperitifs in the ante-room. Van Straten's wish had reached the Mess president as if by magic. The Mess President this calendar quarter was the Regional Co-ordinator Africa, a quiet-spoken man with grey hair and a face uncommonly serene in such a gathering of affluent cut-throats. He raised his eyebrows to the Ice Maiden across the ante-room and, at his nod, motioned the men in to the long dining-room parallel to and overlooking the Thames. The President had gone to the mid-point of the other side of the fine table, showing Van Straten to the seat on his right. Men flowed about choosing their places and sat with a muffled clatter. Blake found himself a seat on the Ice Maiden's side, two away from him, but certainly within full range.

'No doubt everyone knows everyone here today?' said the Ice Maiden in Olympian tones, robbing the Mess President of his functions without turning a hair. 'Ah! But perhaps not everyone has met Hans Hesse here, on my right. He's GM Singapore. No? I thought perhaps not. Well, Hans here, I have it on excellent authority, is visiting us fuddy-duddies in the centre today because he simply *has* to touch us most urgently – and right out of normal budget sequence, mind – for fourteen or fifteen million pounds, because all his refineries have suddenly started to fall down. A brilliant exhibition of sound maintenance, sound planning. The nervous tic you see in his left eye is simply because, as an experienced senior executive, he knows bloody well that he hasn't a snowball's hope in hell of getting it. Sorry? Ah, Hans here says he's *got* it! Surprise, surprise! Indeed, come to think of it, I remember we authorized that this morning. Then that nerve-end of Hans is leaping out of sheer relief, because he knows he's damned lucky and has won against all the odds. Who'd have ever thought he would? Give the man a big hand, gentlemen! Our Man in Singapore –'

Blake was glad to see that only a few near the middle of the table clapped, and in a desultory manner. The Ice Maiden was really selling his Eton and The Guards act to the absolute limit today. What the hell was fuelling him? What drug? It couldn't have been the mere approval of £15,000,000 as emergency aid to Eagle Singapore. That was peanuts for Van Straten. That could never hop him up like this –

'Great power-play,' said the man to Blake's right. 'Maybe this is how he gets his jollies. By screwing his subordinates in public.'

'Cut the blasphemy, friend,' said Blake, 'and concentrate on the wines. They're always good here. They won't turn round and bite you like him.'

The table itself was as usual excellent. The Mess Stewards had already taken all the food orders while the men were still clustered in the ante-room with their gins. There were smoked trout or shrimp cocktail or various soups as starters, then a range from roast pork to side of mutton and Lobster

Thermidor or Mayonnaise to follow. The wines now being offered round the table suggested that even oilmen became discriminating if they knocked about the world enough. The whites ran from a 1971 Chablis Premier Cru from the Fourchaume domaine and a good 1976 Sancerre to a 1973 Pouilly-Fuissé, and the reds from a 1970 Saint-Émilion from Château-Belair to a 1972 Château Gruaud-Larose from Saint-Julien. Blake chose the Sancerre for his smoked trout and the Saint-Émilion for his side of mutton.

'By the way, Hans,' said Van Straten, still at it, 'one man you certainly must know by now is straight opposite you – Ray Furrier, head of Eagle Shipping. He's famous as the man who, admittedly badgered incessantly by one of our more obsessional MDs who shall be nameless, years ago ordered so many Ultra Large and Very Large Crude Carriers for Eagle that, anchored stem to stern, they'll stretch three times round the British Isles and Irish Republic combined – which is probably where we'll finally have to ditch them as surplus.'

Blake glanced across the table and caught Ray Furrier's eye and winked. He was a big decent man and no match for Van Straten in repartee, even were he reckless enough to take him on. Now he simply smiled awkwardly and looked round to each side at his companions, as if concerned that they too might join in on this assault on him. Ray Furrier was not enjoying his lunch. Van Straten as clearly was exulting in his, and in Furrier's discomfort. Why? An extremely just man he might be, and as exacting to himself as to others. But did he always have to *prove* that he dominated? Nel de Jonge, half-right across the table from him, caught Blake's eye at that moment, and raised his eyebrows at him. Nel evidently guessed what he was thinking, and felt much the same way.

So why hasn't the Ice Maiden picked on *me*? thought Blake. Whom he must feel as one of his really Blue Ribbon gut-enemies? Especially after Falcon Aviation? Or has he got some other little surprise in store?

'Of course you know the elegant man to Roy Furrier's left, dear Hans,' Van Straten went on. 'Joost de Haas, Supply Co-ordinator. Yes, I know, a Dutchman, a cousin to my Flemish ancestors. Still, at least he has achieved notoriety by a new route – by marrying a countess. What, gentlemen? All right, all right; the gentlemen all insist no sex at the table. Then, finally, half-left, and that must be at the edge of your range of vision, you'll notice a gaunt and shambling man, his longbow length cruelly wrinkled and wasted. What from? From many years of devilling in the cobwebby offices of the London *Spectator*. He's Murrel Cruikshank by name, Eagle Trade Relations Co-ordinator by function. Just imagine, gentlemen, here is the mastermind who presents Eagle's face to its many publics. You can know him at once in a crowd, Hans, by his erudite magpie croak, a fair reflection of his mind – a drawling, cunning, booky man indeed!'

'Oh, General Van Straten!' cried Cruikshank, in a high and simpering falsetto. 'Oh, General, you *do* carry on so!'

This frankly bizarre effect amazed much of the table into silence. Cruikshank was another rare man who would dice his destiny with one and all, even including the Ice Maiden. Now he got his ripples of laughter, so momentarily outclassing Van Straten. But Van Straten, looking up from his shattered lobster, rejoined swiftly: 'That was *your* press release this morning?'

'Which?'

'You know perfectly well. Our denial that there was any fixing behind the general industry increase in the price of petrol here in the UK from last Monday. I saw it in this morning's *Guardian*, but presumably it's in all the other main dailies too?'

'It is,' said Cruikshank. 'Well, the godhead knew all about it as usual, and I cross-checked it with Eagle UK before release. You didn't like the prose?'

'I didn't like the piety,' said Van Straten.

'Oh, come now, Kobus!' said Cruikshank, another of the very few who dared use the Ice Maiden's Christian name to him in public, possibly because he knew that in the worst event he could always go back gloriously to the *Spectator*. 'Where's the fire? This is routine stuff, isn't it? Labour or some left-wing journalist takes a crack at us, and we reply, all offended. It's standard procedure. It's what's expected of us. If we didn't do it we'd disappoint our publics. Including our shareholders. There's no worse sin, is there?'

'All right,' said Van Straten, 'but *must* you couch it in that Victorian pomposity? "Eagle would never stoop" and so forth? When we all know that in fact Eagle would stoop so fast and far for a buck that the old biddy'd happily bust her bloomers, so long as it wasn't illegal, *patently* illegal, and naturally provided she did get the buck. It's a hard world. So why pretend? We ought to be a lot more like Texaco. They're hard-nosed Texan oilmen flat out for maximum gains. They're pure profit-motive people and that's exactly how they always present themselves. They're completely honest. So they keep their dignity, and they deserve it. It's a good deal cleaner than our unctuous pretence of being here primarily for public service. This spurious holier-than-thou posture! I can't stand that!'

You had to admit it, thought Blake. The man surely had his stature. He even had the good sense to echo Sean O'Higgins acerbic rejection of Oil Industry cant.

'I really can't believe you wrote this crap, Murrel,' said the man.

'Then don't, Kobus,' said Cruikshank. 'I didn't.'

'Ah, I see!' said Van Straten. 'A Lord and Master!'

'Yes.'

'We must see about that,' said Van Straten.

That meant that George Paul, the blood-under-the-finger-nails Regional MD for Europe and the UK, would get it in the neck. There were some really quite appealing sides to the Ice Maiden.

'Oh, one other small thing,' that gentleman went on. 'What about the *logic* of pushing through a price rise in the UK at a moment like this? I know that Eagle UK themselves were *not* in favour of it. Isn't it a bit odd, when we and all the other Majors in the UK have recently announced our last quarter's results, and they have been, to commit a massive understatement, highly satisfactory?'

'Are we talking policy now, Kobus,' asked Cruikshank, 'or still paradigms of prose? If policy, then I think you have a point. An impartial outside critic, say, might have had harsh words indeed for that move, also pushed through by one of our Lords.'

'Such words as, Murrel?'

'Such as: "Greed, bordering on stupidity."'

Van Straten looked at him for just two seconds. Then he said: 'You're still in, Murrel. I see a great future for you in Eagle.'

But not for George Paul, thought Blake. There was not even going to be any dried blood under George Paul's fingernails. George Paul was not going to have any fingernails.

Blake glanced again over his great year's Saint-Émilion at Van Straten. There was no denying the man's messianic quality, though the naked forked-lightning power in him that day might seem to place him more aptly at the other end of paradise, as demoniac. Again, what so charged him? Which decision that, in Nel de Jonge's way of thinking, was utterly basic to his being, and which he had just forced through with great difficulty to gain this uncanny exhilaration, exultation? For his magnetism seemed a little superhuman that day. There was no doubt that many others round that table felt it. Indeed, thought Blake, had a snap vote from all there been called on who among them was most likely to succeed as world emperor, Van Straten would have won hands down; that, whether they liked him or not, and probably most did not.

'Ray,' said Van Straten now, turning again to the search for his odd Holy Grail, 'I think I saw from the papers that Christina Onassis is free again.'

'Yes?' said Ray Furrier cautiously, looking back at him with a strained smile. 'And so?'

'They say she's a very pleasant girl. Intelligent. Attractive. So why not move in, Ray? What a marriage of true interests. A merger between two of the biggest mercantile fleets! What operational savings! There'd have to be economies of scale somewhere. What do you say, Ray?'

Most of the table craned round to see what Ray Furrier would say.

'You mean, *marry* the girl?' said Furrier, his smile now very uncomfortable. Apart from being a good natured and friendly man, he was a confirmed bachelor, and sensitive on the point.

Blake looked back at the goading Van Straten. My God, he thought, Falcon Aviation must really be hurting him again –

'Why not?' said the Ice Maiden. 'Vertical integration's all the rage these days. What about a little old-fashioned horizontal integration?'

Not at all sure that it had got the point, the table dutifully roared with laughter anyway. Van Straten got up and left to that sound, triumphant all the way.

Yet it was Blake who appeared to have the greater occasion for triumph that day. The Office Circular lay on his desk when he reached his office. The messengers must have brought them round during lunch, and now they would be on everyone's desk in that huge building. Blake thought he had seen a sparkle in his secretary's dark brown eyes as he came through her office. Eva had settled down beautifully in her six months in London since her transfer from Eagle Austria. Reaching his desk, he spun the circular round and read it standing, at first casually, then with his attention riveted. It read:

> The Committee of Managing Directors announce their decision to appoint a new Managing Director of the Eagle International Oil Group. He is Mr Philip Blake, currently Regional Co-ordinator for the Middle East. His sphere of influence, until further notice, will be: Functionally: Supplies and Trade Relations. Regionally: the Middle East. The appointment is with effect from July 1. Mr Blake's successor in his former post is –

Blake sat down silently in his swivel chair. This was the aim achieved! Now he was at the absolute peak of his ambition! What more could he want? He had a vivid, completely satisfying and lasting relationship with Leila. He had eight million US dollars in his numbered account in Lausanne, more than he could ever need to spend, and another $2.3 million was coming in yearly from his continuing brokerage fee; this year interest alone on his deposit would reach a million. He had a magnificent house and a very pleasant, convenient and (it seemed) stable marriage. His health was robust as a bulldozer. And now this top accolade in his profession, at the age of forty and he had won it all! Now he could really laugh in the face of the gods, of destiny. It was almost too good to be true.

It was. He should have listened more closely. Blake played for high stakes, total triumph or defeat, life or death. But heaven never came easily. That was basic. The gods were jealous, swift at sleight of hand, top cardsmen. Blake was reckless to let his victory mesmerize him.

Not only did he see his triumph as magnificent, total, and singing with joy, but he even had the epic opportunity of telling his true love personally all about it, thus sharing it generously with her as was right. Leila was arriving from the Kingdom of the Sun late that night, too late for him safely to see her, but they were to meet the next night for dinner at the White Tower in Percy Street – that day and the next Celia would be away in Paris for a fashion convention. Thinking fleetingly of that, it struck Blake that in order of importance, Celia was in fact the second person he should tell. She had, at least so far, always carried out her side of the bargains implicit in their marriage scrupulously and with dignity. She deserved that small recognition. So Blake rang, finding her not in the house but in her boutique in Fitzjohn's Avenue, and told her of it. She seemed ecstatic; well, she had always liked the gold dust of success, of great positions and great names; some of it always rubbed off.

Then the Eagle congratulations began; Eva, his secretary, came in swiftly after his talk to Celia; her eyes shone and she kissed him on the lips. Then men phoned or called in; Blake loved it. Ray Furrier, Nel de Jonge, Joost de Haas, many others. But not Morgan Sperry or Sean O'Higgins, whom despite the difference in rank, he had always felt to be great friends. That saddened him slightly, and struck an off-key note, but the weight of congratulations from others was so heavy that he did not have time to dwell on this odd silence. He left his office at the official closing of business and was driven home. There a few more congratulatory calls came in, and requests from the *Financial Times*, the *Telegraph* and the *Petroleum Economist* for interviews the next day. The whole world seemed to know about his elevation to the godhead.

Again he dined intimately with Celia at home. She was full of praise. Blake loved every minute of that afternoon and evening. After dinner they went quite early to bed. They made love most passionately, as if this were the first days of their marriage, and each quite without guile. It was a day marvellous in its own right, unique, quite without relation to any other, even the morrow. This was a fact, even though at a few fleeting chill fractions of seconds it again all seemed to him a little too good to be true. Still, there was the circular. . .

20

A Fall, and a Breaking on the Rack

The Committee of Managing Directors, under the leadership of the Chairman of the Board, hereby rescind their Office Circular No 47 of yesterday's date regarding possible further appointments to the Eagle International Oil Group's Board. Mr Philip Blake will continue in his present position as Regional Co-ordinator Middle East.

Thus eighteen hours confirmed that it *was* too good to be true. This second circular, unusually, was signed with Kobus van Straten's quick and jagged signature. It lay on Blake's desk in exactly the same position when he arrived first thing the next morning.

Just so that nobody should have the slightest doubt about who really stood behind that decision, thought Blake. *That* was the extremely hard decision that Nel de Jonge had talked about in the Midshipmen's Mess the day before, that Van Straten had just forced through the Board, his victory there injecting so much adrenalin into his veins that he had gone through the entire lunch in that state of unholy exaltation –

Blake's left forefinger and thumb traced his upper lip again and again. He picked up his switchboard phone. It went through Eva.

'Eva? You've seen today's circular?'

'Yes.' She sounded deeply shocked. 'It's a truly terrible thing to do to you!'

'The most perfect humiliation he could inflict. Appoint me publicly, then sack me publicly the next day –'

'I wish I could do something to help!'

'You can. Try to get him for me through his secretary.'

For Van Straten had no direct line and took no calls direct.

Eva came back within thirty seconds.

'His secretary. She says he's away. I'll put her on.'

'Mr Blake?' said the Ice Maiden's secretary sweetly. She knew exactly what was up. All the world would.

'Yes. Mr Van Straten's not in?'

167

'In Paris for two days, Mr Blake. He has to see Mr Fouquet of Eagle Française about Mr Fouquet's plans for his succession.'

'I see. Put me down for ten o'clock on Friday then, would you?'

'You'd like to see him?'

'Yes,' said Blake grimly, stroking his upper lip. 'I would most certainly like to see him!'

He got Eva to try Morgan Sperry, but he had left for Tokyo, Hong Kong, Singapore and Bangkok early the afternoon before. Sean O'Higgins was in though, and would be glad to see him at once. Blake took a lift up promptly to the twenty-first floor. O'Higgin's secretary showed him straight in.

'Well, Philip, it's a damned ugly business.'

Sean O'Higgins, behind his huge clear teak desk, tilted back in his chair and raised his monstrous silver-brown mountain-ledge eye-brows at Blake. He stood up and a broad sinewy hand motioned Blake towards the huddle of deep armchairs and sofa in the corner destined for his VIP visitors. O'Higgins put his head through the intercommunicating doorway to his secretary's office and asked her for coffee. He came back and sat. He was giving Blake all the support he could.

'What the hell happened?' said Blake.

O'Higgins shrugged and furrowed his cliff-like forehead more deeply.

'You were all set,' he said. 'There was nothing to stop us having six MDs instead of five, and as the new one we were giving you the Middle East and Supplies and TR – mainly because of the brilliant work you've done on the Sun Light contract. That's our main artery now, seventy per cent of our total crude intake; God knows what we'd do without it.'

'Well,' said Blake. 'I'm getting a fine reward for it now.'

'That was the idea. The Office Circular was even printed. Well, you saw it. Morgan Sperry pushed it to the hilt, and so did I –'

'Bloody good of you,' said Blake. 'No, I mean it. But what were you going to do with Morgan Sperry? The Far East and Supplies and TR were *his* province. Throw him out?'

'No. You know that for some years we've wanted to intensify our penetration of the North American market. So we were going to split my hemisphere. I'd stay with Latin

America, which God knows is trouble enough on its own, and Morgan would take charge of our assault in North America. Logically enough; he's an American –'

'But?' said Blake.

O'Higgins's secretary came in with the coffee and served it.

'But Falcon Aviation,' said O'Higgins when she had gone. 'Kobus came back obsessed with his belief that the fault for that loss ran partially through you. Nothing like as much as through Byrd – though both Morgan and I found that theory highly doubtful too. But you know Van Straten. He has that total puritanical honesty, those appallingly actuarial concepts of responsibility and accountability. Once he's truly convinced – and he's a truthful man, anyway about his business – then his feelings get a moral patina over them. You can't budge him. His courage in defending his beliefs is implacable; burn him at the stake and you won't change him. He is of the stuff that martyrs and heroes are made from –'

'Make me an MD,' said Blake, 'and I'll be a hero too.'

'I still would,' said O'Higgins, 'and so would Morgan. But after Falcon Aviation Van Straten got ethical about you. His sense of duty totally forbade him to let your appointment, which he had agreed to before, go ahead. And that was that. Morgan and I fought him yesterday until right up to lunch, then he called a vote. And naturally he and friends Paul and Poynter outvoted us –'

'So there's nothing to be done?' said Blake.

'Nothing, I fear,' said O'Higgins.

'For how long, Sean?'

O'Higgins craggy face, wrinkled as an old apple, observed him seriously.

'God knows, Philip. I wish I could tell you. Maybe forever. He'll tend to believe that, because if what he sees as a fault has run through you before, it can do so again, however diligently and loyally you apply yourself. He would consider himself failing in his duty to Eagle and its shareholders – and he knows no higher obligation – if he did not see and treat you now as basically flawed material. It's pure Old Testament, I know. He can't really forgive a fault – and he's as pitiless here on himself as on others – or forget it.'

In the long and painful silence that followed, Blake saw O'Higgins pull out his silver cigarette-case and extract a

Benson and Hedges and light it with a Dunhill lighter. O'Higgins worked at it gingerly, making it something of a ritual. Blake knew that he smoked only two or three times a day, generally after meals, or when he felt himself under considerable stress. His cigarette lit, O'Higgins inhaled deeply, then looked back steadily at Blake.

'This is hard stuff to hear, Philip. Perhaps I'm exaggerating things, though I don't think so. But I think it imperative that you see the situation accurately. I know the strength of your ambitions.'

'Bless you for that too. Funny, he still has that immense presence. One has to hand it to him.'

'Yes, he's a very great man, in his own specialized field. Think what he's done already in his four years as Chairman. He's led us to becoming the most profitable company in the oil business, for our size – a steady twelve to fifteen per cent post-tax return on our capital employed, sometimes much higher. It's a remarkable performance.' O'Higgins looked at him piercingly. 'And remember that he still has just on eight years to run. He's there as Chairman until he's sixty. Unless he commits some great gaffe or is responsible for some really huge misfortune or loss.'

I can think of one, said Blake to himself.

'Eight years is a long time,' he said aloud.

'Yes,' said O'Higgins. 'A long time in which you may get no other chance at the Board. I know what you mean.'

'Am *likely* to get no other chance at the Board,' said Blake.

O'Higgins hesitated, then met Blake's eyes again.

'" *Likely* " is right.' He went on after a moment. 'And there is another pertinent factor, on another level.'

'Which is?'

'Van Straten hates you. You know that. And in your guts you hate him. There's probably not a lot either of you can do about it. It's what the French call a question of skin. I don't know that you can beat it.'

Blake said nothing to that. He watched O'Higgins inhale again deeply.

'Sean,' he said, 'what would you do in my position if you had a good alternative offer of employment?'

O'Higgins shot a look at him from under his overcrowded eyebrows.

'Really good?'

'Top-level,' said Blake. 'High pay. Extremely interesting. And quite a lot of power.'

O'Higgins considered him for some while.

'I'd hate to see you lost to Eagle,' he said. 'You know, remaining as a Regional Co-ordinator at your tender age is no bad deal. Good money. Fascinating job. Power and social position. Pretty good security.'

'No,' said Blake. 'I don't think I'll be doing a Byrd.'

'Then I don't think I'd throw that alternative away,' said O'Higgins carefully, 'if I were you. Not just yet. With our Van Straten scenario as it is.'

'No. Good.'

'Before you make any final decision,' said O'Higgins, 'have a chat to Morgan Sperry first. You've a very good friend there.'

'*Another* very good friend,' said Blake. O'Higgins's wizened faced unfolded into a smile.

'As perhaps some slight demonstration of that,' he said. 'I must tell you the inside story of yesterday's Office Circular, the one that appointed you MD.'

'So?'

'The circular was of course printed and ready to go to everyone's desk by messenger at lunchtime. But then Van Straten called this urgent Board Meeting, mainly on your nomination. We fought it till 1 pm, and you know the sad result: you were not to be appointed, so the circular was not to go out.'

'And?'

'Well, Morgan and I had a little chat straight after the meeting, exchanging ideas. Consequently neither of us passed on any order to Office Administration to stop the circular. So it went out.'

'My God!' said Blake.

'Our reasoning was,' said O'Higgins, 'that once the circular was out on the whole wide world's desk, Van Straten would never dare to countermand it.'

'But Van Straten did.'

'We underestimated his resolve. A man of goddamned iron.'

'Or ice,' said Blake. He looked across at O'Higgins and suddenly burst out laughing. 'My God!' he said. 'It was a bloody good try! You return me my faith in humanity!'

'Eagle always teaches you to use your initiative,' said O'Higgins.

'Well,' said Blake. 'I'm going to use mine. And go home to think this out.'

He got up, and shook O'Higgins's hand.

'Very many thanks,' he said, 'to you and Morgan. Most sincerely.'

By the door, O'Higgins clapped him on the shoulder, smiling.

'And to hell with Eagle!' he said.

'Yes,' said Blake, 'to hell with Eagle!'

Sean O'Higgins watched Blake carved out next to him that last instant by the door. Blake stood tall and utterly still and concentrated. As utterly still as Kobus van Straten in Old Testament judgement. Blake's neat blond hair and sharp blue eyes glittered icy-cold. His body crackled with tension. Here's a man hell-bent on vengeance, thought O'Higgins. Yet Blake, now, *was* Van Straten. O'Higgins's split second of total insight shocked him. What real difference was there between these two men now? Give Blake a matching power, and he would *become* what he most hated, his greatest enemy, a twin Van Straten, with the same terrible stature, the gift or fate to play with apocalyptic powers, the Ice Maiden dedication, to destroy souls or worlds. Would both too triumph, then be totally defeated, to fall vertically, and gleaming white hot as shooting-stars across the awed firmaments, like Lucifer to his inferno? It was to hell with Eagle indeed, and, from the look of it, with Van Straten and Blake too. For a total and inexorable fatality seemed to bind these two.

Blake found the diary purely by accident. He had told Eva to cancel all his appointments that day and got himself driven home to the surprise of Marta and Asunción. He went to his study and sat with his head in his hands. Marta brought him the pot of coffee he had asked for, and when she had gone he began to list the pros and cons of in fact sending Eagle to hell, in favour of his alternative. It would be a huge and painful break; he had now been nineteen years with Eagle, breathed it, eaten it, slept it. It had become an entire life-style, his marriage part of it. He was astonished at the sharp pain which the mere thought of losing Celia caused him. He had begun this at least partly as a marriage of convenience. Now the habit of the years had locked him into a sort of affection. This was true even though theirs was not a monogamous marriage; probably from her side either; he had not forgotten Chris Morgenthau of AFP. But there had been no malice in that; she had carried no naked knives against him, knowingly or unknowingly, to castrate or disembowel. It had been on another level, not very important. Certainly then she mattered to him. Blake had a theory that you could only get to know five or six people really well in your life. He had known his father, that desiccated rector from Sussex. Jimmy Byrd, perhaps, because Blake had been through that crisis with him. Sean O'Higgins and Morgan Sperry, perhaps half a person's worth each. Celia, certainly. Leila, most certainly. So to lose even one from that very short list would be deeply painful.

Jotting his pros and cons, Blake discovered that his fountain-pen had run dry. He had no ink in his study, but Celia generally had one or two ball-points floating around in their bedroom upstairs. As he got up to go up and look, Chunt entered and flung himself at his chest. Chunt must have been somewhere in the large garden behind the house when Blake had arrived, for, demonstrating his uselessness as a watch-dog, he had not even barked. Now, more neurotic than usual after the six months' quarantine which he had just completed, he was not letting Blake out of his sight. Brindled and broad shouldered, his pink tongue panting and his piggy eyes glistening, he hung on Blake's heels, crowding him all the way upstairs. Blake could well have been one of the mere five or six people that Chunt was ever going to get to know really well in his life.

Upstairs in their bedroom, Blake could not discover even one pen floating around. In desperation he went over to Celia's chest-of-drawers. She kept all manner of lingerie and jewelry and bric-a-brac in the top right-hand drawer, which she generally left locked. But he found it open today. There was a splendid froth of underwear at the top, in whites and flesh pinks and sheer blacks, most tiny and provocative with lace. She had a particular weakness for lingerie from Rio de Janeiro, whose manufacturers seemed to have a racy and undying belief in the impossible; how could a pair of female breasts or buttocks ever fit into that? Blake held some of this work of genius against his cheek. The scent of Celia was subtly in it, of herself, of her humanity, as well as the scent of Joy. Then he dug reverently under this gossamer stuff and down into the drawer.

There was a pen! He took it out thankfully, thinking that he must remember to tell Celia of his invasion, and return it to her. He hoped the damned thing would work. It was then that, already half turning away, he recalled the image of the diary he had seen at the bottom of the drawer. It would do for him to try out the pen. He would need only to open it and draw a short line on any white page. He could see no other paper or envelopes around. So he turned back for the diary.

It was handsomely bound in dark blue leather, with little gold-coloured metal L's to protect its outside corners. About three inches broad by five and a half deep, it would no doubt fit conveniently into a handbag. He wondered why it was not there now; probably because, as he knew, she had finally and characteristically left for Paris in something of a rush.

For Paris. Now why should that name suddenly evoke odd reverberating echoes somewhere deep in his mind?

He picked up the diary and turned the front cover casually. The diary opened at where the dark blue cloth marker lay, at exactly one week earlier, the day that Blake had left for Beirut, and two days before Van Straten had. The entry in the diary, in Celia's miniature and extraordinarily neat writing, in fact referred to just those happenings, but in terms that shocked Blake almost out of his mind:

P left for Beirut this evening, so I was able to meet K without fear or subterfuge and dine with him at the Lebanese restaurant near his garçonnière in South Ken. Afterwards a night of exquisite love. K is a man of such immense grandeur, power, and clarity of mind. I bow totally to him, without reserve. I give myself totally to him. Yet it's in no way degrading, but ennobling. I've never lived so fully before. And despite his huge might in the world he can show great kindness and tenderness, at least to me. He pays me high honour too, in telling me many things of his exacting life. He fears P may prove too weak, through earlier friendship, with B in Beirut; an example, he thinks, may have to be made, and he may therefore have to go out there himself. But this, he promises me, won't disrupt our two days together in Paris next week. I look forward to that as I would look forward, blessed, to meeting a god in heaven. For he is that, godlike; a man of fine justice, honest, truly great. And if he holds me in thrall I lie before him, or by him, most willingly; I thank the true God that we met. He has fulfilled me, made sense of my so far empty life. He is my absolute passion. Why have I never felt anything like that with P, or such undying respect? Of course the two are of such different metals –

They are indeed, thought Blake grimly.

And that was where Paris came in. They were there together now. Fouquet's management succession . . .

It was the second time that day that Blake's guts seemed to have dropped clean from him. This time it was not all the way down through the eighteen floors of the epic Eagle Millbank building into the near-Olympic-sized swimming bath thoughtfully provided for all its employees in the basement by a benign management. This time they had dropped sheer to the lip of the abysses of hell. He wondered where the intensity of his anguish now came from. It was not just that he was losing her as a possession. The wound was more deadly. This was no mere Chris-Morganthau-type athletic fuck, or series of fucks, supposing that there had ever really been any. Here the betrayal was much deeper. Here she had gone across totally to the enemy. She had, willingly, mortgaged her spirit. . .

And had the initiative come from Van Straten? Had his motive been just to seduce her great beauty and attractiveness, an almost laudable, or at least understandable, aim in a world of competitive men, if the lady were willing? Or had the greater, the definitive part of that aim been through her to batter and destroy him, by this grave, bitter, and perhaps lethal cutting down of him? And by what eerie logic had she chosen to leave that drawer unlocked, this fatal diary in it, just this day? Somewhere a death-wish deep in her that he would indeed there see and read it?

Blake looked back through the diary to see if he could find the answers, or even an answer. It was clear that the affair had started six months before, just when the Blakes returned to London for his new job. He could find no touch of evil there.

Rather, she spoke of that beginning with an engaging simplicity and innocence. There was no doubt that she had been completely sincere. Perhaps both had been. Stranger things had happened in the history of humanity. Another thing amazed Blake: the sheer beauty, at times, of her writing about her emotions. He read, most painfully, of her deep desire to bear Van Straten's child. It was a lyricism, Blake realized, that he had never himself known how to prompt in her —

Or ever would know. For Celia, that diary, had made up his mind for him. They had had at least that virtue. Now he must without doubt quit Eagle and go to his alternative. It would be a totally new life, with no links back to here. He took the diary. He would go now to a photocopying shop he knew, to get a complete copy made. No, make that two; one for the best divorce lawyer he could find in London.

As Blake turned to go, he caught sight of Chunt. His six months of quarantine seemed to have developed hidden depths in Chunt too. His intuitions now seemed as sharp as laser beams. He had been sitting absolutely motionless watching Blake with his head cocked very slightly to one side. So far as a broad-chested brindled Staffordshire bull-terrier could ever sympathize with a human being, Chunt was doing that with all stops removed.

'Poor little bastard!' he said to Chunt. 'I'm afraid you'll never see me for walks again!'

But that night at dinner in the White Tower he did not tell Leila about Celia's affair with Van Straten, or his own finding of her diary and decision to divorce her. Some sense of delicacy stopped him; the wound was too raw and recent. But he told her about Beirut, and his appointment for what must have been the shortest time on record as a Managing Director. And his decision to get himself declared redundant by Eagle at the absolute maximum terms he could negotiate. They were sitting upstairs, Leila next to him. She was dressed in pure white silk, just covering her shoulders, and close-fitting to her slim waist, then flaring. A plain gold band round her throat and single drops of gold at her earlobes bloomed against her dark olive skin. She turned her head, and her fine high-cheek-boned face regarded him.

'Well, you know where to go. You will be welcome. You've still got your guarantee?'

Blake smiled and pulled the long envelope from his inside left breast pocket. He took the folded sheet of paper from it and opened it and put it on the table in front of them. They glanced through it together. It was under the official letterhead of the Ministry of Oil of the Kingdom of the Sun, and it read:

I, Abdullah bin Ali bin Jibál, Minister of Oil of the Kingdom of the Sun, hereby guarantee that at any time during ten (10) years from today's date, Mr Philip Blake, currently employed by Eagle Oil International Limited of London UK, has the option to take up employment with this Ministry as an Oil Counsellor, reporting directly and exclusively to the Minister. His salary shall start at US$ 200,000 annually, adjustable by changes in the COL Index as published by the official organs of the US Government. His term of employment will be five (5) years initially, automatically renewable for further like periods unless one party gives the other notice to terminate at least one month before the termination of any such period. Other conditions of employment shall be those standard in the Kingdom of the Sun for senior expatriate employees, including: free suitable furnished accommodation, free use of Ministry car, one month's paid holidays annually, free medical attention for himself and any members of his family accompanying him.

It was signed by Abdullah and dated 23 October 1973.

'A far-sighted gentleman, Mr Blake!' said Leila, smiling at him.

'Thank God I was,' said Blake. 'But I didn't have to be exceptionally bright. Just to listen a bit. Because even then I knew that Van Straten was gunning for me. It's a game we play.'

'And which you'll not stop playing?'

'Not if I can help it,' said Blake. 'He has just hit me very hard. Twice, really. So the next strike should be mine. And it should be very heavy, perhaps final. For this one has been a bitter bloody shock. I was within an ace of the top. I was *there* for an instant, even. Then thrown down. Well, at least it has never been dull. I'll miss the Ice Maiden.'

'They're fools,' she said. 'Their loss is our gain.'

A waiter had brought them *merethes*, savoury snacks, brochettes of *souvlaki*, grilled pork, and *dolmathes*, little meat and rice balls rolled in vine leaves. Even more vital, he had brought and uncorked the big bottle of heavy rich red Othello wine, from the Trodos Mountains in Cyprus. Whether they ate red or white meat or fish, Othello was the wine they drank at the White Towers; the law was inviolable. They toasted each other in it, revelling in its heady kick.

'What will you do now?' she asked. 'You'll stay with your wife, of course? With Celia?'

He looked at her sharply, amazed that she seemed to have put her finger on that so swiftly. Leila seemed to listen too.

'She's in Paris till the morning after tomorrow. I'll pack what things I need tomorrow, and move to the flat off Queensway.'

Leila raised her fine eyebrows very slightly and observed her wine. If she had won a subtle victory here, she was, unlike Van Straten, not going to show an exultation in it. She simply said, very quietly:

'Well. I must remember to give it a special Arab blessing tonight, for a new house or tent or home.'

The waiter had brought the *salata horyátiki* now, a full mixture in two china bowls, of lettuce and tomatoes and onion galore and olives and *feta* or white goat's cheese and liberal helpings of olive oil dressing. Right on its heels followed *i aghriopapya*, wild duck, one of the White Tower's master-pieces, almost as lyrical as the prose in their menus. A second bottle of the splendid Othello accompanied it.

'I'll go back in a week,' she said. 'And when shall I tell Abdullah that you'll be coming?'

'As soon as I can,' said Blake. 'I'll start negotiating my exit terms from Eagle tomorrow. I'll tell you how it looks. And I'll ring Abdullah tomorrow to let him know generally how things stand.'

'We must find you a good flat,' she said. 'I know of one in a building near mine. Quite like mine.'

'Marvellous!' he said, his blue eyes sparkling. 'So I go to a magnificent new life, offering everything!'

'But with care in one thing,' she said gravely. 'We should still never again make love there. It's too dangerous. Parts of our society are still not too far from beheading adulterous princesses with golden swords.'

'But I shall still be able to see you there often?'

'Of course. As often as you like. And doubtless in your new work you'll have many opportunities to travel outside the Kingdom. And I can always, as now, meet you wherever you go.'

That restraint saddened him, though he knew it wise. But there was none of it in their love-making in the flat off Queensway afterwards. They were full-blooded and innocent, bound in a long accepted pact. Blake's discovery of the Ice Maiden's six month affair with his wife had not castrated him. That was just a blow of fate, as Van Straten's toppling of him from his brief peak in Eagle had been. Perhaps what mattered most about such blows was how you fought your way back up from them.

Blake saw the man when he had gone ten yards towards his parked Aston-Martin Lagonda. Leila had decided to sleep for an hour before going back to her own flat. It was just on midnight. Blake wanted to get home now so that he could get up early, pack his essential things and leave that house and his former life forever.

He could not miss the man who stood straight out in front of him from the shadows, confronting him. Blake stopped. He could do nothing else. They were a hundred yards from the lights of Queensway.

'Like to try your luck, mate?' asked the man. 'See what fate's got in store for you?'

'Fate?' said Blake, oddly disturbed.

The man smiled at him maliciously.

'Well, you've had your fair share of luck so far, haven't you? Can't complain. I saw the two of you go in. Gave the little lady a good time, did you? I couldn't see, but I could imagine all right!'

He rounded his lips and shot his tongue in and out several times, salaciously.

'Get the hell out of my way!' said Blake. 'What do you want?'

But the man stood immovably. He was almost as tall as Blake, and much more thickly built. He looked like a solid block of muscle from his shoulders straight down. He wore a light black overcoat, tight-fitting and buttoned up to the throat, and Blake could see the shine of his light black shoes. His hands were in his overcoat pockets, and he wore a small black trilby hat pulled down on his bull-necked head. He looked thirty-five or forty, and tough as a nut. His black eyes snapped with energy. Yet something jarred in this thug-like silhouette. He had thrown in a few of the right words for the part, like mate and little lady, but for the rest his English was very pure and U.

'Want?' he said. 'Oh, all the money you have on you will do, as starters.'

'I see. And what was this line about trying my luck?'

The thick man smiled again.

'Oh. At a little fisticuffs, I meant. Though I'm not so sure that it makes good sense now, for a man in your position. You won't look too pretty for some time. Better just give me your cash.'

The man addressed him head-on, a yard off. Blake stepped forward and half left, and hooked short and hard with his right hand to the solar plexus. It was a blow that should have felled an ox. The other simply grunted, and looked back at Blake, and Blake knew then that he was in for a very rough fight indeed. His fist had felt the walls of the man's stomach as resilient as a sandbag.

'I like to keep fit!' the other called out gaily, from the lunatic edge of his paranoia. As some evidence of that, he had dropped now into an easy orthodox boxer's crouch, left hand and foot out forward questing, right hand at guard. For his hands were out of his pockets now, and Blake saw the light leather gloves, and the gold flicker over the right one – *there* was the murder weapon, Blake's greatest danger.

As if certain that Blake's attention would be focused there now, the thick man kicked forward with his left foot, quick as a snake striking, straight up from the ground, with no prior drawing back or hint, for the testicles. It would have ended things there, but Blake saw the blur under him and turned fast instinctively to his right into it, catching the kick on the outside of his left thigh. Before the thick man recovered his momentum, Blake had himself attacked with his right foot, the karate kick from the back leg which consists in lifting the foot laterally out first, then swinging the trunk so as to shoot the heel straight out to the side at the target, the whole weight of the body in line behind it.

Blake caught him full, high on the chest, just too low for the throat or face, just too high for the solar plexus; that blow on any of these must have stopped him. As it was, he went over backwards hard from it. He was too wise, too professional, to hold himself seated splayed out there on the ground with his hands back, wide open to further assault. Instead, he rolled right on over, and back onto his feet, losing little except his trilby, revealing all his hair, thick and black and sleeked straight back.

Now clearly he saw that he must move faster, for a policeman could turn into the street any time from Queensway, or people could appear. So he shuffled in decisively on Blake now, his hands weaving, supple and deadly. Blake caught him again with the same karate kick, though from the left, but he had left it a fraction late, so the other could swing and take Blake's heel high on his right thigh. Still, it had hurt him, for Blake heard him grunt deeply, and saw him falter.

But then he came on. Both men were breathing heavily now. Blake fell back, striking again and again with straight lefts into the man's face, and watching for kicks. But the thick man went boring in deliberately, until Blake had the sudden nightmare conviction that he could never stop him. The other had not even tried seriously yet to hit him. He was biding his time. Desperate, Blake stood his ground, hit the thick man again hard with a straight left, then followed it with a vicious short right to the face. The other's head jerked back and blood came from it. Blake went in close while the thick man's neck muscles were still slack and slashed down hard with the edge of his right hand in a karate chop across the other's carotid and windpipe. The man coughed horribly.

But from too close. He shook his head, and jolted his left fist up into Blake's solar plexus. It was a six-inch punch, but it almost lifted Blake clean off the ground. Nothing like as fit as the other, he could only try to clinch forward into him. There the brass-bound right hand met his face.

On its own, that blow must just about have knocked him out. For he did not really feel the others that followed it, busting his lips and teeth and nose, and most of the bones in the left of his face; or the thick man's knee, now right in close, up to his groin. Blake was busy in a private discussion.

When did a man give up? Anyway for the moment?

Christ, I've given up already, thought Blake. I can't fight this thick bastard any more. I can't fight any more, period.

Bullshit! said Laurie Jakes, ex Welterweight pro, who had been his boxing instructor when he had practised the noble art in his first training year with Eagle in London, mainly to reflate his morale after the skiing accident that had broken his left leg. You can't give up while you're still standing, said Laurie. Why! Remember my rhyme:

It's not the size of the dog in the fight,
But the size of the fight in the dog.

Then I'll lie down, said Blake craftily, and did so.

It's up to you, said Laurie. No man can ever really live another's life. Or save him. You're always alone in the death.

Mostly, said Blake, but I have one very good lady friend. Lover. I think she will go with me as far as she can.

Then don't give up, said Laurie. Few can climb back to the top once they've given up.

I'll fight back up, said Blake. Against God and the Devil combined. And beat them. But not now. Now my guts are shot and my will's all shot. Call again next week.

The trouble with you, said Laurie, is that you're just letting all that blood blind you.

Blind my arse, said Blake crudely. He could see perfectly all right. He was lying flat on his back, and he could hardly miss all the blood over the front of his shirt and jacket. The thick man's face swam a foot or two above him. Blake was sorry to note that it was not very badly marked. It slid out of his field of vision, and he felt a sudden bitter stab in his right side, and heard another rib pop. That was the thick man putting in the boot again, maybe for the last time, a comrade's poignant farewell. Blake felt the other haul him over onto his face and go into his left hip pocket. The man rolled him thoughtfully onto his back again, so that Blake could watch him riffling through the wallet, taking only the banknotes, keeping his gloves on so that he should leave no fingerprints. Then he dropped the wallet with its driving licence and credit cards next to his victim; a gentlemanly touch, thought Blake.

The thick man, his small black trilby replaced neatly on his sleek black hair, took a last look down at Blake, then turned on his heel and walked away towards the lights of Queensway, without looking back. Blake noticed that he limped a little, possible from one of the karate kicks that Blake had delivered him. It was some slight satisfaction. Blake had also noted that the thick man had not sworn or spat at him before he left. That pleased him too. The thick man would not be given to histrionics. He was too professional. Even that last kick in the ribs had doubtless been applied scientifically, without particular malice, to ensure Blake's immobility while the thick man got away. He was quite an artist in his own manner.

But he need not have worried. Blake lay there for a long time, gazing down the road at the lights of Queensway, thinking. Who would have set him up for this? Celia? Hardly. At this point she did not even know that Blake had discovered her affair with the Ice Maiden and was gunning for a divorce. And would she know the contacts to carry it out? It was hardly her style. Van Straten himself? Perhaps just possibly. Certainly the hatred was deep enough. But would that be his style either? Wasn't he the kind who would prefer to carry out his own executions?

Most probably it was just fate itself, and the thick man exactly what his actions suggested. Life had its own tragic rhythms, fatal rhythms. This was just destiny, heavily underscoring the fact of his defeats and fall, his vertical plunge from grace. The blows of fate were supposed to come in threes, weren't they?

No people came from the lights of Queensway towards Blake. Finally he found the strength to haul himself up very slowly on the railings, and to grope his way back along them like a drunken or blinded man to his flat building's gate, to open it, and to grovel the long and bitter pilgrimage along the path to the steps, and up them to the bells at the front door. It was here that Leila found him.

PART THREE

21

Rebirth to a New Religion

'Well, you mended fast,' said Ahmed Feisal, six-foot-one and lean, immaculate in his open-necked white drill jacket, white cotton slacks and polished brown sandals, his clean-cut face mesmeric as a light, his wide-set Turkish light grey eyes electric with energy. 'Yet you say the mugging was only six weeks ago?'

'Yes,' said Philip Blake. 'Of which three in hospital, mainly for plastic surgery. The broken ribs they just taped up.'

'And no idea who did it?'

'Just surmises,' said Blake. 'But most probably he was just another small businessman, using his own initiative – a true spirit of free enterprise. What the hell, it's a world ago now.'

Feisal smiled.

'I hope ours here treats you better.'

'The odds on it look good,' said Blake.

They did. The Arabs in the City of the Sun's main souk that late afternoon in the first days of August 1977 were putting on their best performance of benign and courteous independence. They were almost all men, dressed in dishdashas and *khutras* with *ogals* or *jelabíahs* and skull-caps, or simple open-necked European shorts and slacks. Almost all wore sandals. They were Iraqis and Saudis and Kuwaitis and Bahreinis and Omanis and men from the United Arab Emirates and Yemenis and Egyptians and Syrians, and Pakistanis and Indians and Iranians and Kurds and even a few *Shemsis*. None of them interfered with the two visitors in the least, not even observing them directly. Blake saw few other Europeans. He and Ahmed Feisal sat on wooden chairs at a simple table by a restaurant's entrance and drank *masboot*, the medium dry-sweet Arab coffee for men of moderate taste. This was one of the souk's wider lanes, and roofed, giving blessed shade against the sun;

the temperature was still about 100° F. Both sides of the lane bulged with stalls which offered fresh foods – lettuces, cabbages, cauliflowers, oranges, apples, lemons, tomatoes, *khubs* or unleavened bread. Trailing the buyers were porters, almost all Iranians, great baskets of about their own size on their backs, hung from flat broad straps round their foreheads. Here there were food booths everywhere, glass-fronted, with naked chickens revolving on horizontal layers of spits above small fires which bronzed them like Caucasian sunbathers.

But *was* Ahmed Feisal a man of moderate taste? Could *any* man be who had that messianic quality? Wasn't charisma itself by definition an extreme, an exception? All Blake knew about him so far was that he was head of the legal department of the Kingdom of the Sun's Oil Ministry, and excellent at that job. And a Palestinian. Blake had been sure that he was that when he had first met him, nearly four years before, and Feisal, he recalled, had half mockingly and half in deadly seriousness claimed his Palestinian heritage that evening when jousting with Abdullah in Abdullah's residential castle. Unlike Ibrahim Sabri, the ministry's chief petroleum economist, with his eternal Tonton Macoute dark glasses and raddled complexion and habit of sucking air in audibly through his teeth to stress his points, Feisal had no inhibitions about his origins. On the contrary, he had clearly been strongly in favour of the *fedayeen* and the armed struggle against Israel. *How* strongly?

'And how's the world treating your Palestinian Arabs these days?'

At that, Feisal's excessively handsome face looked at him sharply, then smiled.

'Which world? In the one that considers itself the greatest, the United States, perhaps a shade better – since Jimmy Carter was elected President last year. He made a public statement in March this year in Massachusetts that there had to be a homeland for the Palestine refugees who had suffered for many years, and proposing a Geneva conference. And Kissinger quit the Department of State this January, and hopefully with him his commitment to the Israelis that the US wouldn't negotiate with the Palestine Liberation Organization until the PLO recognizes Israel's right to exist and the Security Council's resolutions 242 and 338. We may get a better deal with Cyrus Vance.'

'And in Israel itself? The West Bank and Gaza Strip?'

'Bad, with Menachem Begin in power heading a Likud coalition since May. He's the ex-Irgun Zvai Leumi leader, and it was the IZL who murdered hundreds of Palestinian women, children and old men at the village of Deir Yassin in the 1948 war – to strike terror into our people and make them flee Palestine. And hanged your two sergeants at Natanya. The West Bank? The Israelis are still repressive and colonizing hard, building new settlements as fast as they can.'

'And can't your PLO beat that?'

'How?' asked Feisal. 'By another outright confrontation? Another try at a lightning war? But nothing could have been more lightning than Sadat's October War nearly four years ago. Or had a greater element of surprise. Yet the Israelis still turned the tables on us. And they're much stronger militarily in all the conventional senses than they've ever been before. No. If we want to beat them by armed force, we need totally new methods, approaches, weapons –'

'There's no other route? Say diplomatic?'

Feisal called for two more *masboot* coffees, then turned back to Blake and shrugged delicately.

'That was the policy adopted by the thirteenth Palestine National Council – PNC – when it met this March in Cairo. The PNC's a sort of Palestinian Parliament in exile. Some hundreds of Palestinians from all areas take part. They elect the all-powerful PLO Executive Committee, and none of the fifteen this year were hard-line Rejectionist Front men. Arafat's Fatah dominated, but at the cost – which may prove far too high – of getting politically into debt to Egypt, whose recent policies of rapprochement towards Israel I find profoundly disturbing. But, to meet your specific question, yes, the Fatah-PLO leadership of the Executive Committee has opted mainly for peace negotiations.'

'Which you think wrong?'

'Which I think politically doomed to failure, if politics is the science of the possible.'

'And that concerns you personally?'

Feisal looked at him.

'Certainly it does, both personally and officially. You do know, don't you, that I'm the official PLO delegate for the Kingdom of the Sun?'

'No, indeed I didn't. And don't Abdullah and the cabinet mind?'

'Not at all. Why should they? They rather encourage me. After all, the strict Fatah-PLO line is non-interference in the internal affairs of the Arab States. Literally applied, that means that we leave them alone. We cause no revolutions. We're a very powerful stabilizing factor. Consider that of the million inhabitants of the Kingdom of the Sun, 250,000 of us, or near a quarter, are Palestinians. And most are professionals like myself, some placed in very key positions in the Kingdom's economy. So just think what total chaos we could cause if, cohesive and well integrated and disciplined as we are as a community, we chose to rebel and rise in anger against the Establishment! If we were even only halfway armed and organized, *no one* could stand against us –'

Blake looked at him with interest. Feisal's voice, usually so lazily cultured and flippant, had positively throbbed with emotion in those last few sentences.

'Would they really deserve such rough handling?' he asked lightly. 'Going by Abdullah and his sister, they seem a pretty progressive lot.'

Feisal glanced at him, and away across the lane, his face taut.

'They could have done so infinitely much more. That's above all true for the Arabian Gulf States, like the Kingdom of the Sun. So often their rulers have been too totally absorbed in spending their astronomic new oil wealth after the 1973 price increases to consider either their own people's advancement or our Palestinian cause –'

'Where have they recently failed you in that?' asked Blake.

Feisal looked at him. The passion and anguish in Feisal's face shocked him. It was like seeing the Ice Maiden weep.

'What do you know of the massacres of our people in Beirut last year?'

'Not much, I'm afraid. I read something of it.'

'On June 22 the right-wing Christian Lebanese militia attacked the last three Palestinian and Shi'ite quarters in Lebanese Christian East Beirut. The Militia overwhelmed the small Palestinian refugee camp of Jisr el Basha on June 28. They took the Muslim quarter of Nabaa on August 6, then after great violence took our bigger refugee camp of Tel ez-

Zaatar on August 12, where thirty thousand surrendered. The Lebanese Christians slaughtered fifteen hundred of them the day they cleared out the camp. Even more dreadful than this massacre of Arabs by Arabs was the fact the *the Syrians were colluding with the Phalangist and Chamoun Lebanese Christian forces*! We know that the Syrian commander even visited the right-wing HQ attacking Tel ez-Zaatar. We appealed to Sadat for urgent mediation. We got no help. Look, from the earliest days when Yasser Arafat and Salah Khalaf and others of us of less stature were setting up the Palestine Students' Union in Cairo, we already knew bitterly that we were really alone in our struggle. We'd get nothing, except probably betrayal, from the Arab States, mostly self-seeking, acutely right-wing and feudal, and riddled with corruption. We saw that already in 1951 –'

'You were there?'

'Yes,' said Feisal. He had taken a silver cigarette-case from the right hip pocket of his white drill jacket, and he offered it now to Blake. Blake smiled and shook his head. Feisal took a cigarette himself, and Blake watched him light it with a silver Dupont lighter. Whatever else the PLO might have been short of in the past it did not seem to be money now. Though of course Feisal was a department head, and the Kingdom's Oil Ministry paid its staff well. Blake wondered why Feisal had chosen to go through this elaborate miniature ritual now. Probably it was to regain a grip on his emotions. He must have realized that he had begun to talk with a good deal of passion. Indeed, he went on now rather more calmly:

'I was at Fuad I University, now Cairo University, from 1951, you see. Studying law, on an Egyptian scholarship for the children of refugees which I was very lucky to get. I had been at a camp near Tel ez-Zaatar since my parents and brothers and sisters and I were thrown out of Haifa in 1948. It was a very primitive small camp. At first there was no electricity, and only two or three water-taps for the whole camp; it meant long queues in the cold and dark. We had two small rooms in a shambling house of mud and rocks, among ten of us; I had seven brothers and sisters. My father died quickly, from dysentery. He had been a worker at the CRL Oil Refinery at Haifa. He wasn't used to mud and filth –'

'How in hell did you live then?' asked Blake.

'Oh, I was fifteen when we got there,' said Feisal. 'Old enough to sell papers in the streets of Beirut after school. And –' He hesitated, and inhaled deeply from his cigarette.

'And?'

'My mother worked. At the only things she had ever learned. Housework, cooking, washing laundry. And opening her legs. She earned a few bucks whenever she could by prostitution. We were too young to have a say in that. And too damned hungry – you get used to anything, you know. Of course we would always have to vacate that one room with her bed. That could mean the cold outside or far too many for comfort in the other room, where we could hear the noises. The smell of the men always seemed to stay on after they'd left. Still, we lived. We survived.'

'Why do you tell me all this? I know there's been enough murder and mayhem and misery in the Middle East.'

'I wonder if you do?' said Feisal. 'Yes, perhaps that's it. I've had a bellyful, you see, of newcomers getting this glamorized view of things here, the Bedouin on his camel, stately galleon of the desert, the Sheikh on his fiery Arab steed, a gentleman to the fingertips. A highly progressive monarchy, with a slickly efficient and up-to-date Oil Ministry. Its Minister a cultivated Oxford man, no less. You've been here just a week now, and that's the picture you must have. It's pretty, but it's *not* the Middle East. The Middle East is these deep treacheries. Arab against Arab, slitting throats for a political whim or a fancied insult, yesterday's friend tomorrow's enemy. The Middle East is five Arab armies each so egocentrically and corruptly led that a tiny new Israeli State can knock the shit out of them in 1948. The Middle East is Hussein's murderous purging of Palestinians from Jordan which by July 1971 had killed three thousand of our guerrillas and civilians and pounded our refugee camps to powder. It's the million Palestinian refugees flung out from our country in 1948 that have grown to two million desperate and hopeless people today. The Middle East is Syria's collusion with the Lebanese Christians who overwhelmed our Tel ez-Zaatar refugee camp and disembowelled its survivors. My mother and some of my sisters had moved to that camp –'

'Oh my God!' said Blake. 'What happened to them?'

Feisal shook his head suddenly, left money on the table, and got up.

'Come on. Do you mind if we walk?'

'Of course not.'

Out of this lane they passed into a very long high building, quite broad, roofed, its walls made of brick, lit by the later afternoon rays of the sun through the high windows, and occasional naked electric bulbs on long black flexes. This was the busiest part of the souk. Both sides were lined with stalls filled with a gay bric-a-brac of consumer goods – television sets and radio-cassettes and transistor radios and clocks and watches and cigarette-lighters and ball point and fountain pens. There were fine carpets from Isfahan and Bokhara and Turkestan. There were western suits and slacks and shirts and shoes as well as dishdashas and embroidered *khutras* and leather sandals. Blake saw fine *jelabiahs* too, finely embellished with silver and gold threaded patterns, and shimmering gold and blue and red and yellow saris. Between every six or seven booths, as if set thoughtfully there to save the gasping avid buyer in his last extremity, was a bar with huge glass bowls on it holding orange and melon and pineapple juices. There was no lack of clients. The Middle East might be a cruel haunt of murder and betrayal, but some at least of its inmates seemed to survive it with good humour and grace.

'I got back into Tel ez-Zaatar two days after it fell,' said Feisal. 'It stank of death. It was as if a sudden fatal gas had smitten them all. For there was no discrimination by age or sex. There were slaughtered fighters and disembowelled old men, and infants and women of all ages, some shot or grenaded, but mostly killed by bayonets or knives. It looked as if tanks had rolled over some of the bodies. And always that terrible sweet smell of dead humans – so much more acrid and penetrating than the stink of dead cows or donkeys or mules, maybe our noses recognize ourselves. And those butchered or squashed bodies – did you ever read a novel called *The Skin* by the Italian Malaparte? The image from a corpse deliberately run over by the tracks of a tank –'

'And your mother? Your sisters?'

'After an hour I found my mother,' said Ahmed Feisal, 'and one sister. My youngest sister, unmarried, who still lived with my mother. They were by a communal water tap, among other bodies. With pails, having no water in the house –'

'Dead?'

Feisal turned and looked at Blake. Feisal had no blood at all in his face. He could have been dead himself.

'At least it was clean with my sister. A small hole in the centre of her forehead, no back to her skull. Quick. Decent, almost; no one had even disarranged her dress. But you couldn't say that about the other girls there. Most had been stabbed, chopped up, mutilated –'

In horror, Blake looked round at him. Feisal had clenched his hands, and his head was down forward on his chest. He half glanced back at Blake.

'My mother? Yes, I found her too. It must have taken three Lebanese Christian heroes to do it. One to hold each leg apart, the third to ram the bayonet up her vagina. It looked like one of these very long World War One bayonets that the French *poilus* used. They must have used terrible force. Only the top of the haft still projected –'

Feisal stopped dead and swung right round with his hands flung up on Blake. It could have been all Blake's fault. Other Arabs in this new twisting alley of the souk divided silently round this sudden island, the less tactful glancing at it curiously.

'Why *that?*' cried Feisal. 'Why *that* to her? Wasn't death enough, after eighteen years, almost half of her adult life, in the hopeless misery of those goddamned refugee camps? Wasn't murder enough? What vicious god demanded that much more?'

They walked on for a while. Against the silence, Blake asked:

'You believe in such a god?'

Feisal glanced at him.

'I believe in Allah. In Islam. Perhaps as something not quite a religion in the Western sense. As a whole view of life, a whole culture, covering every aspect of a man's life, religious, political, social, moral, everything. There's no merely Sunday morality in Islam, you know. It's the same for every instant of the week, the year, your lifetime. Oh yes, I went most diligently to my *kuttab* as a child in Haifa. That's the religious school all little Muslim boys should go to from the age of seven to ten. There you learn almost the whole Koran by heart, every stylized hesitation and elision and accent; you can quote whole suras from it. It becomes the core of your life. The clear iron certainty you always fall back on in the grimmest moments of your life, that you never forget. I fell back on it then, God knows, in Tel ez-Zaatar –'

'There's no way you could have got them out of there before?'

'They wouldn't come,' said Feisal. 'It's a characteristic of the Palestinians in the refugee camps everywhere. They won't accept permanent settlement and integration in Arab societies outside. They cling always to that hugely emotive concept of the final return home. It's totally illusory, of course; their villages have been razed or turned into kibbutzim many years ago. There's no home left. God knows, for example, which Jewish family now occupies our former house near Haifa Port; the new Israeli State put through a pack of laws permitting Israelis to take over deserted Arab property. No, time and again I tried to get my family to come here. I sent them the money for the fares. They wouldn't come; for the camps there was only one home to return to.'

His smile was free of humour.

'Of course we in Fatah and the PLO get tremendous support and many *fedayeen* volunteers from them for precisely that reason. The Palestinian Arabs working in Gulf States like this are less enthusiastic; they're professionals and middle-class, thus less inclined to violent action. Though we have our ways,' Feisal added ominously, 'of keeping them up to scratch on their first loyalties. And of course we tax them, with the Arab States' rulers' accord, between five and seven per cent of their gross incomes for the Palestinian cause. But don't think I did not try to get my mother and sisters out. I never did discover what happened to my other two sisters there. They'll have died too, preferred to die in that carnage –'

Carnage was an apt word here. They were now in the huge open butchery quarter of the souk, surrounded by stalls whose marble or concrete counters were decorated with an astonishing variety of limbs and entrails of camels, sheep and goats, some hanging behind the vendors from huge hooks, and all pinkly nude or bloody. Muslim Arabs would eat any meat except pork, Blake had read, provided the beast had been properly slaughtered. That consisted in slitting its throat and

holding its body while it died, so that its spirit could leave it
decently and with decorum. Here everything was for sale,
including noses, ears, hoofs and all manner of innards. There
was even a row of goat's heads on one counter with their faces
peeled but their brows still luxuriant with shiny black curls
and crowned tiara-like with neat short horns, gazing fixedly at
the passers-by. The huge central concrete slab, Blake had been
told, was for the morning dissection of camel's corpses,
hulking there like shot-up army trucks in a desert war, and
disintegrating to the customers' bids under the myriad expert
slicing knives before one's eyes, like snowballs under a hot sun.

'So where do you go from here?' asked Blake. 'How do you
stop massacring one another in this merciless and bloody
infighting? When do you Arabs get your act together?'

Feisal shrugged.

'Those are harsh words, but a fair question. I don't know.
I'm personally not so sure that there isn't a fatal flaw right at
the heart of the PLO's strategy. Where? Well, on January 1
1968, six months after Israel had shattered the Arab armies in
the June 1967 Six Days War, our Central Committee made an
extremely important public announcement. The Central
Committee's extremely powerful because, even when divisive
hard-line Palestinian guerrilla splinter groups like George
Habash's PFLP, Popular Front for the Liberation of Palestine,
have been absent from the fifteen-man PLO Executive
Committee, they've stayed in the Central Council. Which
means that the Council has talked for every important
Palestinian guerrilla group.

'And that makes what it said on January 1 1968 all the more
vital – that the Council's final aim was no longer the
"liberation of Palestine" but the creation in it of a "secular,
democratic state " where Jews, Christians and Muslims could
live together in absolute equality.'

'So what's wrong with that? It seems to me very fair, very
modern, very democratic.'

'*Democratic*? How goddamned *small*! In your terms, Marks
and Spencers and summer holidays at Brighton!'

'Ah, not *violent* enough? You're really that passionate
about violence? Have you ever *been* violent, in the terms
you're talking about, guerrilla fighting and terrorism? You
were too young for the 1948 War.'

Ahmed Feisal smiled.

'But not too young for the continuing war of attrition with Israel in 1951. Khalid Wazir, from Ramallah in Palestine, was one of Yasser Arafat's contemporaries when Arafat founded the Palestinian Students' Union at Fuad I University in Cairo in 1951. Wazir was already directing guerrilla raids from the Sinai into Israel. I went on two of his missions. In all I shot and killed three kibbutzniks. So, whatever the Israelis do to me now, I've already paid my way.'

Blake raised his eyebrows and looked round at him.

'You didn't want to go on with your guerrilla?'

'I would have been happy to do that. But Arafat's Fatah, and the PLO, sent me to this job here.'

'Yet you don't like the PLO's strategy to found a democratic state in Israel. Why?'

'Because it misses a vital dimension. Who the hell, except perhaps Churchill, could ever really get passionate about democracy? And what kind of democracy was his anyway? And we need passion. To win back Palestine, fair rights for the Palestinians, we really need passion. Believe me.'

'Such as? What kind of passion?'

Feisal looked round at him steadily. They were at the golden edge of the souk. Here were the goldsmith's shops, rich in gold bracelets, necklaces, ear-rings, finger-rings, anklets, beloved of women; diamonds might be a girl's best friends, but gold, as a status symbol, or as portable survival insurance, ran them a close second. Gold, thought Blake, and a clean pair of heels, might be your only escape if Feisal came hard against you –

'*Islamic* passion,' said Feisal. '*That's* the missing dimension. Pan-Arab passion. You can say that Arafat has one objective only: to found an independent Arab national state in *any* liberated part of Palestine, however small. That is, Fatah and the PLO see the liberation of a *secular* Palestine as the road to Arab unity. Nonsense! It should be exactly the other way round. *It's only by Arab unity in the sense of deep, pervading and militant Pan-Islamic faith that we shall ever liberate Palestine*! That, and only that, bringing in that colossal apocalyptic *power* of Islam, as a total all-embracing religion and culture. *That's* what matters! *That* is what will light the flame that sweeps across all the boundaries of all the Arab and

Islamic states, and cauterizes the Zionist race in Israel clean out of existence!'

'And just how are you going to weld together a whole mass of anarchists bent only on massacring one another?' asked Blake. 'For that's your Arab world today. With what magic wand?'

'How?' asked Feisal. 'With what magic, what total dedication, what mystic and absolute readiness to sacrifice one's life for the cause? With a magnificent and I think unstoppable discipline called Islamic Fundamentalism. Once *that* is properly lit here, it will radically change the whole of the Middle East, and indeed the face of the world. It will raze to the ground every feudal and corrupt government. It will bring absolute social justice to a region that has not seen it since Muhammed. It will *of course* completely liberate Palestine. And it will win us back a quality we have sold too cheaply until now: our pride. Our Arab identity. Our history. All *that* we can and must win back!'

'Your Arab identity?'

'You mean, what do I mean by that?' said Feisal. He waved his hand before him. They had come out from the sensuous glittering luxury of the goldsmiths' shops. They had walked along a twisting alley suffused with dusk between high dark mud walls and they had felt the rot of ages under their feet, old newspapers, condoms, rinds of fruit, eggshells, cigarette butts and packs, hardened by steamroller time under a million sandals and naked Arab pads and heels into a highway as tough and resilient as any scientifically laid asphalted arterial road. The scent of urine and faeces drenched it. From this anal channel they had come with sudden shock upon great beauty. There the mosques lay before them, the same that Blake had first seen almost four years before from the other side, from Abdullah's high window, as if from a high mountain. Now again they addressed him, the generous orbs of the domes, the stern stone lace of the crenellated battlements, the stone jets of the minarets reaching up daring as Prometheus to the highest diffused blue arc of the sky. Across this blithe ecstatic masterpiece little black accents pricked with fussy precision – the black iron upwards-pointing crescents at the tops of the domes and minarets, mounted to ward off *Shaitaan*. Here was the epic etched eternal Islamic silhouette. It sang to you with clear clean notes and seduced your soul. Once you had seen it with intensity, as Blake had now seen it twice, you could never forget it.

'Yes. That must indeed be a part of your identity. A proud part. I can see that.'

'Then we'll make a good Muslim Arab of you yet.'

'Before you do that, what Islamic Fundamentalism do you talk of? The Muslim Brotherhood? Hassan el Banna? Social reform and a greater role for Islam?'

Feisal stopped short in visible surprise, and turned a long considering gaze on Blake.

'If you know even that much, then you are no longer a spectator, Mr Blake.'

'Doesn't working in the Kingdom of the Sun make me more than that in any case?' Feisal was still drilling his attention into Blake. If there was a glimmer of respect in his new attitude, there was also a shaft of suspicion. Blake could not speak of his first meeting with Princess Leila, still less of the affair which had engaged him most profoundly with her world. But there were things he could explain to Feisal. 'And don't forget that I spent two years running the Eagle operation in Egypt. That gave me the very best of reasons for learning more about the Fundamentalists. Some of them were after my head!'

Something in Feisal's expression told Blake that here he was learning nothing new.

'Let us agree that you are a player,' he said softly, and a little of the tension went out of his stance. 'Then it remains to be discovered what kind of a player, and on whose side. Perhaps we could start by playing a lesser game. Question and answer. And I shall begin by telling you something you may not know about Hassan el Banna, that great man. You will know that he was shot dead in a Cairo street in 1949 by Farouk's political police. They had begun to be alarmed by the calibre of his following – too many civil servants, teachers, white-collar workers, some of them ready to take power by force. But you may not know that before his death he was sending regular bulletins of advice to the heads of Arab governments. One was the famous *Nahwa en-Nur*, Message Towards the Light, a general lesson on how they should run their states in a proper Islamic manner. You can imagine how Farouk and Company must have loved that!'

Blake laughed. 'Fine!' he said. 'And you're saying that the Muslim Brotherhood wasn't just a national movement – that Islam provides a field of action from here to the Philippines, North Africa to Pakistan, Iran to the Muslim states of the Soviet Union. But tell me, just what *was* this "proper Islamic manner"? What does it mean to you?'

They had come clear out of the Souk now, and into the start of the City of the Sun's splendid network of wide paved roads. Blake's new car was parked just ahead. It was a Chevrolet Camaro, low and sleek and painted metallic silver, with a aerofoil air-brake at the back theoretically to keep its tail down at high speeds. It was six-cylindered and looked capable enough of those. Blake loved it.

'First principles,' said Feisal. 'The Koran and the *Sunna*. Islamic Law. That means selfless public service, ruthless elimination of corruption, total social justice; and in personal ethics the same strict standards of honesty, sexual morality, religious observance.' He worked through his catechism with the practised fondness of a soldier dismantling and cleaning a favourite weapon. 'And the protection and advancement of the true Islamic identity, at the cost of your life if necessary. Do not suppose that Banna was merely a reformer, Mr Blake. He accepted the concept of the *jihád*, the holy war. It was "every Muslim's obligation", he said.'

'And the cruel punishments, the stoning to death of the adulterous women, the cutting off of hands?'

They were by the Camaro now. Feisal, who had gone to the right-hand door, looked across the low metallic roof at Blake. That die-stamped, perfect face remained unmoved.

'Is it really such a high price to pay, if in return you achieve total order, absolute social justice?'

There was no fervour in that voice. Blake recognized the mortuary chill of the utter perfectionist, the political fanatic armoured in his own conviction.

'Now let me ask you something,' said Feisal. 'You have lived in Egypt. No doubt you know some of its State machine from the inside. Is that a stable government, a contented people?'

Blake started the Camaro and pulled away from the kerb. He could feel the surge of huge power under his hands. He met Feisal's question head-on.

'I'll answer you with two events. First, 1974, the Technical

Military Academy Group: it marched on the Academy and fought and took it, aiming to go further, but Sadat's forces counter-attacked and defeated it before it could advance. Yet this was only six months after Sadat's supposedly victorious and popular October War. Sadat put nearly a hundred men on trial, and executed three leaders. But he had only scotched the snake. Last month . . . '

Feisal broke in. 'Last month the *Takfir wal Hijra* group, meaning Atonement and Holy Flight. They kidnapped a former cabinet minister as a hostage against the release of some *Takfir* prisoners. Sadat refused and they executed the minister. In his repression, Sadat killed six and wounded fifty-seven, then executed five of the 258 accused. Very well, you have a little learning.'

Blake could not mistake Feisal's point: if there was danger here, it was to himself.

'You were asking about stability.' He kept his voice as cool as Feisal's. 'At the trial, it turned out that *Takfir* had something like four thousand activists, spread through some of the most important sectors of Egyptian society, the middle classes, the students.' He had swung the Camaro past the Oil Ministry building in Jerusalem Road, and was pointing towards the old Arab residential quarter where Feisal had his house. 'You know better than I do what that means.'

'Did you know that the leaders of both those groups had been Muslim Brothers in their youth?' Feisal's tone was suddenly friendly, as if Blake had passed some preliminary test. 'Every member was trained and conditioned to be a *shahid*, a martyr, if necessary. What created such a sense of mission? The Egyptian political system is corrupt and inept. The West, Zionism and communism have defeated and humiliated it externally. Internally it has sold out to Western legal codes, and its leaders to Western life-styles, flouting the *Shari'a*, Islamic Law. Add to that Sadat's increasing flirtation with Israel, and all this on a base of poverty, disease, illiteracy. . . The Academy group thought they needed to wipe out only Egypt's leadership. The Atonement group saw their whole society as a new *Jahilíyya* – the grim period of idolatry, corruption and ignorance before Muhammed. Everything had to be ripped out and rebuilt.'

He turned one hand palm-upward in a gesture of stoic patience.

'Both of the groups you mentioned failed. My judgement is that they will be back, redoubled, they or their twins or their daughters. That colossal Pan-Islamic power is still latent there, as it is elsewhere. We must simply learn how to fire it, and direct it. We too need a *jihád*.'

'So you will win back your Palestine?'

'So we shall win back our Palestine!' said Ahmed Feisal, his grey eyes glittering. 'And much more. *Insh'Allah*! If God wills!'

'Much more?'

Feisal turned and stared at him arrogantly, evidently amazed at Blake's obtuseness.

'The whole of the Arab Middle East. The whole of the *Pan-Islamic* Middle East, including Iran! Whoever binds all that together, in final true Pan-Islamic unity, rules it! And puts us on the first step back to that epic majesty which we showed above all others in the Middle Ages! Back, *justly* to our real, our central role on the world's stage!'

Blake could feel the immense exhilaration bursting out of the man like a great naked charge of electricity. Get too near that, thought Blake, and it will sure as hell burn me! But the sheer swell of Feisal's ideas fascinated him.

He had drawn the car up now in front of Feisal's house. It faced right on the road, and after that that tepid opaque sea. The house had what passed for a garden at the front, mainly sand, but the building itself convinced. Single-storeyed, it looked big and strong, pure Arab, with thick stone walls that would keep it cool within, and cedarwood-beamed ceilings. Blake had never seen inside it. He was not that intimate with Feisal yet. He believed it contained a wife and two children. He might meet the children in due course, but the wife, Arabs being Arabs, would probably not be for a year or so, if ever.

'So why do you tell me all this?' he said. 'You want to recruit me?'

Ahmed Feisal looked square round at him.

'Maybe. Why not? When I met you first in Abdullah's office four years ago I felt you were a gambler. Not just for money. Much more with history, events. You like to move big things around, pull tricks on fate. And people. It's a solitary, privileged game. Well, I could guarantee you that. A really big game. So big it could rock the world. You could be part of history all right, of something no one would ever forget.'

'I'm flattered you think you could use me.'

'Oh,' said Feisal, 'we take and use what weapons come to our hand, you know. For as long as they serve, of course.'

Blake laughed.

'Well, it's an amusing thought. Tell me, speaking of weapons. You're a diligent man. D'you have training camps in the desert here for your Fatah terrorists? I know that you've a big military force already, to be taken seriously – that, for example, you already had some fifty thousand guerrillas trained in Jordan by 1970. Do you operate on the same sort of scale here?'

Feisal eyed him quizzically, and put his left forefinger to the side of his nose.

'I really think I need notice of that question, you know.'

'All right. Well, to think it's all really a matter of vengeance.'

'Perhaps not all,' said Feisal. 'But, yes, certainly partly. Against those Lebanese Christian butchers for what they did to my mother and sisters. That's an imperative, believe me. A moral obligation. And against the Israelis, for throwing us out of Palestine to cause that whole misery of refugee camps in the first place. Yes, it's certainly vengeance in part. An old Arab custom.'

'Oh. I don't belittle vengeance in any way,' said Blake. 'Not at all. I mean to take a pretty piece of it myself one of these fine days. Not here, of course. In London. An old friend.'

'Indeed?'

'Colleague, is better,' said Blake. 'In just over a year.'

'*Barakát*! said Feisal amiably. 'Blessings and good luck!'

22

A Vengeance

The six Managing Directors of the Board of the Eagle International Oil Company Limited sat at the elegant oval mahogany table in their twentieth-floor Board Room in Millbank and gazed simultaneously down at a single piece of paper. They looked transfixed. They might have been killed stone dead in their chairs there the instant before by a particularly efficient nerve-gas. It was hard even to see if they breathed. The timing was brilliant. This was the last working day of July 1978. The date on that single page, whose registered original the Ice Maiden held, the others photo-copies, was four days before. The text read simply:

> The Kingdom of the Sun, joint signatory with Eagle Oil International Ltd of the supply contract for 500,000 barrels a day (bd), later modified to 700,000 bd, of Sun Light 34 API Low Sulphur Crude Oil, dated October 22 1973 and effective November 1 1973 for five (5) calendar years at prices and under conditions of credit periodically determined by the Organization of Petroleum Exporting Countries (OPEC) hereby, in terms of Article 7.2(e) of that contract, gives notice of three (3) calendar months of its decision to terminate the contract as from midnight October 31 1978.
>
> Signed: Abdullah bin Ali bin Jibál,
> Minister of Oil.

All five of the other MDs turned as one man and stared at Van Straten at the head of the oval table. However silent, their indictment seemed absolutely categoric. Even his usually loyal-to-the-death acolytes, the Armenian-tinted Edward Poynter, and the hair-netted George Paul with the red fur on his fingers, looked at him with unqualified hostility. They could recognize the source of this lethal blow. The Ice Maiden had provoked that, and it could bankrupt Eagle and obliterate it from the face of the oil world. It was a cruel poetic justice. Against that cold blast of condemnation, Van Straten crouched very slightly into his posture of utter animal stillness. His full head of silver hair confronted them like a burnished casque. The vertical lines of muscle bracketing his mouth bulged and set rigid. His chill grey eye flung them back.

'This is *nothing*! We can ride this. As we've ridden *everything*. And come through –'

But that contempt was not biting now.

'I doubt that,' said Morgan Sperry quietly, high-browed, fine-featured, tough as tempered steel now. The Ice Maiden shot a glance of pure venom at him.

'Why, maybe this advice isn't even *legal*! Legally binding. Surely we can fight it?'

Sean O'Higgins beamed his monstrous mountain-ledge eyebrows on him.

'Come off it, Kobus! Their right to give three months' notice prior to termination is absolute and unreserved. As ours would be. They don't have to give any reasons. No, we can't fight it. We'd be laughed out of court!'

'This could hardly have happened at a worse moment,' said Morgan Sperry. 'That's seventy per cent of our total crude input gone in one swoop. And the world shortage of crude must go on for the next two or three years at least. I took a reading from the Foreign Office yesterday on Iran. They think it could blow at any time. They don't rule out a mass revolution, an entirely new Islamic State, under Islamic Fundamentalism. Iran's the second biggest oil producer in the Arab Gulf. Knock her out, even just disturb her gravely, and we can see further huge shortages of crude. Worse in absolute cash terms than even the disastrous 1973 to 1974 increases. In that context, trying to find a new 700,000 bd of suitable crude within three months is going to cost us an arm and a leg in premiums. Maybe two arms and two legs. Maybe our whole existence.'

'That swine,' said Van Straten, his hands, all his body deadly still, only his lips just moving, 'deliberately put us in that position of acute vulnerability! It was *he* who got us taking half our total crude offtake from the Kingdom of the Sun in the first place. And, more recently, displayed the devilish ingenuity of lifting that vulnerability from 500,000 to 700,000 bd!'

Edward Poynter, groomed and handsome as a film star, his temples exquisitely brushed with silver, rubbed his right fingernails on his left lapel, inspected them, then looked back at the Ice Maiden.

'We could of course still have had those 700,000 bd securely with us. If we'd kept him.'

At this, Poynter's first small betrayal of Van Straten, George Paul looked at him sharply. Yet, so far at least, no celestial thunderbolt had struck him down. Evidently keen to see if he could do that himself, Paul also glanced at Van Straten and said:

'An outstandingly good crude too, Sun Light, for our refinery patterns. Which of course almost certainly the next crude won't be. If we can find one.'

Van Straten looked away from him in disgust, and back at Sperry.

'Has this swine no loyalty at all to Eagle? Has no one tried to reach him, talk to him?'

'I did,' said Morgan Sperry. 'The moment you circulated this paper to us an hour before this meeting. I got through to the Oil Ministry in the City of the Sun almost at once. They were the soul of politeness. Regretfully Mr Blake was not in the country. No, no one knew just where he was. Or when he would be back. And the Minister? No, unfortunately Sheikh Abdullah was not available for comment. And that,' said Sperry succinctly, 'is that. We shall get no other answer whatever we do, and whomever we try to see. They will simply not go back on their decision.'

For a few instants, Van Straten had gone quite white. He might suddenly have been hearing eerie echoes.

'For God's sake!' he said then. 'Where on earth has it gone? You can't just switch off 700,000 bd of good crude like that from one day to the other! Who've they *sold* it to?'

Morgan Sperry looked back at him in silence for a while. Though as a very good Company man he must have seen this moment as most grave for Eagle, possibly fatal, yet it might seem that Sperry was very near to enjoying himself.

'It just might be Tulsa,' he said. 'There's their new refining capacity coming on stream at Rotterdam. Just a possibility, but it does make sense logistically.'

'Tulsa?' said Van Straten. He had gone very white again.

'Certainly it makes sense logistically,' murmured the sixth MD reverently. He had a scaly but benign quality, and looked thin and wizened behind his rimless glasses. It was Nel de Jonge. Unlike Paul and Poynter, he had in no way moved to betray his former boss. But he had too much reverence for the truth to avoid it now either.

'Well, said Morgan Sperry, 'we'd better start looking for alternatives. This is going to be a crippling, a murderously costly business.'

'So true is that,' said Sean O'Higgins, 'so grave the loss of our 700,000 bd Sun Light contract, that I think that without doubt this constitutes an emergency —'

To emphasize that, O'Higgins raised his two big broad-backed hands to the level of his shoulders, and his seamed face addressed the Ice Maiden like a cliff.

'— Therefore I propose that we urgently call an emergency General Shareholders' Meeting —'

That would be brutal, forcing the issue. That would want blood, demand that a head fall. Every one of the six men in that Board Room knew whose it would be. There was a serious flaw in this house. Sheer common sense, a wisdom as enshrined as the Old Testament's, required that it be rooted out. In his diligent and thoughtful manner of sapping away slowly at his enemy's foundations, Philip Blake had done a thorough job. Any Arab tribe would have been proud of him.

But not the Ice Maiden. For once this immaculate and superlatively disciplined gentleman had frayed a little at the edges, shown a palpable hint of humanity, in the form of sheer anguished human anger, a shriek against the utter injustice of gods and destiny:

'And no one can even tell me where the little bastard *is*!'

23
A House on Hydra

Blake and Leila were just getting off the Flying Dolphin hydrofoil, having left the small harbour of Zea, by Piraeus, an hour and forty minutes earlier. Blake had been in Greece with Leila before, in Athens and Crete and the magnificently primitive island of Karpathos near Rhodes, but this time he had something new to show her. Poros, the only other island at which the Dolphin had stopped en route that morning, had impressed her. She had gazed with delight at the pine-drenched slopes of this second Saronic Island, the high chapel bravely topping the clusters of houses on the small hill of the port, the narrow strait of a few hundred metres separating it from the Peloponnese mainland, and the crystal-clear waters along its beaches. Hydra, the third Saronic Island, first provoked precisely the opposite reactions. All she saw of it was rock.

This stark introduction was no accident. It was no bad policy to cast people down before you raised them high. That etched in dramatic depth to your subject. So Blake had taken Leila to the port side opening halfway along the hydrofoil's hull for her virgin glimpse of Hydra. The Russians who had built these craft had evidently not thought it essential that their passengers see where they were going, the portholes were frugal. Hydra lay two or three kilometres off, stretching some twenty-four kilometres east to west. It had the impact of a high blank wall. Hydra could have been the tip of an extended iceberg, or the iron-grey blade of a long half-submerged knife. It was obviously totally hostile to life. She could not see a tree upon it. Hydra was bald as a skull. It was bleak, uncompromising, forbidding. It kicked you in the crutch.

'*Walláhi*!' said Leila. 'God Almighty!'

Blake watched her with interest.

'Quite an effect, don't you think? Original.'

'It's all of *that*! You really bought a house *here*, Philip? I can't even see any *towns* on it, let alone trees!'

'Well, there's only Hydra itself, really, and a couple of small harbours either side of it. Nothing much else. And of course this eastern side of the island may look a trifle barren.'

'It may indeed,' said Leila, looking at the leaden cliffs which plummeted into the sea. 'But what have you done with Hydra port itself, then?'

'Oh. Well, you see that white tower up on that slope? That's a disused windmill just this side of it. Hydra port's stuck away behind it in a bay.'

'And your house?'

'Quite high above that. Leila, we'd better go in for the suitcases. When they say the hydrofoils touch at these ports, they mean touch. It's about thirty seconds.'

Their luggage was buried; the hydrofoil was full. When they had cleared it they were twelve from the head of the queue. There Leila could see little, save that they were in a harbour. The hydrofoil had dropped down full and awkwardly onto its hull now, like a fat skater falling flat on his face. Its port side slid to the quay, they tied up fast and the queue moved off. A scrum of passengers for Spetses and points west waited impatiently for them to disembark. Once well clear, Leila stopped with Blake on the cobbled quay and looked around.

'This is something else!' she exclaimed.

She saw the harbour as a hollow square, with Blake and herself at the low left corner. Hotels, bars, restaurants, gift shops lined the left quay; Hotels Delfini and Argo, Antonio's Bar, Hydrohous, Spaghetteria. At this late morning hour the many small tables in front of them were filled with tourists, sitting soberly around as though paid to do so; end July was peak of the season. Along the base of the harbour ran goldsmiths, grocers, a bakery, two banks, bookshops and more gift shops. Near the right end was the trim clocktower of a monastery. People strolled over that wide cobbled quay or sat at tables. Donkeymen stood with their beasts; the island's only commercial transport, said Blake; all motor transport was banned. Except for this first quay reserved for the hydrofoils and obese white cruise liners, all others, and the two long piers jetting into the harbour from the other side, were packed with seacraft, mainly luxury. There were yachts, motor-sailers, cabin-cruisers from almost every seafaring country, from an ocean-going 200-tonner with a small helicopter mounted aft to more usual craft of thirty feet. Their names sang a poetry: *Four Winds*, Barbados; *Scimitar*,

Tangier; *Martini Two*, Limassol; *Toby Jug*, Piraeus; *Alouette*, Marseille; *Albatross*, Nantucket; *Roaring Forty*, London; *The Cloud*, Valetta; *Life Song*, Plymouth. At the shimmering emerald level of the water, nets of sunlight spangled their hulls.

In front of the clocktower the cut of the seacraft changed. A flock of islanders' caiques were moored there. They were small deep-bosomed craft, single-masted, some with an austere cabin aft, like a cut-down sentry-box. Their decks curved up to the prow and stern. Often a high broad line of colour stressed this curve, just below deck level; red, blue, black or gold; a bold buoyant sweep that lifted the heart. But Leila stared most at the tall patrician houses at the other side of the harbour. They rose tier upon tier to the top of the hill. Their walls were stone-coloured or white or cream or light rose or astringent red. They were cubic and cubist, their windows very regularly patterned. Almost every shutter was a clean light blue. These houses were modest and understated, with good trees in their gardens, some the jets of cypresses, their beauty icy sharp, nearly black.

'Those too,' said Leila. 'Who built them?'

'The houses? Mainly shipowners, from the age of sail. You know Hydra has a strong naval tradition. The big grey building behind us is a famous Greek merchant marine academy. Though the Hydriots weren't always sailors. The first here were Albanians whom the Turks had flung off the mainland. These refugees had no idea about the sea. Then the Algerians raided here and took them off to work in their shipyards. When they were ransomed they came back and tried out what they'd learned. From there it was all one way. They became great sea-captains and traders, and pirates when it paid: good practice for the Wars of Independence against the Turks. That was Hydra's peak; Greece got her navy mainly from Hydra and Spetses. That's also why there are so few trees here – most went into building those warships. Then came the steel steamship. That killed Hydra. Now tourism's giving it a shot in the arm.'

'I can see why. That's a beautifully structured hill, for example. It's got terrific harmony.'

'Try the rest of the town. Look above the monastery. See how the buildings fall back, level upon level, like your shipowners' houses? My house is up there, behind the big red basilica. That was Kiafa, the first settlement here, round 1640. My house was in the first line, overlooking the port, where the invaders would probably have come from. Look half-left above the Spaghetteria too. It's the most recent part of Hydra, with just the same form, tiers upon tiers falling back, but always concentrating their look down at the centre of the port.'

'My God, a Greek amphitheatre!' cried Leila. 'Did they plan it like that?'

'Maybe not deliberately, just by intuition. But there indeed it is.'

'With a magnificent Chinese backdrop of hills behind it, range upon range, all circling, looking down, on this one distilled tiered place! Lovely!'

'Wait till I take you up to our Profiti Ilías Monastery,' said Blake, 'and the convent close by. They're high up over the shoulder of that hill in front, at nearly two thousand feet. You get fine views from there.'

'And no motor vehicles on the island by law? What bliss!'

'Save for two to collect the rubbish.'

A wiry small man bore down on them on a large donkey, towing two others. He looked windswept, with a leathery wrinkled face, cropped white hair, and piercing blue eyes. He rode sidesaddle.

'*Kyrie Philip!*' he said smiling, and dismounted. He took Blake's hand.

'Leila, Cristo, my donkeyman. Cristo, *mia fili mou.*'

'*Kalóstone!*' said Cristo, and to Blake: '*Sto spiti sas?*'

'*Né, parakaló,*' said Blake, and Cristo loaded their suitcases onto his second donkey and sprang back side saddle onto the first. '*Misi ora,*' he announced, over his shoulder.

'*Endáksi.*'

Blake added to Leila: 'Meaning that the lad will have our bags up there for us in half an hour.' And he led her up the steps just after the clocktower, past the Three Brothers taverna and into narrow cobbled alleys of hundreds of steps, happily gradual. The houses on either side were clean and crisp, rarely more than two storey; the architectural controls were strict. Leila saw churches and chapels everywhere. A donkey's bray floated across the warm air, full of humanity, stoic chant to the pains of survival. They climbed for thirteen minutes.

'There!'

A lateral cobbled path. The house was left, across open ground. It was white, cubic, of two storeys, with a red tiled roof. A high stone wall, an elegant white stripe along its top, circled round and down well in front of it, following the contours. Leila was sweating heavily.

'Quiet, isn't it?' said Blake with pride. 'The tourists never get up here.'

'I can see why.'

The path twisted up behind the house. Blake opened the wooden main door. They walked onto the terrace. It stretched for twelve metres, by six broad. They stood at the far edge.

It was like riding on a magic carpet. Leila saw straight ahead the tip of the hill that had mesmerized her in the port, where the chaste patrician mansions scrambled. She saw it now from due south, six hundred metres off, a white chapel crowning it. To its right the hill fell steeply into Hydra port. To its left it swooped, held its breath at the fat white carcass of a windmill, then plunged again. Past the hill she could see an eight-kilometre band of very blue sea, then the long coast of the Peloponnese.

'The small bay there, down to the left under the windmill?'

'Kaminia,' said Blake, 'a fishing village. That's a chapel on its island, not a house. And about due west is Vlichós Island, another chapel on it, another fishing village opposite. You've noticed the many chapels? We've more than two hundred to a fixed population of three thousand; a chapel to every two or three families. The Devil has a hard time to win a soul here.'

She laughed. Indeed, from that point she could see fifteen crosses. Other shapes were as incisive. Most of the cubic, two-storeyed houses were emphatically white, a few stone-coloured. All had brown or light red tiles. The basilicas' octagonal towers were a tart brick red. The trees were bushy, deep green, the upwards penstrokes of the cypresses eloquent. The open ground was dark with grey rock or gold with scrub. A cliff of leaden rock fell sheer from the hilltop chapel. The midday light prickled life into every surface. It was a painter's light, infusing a glow into everything. The whole scene was cubism again, mordant, and exhilarating unity. Leila could have burst into song.

'But I'm hot,' she said. 'Can I shower before we see the house?'

'Of course. The little white shed there, carrying my trellis and vine.'

The shower was white-tiled and neat, the hot water instant. Afterwards she turned it dead cold. The fine icy needles probed her skin, massaged her. She came out tingling.

Blake had opened the house's front door. The hall's floor was painted a brilliantly shiny white, as stimulating as the shower. He met her there.

'Let me show you downstairs first. It's the historic part.'

An acrobatic wooden staircase, evidently an afterthought, led them down to a big hall with the well-like top of a cistern in the far right corner. She rapped on its wooden hatch. It boomed impressively, and echoed Blake's voice when he spoke.

'Useful as a reserve,' he said. 'Hydra has to get most of its water from the mainland, from a waterboat. It can break down or go mad.'

'And this?'

'The second entrance. Certainly the original one. It takes you out just in front of the neighbours, by the arch you saw.'

She saw that Hydra's mania for sculptured tiers reigned here too. This floor was not just split-level, but double that. Blake turned left and went down three steps and past a door to the right: 'The second loo and shower.'

Past this level's gleaming white floor, Blake dived down three more steps. Another glowing white plaque, two windows like arrowslits in the thick wall, the same luminous view of the valley, hilltop, and far sea. 'That bed's for any third guest or couple,' said Blake informatively.

'The fireplace works?'

'Sure. Build your fire in the back left-hand corner. And the kitchen's behind you.'

'I like your shelves hanging on cords. And the black-creosoted ceiling beams.'

'It was built to last, like a bunker. That back wall's dug right into the hill. And the beams are cedarwood.'

She liked the prints on the walls too; Gauguin, Van Gogh, Seurat, Modigliani.

'So nearly four hundred years old,' said Blake. 'Upstairs is a mere upstart, only two hundred. But come and see.'

He showed her the small second bedroom off the upstairs hall, then the main room, tall and spacious. The ceiling was some five metres high, the sea wall seven wide, the other nine. Two big windows looked to the sea, and one east. The walls were whitewashed, the floor glittering shiny white, with two matched Bokhara rugs in dark sparkling reds. Most of the prints here were *fauves*; Matisse, Derain, Van Dongen, Vlaminck, Rouault. A seascape in oil a metre and a half wide by a metre by an expatriate island painter, Motley, dominated the base wall, its clouds pink-edged, subtle, and evocative. The room's left wall twisted left halfway and ran two metres to the west outer wall. The double bed there looked straight out of the sea wall's left window.

'*Walláhi*! Waking here would be like looking straight into the eye of God!'

'Long may you so commune,' said Blake. 'We ought to baptize that!'

He was back in a minute with long-stemmed tulip-shaped crystal glasses and a two-litre bottle misted with cold.

'Retsina?'

'No, aretsínato; I buy it in bulk. A good neighbour turns on my fridge downstairs and stocks it lightly before I come. He holds my spare set of keys, should you ever come again alone. By the arch. So *Prost*!'

'*Prost*, indeed! Philip, I love your house. This island. Let's plan our day!'

'Well, I could walk you across to Vlichós. It's about four kilometres due west. We can lunch at a taverna there, by the sea. Then come back along the coast to one of the small hidden bays. We can swim naked there.'

'Marvellous!'

'First I'll shower too, quickly.'

As he rose, Cristo arrived with the cases. Blake paid him, and then took a shower while she unpacked. After that, they took the lateral path west. It ran first through arched houses. Its cobbles were set solid, as polished as mannequins' fingernails. Marigula stood in her grocery's doorway on the left, arms akimbo. Marigula presided, short in black, adamant as olive-wood, her eyes pandaed by pouches, her cheeks flecked by the black-brown freckles of age. She looked at Blake wisely, she smiled benignly.

'*Paw isoon, Kyrie Philip?*'

'*Sto Kolpo Araviko, Kyria Marigula.*'

'And how long will you stay this time?'

'Fifteen days, God be thanked! And this is my friend, Leila.'

'*Yásas!*' said Marigula shaking her hand. 'She looks a fine lady.'

'So she is,' said Blake. '*Adío.*'

'*Adío.*'

In two hundred metres they stood at an arrowhead above a sharp falling stream of steps. At the sea to their right, iron hills met like pyramids colliding. They enclosed the small bay of Kaminia.

'We'll walk back through there tonight.'

Blake led down. The steps levelled out past a church with a bent iron cross; a stone from Satan's sling, perhaps. They left the town's outskirts, and were between Hydra's few tilled fields, a sheep pen, a goat pen. Whorled and tormented olive trees scrawled the sparse lines of their signatures across this barren land. They passed a cemetery on their left. To their right across a field was a chapel. Its sharp walls ached white. The hills blocked off the sea. Leftwards they rose steeply, salted with scrub, contours of iron-grey rock and boulders running through them like sinews.

'It's harsh land,' she said.

He glanced round at her.

'It's very old land,' he said. 'Up there left's Mount Ere, over six hundred metres, nearly two thousand feet. A Mycenaean outpost looked out from high up there once. That puts the first human life here thousands of years BC. And it has its own old evil. *Shaitaan* lurks here too. At night in the hills you can feel him. And early you can sometimes find very odd patterns of branches and stones on these paths – I run early quite often to Vlichós. Animistic voodoo, perhaps. Black magic.'

Long stone-set steps downwards, caves in the hill to the left. Ahead a great V and the sea. A huge rock, shaped like a monstrous whale, reared up out of it kilometres away. 'Dokos,' said Blake. 'Crusaders built a castle on it.' They came to Vlichós, through a high moth-eaten arch over a ravine which fanned out then into a wide pebbled beach. To the left a line of houses drove down to the sea. Halfway along a giant banner read TAVERNA VLICHÓS. Three caiques were drawn up at the left of the beach, their decks curved like string bows and edged in red. A fourth floated fifteen metres out, at the sea's first colour change from light to darker blue. Its mast tickled like a metronome on the tide. They smelt the sea.

'Our taverna's just round the corner to the left,' said Blake.

They sat in the sun above the crystal-clear water of a jetty and tiny bar. A huge taciturn Greek served them *kalamares* and a Greek salad and a kilo carafe of draft retsina, slightly warm. The small squids were succulent under their fried bread-crumb coating. They drank small cups of strong Greek coffee, then walked east across the pebbles past the three stranded caiques and the wild one that floated free. Gold-brown nets were spread out in the sun. They climbed the sharp gorse-tufted hill to a stone-walled rampart. From here, sixty metres up, they could see far along the northern edge of this rock island. A narrow rocky path ran east. In places the cliff fell sheer to small bays held like rough-cut jewels between giant slabs and blocks and shattered white pillars of rock. The sea was calm, ice-clear.

Two hundred metres along Blake led her down left, over a ridge of tilled land, then over a coarse wall into grey-white rock and gorse, and down again round left in a steep descent. They were in a small bay held in by near-vertical rock walls.

'You can swim or sunbathe naked here all you want,' he said. 'No one can see you from the path unless you swim far out.'

She stepped to the edge. Someone had set a line of rocks here, perhaps to stop the sea scouring out the tiny metre-wide beach. The water was deep enough for you to dive straight in. It was a very light emerald, shading to aquamarine, and so transparent that it was almost radiant. It could have had its own internal sources of light.

'Swim now?'

She looked round. 'Why not?'

Blake had stripped. He stood tall and muscled and teak-brown, he swam and water-skied a lot in even the Kingdom's ominous sea. The white slash of skin at his hips bisected him. She saw the gold V of his pubic hair, darker than the hair on his head. Leila stripped too, and took off her flat platinum necklace and her four-carat diamond ring. She stood companionably naked with him, slimmer and far slighter, but her olive-brown perfect all over.

'It's a sheer joy here,' she said, almost purring. 'It's like your Eden!'

Blake laughed and turned and dived in. He came up and swam. She saw the water polish his brown shoulders. She dived in too. The water embraced her sweetly as another skin. She swam out vigorously, sleek as a seal, really using her feet, not just trailing them after her like tired kids in a park. The sea-bottom dropped away starkly to dark blue depths. She could see down surprisingly far. A scuba-diver down there with his mask would see forty metres easily.

She and Blake swam back together. The hot sun dried them on the flat rocks.

'Retsina? Nice and iced for the picnic?'

'How did you manage that?' she asked, marvelling.

Blake leant over to his small blue back-pack and pulled out the four frosted half-litre Kourtaki retsina bottles, capped like beer, and two paper cups. He set three of the bottles in a cool rock-pool in the shade, then came back and opened the fourth with his Swiss Army penknife. He poured.

'Cheers!'

'*Prost!*'

The pine-tang of the resin leached her tongue. It went with the sea and the sun. She and Philip Blake lay together face down on the hot flat rocks, like survivors reviving. After the second bottle of retsina they lay gently in each other's arms. They made love passionately under the splendid hot sun. Their naked limbs threshed on the hot flat rocks. They were like long wet fish just landed. Afterwards the cool sea took them. They hung above its dark blue infinities.

After one such swim as they lay contentedly on the hot rocks she asked him:

'Philip, you've been just on a year with us full-time now, in the Kingdom of the Sun. How are you liking it? And us?'

He turned on his left elbow towards her, frowning slightly.

'Fine. An oil ministry's quite a powerful weapon. Though my *really* hard work was done in my first few months from August last year. You know, to convince Tulsa Oil International to take Eagle's 700,000 bd of Sun Light on a five-year-renewable contract from November 1 this year, and to convince Abdullah that Tulsa would prove at least as good a customer as Eagle; and to keep the whole deal top-secret until we sent Eagle our registered three-month notice of termination last week. Well, all that's clear now, *Elkhamdulillah*! I'd like to see Van Straten's face at this very moment!'

'Yes, that's a vengeance worthy of a true Arab! It's quite a victory. But, having achieved that, you don't see anything really challenging enough left in the Oil Ministry to keep you fully stretched now?'

'Oh, I expect I'll still find that there's a tremendous lot to do,' said Blake, not very heartily.

It was precisely because he believed that that would *not* be true that Blake had added a twist to the new Tulsa contract that he had told nobody about except the enchanted Ahmed Feisal. This twist was that Tulsa, as well as paying the Kingdom of the Sun the standard OPEC price for their 700,000 bd of Sun Light from this November 1, just three months off now, would also, anyway for the first five years of the contract, pay ten cents a barrel or $2.6 million a year to a numbered bank account in Switzerland, to which only Feisal would have access for his PLO-Fatah purposes. Tulsa, in a world still obsessionally persuaded that oil was going to be critically short for many years forward, was only too delighted to pay this secret fee.

By this move Blake, to whom the skilful and subtle management of large vital organizations and forces was probably the prime passion in his life, had thrown a bridge forward to a dark world of subversion and terrorism, which he could explore should he wish to go beyond his present eminently productive work. The world of PLO-Fatah resistance was bubbling. Sadat had made his fantastic trip in an unarmed aircraft to Jerusalem on November 19 the year before and offered Israel peace in his Knesset speech the next day. From July 18 of this year of 1978 Egypt and Israel had been busy negotiating in the strongly protected Leeds Castle in England. From that would come accords, Blake guessed, by which Egypt would get back the Sinai and in return not insist too toughly that Israel get out of the Palestinian Arabs' West Bank and Gaza Strip. Also, Israel had invaded Southern Lebanon on March 14 this year, ostensibly in reprisal for a raid by an eight-man Fatah commando that caused thirty-seven deaths. The Israelis had invaded with 25,000 troops and killed some eight hundred Lebanese and Palestinians and razed many villages. Despite Security Council Resolution 425 five days later, they had not withdrawn until June 13, after cocking myriad snoots at Assad's regular Syrian troops stationed within Lebanon who failed to fire a single shot against them, and after leaving Major Haddad's pro-Israeli and Israeli-equipped militia securely in command of the southern strip of Lebanon bordering Israel. Meanwhile the fighting in Beirut between the mainly Syrian Arab Deterrent Force and Lebanese Muslims on the one hand, and Christian Lebanese on the other, had grown really vicious, the Phalangists carving out a full-blooded mini-republic in the east of the city. Blake was sure that giant political events were shaping in the Middle East.

'Do you think that you will settle in our Kingdom for always now?' asked Leila, sleek in her olive-brown beauty on her hot flat rock.

'Why not?' said Blake. 'It's been just about perfect so far, working on and bringing off that contract switch from Eagle to Tulsa. Seeing you socially quite often. And learning your country a little.'

Blake had made a point of doing that as thoroughly as he could. He had visited almost every square metre of the small kingdom, gone falconing often with Abdullah in the desert, and ridden there long days with him on his horses. He had befriended the craftsmen who built their fine curved wooden hulls for the dhows that would sail to Zanzibar and Dar es Salaam. He also regularly studied his Arabic at the university's evening classes. Blake loved the language. He found a splendid architectonic grace and balance in it, like that in Islam itself, whose very austerities, its deserts and Bedu and falcons and solitary far-sailing dhows, its Koranic disciplines and month-long Ramadhan fasts, its sharp silhouettes of vaulting domes of mosques and minarets, had their own clean grave appeal and beauty.

'Well, I've thought it before,' said Leila. 'You'll make a pretty good Arab.'

Blake smiled. 'The only drawback,' he said, 'is not being

able to make love to you there. Still, one shouldn't ask for too much. And our trips away like this have been marvellous. *Elkhamdulillah*.'

'There *would* be one way we could make love there, of course,' said Leila.

Blake looked at her and refilled her cup with retsina from the third bottle. 'Oh yes,' he said, without amplification.

Blake might be in love with Islam, but not to the point of negating his own hard-won identity. He was not religious, but he instinctively and categorically resisted any idea of becoming a Muslim. For of course he knew what Leila meant. In the *Dar el Islam*, House of Islam, a Muslim man could marry a girl of any religion, be she Christian or Jewish or whatever. There was no truck with feminine rights in this respect in Islam. It was the man who wore the trousers, or dishdasha. He ruled the roost, whatever his religion. So if he was *not* Muslim but wanted to marry a Muslim girl, he had first to become a Muslim himself. However deeply and genuinely Blake loved Leila, he would not go that far. Blake still had big things to do, within his own stature.

So they swam and swam again that afternoon, resting between on those amiable rocks. They spaced the rest of the retsina out intelligently across the hours. It gave them a small lasting ecstasy, stippled with sleep. They stayed until the sun began to set in that small bay.

Then they climbed the steep rock, and back over the tilled shoulder to the path, turning left onto it. It clung loyally to the iron-grey cliff at that height. At times Leila's eyes pierced vertically down into the water. The evening glow suffused it. It was lapis lazuli and chaste. You could fall here to a fine death, she thought. That crystal water would bear you up intact forever, immortal as a bee in amber.

Round a granite bend Kaminia broke on their sight. It was a frozen burst of sharp white cubes, ranged in stiff diagonals which dived into the sea, and spiked with cypresses. A pebble beach left held a few late bathers. A breakwater guarded the miniature harbour. Fifteen newly painted caiques were moored in it muttering at their ropes. Gold fishing-nets dried on the harbour wall. The path sloped up again and after five hundred metres curved round the last bay before Hydra Port. Here ramparts were set high. Long black cannon impaled their embrasures, surveying. The path looked over them and huge boulders below. There were concrete steps and slabs here for bathers, by clear deep water. A late hydrofoil bumbled by in the middle distance, a long yellow-blue slug on squat stilts.

Round the corner to the right into the port, Leila stopped at the impact. There was the whole hollow square of the harbour, the serried hills embracing it. The twilight was a live force. It injected a glow into the whole scene. Boats filled the port, many fully lit. The main pier began at Leila's left, going straight out. She saw a neat cabin-cruiser of some 37 feet, white; *The Baron*, of Valetta. A trim silver-haired man in a swimsuit was up on the flying-bridge, a striking Nordic blonde seated in the stern; perhaps the two came with the boat on purchase. She saw shops to the right, Lagoudera Greek Art, Midas Gold. The shops and bars and tavernas were lit all round the harbour, a wide body of silver light at ground level, under the darkened buildings and high hills. That, with the twilight, gave an extraordinary upwards surge. Blake and she might have stood before some gigantic spacecraft just about to take off.

They strolled on round the harbour, glancing in at the shop windows, reading the faces of the many people in the fluid silver light. At the far corner Blake led her up a cobbled alley past the Flying Dolphin office to an arrowhead. A notice said: Bill's Bar.

'Where the smart set meets,' said Blake. 'I'm not one of them. I had a hard enough time as it was, keeping up with my ex-wife's set.'

'What happened to her?' asked Leila.

He shrugged. 'Her lover left her. But she'll survive, of course. She has her passion for fashion.'

He took Leila into the bar, and they ordered iced white *aretsínatos*. He presented her to Bill, of medium height, neat, a composed fifty with iron-grey hair. He was genial. Blake pointed out some of the island's good painters at the bar; Anthony Kingsmill, a genius when he wanted; Bill Parnell and Mario the Cypriot, always good. They went out, turned left.

The alley narrowed. Shops dropped out of it. They crossed an open cobbled square. Abruptly they were out into a cobbled courtyard twenty-five metres wide by twenty. Three large bushy trees occupied it. Three metres up their branches spread widely, and were cunningly roped together for a roof. Across was a large cubic building, with above the doorway TAVERNA DOUSKOS. A big plate glass window like a fish tank to the left displayed liquors and Greek wines in variety.

Blake led her between the tables to the building. Inside were two vast glass counters holding the evening's menu; in Greece you ate what you saw and chose. There was lobster, red mullet, souvlaki, lamb on the spit, boiled meat balls with rice, bifteki and mousaka. They chose red mullet and *salata horyátiki* and went out to a table to wait for it. There Blake ordered a dry white Santa Laura 1973, ice-cold. It was welcome as the cool luminous water of the little bay. It lasted a third of the way into the red mullet. They turned then to a Cellar Leiko, rather drier. Afterwards they walked mellowly across the lap of the town, and past the green park in front of the Hotel Xenia Palace. Two guitarists sat on the balcony of the taverna to the right, singing *bouzoukias* sadly to the diners. Long after, when they were far up the hill, Leila could still hear their voices and guitars.

So they came back to Blake's house. He opened the terrace door and they walked to its outer edge. It was utterly quiet. They could hear nothing from the port. They saw the web of sparse lights in and across the valley, and beyond them the far lights on the Peloponnese coast, from the Hydra Beach resort, and the glow in the sky from the town of Ermione, twenty kilometres to the north-west. Lights sprayed statically in the band of Aegean sea too, probably from Hydra fishing-boats. Instinctively Leila looked up behind her. The hill above was completely dark.

'Here no one overlooks us,' said Blake. 'The only building there is a church. It's like our little bay after Vlichós.'

But she shivered, looking over her shoulder into the heavy darkness.

'Such an old island,' she said, 'of such beauty. But certainly with evil in it.'

'Yes,' he said. 'It's old. And there's evil, yes. But then surely there's evil everywhere –'

For some while they gazed down together into the darkness, between the thin scatter of lights. Then he said, apparently apropos of nothing:

'I wonder what Ahmed Feisal's doing now?'

She looked round and up at him.

'These Palestinian Arabs,' she said, 'they can be very complex men.'

'Complex indeed,' said Blake, for once misreading her. 'I find him fascinating.'

Blake waited a week before he phoned Morgan Sperry and learned of the Emergency Shareholders' General Meeting on the subject of Eagle's dramatic forfeiture of its Sun Light supply contract, the crippling costs it was having to suffer to replace it, and the resulting loss of market position which would probably prove permanent. The net issue, Sperry said, was that Kobus van Straten had resigned. He had done that without hesitation, with great dignity. One had had the conviction, Sperry told him, that there, whatever his faults, went a truly great man. And he went forever, for if you left the élite oil command at that celestial international level, you virtually never came back.

That might be, thought Blake, but the consequences, as he saw them, were hardly tragic. They were that Morgan Sperry was now Chairman of the Eagle Board, and Sean O'Higgins his deputy.

Typically, one of the first things that Sperry had done in his new Olympian position was to give the so-far ill-fated Jimmy Byrd, whom Van Straten had reduced to nothing after the Falcon Aviation fiasco in Beirut, a second chance. He had named Byrd Eagle's manager in Tanzania. It was a smaller post than Beirut, but at least it was a step back upwards. Jimmy Byrd had finally got his own command back, and consequently his pride and dignity as a man.

If I have done no other good work in my life, thought Blake, I should go down with a plus sign in the grudging divine accounting for this. Still, though he had hated him most frankly, he was secretly rather sorry to see the Ice Maiden ejected. Blake would really miss him from his universe. No one could deny that Kobus van Straten was a man of heroic proportions, even if he had something of that chill lethal touch of the perfectionist. After all, thought Blake, someone like Ahmed Feisal had that too . . .

PART FOUR

24
Reflections of a Southern Baptist

'We can only pray to God,' boomed Horace B. Murgatroyd, pointing his right forefinger upwards into the Kingdom of the Sun's night sky to clarify his meaning to even the dumbest amongst his huge audience, 'that this vicious and bloody war between your sister Arab nations Iraq and Iran, at each other's throats for five murderous months now, may be brought swiftly and mercifully to a close. Do we not all agree?'

The several hundred men and women gathered at the feet of the virgin US Ambassador in the vast gardens of the US Embassy in the City of the Sun this National Day of March 1 1981 roared back to him politely in assent. The Kingdom of the Sun was militarily too small a power to be able to usefully intervene in the conflict anyway, so this virtuous expression of moral disapproval was as apt a reaction as any. Blake could see almost everyone he knew in the Kingdom in this crowd, all the Western ambassadors and those from Russia and Mainland China, the heads of the various UN Missions, those of the main commercial concerns and of all the government ministries and important departments.

'Iranians are not Arabs,' said Ahmed Feisal audibly.

Blake stood in a small group with him and Abdullah and Leila bin Ali bin Jibál. They, and the hundreds of other guests, could not have avoided listening to Horace B. Murgatroyd even if they had tried, for three lines of *Shemsi* troops, mostly brawny Bedu from the desert, pinned them in away from the Embassy entrance, over the wide lawns and ornamental paths, and against the broad stairway up to the Embassy's main doors, in front of which stood the horn-rimmed Ambassador, concentrating heavily on the lamp-lit lectern before him which contained his somewhat emotional but certainly beautifully cadenced speech. However obviously Horace loved his own ornate speeches, there was clearly a practical side to him which admitted the rare possibility that others might not. Hence his use of the *Shemsi* troops as a *cordon sanitaire*. It was like the Israelis' wily use of Major Haddad's militia in the southern strip of the Lebanon bordering Israel, the only difference being that the Israelis thereby intended to keep Fatah and other Arab terrorists from getting into their premises, while Horace's purpose was to stop his guests from getting out.

His choice of these *Shemsi* troops was astute. They were clearly picked men, tall and lean and trim from hard physical training. There was thus no doubt that they could do the job. They were also dramatically satisfying, adding richly to the spectacle. They wore smart dark khaki-drill uniforms, the tunics short-sleeved and open-necked and their gold buttons brilliant, the creases knife-edged in pants that went down neatly into highly polished supple black paratroopers' boots. The black leather belts round their waists and straps over their left shoulders were as shiny. They wore red-and-white chequered *kefiyyahs* on their heads, held down by the black rings of *ogals*, like the Bedu troops of Jordan's crack Arab Legion. They were a spick-and-span military force. Only their main equipment seemed odd at first sight. For they all carried Scottish bagpipes. The Kingdom of the Sun, like say Kuwait, had once had a British Imperial Presence. In each case, the British regiments had included Scots and their pipers, and by some strange Celtic affinity the Arabs in both countries had leapt at once to the skirl of the pipes, drawing it to their bosoms and making it their own, buying their own bagpipes and training their own best men up in playing them; thus had British Imperial culture immortalized itself yet again. These might seem strange weapons with which to repel boarders or hold back itinerant escapees, but just in case they needed more conventional support each *Shemsi* piper also carried a polished black holster on the right side of his belt which held a 9 mm Browning automatic pistol with two spare filled magazines. These three smart lines of stalwart men stood now silently At Ease as Horace droned on.

'Of course nothing is ever really new in the Middle East,' thundered Horace, demonstrating his extensive one month's experience of the region. 'This blazing war, with its shocking casualty figures on both sides, stems as you know from

Saddam Hussein's taking of power in Iraq in July 1979, and his break, together with King Hussein of Jordan, away from Assad's branch of Baath socialism in Syria –'

Horace pronounced the world socialism as though it tasted like gall in his mouth, but even he desisted from being really rude about Assad, Russia's major client in the area; remarkably, Russia's Ambassador had come to the party too.

'This break of Saddam Hussein of Iraq from Syria led in turn to grave friction between Iraq and the new revolutionaries in Iran, then to this bloodbath of open war. Now, these new revolutionaries in Iran –'

Horace, momentarily overcome, breathed heavily and raised his head from his papers and stared gloomily through his pebble lenses at his large audience instead. His stertorous breathing whistled eerily over the loudspeakers set strategically about the gardens.

'– are those who in the first days of 1979, just over two years ago, threw out the Shah, that world figure whose prime objective was to modernize and Westernize his potentially great country as fast as he could –'

'Too fast,' said Feisal, 'and too drastically. And he had other less palatable objectives too. Like building up a fabulous personal wealth outside his country.'

Abdullah glanced at him warningly.

'That has changed the whole balance of power in the Middle East,' Horace boomed on, 'and indeed in the entire world. This with Ayatollah Khomeini in command, is the first fully Islamic State in modern times. The first to be ruled totally and without exception by Islamic Law. A formidable concept,' commented Horace, looking around suspiciously from side to side, his almost cubic head rolling on the almost non-existent bull neck set into thick shoulders, as if trying to smell out anyone idiotic enough to try to contradict him, 'in the sense that, whatever these Iranian revolutionaries have done to American capital engaged there, or to our Tehran Embassy staff – and this has sometimes appeared unbearable to the civilized eye – yet they have displayed a dedication to their new cause, a total commitment, an almost laughing readiness to sacrifice their lives for it in, for example, their human-wave attacks from boys of from fourteen or fifteen up upon the well-armed and efficient Iraqi lines, such that we should be certifiably mad were we not to take due account of this colossal phenomenon and act accordingly –'

Clearly Horace himself was not going to be certified mad on this score, thought Blake, for Horace was now bowed spectacularly forward over his lectern, the gravity of the situation heavily upon him. Yet neither Blake nor anyone else in the audience smiled at this exaggerated but apparently instinctive mime. Horace was too massive to be merely comic. There was, rather, something monolithic and ominous about him. He was a big man, heavy-shouldered, barrel-chested, thick-thighed; it was the body of a weight-lifter in the top divisions. His hair was grey, cropped so close that he appeared nearly bald. Under that bullet brow his slate-grey eyes could move about amazingly swiftly, his head often not following them, but staying set rock-steady. He could look then like some cornered and extremely dangerous animal; a wild boar, say, a rhino, a buffalo.

'I detect a note near admiration in his voice,' said Feisal more quietly. 'Can it be that we have here an American Ambassador who actually approves of Islamic Fundamentalists?'

'He's a Southern Baptist, remember,' said Blake. 'From Alabama or some such. So he probably knows all about puritanical disciplines.'

'He's not a professional diplomat?' asked Feisal.

'Not a chance!' said Blake. 'I heard he was among the first of Reagan's purely pork-barrel nominations. He was a supermarket baron, but always a very staunch Republican too, with a lot of active interest behind the scenes in City Hall, and always ready to back up his preferences with thick wads of dollars. He could afford to; he's a millionaire many times over.'

'We must be able to face up to these huge new movements in the world's history,' said the Southern Baptist multi-millionaire stoutly. 'Those of us here tonight who are from my country are come to help you in any way we can to do that, to maintain our western Chris– our Western form of civilization, and I of course include in my definition here your, ah, *advanced* culture in the Kingdom of the Sun, with your enlightened and excellent Amir and Crown Prince and Amir-appointed cabinet, and your, ah, semi-elected National Assembly –'

'*Semi* is right,' whispered Feisal into Blake's ear.

It was indeed, Blake knew. The hundred members of the National Assembly had all to be pure *Shemsis*, graduates at least of high schools but preferably universities, and owners of significant property. The list of candidates for the four-yearly elections had moreover to be fully approved by the Amir. That left the Assembly's role in governing mainly cosmetic and rubber-stamp. The true power stayed in the hands of the Amir and Crown Prince and the cabinet or other counsellors whom they summoned. This group took all key decisions in their diwanías – the word came from the Persian divan – in the Amir's or Crown Prince's palaces. They sat round on cushions or the rich carpets of a room with their backs against the walls and drank Arab tea or coffee, and they ran the Kingdom's business in astonishing detail and with remarkable efficiency. It was just the State's good luck, thought Blake, that some of these counsellors were of the very high standard of Abdullah, with his close personal links with the Royal family.

'You-all will know,' said Horace B. Murgatroyd heavily, 'that we always see our friends right in the end. Even if –' and he stared down at his audience through his powerful pebble-lenses – 'it sometimes takes us a while. As it has taken us four hundred and forty-four days to achieve the release of our fifty-two hostages from their imprisonment in Tehran in November 1979. Still, we have *got them all out*, unharmed –'

'Not the happiest of examples, I would have thought,' whispered Ahmed Feisal. 'After the disastrous failure of the American rescue attempt by helicopter, that James Bond fiasco!'

Horace peered down at his lamplit notes.

'And I think we can justly claim some successes. The announcement of our prior President's highest diplomatic feat, the Camp David Accords, on September 17 1978. And President Sadat of Egypt's actual *signature* of his peace treaty with Israel on March 26 the next year – by which both he and Mr Begin of Israel won the Nobel Peace Prize, most fairly and I think honourably. Of such achievements surely we can be proud?'

The question-mark in his voice, thought Blake, was unfortunate.

'Doesn't he realize,' said Feisal *sotto voce* by him, 'that the

Egyptian-Israeli peace treaty is not widely popular round here? No Israeli withdrawal from East Jerusalem. No clear concession to Arab rights in the West Bank and Gaza Strip. This same Sadat that let the Americans use Egypt as a springboard for their punctured Boy Scout helicopter raid on Iran, a sister Muslim republic!'

Blake noted that Abdullah and Leila had edged away somewhat from the highly critical Ahmed Feisal. He also noticed that he himself had instinctively stayed. Feisal's barbed commentary amused him. Blake was drawn to the man, with his perfect features and neat small white teeth and faultless English and quick sophisticated wit.

'All right,' he said quietly, talking back to Feisal for the first time, conniving implicitly with him, accepting the half-glances from the slight stiffening in the postures of Abdullah and Leila towards him; Feisal was after all proving the more stimulating, the more seductive, anyway for the moment. 'But you've paid him back in full measure, haven't you? In terms of your Baghdad Summit, once he'd signed the treaty you flung Egypt out of the Arab League, transferred its centre from Cairo to Tunis, and boycotted any Egyptian organizations that worked with Israel. And your League voted $3.5 *billion* a year to your front-line states against Israel – of which your PLO has been getting a good share –'

'Fair,' said Feisal, and smiled, and turned back to Horace.

'. . . mission,' Horace was saying. 'We in the United States of America know that we have a huge responsibility for maintaining and promoting peace in all the world in our time. A *fair* peace. And democracy,' he added hurriedly. 'We recognize and fully assume that responsibility. We have these world-shaking events. The bloody, the momentous revolution in Iran. We're fully aware of that, let no one mislead you. We know. We have our mission – '

'But where does it take us?' asked Feisal. 'What is it?'

'– The murderous carnage of that revolution,' thundered Horace, 'has as I say changed the whole balance of power in the Middle East. From it a new and most formidable force has appeared, perhaps the most dedicated, disciplined and dangerous of any in the world today. It could destroy us all if we do not learn how to come to terms with it. That force is –'

Horace halted, and stared down at his audience, his broad

and powerful hands open and raised to a level with his shoulders, so that it was as if a battery of three square white faces gazed down emphatically now. Horace could have been a born Deep Southern Baptist minister too. Blake could see how raptly the people listened to him. Horace had snared them with his rhythms, stunned them with his sudden thunderings, enthralled them with his abrupt silences, as now. Horace, he thought, could have raised a pretty bloody riot himself, tumbled a monarchy, masterminded a lynching – '

'– the Islamic Fundamentalists!' roared Horace in crescendo. 'So let us all look to our defences!'

'The man's right, of course,' said Feisal quietly. 'Khomeini's revolution is the single major – and favourable – event here since Israel thrashed our five Arab armies in 1948. And our Fatah guerrillas have rightfully rejoiced at it – we gave many of their activists military training in our camps and our trainers still help in the Revolutionary Guard-run Schools of Death throughout Iran, hardening the young volunteer Fundament-alist activists that come from Iraq, Syria, Kuwait, Saudi, Bahrein, the Emirates and every other Gulf country and from many more distant . . . '

'– Enemies,' said Horace B. Murgatroyd sternly. 'We know our enemies. We see them!'

He gazed out above his lectern illustratively, to such effect that the Soviet Ambassador, a tough gentleman of fifty and allegedly a KGB colonel, flinched visibly, and his Chinese equivalent, a venerable greyhead who was wearing his best Mao tunic for the occasion, and who had been following Horace's muscular prose only with difficulty, dropped him a small curtsy under the illusion that Horace had singled him out for a compliment.

But Horace did not see that. In a flash he was seeing, not the three trim lines of Bedu pipers, locking his audience in to him, their red-and-white chequered *khutras* dramatic, but the image those cowls had triggered in his mind. This was of lines of men in long white gowns with flowing sleeves and tall white three-horned hoods, wrapped with red string, with black holes for eyes, noses, mouths, again trimmed in red. Every third man carried a tall fiery cross impregnated with kerosene, casting huge fitful pointed shadows across this wide waste plucked cotton field deep down South. These 1938 uniforms were identical to those of the first Ku Klux Klan *kyklos*, circle, the Invisible Empire formed in 1866–7 covering every state in the Confederacy, and the zeal of their wearers was as intense as those of the Second Klan born on Stone Mountain by Atlanta in October 1915 and whose membership peaked at some five million by 1925, their Holy Grail to denounce, abduct, whip, sometimes kill Negroes, bootleggers, adulterers, Jews, pacifists, radicals, Catholics and evolutionists.

Horace B. Murgatroyd, aged twelve, was again raised above an audience. He was with his father, who was Grand Titan of the Province or county. Horace's father sat magisterially at a small wooden table on the open low-sided back of a big truck. The boy, in the cab, peered through its rear window. The truck was an odd but practical tribunal. Everyone could see what was to be done.

The Nigra was up there with Horace's father, his wrists tied tightly behind him, with a rope wound many times round his biceps and elbows, immobilizing his torso like a straitjacket. He was barefoot and they had not bound his legs; there was a purpose to that. Three of the biggest and heaviest Klansmen were up with him on guard, for he was a big man too, a big buck Nigra, six foot and two hundred pounds and thirty years old. You heard the charge, Horace's father told him, how do you plead? Ah ain't denyin', said the Nigra, I took her cos she *axed* me. She *axed* me into her house, see? Sah. Well, said the Judge, that's all we want. You men heard him; the plea is guilty. He turned to the three on the truck. So fix it, men, so he cain't do it again –

There was a deep heavy roar from the men on the ground. Those on the truck held the Nigra. He was a big bull buck, but grey-faced now. He wrestled with the ropes round him, but one of the men took the broom-handle in the truck and jabbed it up viciously into the Nigra's solar plexus and he doubled up in agony. They flung him down and two ripped off his cotton pants. They always said the Nigras had them extra big, but Horace saw that this was like a length of hosepipe. The audience had crowded in; the truck's back flap was down so they could see. The third man took the heavy butcher's cleaver, and the Nigra screamed like an animal in slaughter. Got to defend the purity of our white Protestant womanhood, said

Horace's father didactically, a Sacred Trust, a Mission. We must get back to aah first principles, safeguard aah pure Christian values and way of life agin all that these goddam liberatin' Yankees can throw at us, in the form of upstart dam Catholics, Jews, and of course *Nigras* –

There was another savage roar from the massed men on the ground. The big buck Nigra was less bull now. Horace could see him lying and weeping endlessly and almost without sound, his bloody testicles beside him on the truck floor like small skinned animals. The white-hooded-torch-bearing men had forgotten him by now. He had served, for his moment. They had had their exaltation, reasserted their embattled identity. Horace's father glanced down at him and said: 'Ain't nothin *personal*, mind.' The men roared again –

Horace's Bedu-trapped audience on the US Embassy lawns roared in applause now too, for he had just finished his somewhat circuitous sermon by proposing a toast to the Kingdom of the Sun and its Amir and Crown Prince, who were celebrating their National Day in their own palaces in their own way. The various ambassadors, business tycoons, departmental heads, wives and mistresses, most of them clearly still in a state of mild shock from Horace's dire and lowering verbal pictures, his Biblical thunderbolts, his heavy rhythmic Greek-tragic sense of doom, his killer's lust for purity, lifted their glasses obediently back to him, their alcoholic content ranging all the way from zero to total, reflecting their holders' degree of public Islamic orthodoxy. Nor was this the only reaction to Horace's powerful performance. At its ringing climax the Bedu pipers, as one man, swung into the Kingdom of the Sun's national anthem, a touching theme suspiciously like the Bonny Bonny Banks of Loch Lomond, and to which, as Blake had discovered, the usual passionate and humourless lyrics had been written. This theme, which the Bedu pipers delivered with great verve and volume, caught and for some minutes painfully paralysed most of the guests with their drinking arms outstretched towards Horace. At last the pipes died away. Duty was done for the day, and now joy could be unconfined.

Among the first demonstrations of that was the fact that Horace had now come down his steps and was mingling freely with the mob, gracious as a musical comedy star after a successful première. Blake saw him coming.

'Evening, Mr Ambassador.'

Blake watched Horace B. Murgatroyd stop dead in front of him. Again he had that impression of an intense naked force, something primitive and ageless, cunning, developed to its absolute physical peak many aeons before, and frozen there wisely for all time at that level of perfection; a shark, say, or a rhinoceros. He could indeed have been a rhino, taking stock, in that split second before he horned the ground and charged, his heavy lethal head still and solid as a boulder, his little pig slate-grey eyes switching.

'Glad to see you here, Mr Blake. Sure, I remember you.'

Blake had met him at the welcoming cocktail-party which the British Ambassador had given for Horace.

'I don't know if you've met Ahmed Feisal here, the head of the Oil Ministry's legal department – '

'No, I haven't yet had the pleasure. Mr Feisal. Mr Ahmed Feisal.'

Horace switched the glass from his right to his left hand and shook Feisal's hand vigorously. Blake saw Feisal, no weakling himself, wince at that grasp. Horace's glass in his left hand was charged full of pale gold liquid; Jack Daniels rye whisky, Blake guessed, from having seen him drink it before. He could put it away like water, and it seemed to have no effect on his iron frame.

'And Sheikh Abdullah bin Ali bin Jibál, the Minister of Oil, and his sister, Princess Leila.'

'Yes, I *have* had the pleasure, anyway of meeting Sheikh Abdullah, at that dinner-party which your Foreign Minister kindly gave for me. Not yet your charming sister, Princess Leila –'

He had, Blake noted, an adroit speed in the way he moved, surprisingly graceful in so bulky a man. And he got all his names exactly right. Horace was in no way as simple as he might at first sight seem.

'You think I was a tad too outspoken in that talk, Sheikh?' asked Horace, evidently not a man to discount the possibilities of a direct approach.

Abdullah smiled.

'You mean in your description of the Iranian Revolution as the really major, even cataclysmic, event in the recent history of the world? No, I don't think so, Mr Murgatroyd. It is without any shadow of a doubt exactly that. And we must all be duly wary of its consequences. Particularly we here in the Arabian Gulf –'

'Would you be as concerned, Princess?'

'As my brother?' said Leila. 'Certainly! Islamic Fundamentalism is indeed a gigantic new force here, and we should be criminally at fault if we ignored it.'

'Ah. Which argues, Princess, that you have taken measures to face up to it?'

'Yes.'

'And what, may I ask, would those be?'

Leila looked straight at him, perhaps, thought Blake, to see if he was needling her. But Horace was monolithic and dead serious and, from his questions, evidently astute. Nothing more intellectually sophisticated than the pork-barrel might have brought Reagan to nominate him, and he might have been sent as Ambassador to the Kingdom of the Sun in the pious hope that its relatively small size must automatically constrain his abilities to create chaos, but in fact, here and now, Horace was impressive, smart in his light white linen dinner-jacket and knife-edged black pants. Leila made a nice foil to his trim bulk. She was dressed in a silver chiffon Dior drape which discreetly covered her from neck to just below her knees, the wrist-length sleeves bouffant, her slim waist disguised. So was her lustrous black hair, under the silver cowl, sufficiently to blunt men's crude and rampant sexual desires. Her high cheekbones, fine features and shining jet-black eyes addressed Horace's near-bald-grey-cropped bullet head.

'Islamic Fundamentalism thrives on human misery and social injustice. I don't pretend that there are not other causes. But at least we can do something concrete about the first two. What have we done? I'm not sure how much you know, Mr Murgatroyd, about the immense investment programme we've had running now for several years? It's virtually to re-build the social infrastructure for *all* of the two-thirds of our inhabitants who are *not* born *Shemsis* – these last so far being the highly privileged, with full political and property rights.

That means that for our *under-privileged* we're building complete new road networks, housing estates, shopping centres, power-stations, hospitals, clinics, schools, sports and recreation parks, so that every inhabitant here can have a decent life. We already, you know, give hospital treatment free to everyone, and free schooling for many years. And politically –'

She glanced at her brother, and Abdullah smiled.

'– we hope soon to take the first steps in according political rights, the right to vote and own property, to those not born *Shemsi* too.'

There was a rather long silence. To breach it, Abdullah said: 'We have of course full and very detailed figures on all these social infrastructure rebuilding plans of ours, and year-by-year comparisons of achievements against targets. I'm glad to say we're well *ahead* of the targets so far. I'd be very happy, Mr Murgatroyd, to have the Amir's Planning Office send you over a complete set of the programmes and figures.'

Abdullah himself was looking very regal that evening, with his six foot three long lean eager body, hawk-like olive face and his sister's vivid black eyes. He was dressed in the National Day's honour in a gold-coloured dishdasha with splendid gold-thread-embroidered patterns down the front, and a fine gold *kefiyyah* crowned by rings of gold *ogals*. He, like Leila, was as usual acting like a good orthodox Muslim in public; each held nothing more alcoholic than a tall glass of Horace's orange juice in his hand.

'Sure, thanks, Sheikh,' Horace said. 'I see. A kinda *socialism*, is the way you're going, it sounds to me –'

He drained off the entire large slug of Jack Daniels whisky in his glass in one swift movement, then, in what looked like a practised and skilled extension to it, put his hand out promptly horizontally like a steel bar. As immediately an Arab waiter was there to refill it. The effect was slightly disturbing but epistemologically very clear. Horace B. Murgatroyd did not find socialism the most appealing and valuable political philosophy in the world.

'And what do *you* feel about this rebirth of Fundamentalism, Mr Feisal?'

Feisal looked at him, then at Abdullah, then back at Horace, deliberately. Ahmed Feisal, like Blake, was dressed in a lounge suit that evening, though while Blake's was a sober dark blue, his was of a more exotic dark pearl. In it, with his good height and figure, and his excessively good looks, he looked both elegant and supremely self-assured. He was also clearly rating himself as more international, less parochially Kingdom of the Sun, than Abdullah and Leila, for he, like Blake, held his glass of whisky and water in his hand without discernible inhibition. He now spoke carefully, in a way which Blake saw as designed both courageously to express his own true views and yet not to upset either of the two sharply differing political groups before him.

'You have to see me as what I am, Mr Ambassador. A Palestinian Arab. Which means a forced exile without a true homeland – though the Kingdom of the Sun, and its esteemed rulers – ' and he inclined his brow gravely and justly to Abdullah and Leila, ' – have indeed been most generous with their hospitality, in the best Arab and Islamic traditions. So my view may be biased, of this I fairly should warn you. I am, perhaps because I am a member of a people dispossessed – and that is the simple fact of the matter, however searing and complex and total it may be in its emotional depth and pain – most of all struck as regards the Islamic Revolution in Iran by the extraordinary courage, discipline and dedication shown by its activists, its passionate desire to regain its own pride and identity in its own land – its return in short to the shining purity of its own first principles. In this they have surely set an example to the world. Theirs are the *simplest* truths, however profound. As in the end the truth about my country, Palestine, is simple. However complex and cruel its pains.'

There was a silence. All four of his companions stared at Feisal. Then Horace said:

'Pride and identity in your own land, in your own true customs. Yes. A return to the purity of your own first principles, yes. I can read those. I like that, Mr Feisal.'

'But perhaps we shouldn't altogether forget, Mr Murgatroyd,' said Abdullah, with what Blake saw as a rather strained smile, 'that the actual business of government is severely practical. We spend most of our time moving from moderately accurate analyses of the available facts – which are always limited – to moderate decisions and solutions. But isn't that life? We're not perfect, just pragmatic. There's really no glamour to it. We just don't have the space for the fine thoughts and lyrics of Ahmed here – '

'Pragmatic you sure as hell are,' replied Horace with vigour. 'I know what a goddam shotgun bargain you OPEC crude oil producers have driven with us poor consuming countries. You've really screwed us there, including my own land the United States, and slung us and the world into a major recession. Some pragmatism.'

'It's a hard world,' said Abdullah. 'But just think of how many years you screwed us by undervaluing our oil!'

'I know about screwing,' said Horace. 'I've been a business-man myself, remember? I've learnt about screwing.'

Horace certainly looked it, thought Blake. He wondered if Horace screwed anything but business competitors. A wife? But there was no sign of one. Somehow, thought Blake, Horace seemed to make better sense without. There was that rumour somewhere that Horace had lost one, some said by suicide. Anyway, he seemed intact on his own.

'Well,' said Abdullah equably, 'maybe you just like screwing. We all do what we want in the end, you know.'

'Sure,' said Horace. 'But – '

'But?'

'Maybe,' said Horace, and he glanced then at Ahmed Feisal, 'even beyond screwing, I just still prefer lyricism in the end. In the death, as they say.'

25
Pride, and a Fatal Fall

'Has the lyricism gone, Philip,' asked Princess Leila Jibál of the Kingdom of the Sun, in the Nile Hilton's Tavern Bar in Cairo, that evening of October 5 1981. Philip Blake looked back at her with his eyebrows raised.

'Which? Between us?'

'Between us, Philip.'

'God forbid!' said Blake. 'Not for me! You're far too perfect for that.'

She looked it. They sat in armchairs by a small table in the expensive submarine gloom. The Tavern Bar's big main horseshoe counter was behind them, and another scatter of small tables beyond that. A piano played. Outside, the Hilton stared straight across the Corniche and over the Nile at the Island of Gezira, sparkling with lights at this hour from its famous Sporting Club, its myriad ambassadorial residences, its many shops and blocks of flats. Here the Nile, two to three hundred metres wide, flowed south to north, left to right, still carrying the occasional felucca – that tall curved arrowhead of white sail on the black water, its skilled crew slipping its mast nimbly back to horizontal at each bridge. Just to the right was Cairo's newest bridge, the Sixth of October, its title a memorial to the date on which Sadat and Syria and their allies had launched their 1973 war, which Sadat and Egypt always referred to fancifully as victorious, against Israel.

On this eve of the eighth anniversary of that war's outbreak, Leila showed no mark of the passage of those years. At thirty-six, she had a beauty that was simply now more rounded and confident, with a fine bloom on it. She sat by Blake with the splendid black eyes in her oval face set on him, its olive skin framed by the falling waves of shining jet black hair. She wore a diaphanous turquoise scarf loosely tied over it and tied lightly under her chin, a concession to orthodox Islam's unremitting assault upon that libidinous cascade. In harmony with the shade of that scarf and its genuflection to sexual modesty was her vivid deep turquoise dress, of light silk, and cocktail length, appropriately high-necked, long-sleeved and loose-fitting, allowing only a faint if provocative hint of her high firm breasts to appear. A broad belt of the same deep turquoise silk gathered the dress at her slim waist, its buckle in front big and silver. That tint was picked up again by her sandals, high-heeled and silver, and her long drop earrings, slim silver vertical bars ending in emeralds mounted in silver filigree.

'And you're still not tired of Islamic culture either?' she asked. 'Despite the heavy booster shot of it that we had this afternoon, under that very hot sun?'

'Not nearly,' said Blake. 'It was marvellous to see it again.'

That afternoon the chauffeured BMW that the Egyptian Oil Ministry had put at their disposal had driven them east from Opera Square and along Sharia el Azhar. On their right they had passed the university of that name, the oldest in the Arab world, and still the finest for Islamic teaching. In its vast open courtyard the 'Ulama, the Learned, sat and taught their rings of disciples like Socrates. Beyond the twin-arched Gate of the Barbers entrance, Leila and Blake had seen El Azhar's great warm-breasted dome and its two lyrical slim stone pencils of minarets which pierced up into the hot cloudless blue sky. To their left were the twisting narrow alleys and thousand crouching shops of Khan el Khalili and the Muski, packed with gaudy bric-a-brac and a million ornaments, the greatest rip-off centres of the city.

From here the BMW had driven them on to something infinitely more genuine. They had dipped under the wide Salah Salem Avenue which led left and north to the international airport, and right to the Citadel which Saladin built in the late twelfth century, and they had lifted up into the Northern Cemetery, its encircling background and grim sand-coloured Hills of Muqattam, rim of the giant bleak dustbowl into which the winds and breezes blew fine sand endlessly from the surrounding deserts, and where twelve million Cairenes sweated and suffered and had their being. They drove between the domed tombs of Tartar and fourteenth-century princesses, then turned north to the splendid architectural complex of the Qaitbai Mosque and bull's-eye grey and white horizontally striped Mausoleum. They stopped and went into the cool distilled vaulted silence, and saw the intricately interlinked script of squares and curls and circles and whorls and stars which decorated the walls, and climbed magnificently up within the inner curves of the domes. This soaring balance could catch the watcher by the throat and heart. This was the essence and true spirit of Islam, a superb architecture, soberly graceful, its insistence on form so great, as the purest manifestation of the harmonies of the divine plan, that it abstained from any representation of the human face or form, let alone those of Allah or Muhammed. Islam's true signature in its sacred buildings was as gravely classical as written Arabic itself. Leila watched Blake absorb it within these quiet magic temples for an hour. Afterwards, outside by the car, she saw him turn and gaze a long moment at this beloved etched Islamic silhouette.

'Have another drink,' said Blake.

'Thank you,' said Leila. 'Then another orange.' And Blake called a waiter and ordered that, and another vodka-tonic for himself. For they were still very sensitive to protect her Islamic reputation, even in relatively liberal Egypt. Thus not only did she not drink any alcohol in public here, but they had also been careful to hire separate suites in the hotel, though in fact she spent every night in his arms in his – a subterfuge which seemed to them a small price to pay for being together.

'I heard the news while you were showering and changing,' she said. 'Fatah's Revolutionary Council in Beirut seem to have come to no definite conclusion whatsoever about Arafat's talks with Prince Fahd in Saudi ten days ago about the Fahd Plan.'

Blake frowned heavily.

'Arafat and his shambling Fatah never seem able to decide about anything. So history will pass them by. Fahd's is a hell of a good peace plan. It would get the Israelis out of all the land they took in the 1967 Six Days War and create a Palestinian state on the West Bank under UN supervision. The Arabs would have to recognize Israel, sure, but that's a cheap price to pay. Israel's *there* anyway, and she isn't just going to get up and go away to suit Mr flaming Arafat's fancy. And all the time he stalls, Begin and Sharon get right on colonizing the West Bank with Jewish settlements – soon there won't be any land left to make an Arab state *with*! And all Arafat and Fatah seem to do is made grandiloquent threats they can't carry out, like liquidating the Israeli Zionist Entity militarily, politically, economically, and even ideologically. My *foot*!'

'My name's not Yasser Arafat, mind,' said Leila mildly.

Blake looked amazed, then roared with laughter and put his hand over hers.

'Forgive me! I got carried away, sympathetic though I am. But what points up Arab impotence is your enemies' tenacity. Look how the right-wing Christian Lebanese Phalangists have been shattering Muslim West Beirut with car-bombs for the last two years. Look at Israel – however much Likud and Labour fight internally, they act as one highly efficient bloc to the world outside. They spend *one year* training selected pilots, then just under four months ago they fly five hundred miles undetected into Arab territory and take out Iraq's nuclear reactor north of Baghdad clean as a whistle and with minimum casualties. When the Joint Forces in Lebanon – including the PLO – shelled an Israeli settlement in Galilee in June, the Israeli air force went back at once and killed three hundred in the Joint Forces zones. They made their point. Arafat and Fatah don't. If the Palestinian Arabs really want to carve themselves a homeland again, they're going to have to use a very different kind of power. I can understand why Ahmed Feisal back in the Kingdom feels as dissatisfied with the PLO as he evidently does these days. Were he in charge, I think we'd see something very much more vigorous and direct and effective. I think I'd feel the same as he, were I in his shoes – '

There was a long silence. Then Leila said: 'Philip – '

'Yes?'

'Please bear with me a little, Philip. Be careful with Ahmed Feisal – '

'Careful? Why careful?'

She looked away, then back at him.

'I'm not sure. But you may get more action from him than you bargained for. Than *we* bargained for. Philip, don't get too close to him – '

'But what worries you about him? That he's passionate about Palestine? You can hardly blame him for that. It was his home, and he was thrown out of it. He had his mother and sisters slaughtered by right-wing Christian Lebanese militias, allies of the Israelis, in Tel ez Zaatar refugee camp in Beirut. The mother mutilated sexually. No one can get those back for him. But sure, he wants his country back. That at least – '

'Philip, he wants power. He'd want that, whatever had happened to him in his life. That's basic to him. He's very deep. Too deep. I sense huge violence there.'

'You can hardly blame a man for being deep, Leila.'

'Well, I don't know. He frightens me. There's not much human compassion there. I can't trust him. Be careful of him, Philip. For *our* sake. For your own – '

Blake looked back at her, then shrugged slightly, and took a pull at his vodka-tonic.

'You said your morning was all right,' she said, deflecting to safer ground, 'with the Egyptian Oil Ministry?'

'Yes,' he said. 'It's not a great thing, in the context of what we've been talking about. But we've got the deal through, on terms very favourable to us. It's just a crude interchange, quite small, fifty thousand barrels a day. We give them Sun Light, because they're desperate for low sulphur. They give us that much back of higher sulphur and lower API – but plus twenty per cent, or sixty thousand bd in all. We've got much better cracking facilities at Mina es-Salaam than they have at the Egyptian refineries. So, even discounting the extra transport costs, we still come out well ahead on the deal. *And* help the Egyptians. It's good Islam all round.'

'That's where you're a boon to us,' said Leila. 'You're experienced and high-powered enough to push this sort of thing through, and you're still safely an expatriate officially. The only other people we could have sent would have been Abdullah himself, or his Under-Secretary Kamal Daud, or perhaps Ahmed Feisal, though he's no crude oil expert. But any of those would have been dangerously high-profile, right against the official Arab League boycott of Egypt. With you we can get away with it.'

Blake smiled. 'Glad to help,' he said. 'And it gives me the chance to be here freely with you. Not that your Arab League boycott looks to me all that fierce. Neither Saudi nor Kuwait nor any of the other big money boys have pulled a cent out of their vast sums in the Arab Investment banks or other joint ventures centred here – nor have they stopped sending their thousands of rich Arabs for the Egyptian fleshpots, nor their thousands of students to the excellent universities – any more than the Egyptians have refused to go on admitting them. Everyone's really being very Arab about the whole thing.'

'You've still pushed something worthwhile through for the Kingdom, Philip.'

'Well, just a civilized size.' He smiled again. 'The same volume, in fact, that you've very kindly been selling me personally for the last eight years, and which has made me a multi-millionaire. I'm very heavily in your and your brother's debt.'

'You've earned it,' said Leila. 'And it's a well-guarded secret. Only Abdullah keeps a record of the sales and channels the money to the Kingdom's Treasury.'

'And I value that discretion,' said Blake cheerfully.

Despite his earlier slight brush with Leila about Ahmed Feisal, he was looking very much at his ease. Success suited Blake. It brought out the best in him. He sat, pleasantly relaxed in his lightweight white Shantung silk suit from Fatina in the Plaza Trevi in Rome, his tie a Giorgio Armani silk, the background light blue, a regular pattern of gold spots across it, his cuff-links Takashimaya pearl, and his shoes very dark tan Bally from Switzerland. His strong right hand held his second vodka-and-tonic as though it were highly fashionable too, and his flat blue sniper's eyes gazed out tranquilly, not discernibly marred by doubt or inhibition, upon a generally receptive and subservient word. At forty-four, Blake felt that he was on the way to owning a fair part of it anyway. In his public life he was right-hand man to the Minister of Oil of a respectably sized crude oil producer in the Arabian Gulf. Behind the scenes he was also a valued aide to the sophisticated leader of the extremely powerful and expanding Militant Palestinian movement in that country – a vibrant and fascinating shape for the future. He was a multi-millionaire in his own right. Blake also had his full health, save for that minor deformity to his left leg. More, he had Leila.

'And tomorrow?' she said, taking her flat platinum case out of her handbag and opening the case for a Balkan Sobranie Virginia. Blake lit it for her and she nodded her thanks.

'Well,' said Blake, 'tomorrow morning latish we go and watch the mass military march-past and fly-over at Nasr City on the north-eastern outskirts of Cairo, to mark the eighth anniversary of Sadat's gloriously victorious war against Israel.'

'Just war would do,' said Leila.

'Well, he's got to keep the lads happy. So in celebration of our signing this crude interchange agreement this morning, the Minister gave me two seats for tomorrow in the reviewing stand just next to the one where Sadat and all the rest of the top brass will be. If the seats are that good, it would be a shame not to use them. And it might even be quite an impressive ceremony. The Ministry has arranged too that there'll be a military guide for us next to our two seats.'

'You've talked me into it,' said Leila lightly. 'All right, by all means let's go.'

'Fine,' said Blake. 'It all helps to know what's changed in the country. For me, anyway. To take its temperature, if you like.'

'And how *is* its temperature, Philip?'

He looked at her shrewdly, then ordered a third drink for both.

'You want the short tour or the long? Better make it the short, if we're to get to the Arabesque in time for dinner. Okay, let's take it we're agreed on the basics. The economy's shot to hell – falling earnings, say seven billion dollars last year, and rising imports, near nine billion. That's a permanent balance of payments deficit, a population up from 26 million in 1952 to 44 million now. Egypt imports nearly three-quarters of its food by value, and only four per cent of the land is arable. Nasser nationalized everything in sight, and the legacy of that is the world's worst bureaucracy, three million of them, mostly useless time-servers.'

'Why doesn't that make them dangerous to do business with?'

'It's a straight swap we're making with our crude interchange,' Blake reminded her. 'If they slip on sending their own shipments, then we stop ours. There's no risk. And we gain hard economically while the deal lasts.'

When Philip had made the decision to work for the Kingdom of the Sun, he had promised himself that within five years he would know as much about the Arab world as any of his new colleagues, and Leila had watched him more than once as he cut through books, reports, statistics with a concentration that locked him inside invisible walls until he switched it off. She could see in that hot pursuit of knowledge the force which had taken him so high at Eagle and had finally matched him against the armoured certainties of Kobus van Straten. In the Kingdom of the Sun, much though her brother and the Amir himself respected Philip, yet he was only an adviser. She felt the discrepancy between that function and the depth of his fascination with the Islamic world, and she knew that he was no academic, to strive so hard for understanding only for its own sake.

'What about the politics of Egypt?' she prompted him. 'What's in the air?'

'You feel it too, don't you?' He scanned the lights of Gezira, over the quiet river, as though they too offered some vital data if you knew the code. 'Egypt could be the pace-setter for the whole Arab world, as she was under Saladin and the Mamelukes. Only this time we could see a bleaker influence, as the ostensibly moderate State which broadcasts Islamic Fundamentalism out to the whole Arab Middle East.'

'Oh, you're exaggerating, Philip! Imagining a Frankenstein!'

'The monster's there already, Leila. All round us. Not just Iran. What about that bloody occupation of Mecca's Mosque two years ago? The Saudis tried to play it down, a minor nuisance. Nonsense! The rebels held it for ten days against the whole might of the Saudi armed forces, with hundreds killed on both sides. These were Fundamentalists trying to topple a totally feudal monarchy, and they damned nearly won. Name a country where they're *not* a growing force, a Muslim country. They have people in the governments of Kuwait and Pakistan. Khadaffi's Libya is at base totally Fundamentalist: puritanical, highly orthodox religiously, exporting revolution and terrorism, anti-Western, Pan-Islamic. Indonesia has the world's fifth largest population, and nine-tenths of them are Muslims. What a potential there, if Fundamentalism should become a banner for the disaffected.'

'And Egypt?'

'I won't play you back everything I've learned from you, ever since Vienna, or the armed uprisings we saw here in the Seventies. Now we have Sadat's peace with Israel. Remember that swipe at him in the Brotherhood's paper, *Dawa*? When they quoted that bit in the *Shari'a* that rules that if land is stolen from Muslims and they could fight to get it back but don't, then all are evil beyond redemption.'

'Meaning Sadat, no doubt of it,' said Leila. 'The West Bank and Gaza Strip, at the very least, are clearly Arab and clearly in Israeli hands. Egypt has by far the biggest Arab army in the Middle East, and not only does she choose not to fight, she implicitly agrees at Camp David that Israel need not return them fully and at once.'

'That's poison for Sadat,' Blake agreed. 'So stir that into all the other poisons working in a city like this, twelve million alien souls compressed in an arid dustbowl of desert. A concrete jungle, a rat-run of alleys haunted by vice and sickness and easy death. How can Egypt keep graduating a hundred thousand students every year, in line with Nasser's reforms, then offer them no jobs, or menial ones – eight years' medical studies, a bitterly hard-earned degree, and the new doctor may end as a sixty-dollars-a-month government medical clerk. Multiply that by thousands and you have a pool of total disillusion for Fundamentalism to fish in. Why not rip out this whole unjust society, and replace it by the crystal purity of the *Shari'a*?'

'I think Sadat's had something of a warning already,' said Leila, taking her second Balkan Sobranie while Blake reached for his lighter. 'Did you know? Our intelligence passed it on to me in the Kingdom: they still have their ears very close to the ground here. They say that when Begin met Sadat in Alexandria last month about implementing the Camp David accords, he told Sadat that Israel's Mossad Intelligence service had picked up definite evidence of an attempt on his life, probably Fundamentalist. That may be part of the reason why Sadat arrested some sixteen hundred people last month, right through the spectrum of his political opposition. What an effective way to bind his enemies together!'

'You're right. He may have alienated too many hostile forces. It's not just the fanatical nationalists, the people who resent his peace treaty with Egypt. I think he has tried to move Egypt towards the West too fast – like the Shah in Iran. His Open Door *Infitah* economic policy has sucked Western consumerism and sexual permissiveness into the country, and that's another poison in the mix. All those pictures of Sadat in his Pierre Cardin suits, Jihan in her chic Parisian fashions that no ordinary Egyptian woman could come anywhere near to identifying with. Advertisements for a retreat from Islam.'

'Yet a great man still, Sadat. You would not question that?'

'Oh, I'd say so without doubt. To be the one Arab of the 150 million massed about Israel who had the guts and political genius to fly in there unarmed and talk peace? To run so hard against the tide? You may not like Israel or the treaty, but you can't deny the size or significance of what Sadat has done. For that, he deserves his Nobel Prize, and his place in history.'

'And so we conclude the short tour?' Leila put out her cigarette and rose to her feet as sedately as a Princess should.

Blake finished his vodka-and-tonic as he stood to escort her. 'It is concluded.'

26
The Man Who Stood up for His Death

Next day just before 1 pm under a brilliant blue October sky that great historic figure sat in the middle of the front row of the Presidential reviewing stand and watched the massive Egyptian military parade and air force fly past. Muhammed Anwar es-Sadat had dressed himself as Egyptian Supreme Commander in his shiny royal-blue field-marshal's uniform. He wore a dark green silk sash over his right shoulder, with stars of gold and Egypt's gold eagle on it. His royal blue dress cap carried the same badge of crossed swords and laurel leaves beloved of British High Command officers, and its black peak was braided in gold. His epaulettes were heavily gold-braided too, and his left breast replete with medals. At this throat he wore Egypt's highest military decoration, the Star of Sinai, a fine silver-bordered eight-pointed ebony black star some six centimetres across with just 'Sinai 1973' in silver in Arabic on it. He had some claim to wear it, for by his leadership he had quite certainly recovered that area for Egypt, at whatever continuing cost to the Palestinian Arabs on the West Bank and in the Gaza Strip.

Sadat also wore his thick clipped black moustache and his very dark olive *fellah*'s face. He stared steadily to the front with an appropriately stern military expression of resolve. Sadat had always had a born actor's acute sense of occasion. No one ever beat his head on the ground more piously at the public prayers on a Friday at Cairo's major congregational mosque of Sayyidna el Hussein, the Prophet's grandson, which lay across the throbbing Sharia el Azhar from the university of that name, to emerge with a photogenic dust-mark on his brow. That brow was clear now, as Sadat turned from time to time to comment briefly on the parade and its multiple modern armaments to his Vice-President Hosni Mubárak on his right and his Defence Minister General Abdul Halim Abu Ghazala on his left. The reviewing stands held another 2,000 seats for the reat of Eygpt's leaders and for the world's ambassadors and its military and air attachés.

Here too were Princess Leila Jibál of the Kingdom of the Sun, and Philip Blake of its Ministry of Oil. They sat at the edge of the stand nearest to Sadat's and to his right, and beside Blake sat an attentive young Egyptian artillery officer, Captain Hassan Wahba. Lean and fit with fine Nilotic features, light olive skin, and light grey eyes – not Arab, those, but again a mark of the Ottoman Turk in his ancestry. He impressed Leila with his excellent command of English. She saw too that his khaki uniform was impeccable, no automatic holster blurring its line. Leila herself was dressed very classically. She wore a close-fitting light cotton skirt, to just below her knees, and dark cream in colour. The cream jacket, matching her skirt, and long-sleeved, was also crisply tailored to her bust and waist. Her shoes were black, and semi-high-heeled, apt for walking. A wide-brimmed hat of shiny black straw, very plain and set straight, shaded her face. She had a diamond brooch at her throat, a seagull with outstretched wings, and her silver Cartier watch on its plain platinum band on her left wrist; no other jewelry. Blake beside her was in a light grey cotton suit from Brown's of London and a pure silk Armani tie. Leila sat and smoked a Balkan Sobranie from her flat platinum case discreetly; no one had forbidden it. She still glowed from their love-making the night before.

Leila looked down at the broad flight of steps between their stand and Sadat's and which reached down to the level of the parade-ground. Little Egyptian children were playing on the steps, waving small paper Egyptian flags – like French tricolours up-ended, she thought, the stripes horizontal instead of vertical, and black instead of dark blue, and with the gold Egyptian eagle in the centre of the white band. She could hear Captain Wahba reeling off to Blake technical descriptions of the passing armaments. The parade had been running for well over an hour. She wondered gloomily how long it would still last. Though, she reminded herself guiltily, the Egyptians deserved some of the kudos they were giving themselves. Exactly eight years ago, within one hour, at 2 pm, Hosni Mubárak as Egyptian Air Force Commander had launched his 222 jet aircraft's twenty-minute strike across the Suez Canal which, with the very heavy artillery barrage, breached Israel's Bar Lev Line enough to let through many thousands of Egypt's commandos with their rubber boats, followed by the great bulk of Egypt's assault tanks and army divisions. Even if Israel had superhumanly, and with vast American air-bridged support, won back the initiative against both Egypt and Syria, and indeed thrown Sharon's armoured division counter-attacking back over the canal to crucify Egypt, she, led by Sadat, had still bruised Israel badly, dented its myth of military invincibility, and won back some Arab pride and confidence.

'You're now seeing the result of Sadat's post-1973 policy of diversifying his sources of arms supplies,' Captain Wahba was saying to Blake. 'You've seen our Russian T-55 and American M-60 tanks, and the Russian MIG-17s that started the air display. Now –' he squinted up and pointed, 'come our French Mirage 5Es – '

Leila looked up with Blake. The six delta-winged jets were flying over deafeningly low.

'And the guns in front now?' shouted Blake, pointing back at the parade-ground, where four big open-backed trucks were towing very long-muzzled guns. Four lines of trucks towing the same guns followed.

'They're Soviet Zil-151 trucks,' Captain Wahba screamed back. 'And the guns are Korean-made 130 mm anti-tank cannons.'

Leila was idly watching the trucks. She saw one in the nearest column pull to its right out of its line and stop. Nobody seemed much concerned; she had seen two mechanical breakdowns earlier. Most spectators anyway seemed mes-merized by the low-flying Mirages. The stopped truck was dead opposite and some 25 metres from Sadat.

She saw the uniformed officer jump down from the passenger side of the cab. He was a tall man, well built, with black hair under his khaki beret, and a strong black moustache. Amazed, she saw him swing back his right arm and fling a pineapple-shaped object straight at Sadat's reviewing stand. Then he flung another. Leila saw both land well within the stand, but nothing happened after that.

Except on the truck. She saw three men on its flat back, presumably part of the gun-team, crouch and fire at Sadat and his stand with automatic rifles, she guessed Kalashnikov AK-47s; some of the paramilitary police in the Kingdom of the Sun had them. The three men jumped down and charged in, shooting and hurling two more grenades; both exploded loudly and in smoke, one just in front of the stand ahead of Sadat. Some of its shrapnel must have hit him and the men by him.

For Sadat had stood up. The big uniformed officer by the cab had dived back into it for a submachinegun. He came in fast, firing it. Sadat must have thought he was running in to salute him. Sadat always stood to take such salutes. Vice-President Hosni Mubárak and General Abu Ghazala stood too, courteously. Leila saw both men then clearly grasp what was happening. They dived on Sadat to pull him down. Men leapt in to cover him with chairs.

Most spectators were still stunned with surprise. Now some sprang into action. Captain Wahba screamed 'Assassination!' and hurled himself at Blake and brought him down. Blake grabbed Leila and held her to the ground too. But she still had her eyes high enough to survey the battlefield. So she stayed. *Maktub* was *maktub*. If it wasn't written, she would not die here.

But others did. The second assassin, ahead of the big officer with the submachinegun, had run to the right of Sadat's stand, its front a shallow convex wall some fifteen metres wide by one and a half high. He ran up the steps there and turned inwards. Now above and behind this fragile shield, he fired the full magazine of his automatic rifle down into the bodies half sprawled under their chairs. Leila saw two men, evidently security, crouch and fire their pistols at him from the middle of the third row, but they did not stop him.

He looked half-right. The big officer with the submachine-gun still ran in to the stand's centre, firing bursts from his shoulder towards Sadat. A security guard there fired back. The officer loomed over the front wall. He fired slightly downwards, his gun an ugly extension to his body, his silhouette thick and murderous. The third assassin ran in hunched to the left of the main stand. A man lay on the steps there with a still camera. The third assassin shot him deliberately.

'Why *that*?' screamed Leila. 'Why pick on him?' The man had lain peacefully near her, and she felt personally affronted.

'Muhammed Rashwan,' Captain Wahba cried back, twisting his neck to see. 'Sadat's personal photographer.' Rashwan was famous for his pictures of Sadat in pious poses at prayer and in intimate ones, as when shaving.

'So who would kill *him*?'

'The *Ikhwan*,' said Wahba soberly. 'It's the Brothers. Fundamentalists.'

Leila saw that the fourth assassin had arrived on scene too. He and the second were at the front wall. They raised their Kalashnikov automatic rifles above their heads and rained their fire down like nails into the assembled bodies. The officer with his strong black moustache and submachinegun had fallen back, holding his side, probably wounded. Now the assassins ran, their work done. The security guards and military police and soldiers streamed after them, shouting bravely, efficient after the event. In the other stands the people had fled or tumbled over one another for cover. The stands looked to Leila like refugee camps swept by gales. Blake and she got up and they watched the people come back to life. Some could not. There were many wounded beyond the dead. She saw one, who Wahba said was the Belgian Ambassador, on the ground unconscious and bleeding heavily, a woman attending him.

But the greatest focus was on Sadat. They pulled him out gently. Leila could see that he was in a coma, bleeding heavily from the mouth. His left chest, left thigh, and right arm were also badly bloodied, from bullets or grenade shrapnel. Men carried him behind the stands. A helicopter lifted off at once – to fly him the fourteen kilometres to the Maadi Military Hospital by the Nile, said Wahba. In the hush after all the shooting, half shattered by three Czech jets flying low overhead who knew no better, the voice of the parade's military commentator still came brokenly over the air.

'Oh Egypt, oh treachery. Oh Egypt, oh treachery,' the commentator kept repeating.

'My God, it can be fast,' said Blake. 'I timed it on my watch, you know. The whole thing began and ended in forty-five seconds.'

Leila looked at him. He seemed faintly exhilarated. He might just have watched a good gladiatorial combat. It couldn't happen to him.

'Yes,' she said. 'He's very dead now. Whatever they do.'

'Yes.'

'Once a big man falls, he can fall awfully hard.'

'I must remember that,' said Blake, just keeping the glint from his eye, the faint mockery from his tone, out of respect for the dead.

27

The Long Arm of Mossad

'It happened at three this afternoon, you say?'

Ahmed Feisal stood with Philip Blake and looked down at the corpse. This was a man of about thirty-five, quite tall and slim, in hard physical condition from the look of it, and dressed neatly in Western-style light cotton slacks, open-necked shirt and leather sandals. His complexion was very light olive. That and his lack of dishdasha made him Palestinian Arab, not *Shemsi*. He sat quite precisely on the top step with his back against the wall just next to his open front door, his head forward on his chest. In the shade there, he could have been sitting quietly this Friday – therefore rest-day – in December 1983, perhaps ruminating with mild complacency about the pleasures of having his own house – for this was one of the sub-economic but smart and functional housing units of the Kingdom of the Sun's capital-intensive and progressive programme to give the best living conditions and sense of belonging reasonably possible to all non- *Shemsis* resident and working in it. Feisal had noted that this excellently designed semi-prefab had its own front garden too, with a metre-high wall cutting it comfortably off from the sandy earth outside and the main road, and some dark green shrubs and a couple of low trees within it. It was even in a pretty good area, well served by a huge new shopping complex complete with a school and clinic, and not far from the fashionable suburb where Blake had his flat, on the fourth floor of a splendid modern building that looked straight down onto the sea.

So, thought Feisal, the man sitting in front of him, his compatriot, had every right to look proud. He had got, if not everything, then at least a great deal, including the very pretty and remarkably controlled young daughter of fourteen or so now standing beside him. He was also a brave and highly skilled man who had recently carried out a spectacularly effective piece of work for which Feisal had been the first to congratulate and duly reward him. He lacked only one really basic asset, and that was his life. The exact small black hole in the centre of his forehead confirmed that. Probably a 7.65 mm, thought Feisal; certainly a hand-gun, with a silencer. It could even have been .22 calibre.

'*F'il saat ith-thalitha*,' said the girl. 'Yes, at three. Somebody rang the bell. Just once. He went to the door. I was in the sitting-room, doing my housework. He didn't come back there, but I thought nothing of it. He often works in his study on his own.'

She paused. Feisal glanced at Blake; he had probably got most of that. He knew that for years now Blake had been going religiously to the University of the Kingdom of the Sun's evening classes in Arabic. Blake was no fool, but Arabic was a bitterly difficult language for *ajánib*, foreigners. Blake nodded quickly, and he turned back to the girl, sober and composed in her pale blue western-style dress.

'And?'

'After an hour, I went to the bathroom, past his study. He wasn't there. So I went to the front door, and found – '

'Just sitting like this, dead?'

She nodded her head.

'No sign of anyone near him? No notes, nothing?'

'Nothing. There was just the bullet-hole in his head.'

'And he was dead when you found him? You're sure?'

She looked at him steadily. Her small pretty face, thought Feisal, was compact and pragmatic, like a button. 'I know the dead,' she said. 'Though I felt his pulse and heart. Nothing. I was at Tel ez-Zaatar, you see.'

' *Ya khassára*!' said Feisal. 'I saw it after it fell! You had no one with you here?'

'No. I think you know my mother's a theatre sister. She's on the emergency ward in the Sarmieh Hospital till six. And my two younger brothers are at a friend's house.'

'You've notified the police?'

Her eyes widened a fraction.

'His strict instructions were to call you first. *Whatever* happened.'

'Quite right. Well done. You've behaved like a true *fidáyya*, a true commando. You've not even wept – '

'Well,' she said reasonably, 'he was not my natural father, you understand, though he was a good man to us and my mother. My father died with the Fatah fighters at Karámah.'

'Then greatness has indeed touched this house,' said Feisal reverently. 'Both in this sacrifice for our cause, and in that.'

Blake had learned enough about the postwar history of the Palestinian people to know that Fatah had shown true heroism at Karámah. The Israelis, after their brilliant and murderously successful Six Days War in June 1967 and occupation of the West Bank, Eastern Jerusalem, Golan Heights, Gaza Strip and Sinai, had cleaned the Palestinian guerrillas out of the West Bank so that by early the following year they were taking the war to Fatah encampments within Jordan itself. By an intelligence leak, the Jordanian army learnt of a massive new Israeli attack planned against Fatah's field HQ at the village of Karámah just inside Jordan. Fatah had only some three hundred shock troops there, but they were thoroughly prepared and determined to make an exemplary stand; they felt they had run often enough. They also had excellent Jordanian artillery support. When the powerful Israeli armoured thrust developed up the Jordan Valley at dawn on March 21 1968, complete with infantry and air cover, the Fatah men in Karámah put up an astounding last-ditch defence against this force numerically some fifty to sixty times its size, inflicting casualties on it that it had never expected. Fatah's own losses were grievous, with 120 killed. Their motivation had been magnificent, as high as their intellectual flight: of those 120 killed in action, ninety-nine were university graduates. In Arabic *karámah* meant nobility, dignity, honour. By their bravery there, Fatah had won back some of those rare qualities for the Arab nation.

'*This* one,' said the girl, 'was a valiant man too. He fought in Tel ez-Zaatar, and he got us out and brought us here just before the Phalangists stormed it.'

'I know what he's done,' said Feisal. 'I know his worth. We'll make them pay many times that weight. You can tell the police of it now. Tell them too that I've been here. They know me.'

'*Taht amrak*,' she said. 'At your command. Would you and your friend like to come in for some coffee while I do so?'

There was something to be said for the Arab culture after all, thought Feisal, if its iron laws of courtesy and hospitality held up even at moments like this. Aloud he said: 'Many thanks, but we have work to do at once. Please tell your mother that I shall contact her as soon as I can, to help.'

'*Effendim*.'

She turned at once and went in, not shutting the door; perhaps, thought Feisal, mere robbery could seem only a triviality to her now. He glanced down. The dead man sat immobile, cheerfully considering his handsome house and garden, proof of his arrival as a Fatah hero. He was evidently as innately polite as his step-daughter. He had had the civility and grace not even to show a single drop of blood on his clothes or steps, just that neat small hole dead centre on his brow which might have been drilled there by some skilled and well-intentioned surgeon.

'You don't want to search him or anything?' asked Blake, in English.

'There's not really much point,' said Feisal, turning to go. 'I know who must have done it. And why. We have our common language in these things, you know. To be certain I need to visit three other places in this city. Have you the time and interest to come with me?'

'Of course,' said Blake. 'It's Friday. And I'd like to know what this means.'

'You will,' said Feisal.

They climbed into Blake's metallic silver Camaro with its low sleek lines and melodramatic air-brake at the rear, and Blake turned on the ignition.

'Where to?'

'I think the next logical one's just by the Dhow Port. D'you know it?'

'Of course.'

Blake took the car easily out of the hard rocky earth onto the wide asphalted road. It was a first-rate highway. There was nothing small, thought Feisal, about Abdullah's and Leila's and the Crown Prince's and the Amir's progressive and vastly costly programme to build the two-thirds of the population who weren't *Shemsi* by birth integrally into the Kingdom of the Sun, politically and emotionally, by giving them houses and land and the right to own them, magnificent shopping centre complexes and hospitals and clinics and schools and recreation centres and road highway networks. There was only one drawback to it, but it was a severe one.

It wasn't going to work.

Not if Ahmed Feisal could help it.

Because it *wasn't* the essential. The essential was always the same. To free Palestine, *all* of Palestine, from the goddamned Zionists who had invaded it. And win back for every Arab everywhere the nobility, dignity and honour that Fatah had won back at Karámah. At *any* cost. Certainly at the cost of using a man like Philip Blake to the absolute utmost, if he lent himself to it. Even if you happened to like the man because of his unorthodox wildcatter qualities, his piratical leanings, his epic, perhaps tragic, contours, his nomadic nonchalance even when detribalized, his occasional mordant black wit. Whether he knew it or not, Blake moved with history, instinctively or just a jump ahead of it. It was one of the main things that had attracted Feisal to him from the start. For wasn't that really the name of the game, to read history right to get that most magic sum right? And maybe at times you had to nudge history just a bit, as in this business of freeing Palestine at any cost. Even at the cost of betraying, or at least bypassing, your own mother organizations, the PLO and Fatah, if you were as convinced as Feisal was that they were now getting it all wrong, all round their necks –

And Horace B. Murgatroyd. That was another key man he could use. *Had* used. Was using. Like Blake. No, *not* like Blake. Of a different order. US Ambassador Horace B. Murgatroyd. What did the B stand for? Bestial? Barbaric? Brutal? Or just Basic? For there was something terrifyingly primitive about the man, there was no doubt about it. Prehistoric, primeval, monolithic, ominous. Never to be taken lightly, always highly dangerous, unpredictable. And with a speed, efficiency, almost lightness of movement obscene in that malevolent squat bulk. Though most often the solid almost cubic head would be set absolutely still, in deadly quiet, the little slate-coloured pig eyes switching cunningly from side to side, with the more powerful sense of smell icily charting danger, or dictating it mortally. For Horace had his lethal side all right. With that Herculean yet quick and agile build, he had to be a very physical person. Horace was what his body told you. He *was* that incredible primitive strength, that astute direct mind. Born in the US, Horace could not possibly have been anything but a Southern Baptist. There was the sweet oiled click of inevitability to that. Horace was so physical that the gap between him and concrete reality was very short indeed. That space could admit only the most stripped and immediate set of certainties. Horace *had* to be a Fundamentalist. That makes us brothers beneath the skin, thought Feisal cynically. If at somewhat different levels of subtlety. You could always, he thought, call Horace a Poor Man's Feisal –

Despite that cruelty, Feisal knew that the affinity was genuine, and moreover strongly to his advantage. There was no doubt that Horace felt it, or that his sympathy with Feisal extended to Blake. Ever since Horace's Embassy party for the Kingdom's National Day almost three years before, he had been host to the two of them often. He had invited them, not just and invariably to his many official cocktail parties, but also and nearly as frequently to private tête-à-tête dinners which no one else attended and which were notable, not only for the good food – Horace had an excellent Lebanese chef – but also for the surprisingly rich cellar, inherited from Horace's sybaritic predecessor. These dinners rapidly became something of an institution, normally on the last Wednesday of each month. In them, over time, he showed a remarkable interest in, and deference to, his two guests' views, and particularly Feisal's. It was as if he were using them intelligently as skilled political and economic counsellors for the Kingdom of the Sun and for the Middle East as a whole; he evidently did not think a great deal of his own Embassy staff, or that he could glean much wisdom from his fellow ambassadors, or for that matter from his natural local contact, the Kingdom's Foreign Minister.

Indeed, Horace seemed to feel an equally instinctive and deep-seated antipathy for the Kingdom of the Sun's Establishment as such, and notably as it was represented by, for example, Sheikh Abdullah and his sister Princess Leila Jibál. Perhaps, thought Feisal, it was a peasant's natural reaction to royalty – for it cried out to the high heavens that Horace was of rugged peasant stock – what on earth now would Murgatroyd be? Irish? – or it could be his contempt as a Supermarket king, a tough American businessman, for the Oxford sophistication and accent which they so unmistakably carried – or both of these. Clearly, in any event, he felt them alien, not of his clan. One night late Horace, in his cups – and Feisal made a point of matching his and Blake's drinking glass for glass in these special dinners, which he saw as probably vital for his long-term cause – had made a point of mimicking Abdullah's and Leila's accents, and mocking them viciously. Blake had stayed silent through that, evidently not liking it at all, but Feisal had laughed politely, though being careful to mask his own true intense inner delight. For Horace's strongly emotional opposition to the Kingdom of the Sun's Establishment policies was precisely one of the two attitudes of his which Feisal needed if his long-term, extremely ambitious plans were ever to succeed.

The other attitude Horace revealed slowly but without the slightest shadow of doubt over time, and practically all on his own. He had really, thought Feisal, required almost no enticing at all, save of the subtlest and most skilful kind – which was the quality Feisal had known he must use, in order not to arouse Blake's suspicions. What Horace brought out, as a result of this mild encouragement, and only by a phrase or short comment here, a pointed silence there, was that he had a deeply entrenched and irrevocable mistrust – and he could and would produce an immensely rich and varied and irrefutable mass of evidence to justify it if ever so requested – of Catholics, Nigras and Jews. Mindful of Feisal, Horace had of course swiftly qualified his very first reference to blacks by making it crystal-clear that he naturally saw Arabs as falling into a very different and infinitely loftier category, as members of a remarkable civilization which had reached impressive heights in the twelfth century with leaders like Saladin and such, art and theology and architecture and philosophy and so on, very advanced as a culture, though it seemed to have slid back rather drastically ever since, hadn't it? All the same, it would still be perfectly reasonable, wouldn't it, to see the Arabs today as sort of Honorary Europeans, or Americans?

Feisal, feeling Blake smiling covertly beside him, still took this in his stride. What mattered to him was the third racial target Horace had named. For Feisal's plans to succeed, he needed Horace to be inflexibly anti-semitic too. From the look of it, Feisal had no work to do at all in this regard. Horace had done it all already for him. Feisal was sincerely thankful for his good luck. He knew he must take all the help he could get, from fate, God, or the Devil. For his enemy was every bit as efficient, tenacious, guileful, subtle, multifacetic, dedicated and implacable as he. The highly competent killing whose results he had just witnessed proved that. He knew moreover that he was very likely to be finding more such evidence.

'Some kind of blood brother vengeance?' asked Blake, beside him, driving the formidably-powered metallic-silver Camaro. No doubt Leila liked riding around in it too, thought Feisal. Feisal knew all about Blake and Leila.

'Something like that,' he replied. 'That's the way the Kingdom's police will see it, anyway. A settlement of accounts. Which of course is almost certainly what it was. Fairly private. So the police won't do anything much about it. It's a sound system. They don't interfere with us, we don't interfere with them. Yet.'

He wondered why he had added that last word, which was foolhardy, and he glanced quickly to his side at Blake. But Blake seemed concentrated on driving his straight-six-cylinder Camaro as fast as he reasonably could between the fairly heavy and lazy traffic. The inhabitants of the Kingdom of the Sun liked to wander about in their cars showing them off of a

Friday, and these days just about every *Shemsi* family had at least one car, and many non-*Shemsi* families too. Blake had got down onto the Beach Road by now, having passed the huge and luxurious complex of flats and fashion shops and supermarket and laundry and bookseller and butcher's and baker's and swimming-pools and marina where he lived. Feisal had left the phone number of Blake's flat with his Fatah man on duty, which is where Fatah had located him when he came back there for a brandy after his lunch with Blake at a nearby Lebanese restaurant.

'When will you know for sure?' asked Blake.

'If it's a settlement of accounts? When we see the second man. If he's still around. Just one killing could be anything in this part of the world. But here two's already enemy action.'

Three kilometres out in that ominous still opaque sea the great merchantmen still hung at anchor in the prevailing current, their bows all pointing identically and obediently at the capital city of the Sun's distant and evasive port. And no doubt, thought Feisal, who hated sharks almost as much as he did Zionists, those incredibly swift and silent and aero-dynamic arrowhead monsters that never slept, with their eyes mounted out on those flat stubby wings sprouting out from their heads, and those obscenely efficient nostrils along all the front of them, able to pick up and zero in on a blood-slick kilometres away, were patrolling now constantly in their many serried layers, waiting for bodies, waiting for prey. And one day my men will be as superbly efficient, as deadly, with no coefficient of drag at all, Feisal promised himself, when they are fully integrated in my new movement, trained to destroy with its new equipment as precisely and effortlessly as these –

'Still a lot of ships hanging out there to unload,' said Blake, who had evidently been listening to him think, Feisal hoped not all the way.

'Yes,' he replied. 'With all the most marvellous luxuries that the world can produce. Rolls-Royces and Cadillacs and the world's finest clothes and jewelry from Paris and Rome and London and New York, the most expensive furnishings and TVs, cameras and carpets. All that the most avaricious *Shemsi* heart could desire – '

He had not been able to keep that note of bitterness from his voice. Blake heard it at once.

'While these astronomical sums should have gone instead to liberate Palestine?'

'Yes. I'm sorry; mine's a dull theme, isn't it? But just a fraction could probably do it, properly applied. With enough willpower, determination. Instead, most Arab producing countries have concerned themselves most desperately with finding how on earth they can spend their vast new fortunes from the fantastic crude oil price rises of 1973, and again in 1979 when the Iran–Iraq war started, on frivolities like these – '

'These days of fabled oil riches may not last forever,' said Blake.

'You mean the OPEC crude postings have got to come down again? Yes, I knew that the spot prices of the Arab Light marker have been dropping fairly hard since June.'

'Hard is right,' said Blake. 'The Arab Light spot nearly touched 30 dollars a barrel mid year. The latest spot's round twenty-seven dollars, ten per cent down in six months. The OPEC posting for Arab Light – so therefore for our Sun Light too – will almost certainly have to come down again early next year. It's too high at the twenty-nine dollars level, as it was at thirty-four dollars through 1982. Just think, before the 1970s we were all quite used to two dollars per barrel crude. That 1982 level was *seventeen times* that!'

'So the crude prices will have to come down. That will hurt the big Arab producers!' said Feisal, not without a certain satisfaction. 'Well, it would do them no harm spiritually to be forced back to a desert economy. *That* might help open their eyes! It might help them to get their moral perspectives right!'

'I doubt if prices will drop so far as actually to force them back to a desert economy,' said Blake equably, 'but they've certainly got to come down hard over the next few years. Simply because we really have half-strangled, if not actually killed, the goose that lays the golden egg. We've got the crude oil prices so high that we have effectively compelled the world to seek and find alternative energy sources – nuclear, coal, hydro, solar. So we've actually *cut back* total oil demand. And we're still, just, finding more oil worldwide than is going out of production. But don't worry, Ahmed. You're still certain of your ten cents a barrel contribution for your PLO activities on Tulsa's 700,000 bd of Sun Light forward until October 30

1988 – anyway on paper; you know Tulsa were very happy to renew the contract on the same terms for another five years when its first term ended this October 30. So you can still operate.'

'I'm more deeply grateful for that than I can say.'

That was true enough, thought Feisal. That $26 million annually during the last five years, and hopefully for another five, would go exclusively to fund his Plan. The PLO knew nothing of it. Feisal was funding his usual PLO-Fatah activities from the taxes he levied on the Palestinian Arabs working in the Kingdom of the Sun, the bulk of which, most strictly accounted for (there was nothing in the least easygoing about Arafat in this respect), Feisal regularly transferred to Fatah's HQ, now in Tunis. Fatah and the PLO, he thought a trifle grimly, were already doing pretty damned well as it was. They were now respectable Big Business, with fixed and flat dividend-paying investments of more than $6 billion in the US and other major stocks markets. Feisal knew that Fatah and the PLO had been getting handsome contributions from other Arabs, often as guilt-tinged blood-money, for many years; they were now consummate wizards in extracting them almost painlessly. By the start of 1968, just on sixteen years before, they had already convinced King Feisal of Saudi Arabia to soak the Palestinians working there with a tax for Fatah which brought in some 18 million dollars annually. Just after that Fatah had visited Libya and hit the government and business sectors there for heavy and regular contributions. And the Ninth Arab Summit at Baghdad from November 2 to 5 1978, horrified out of their wits at Sadat's peace treaty with Israel, had voted no less than 3½ *billion* dollars annually to those Arab nations still abutting Israel on a more or less militant footing. Of this, the PLO had regularly been getting the princely sum of 250 million annually, plus the rights shared with Jordan to administer another 150 million a year for promoting resistance against Israel by the peoples of the occupied territories. So Fatah and the PLO were in good financial shape. There was no reason why they should get any of the many millions Blake had diverted to Feisal, and every reason why they should *not*. They would never, understandably, tolerate Feisal's Plan anyway –

He glanced round briefly at Blake. So in its achievement, he thought ironically, these too have their essential roles, Horace B. Murgatroyd, Philip Blake. These *kuffár*, these infidels. Particularly Blake, who so needs to be part of the action, part of the world's history, or just a short jump ahead of it. And so he will be.

Blake glanced back at once, then looked back over the driving-wheel. He was continually alert. I must remember always to be very careful, thought Feisal. But Blake said only:

'I'd say they'd drop to about the March–April 1974 level. The crude oil prices I mean. It'll take two or three more years though. From today, in Arab Light or Arab Sun terms, around twenty-nine dollars a barrel to say eleven or twelve dollars. Why? Because that's about where our whiz-kids' think-tank in Eagle told us they ought to be, seen against the true costs of all other energy sources. After that, it was only the Iranian Revolution in 1979 and the Iran–Iraq War from the next year that threw things out of kilter again. It might drop lower than eleven dollars through panic, but I doubt if it'd do that for very long.'

'So how hard is this going to hit our friends in the Kingdom here?' asked Feisal.

Blake smiled.

'Of course they'll hate getting less for their product. Who wouldn't? But it won't kill them. In fact it'll hardly hurt them at all. They don't really have to sell another barrel of oil at any price, and they'd still survive comfortably. Why? Because they've already put into the ground and paid for eighty per cent of the ten-billion-dollar new economic infrastructure for the formerly under-privileged. And they've astutely and constantly been investing in blue chips stocks and shares in the US, Japan and Europe all these fat years. Abdullah told me the up-to-date total the other day. It's just over forty billion, and they're getting a net return between eleven and twelve per cent per annum. That's around four and a half *billion* dollars income annually, even if they never sell another drop of oil. Among the say fifty thousand *Shemsi* families, that's ninety-five thousand dollars per *Shemsi* family per year. Or suppose you shared that total net income out among *every* family in the Kingdom, to the most recent and poorest Iranian, then every single family'd still stand to get some thirty thousand a year. Not bad, for doing nothing. So the Kingdom of the Sun could just sit on its hands and laugh.'

'They're not going to do that,' said Feisal curtly, so that Blake glanced round at him again, quickly. Feisal stared straight ahead through the windscreen. He had other projects for the Kingdom of the Sun. That was *not* the way it would be governed. There were other things to do with astronomic wealth than sit on it.

They were at the Dhow Port now. Three or four were moored at the quays, their sails sweetly furled; cloves-traffickers from Zanzibar, perhaps, from Pemba.

'It's straight past the Dhow Port,' said Feisal, 'and past the Dhow-building Yards. The old Arab stone houses just beyond. The second.'

The Dhow-building Yards were to their right. There were three skeleton hulls in there, the first decks just being laid. They curved with superb grace. The dhows looked like whales being structured, all the intricate bones set precisely about the strong springy spine, now just the tough skin to come.

'People know already,' said Feisal. 'They've found him. It's as I feared.'

The second house was solidly built, like Feisal's own, of thick stone walls. Even in this constant cruel heat, it would be cool inside. Not, thought Feisal sadly, that its owner would be likely to be bothering about that now –

He thrust through the people crowding the front path to the house. Two uniformed policemen were at the half-opened door, keeping them out. Feisal, with Blake just behind him, addressed the first policeman:

'Your officer's inside? Please call him. Tell him it's Ahmed Feisal.'

'*Effendim.*'

He was back within thirty seconds with the officer, a young captain.

'Ah, Captain Azzam. Ahmed Feisal. And my Ministry colleague, Mr Blake. It looks bad?'

'Dr Feisal, of course. Yes. This is your territory, I fear. We've touched nothing. Please come in.'

The welcome shadows within were like an embrace. Feisal glanced up; the same black-beamed ceiling, creosoted. Ahead in that first room he saw the body.

It was of a man, perhaps forty, sitting apparently perfectly at his ease in an armchair. Like the first, he looked tall, lean, and hard. He also wore neatly pressed slacks, an open-necked and short-sleeved shirt, and sandals, in the Palestinian Arab style, rather than the *Shemsi*, and he too had a very light olive complexion. His well-muscled forearms rested comfortably forward on his thighs, the hands relaxed opened, the chromium-cased Rolex watch still untouched on his left wrist; nobody had come here to steal. This too looked an edifying picture of a Muslim on his Friday rest-day, his *'asr*, mid-afternoon prayer, already decently completed. The only thing wrong was that his throat was slit from ear to ear, the blood from it drenching his otherwise impeccable leisure clothes and that friendly armchair in which he sat. Someone of prodigious skill and strength must have picked that front-door lock or broken it silently, then entered without the slightest sound, and taken and slaughtered that victim from behind in this chair, holding him like a vice and drawing the keen blade across his throat with a speed and ferocity that must have hissed.

'It's like a *dhabíha*,' said Feisal. 'A formal blood-sacrifice.'

'Indeed,' said Captain Azzam. 'And the ritual butcher left no clues, no notes.'

'He didn't have to,' said Feisal.

Azzam looked at him curiously for a moment.

'No,' he said then. 'I see.'

'His wife and children were away?'

'Yes. We understand with her sister, in that new complex of flats by the airport. Nobody has told her yet.'

'Then please find and tell her. As gently as you can. And that I'll come to see her as soon as I can, to help. Meanwhile I've work to do, two other men to check on. Where's the phone?'

'In the hall, *Effendim*.'

Feisal went through to it rapidly and dialled a number.

'Hotel Semiramis? Mr Khalaf, please. It's urgent.'

There was a wait. The voice came back at the other end.

'What?' said Feisal. 'No reply, and his bedroom door's locked? Look, get your nearest police *at once*! Yes, this is a police matter. You get his door open immediately, with your pass-key. And warn an ambulance to stand by. My name is Ahmed Feisal, Ministry of Oil. Tell the police. And I'm coming round at once – '

He came back fast into the room to Azzam.

'Captain, here's a fourth name. And address. Please get a patrol-car there as fast as you can. It's life and death. Almost certainly death. I'm going to the one at the Semiramis, *now*!'

He and Blake ran out to the Camaro.

'Go like the wind!' he said to Blake. 'It's the other side of the city. Not far from the Broadcasting Building. Don't worry about the speed limits. I'll answer for those.'

Blake took him literally, he was glad to see. He screamed past the other traffic like a racing-driver, very fast, but always in control. So much so that he could still half-glance round at Feisal and ask:

'So yet another *dhabíha*, sacrificial victim, Feisal?'

Feisal's lips tightened.

'Yes. Even to the point of his slaughterer holding him rigid while he died, so that his spirit could escape straight and with dignity from his body.'

'Thoughtful,' said Blake, narrowly avoiding a rare Mini-Minor which had emerged suddenly from a blind side-turning. Feisal looked back at this big Englishman with his flat blond hair and sharp blue eyes and apparently inbuilt quirk of mockery.

'Professional,' said Feisal. 'A nice economy of effort. Not a foot wrong so far.'

'So what's it all about?' said Blake.

Feisal held onto his seat as Blake swerved them past a huge and infinitely long petrol bowser, tucking the Camaro in front of it just before an advancing pack lorry hit them.

'You remember that hijack at Athens Airport four weeks ago, no, five? The El Al Boeing that was supposed to be flying back to Tel Aviv, only four hijackers deflected it to Libya instead?'

'Oh, sure. And blew it up there.'

'After releasing all women and kids and non-Israeli men. They just kept the Israeli men. For exchange with fifty Fatah prisoners that Israel was holding. Likud wouldn't play, so they executed four of the Israelis. That didn't change Israel's mind either, so they let the others go, then blew up the Boeing. And went home.'

'I see. Israel having taken their names and addresses.'

'Israel, meaning their goddamned Mossad Intelligence,

having *found out* their names and addresses, God knows how, and cooked up a return party. Which you're witnessing.'

'Christ!' said Blake.

'No,' said Feisal. 'It's more the Old Testament. An eye for an eye. The hijackers killed four Israeli men. And they are four. Meet my friends.'

The third of Feisal's friends was not a pretty sight. He had the same Western-style clothes as the first two, the same light olive skin, the same lean air of constant training. However, he was perceptibly lighter in build. Perhaps this was why his executioners had decided that they could safely hang him from the strong curtain-rail above his door. As it was, his bound feet reached to within centimetres of the floor. That binding, with the cord wrapped tightly round his wrists behind his back, robbed the scene of any suspicion of suicide. His killers had not broken his neck. There would anyway have been too short a drop from that peg to achieve that result. Besides, it was hardly likely that his executioners would have been concerned that he suffered. There could be no doubt that he had. His whole face was cyanosed, even his lips bulging and the same vicious blue-black, and his swollen tongue protruding horribly. His eyes were rolled back until only the whites showed, and they were heavily suffused with blood. The police lieutenant already there when Feisal and Blake arrived told them how this hanging body, like a carcass in an abattoir suspended from a large black iron hook, was the first thing he banged into after he and his men had broken down the door, bolted from within. The killers had presumably left by the fire-escape outside the window, which was their simplest route inward too, to carry out their sentence of death.

'After this,' said Feisal, 'my fourth man's a formality. He *couldn't* still be alive. Still, we may as well go round, to have the full picture. I'll ring first.'

He went down to the hotel vestibule, Blake just behind him, and dialled a number. Within seconds he had put the phone down again and turned.

'Yes,' he said. 'They've found him.' He added grimly. 'We have no need to hurry.'

'It's too late to get that Mossad commando too?'

Feisal looked at Blake and shrugged.

'Almost certainly. The four killings appear to have been

synchronized for 3 pm. It's now just on five, so they've got a two-hour head-start. They'll be lying up in some safe house till dusk, then they'll get out by small rubber boat to the submarine that brought them in. By daylight tomorrow the submarine'll be in deep water where we can't see or touch it – quite a lot of the Arabian Gulf is around a hundred metres water depth, and once she was past the Strait of Hormuz and Gulf of Oman she'd be into the Arabian Sea and over a thousand metres of water. Or they'll get out to a rocky strip of desert to the west and a low-flying short-take-off plane with extra fuel tanks'll take them the 1,400 km back to Israel. Or else they'll simply drift across as Bedu south of El Hijarah, probably following Tapline. They've their special Arabic Section, you know, some of them really indistinguishable from true Arabs. But you're right; one has to go through the motions – '

He turned to the phone again and dialled Police Head-quarters.

'Captain Azzam? Feisal. The blood sacrifice we saw was the second of four. I've see three and have confirmed that the fourth is dead. Yes, certainly a Mossad commando; you know who our four were. So could you please get out a general search, all regular police and border police and troops, naval units and air force? Probably a group of six to eight, heavily armed and able to pass as Arabs. These men are very dangerous; shoot at the slightest suspicion – '

At shadows, he thought bitterly. They would be shooting at shadows. They would never see that Mossad group.

Back in the metallic-silver Camaro, pointing as Feisal directed at a nearby suburb, Blake asked:

'If the Israelis are *that* efficient and invulnerable, then does it really make sense to needle them with hijackings and similar violent assaults?'

'They're not invulnerable!' Feisal replied savagely. 'And, believe me, I'll prove that if it's the last thing I do! And what the hell do you want us to do? We've *got* to carry the fight to Israel now, anywhere in the world, all the time, from countries like the Kingdom of the Sun. Why? Just *think* a little of what's been happening over the last few years. On June 3 last year a Palestinian Arab gunman shot the Israeli Ambassaor in London and paralysed him for life. Next day Israel flung in masses of F-16 aircraft to shatter Palestinian Arab refugee camps and other targets in Beirut and South Lebanon, causing casualties of something like sixty-five dead and two hundred wounded. So Palestinian Arab artillery fired back into Northern Israel.'

Feisal smiled his cold appreciation of a ruthless enemy.

'The Israelis must have been waiting for just that pretext, for only two days later they launched their so-called "Operation Peace in Galilee" and put hundreds of thousands of their best regular troops and *miluím* reservists into an assault that would cost them thousands dead and tens of thousands wounded, and allegedly provoke the resignation of Begin in deep depression and his total disappearance from active politics. The Israelis punched their way incredibly fast all the way up the Lebanon to Beirut. Within eight days Israeli armour and commandos had met the Phalangist Christian militia in and near East Beirut who had been fighting Israel's battles for her already for six years. From there General Sharon, of Suez Canal fame, now demanded the PLO's unconditional surrender in Beirut and evacuation totally unarmed from Lebanon.'

Blake could detect no tremor of emotion in Feisal's voice. He was reminded again, as he had been reminded throughout this tour of the quiet killings, of the years of harsh defeat which had to produce so obdurate a mask. Feisal resumed his dispassionate summary.

'After King Hussein's ejection of the PLO from Jordan in 1970–71, Sharon's demand represented total disaster. The PLO-Fatah would now remain *with no base whatsoever contiguous with Israel* from which to attack her. Yet what else could the PLO-Fatah do? They had three-quarters of Israel's entire armed forces and Israel's Phalangist allies round their necks, and no one else was going to lift a finger to help them. Only five thousand Syrian troops had fought in this battle, and Assad was certainly not going to risk committing any more in so grim a military situation. And *none* of the other Arab States had helped. So Arafat could only accept defeat, though at least he negotiated that his men would go carrying their personal arms.

'So, on August 21 1982 began the first evacuation of the twelve thousand PLO fighters by sea from Beirut harbour. On

August 30 Arafat followed them. Lebanese government dignitaries accompanied him to his ship, and ringing speeches were made on both sides, but this expulsion was still a bitter humiliation.'

'No doubt it was,' said Blake. 'But there was not much else he could do except fight to the death.'

'In fact he told Reagan's trouble-shooter, Philip Habib, that the PLO would do just that unless they got an American and International guarantee of the safety of the civilians they left behind, including their own wives and children. And Habib gave him that in writing.'

'Fair enough,' said Blake. He was still driving like Stirling Moss, probably out of sheer force of habit. 'But the Israelis didn't humiliate just Arafat and his PLO-Fatah. What about Syria? For the five years solid from 1977 the Israeli aircraft overflying the Bekaa Valley in Lebanon shot practically every single Syrian aircraft sent against them out of the sky. Till the Syrians imported their Sam-6 air defence missile batteries that the Russians supplied. Then Habib convinces them to take their Sam-6's *out* of the Bekaa Valley again.'

'And it wasn't just humiliation,' said Feisal. 'Humiliation doesn't murder you. But what the Israelis and Phalangists perpetrated despite that written guarantee did. Just over six years after Gemayyel's Phalangists and Chamoun's Tigers militias had stormed the Tel ez-Zaatar refugee camp in East Beirut, where I lost my mother mutilated and my sisters massacred, the Phalangists did the same thing at the Sabra and Shatila refugee camps, this time with the aid of an encircling ring of Israeli tanks, ostensibly to root out any remaining terrorists. Instead from September 16 to 18 they slaughtered three thousand civilian men, women and children. They shot whole families to pieces in their homes, raped girls then chopped them up, brained or disembowelled infants. After that you seriously ask me why we go on mounting every possible commando action we can from any base we can find? What the hell else do you expect us to do? Write a polite note of protest to the UN and Reagan?'

'Well,' said Blake, 'at least Reagan produced a peace plan for you.'

'With what a superb sense of timing!' Feisal retorted. 'On September 1 last year, two days after Arafat had been kicked out of Lebanon! Besides Reagan's was quite a fall-back from say Fahd's plan. Reagan's didn't even insist on Israel pulling right back to the pre-1967 lines, or on a truly independent Palestinian Arab Nation-State – just on some kind of federation between the West Bank and Jordan, and on a halt to Israel's fanatical building of Jewish settlements in the occupied territories. At an implied cost much too high; our formal recognition of Israel's right to exist.'

'Christ!' said Blake. 'But the State of Israel's a goddamned fact, Ahmed! It's not going to dissolve just because you don't like it! With the full support of the US behind it? Look, even the Russians see that! That's behind the six-point peace plan they announced mid-September last year, which was very near the Fahd Plan. Which itself recognized Israel's existence, even if it did in return require full Israeli withdrawal from her 1967 conquests. And you yourselves, every member of the Arab League save Libya, but including Arafat, approved that Fahd Plan slightly revised at the Arab Summit at Fez early that same September – '

'So what?' Feisal broke in crudely. '*All* those peace discussions were simply shocked and mocked into oblivion by what the Phalangists did with that ring of Israeli armour supporting them in their massacres in Sabra and Shatila from that September 16 to 18. To my mind that makes utter nonsense of any further peace negotiations. You said that Israel wouldn't just disappear. You are absolutely right. So we are going to have to *make* her. By sheer physical force. By outright naked violence. Equally pitiless, at *whatever* the cost!'

The sight of the fourth hijacker suggested that violence was no monopoly of Feisal's. Again the police were there in force already, keeping the morbidly curious away from the inside of the house. For the hijacker was in his own inner patio. It had a fountain and a concrete basin, now dry, and circled by pointed iron railings – perhaps designed to keep cats away from the goldfish in the pond which the affluent former owner might have maintained. The fourth hijacker had evidently had no use for goldfish. He too was between thirty and forty in age, neatly dressed in Western clothes, of light olive complexion, and lean and fit from hard physical training; indeed, of that standard model which Feisal, having largely formed it, knew well. But the Mossad executioners had found a use for the iron railings.

They had impaled the fourth hijacker on them, face upwards. His eyes were still open and staring, in an expression of enormous surprise, and his mouth slack. Three of the sharp points of the railings, down to the ends of the barbs, projected up out of the chest, holding him as securely as a well-gaffed fish. Below him, the concrete basin was serving its original purpose. Like the second hijacker he seemed to have been endowed with a remarkable volume of blood.

'No clues, no traces of them,' said the police sergeant with them gloomily. He was a tall hawk-like man of indeterminate age, almost certainly a Bedu from his accent. That was the great virtue of being born a *Shemsi*, thought Feisal; even if you had just been dragged out of the desert and off your camel, the *míri*, the government, would always find a job for you somewhere.

'There wouldn't be,' said Feisal. 'They're professionals. Now you're going to tell me it must have happened around three o'clock and that his wife and children weren't here.'

The tall hawk-like Bedu sergeant looked at him in amazement. 'No, the wife and children were here all right,' he said, 'but, yes, she said it happened at exactly three. But how did you know that, *Effendim?*'

'Because we've had three other identical murders here today at that hour,' said Feisal. 'We have efficient enemies. But this time the wife and children were here? What does she say happened?'

'Three men came to the door at exactly three. She went to see who it was because her husband was in the bathroom. She says she was sure they were Arabs. They were dressed like Palestinians and spoke Arabic like Palestinians, except one might have been Egyptian. They said they were from a sister organization to her husband's. The same business, they said. When her husband came the two biggest ones took him and hit him in the stomach and neck so that he fell and was unconscious. Then they tied cloth round his mouth so that he could not scream when he woke, and they tied his wrists, and the two bigger men carried him to the courtyard. The third man took her and the children – small, of five and six years – to her bedroom. There he simply watched them, warning them that he would have to tie them up if they were not quiet. She stressed particularly that the third man was most careful in no way to affront her modesty. That impressed her. She heard only a kind of strangled scream from the patio. Then the two other men came back into the house and called, and the third man went, and they were gone. She ran to the patio. When she saw her husband she went into total hysterics. At least she had shut the bedroom door so that the children could not come. Neighbours came at last at her screams, then they called us. But we arrived only some forty minutes after the death.'

'The murderers gave her no hint how they had come, or how they would go home?'

'Nothing,' said the Bedu sergeant. 'We could get little from her save the barest facts. She stayed hysterical, and we sent her to the hospital. Neighbours have taken the children.'

'I've asked Captain Azzam at Police Headquarters to order a full urgent search for these vicious and violent killers,' said Feisal. 'Let us hope strongly and with piety that we find them, so that we can mete out their just punishment to them according to our Law.'

'*Insh'Allah*!' replied the sergeant reverently.

'Let us indeed hope that it is God's will,' said Feisal. 'And until that is ascertained we might as well all go home.'

'*Hathrítak*!' commented the Bedu, drawing himself up to his full height and saluting smartly. 'Your Excellency!'

His Excellency moved back through the milling crowd with Blake to the Camaro. 'Where to?' asked Blake, turning on the ignition.

'It'd better be back to my house, please. I'll have to get a full report off at once to the PLO HQ in Tunis.'

'Sure,' said Blake. 'Well, thanks for the tour. Sorry it's been so rough on you.'

'You've always said you wanted to see what really happens in the Middle East,' said Feisal. 'So meet reality. For you're really seeing the bedrock facts stripped bare now.'

'It's fascinating,' said Blake. 'You know, I'd really rather like to play too.'

'You've *been* playing!' said Feisal. 'That twenty-six million dollars you've been delivering to me annually for the last five years and propose to go on passing me for the next five will finance a truly serious assault, believe me. So, I'll never forget that about you. Whatever happens. Or has to happen.'

'That sounds a bit premonitory!'

'Well, it's a hard world, Philip; we both know that. Look, I've taken you into my segment of it fairly carefully and slowly so far. Except for this afternoon. You could call that a crash course. You seem to have taken it fairly calmly. You qualify; I don't see you losing your nerve.'

'It's just that my facial muscles are atrophied, Ahmed. It's my public-school upbringing.'

'Well, that background may well advise you not to come in any further. It's a rough sea, with some nasty hidden currents. But if you want to see the lot, I'll show it to you. You're a free man, though, Philip. It's absolutely your decision, and I wouldn't influence you one way or another. There's no reason at all why you should do any more for us than you've already done.'

'I hate to pull out of things halfway, you know,' said Blake. 'I'd rather take my chance and buy the lot. Even if there's a man-eating tiger lurking in the package. So could I see the lot, please, Doctor?'

Feisal turned in his seat and looked at Blake very seriously for some while. Finally he said: 'All right. So be it, Philip. I hope it's the right decision for you. Can you get away from the Ministry for say three hours from ten-thirty tomorrow morning?'

'I expect so,' said Blake. 'I can't think of anything urgent on the programme. I'll ask Abdullah, of course, though I doubt that he'd object.'

'Fine,' said Feisal. 'Though I'd rather you didn't tell him you were going out with me.'

Blake glanced to the right at him over his driving-wheel.

'As you wish,' he said.

'I'd just rather keep him out of this,' said Feisal. 'He knows what I do for Fatah and the PLO, of course. That's no secret to him. But I don't see any reason why he should have to know about any part you may play in it.'

Blake said nothing. After a minute Feisal added. 'Poor Abdullah!'

Blake looked round at him again, this time sharply.

'Why *poor* Abdullah? He's an excellent man. And a great friend of mine.'

'Yes, I know that,' said Feisal. 'But – '

'But?' queried Blake, insisting.

273

'But,' repeated Feisal. 'Well, I suppose it's all a question of timing. It so often is.'

'So go on.'

Feisal looked round levelly at him.

'I think that Abdullah will lose out on history. I think that Abdullah will miss the bus.'

28

A School for Death

The desert looked after its own, thought Philip Blake, his eyes sweeping it ceaselessly. It revealed nothing, told nothing. If you trod footsteps across it, the desert wind, soft as a maiden's breath or keen as the razor edge of a scimitar, filled and obliterated them effortlessly with soft fine sand. You could build bold highways across it, erect tall proud cities in it, but unless your legions swept back this subtle and insidious enemy tirelessly, it would sooner or later engulf and bury you, laying you decently beside the myriad other bleached bones already beneath it, and leaving no trace. The African jungle invaded as decisively, but that was a vivid force of exuberant green life, or luxuriant roots and creepers and bursting plants. Here the invader wore the pale yellow escutcheon of death, under the clanging brassy eye of a murderous molten sun, in a waste flat world with no landmarks, no slightest drop of water. This seemed the final void, pitiless, treacherous and secret.

And thus no mean site for a terrorist training camp, Blake decided. He had driven Feisal up to the north that morning, from the Ministry of Oil in the City of the Sun to Mina es-Salaam, the Port of Peace, where the Kingdom's glittering 200,000 bd refinery stood, and its superbly efficient Bechtel-built tanker-loading terminals elbowed out into the ominous sea. Here Blake had parked his Camaro in the rare shade beside the Refinery Manager's office, and switched into the front passenger seat of the four-wheel-drive jeep that Feisal had had waiting there. So Feisal had driven them then twenty minutes further north along the coast highway, then suddenly, at no sign or bend in the metalled road that Blake could see, turned due west off it and into this alien wasteland. Ten minutes into it Blake saw the Bedu. They were dead north, ninety degrees to his right. Their black skin tents were scattered three hundred metres off. Various poles of different lengths held each up, their edges pegged down into the sand. They had a curiously haphazard air, like sun-blackened leaves flung down in a storm. There was no sign of men about them, but women's eyes almost certainly watched from within. A few camels flecked the desert behind them, their long-necked heads confidently down to the sand, grazing on God knew what.

'Where are the men?' he asked.

'They'll be off with their flocks somewhere,' said Feisal. 'There's a small oasis further north-east.'

'They don't bother your camp?'

'They steer clear of it.'

Blake saw why when they got there, fifteen minutes later, following the faintest of tracks across mainly rocky ground. The camp sprang up out of nothing, a huge rectangle on barren land guarded by twin fences of tall barbed-wire mounted up strong iron poles, the top sixty centimetres of which projected outwards at forty-five degrees to carry the last wicked strands of wire. Eight-metre watchtowers stood at each corner and halfway along the longer sides of the rectangle, each a high hut like a crow's nest, with what looked like a fixed .50 calibre Browning machinegun with twin searchlights beside it, and two men in khaki overalls and red-and-white *kefiyyahs* crowned by black *ogals* in it, submachineguns or automatic rifles slung across their backs. The main gate was midway between two of these formidable concentrations of fire-power in the shorter eastern leg of this rectangle. All down the longer southern leg to the left were khaki tents, their colour blending perfectly with the desert. They were exactly marshalled, all flaps open identically for airing or inspection; they could have been a British Guards regiment on parade; it was evident that discipline here was at the highest pitch. As, Blake saw, was activity. For the whole of the northern part of the camp ahead to his right seemed in constant heaving turbulence. It was only after half a minute that his eye began to crystallize out the separate and very meaningful movements to this stern ballet.

'That's a hell of a lot of men! How many, roughly?'

'Five hundred, at any one time,' answered Feisal. 'About ten per cent of that are instructors and fixed camp staff.'

'So that at any one moment you're giving full-time training to four hundred and fifty guerillas, *fedayeen*? How long's the course?'

'Say three months, on the average, twelve to fourteen hours a day. More to our really hot specialists. That makes them pros all right. Remember every one's a volunteer. Many have lost family, say in refugee camps, as I did. So their motivation is very high. They're *very* keen to learn. By the time they get out of here they can really use Kalashnikov AK-47 and American M-1 automatic rifles, even strip them in the dark and put them correctly together again. And all the most widely used submachineguns and handguns. They can make and use explosives efficiently. We even give them shock courses in finding their way out of deserts. Then we drop them in one. It's a graduation test. Some die, but most get out. Then they've really learned something. We drill them pretty mercilessly in judo and karate. And we indoctrinate them, you may say heavily. I probably go far beyond the PLO-Fatah standards on this. It's my specialty. I think it's vital. Without it we won't beat Israel. With it, we shall – '

'Even Israel could hardly break into *this* camp!'

'Don't be too sure,' said Feisal. 'Even though that fence is electrified too. I've another camp identical to this to the south, you know. Why not just one big one? Again Israel. I daren't keep all my eggs in one basket. You saw yesterday what Mossad can do.'

The camp gate swung open. A tall slim man came out to them.

'Salah Khalíl, our camp commandant,' said Feisal. 'Salah, this is the civilized Englishman I was telling you about. Philip Blake.'

Salah Khalíl came to Blake's side of the jeep and shook hands with him. Blake felt an extremely firm grip. Khalíl was not making a macho contest of it. He was just stating clearly who he was, and that was six foot of whipcord and sunburnt skin, with brown hair and bright blue eyes; some Englishman or Irishman or Circassian must have climbed into his family tree somewhere.

'Welcome to Little Mecca, Mr Blake.'

'Many thanks. Little Mecca?'

'Because that's where Muhammed started off from in flight and apparent defeat, which he then by rigorous training and discipline turned into outright, even worldwide, victory.'

His English was perfect.

'Forgive his Sandhurst subaltern act,' said Feisal crudely. 'Salah used to be an Inspector in the Palestine Police. He could never get over it.'

Salah Khalíl smiled.

'Well, the best of British luck to you both,' said Blake. 'And may I please be allowed to see your camp?'

'Give the man the Grand Tour, Salah,' said Feisal. 'Show him the works. He's quite a friend of ours. Has indeed helped us so greatly that we may indeed finally be able to change the face of the word – '

'Would you like meanwhile to rest in the shade of my tent?' Salah Khalíl asked him.

'No, I'd like to come too,' said Feisal.

'*Ya Salaam!*' Khalíl exclaimed. 'It's always an honour, Ahmed, but this must be about your five hundredth time! You'll kill yourself! I know how hard you've worked for us – '

'Salah's my best press agent,' said Feisal, parking his jeep inside the gate and just to the right.

The three men began to walk. First to his right Blake saw the canvas tarpaulins which covered a space of some twenty metres by twenty. Twenty men faced one another in couples upon them, all in judo kimono and three-quarter-length canvas pants. All wore green sashes, thus were already well up in the hierarchy of expertise. Two Japanese stood with them – probably Blake guessed, from the Japanese Red Army – squat men with powerful shoulder and forearm muscles and wearing black belts. They were working on the Spring-Hip throw, that ballet-like crisp movement in which the attacker twists suddenly with his back to his opponent and takes his body onto all one side of his own, then with that leg and thigh and by a quick jerk down of his torso standing on his master front leg throws his rival neatly over his shoulder to land, if unskilled in breakfalls, on his head and with luck snap his neck. So the first Japanese threw the other superbly, and his opponent tucked his head in and rolled as he hit the ground, and was up sweetly on his feet in an instant, smooth and deadly to fight again. Then Blake watched the one line of men throw the other, with nearly the same elegant precision.

'How much of this do they do daily?'

'Two hours,' said Khalíl. 'Then two hours karate, two hours weapons training, two hours explosives, then two hours exercises and run in the desert. And two hours indoctrination in that big marquee to your right. Ahmed insists on that, quite rightly. We're proud to have our men significantly more strongly motivated than, we think, *any* other PLO-Fatah group anywhere in the world. When a man comes out of here, he's not only magnificently highly trained and fit, but also literally ready to die for us, for Ahmed specifically.'

'They're probably so tough by then that they wouldn't even feel it,' said Blake. 'In all the other judo training I've ever seen or done, you have padded mats to fall on. Here I see your tarpaulins are flat on the ground. And there's very little soft desert sand around here.'

'Oh, they harden themselves to it,' said Khalíl.

The Karate class at the next tarpaulin were clearly doing the same thing. Here the twenty or so pupils were wearing the same pattern of judo canvas clothes, and red, green and brown sashes. Again the black-belted instructors looked Japanese, or perhaps Korean; very hard men indeed. The instructors had just taken the class through the fourth kata, that intricate ritual ballet of fighting poses, then attacking strides forward and strikes with the edge of the hand and the instep or hard sole of the foot. Then the class broke up into couples for fighting practice, the stabs with rigid fingertips or chops with the heel of the hand, the three main types of kick, for the stomach and genitals, the chest, and the throat or face, the whole weight of the body always behind each such precise kick. Standard karate practice halted the blow or kick in the air millimetres from the target. Here the strikes were actually landing – certainly not with full force, which would have caused too many casualties, yet still and deliberately with some force; anyone who could walk out of that camp gate after this full three-month course would prove a formidable customer, even with no weapon in his hands. Blake stood a moment and surveyed these schools for scientific mayhem. He could count nine separate tarpaulins of judo and karate classes. This was manufacturing highly skilled terrorists in bulk. Feisal and Khalíl and their Kingdom colleagues just needed to do this for long enough and they had to break Israel's nerve and destroy it. Particularly if these shock troops were also, as Khalíl said, indoctrinated to the point of willingly sacrificing their lives for Feisal's cause.

'They're all Palestinian Arabs?' Blake asked.

'Eighty per cent plus,' answered Feisal. 'Remember that among our most dedicated and zealous recruits are the young men and women who have grown up in the Arab refugee camps. The camps have always been the best source for our PLO-Fatah guerrillas. Poverty, misery, humiliation, frustration, cruelty have always served as excellent recruiting sergeants. The other fifteen to twenty per cent are young intellectuals, not *invariably* Arab, from almost everywhere you'd care to name, who are convinced that we Palestinian Arabs have had a very raw deal, and who feel passionately enough about it to risk their lives to try to put it right.'

A woman in the karate class caught Blake's eye. She had suddenly spun a complete circle on the spot and ended it chopping her male opponent across the carotid artery with the heel of her right hand. The man dropped like a log. The Korean instructor ran over to them.

'Sex rears it head again,' said Blake. 'In fact until this moment I'd hardly even noticed there were women among your recruits.'

'Indeed there are,' said Khalíl. 'Generally between ten and twenty per cent. You wouldn't have noticed them too much here because the fashion's to keep their hair short and dress in shirts and pants or khaki overalls like the men. This particular event probably *was* sexual – I think he made a pass at a nipple – but it's rare. Most of them have got other things on their minds. The women eat with the men and train with the men and relax with them. They just sleep in separate tents. And they often make excellent fighters, like the eighteen-year-old Dalal Mughrabi who led that commando team that hijacked the bus on the Israeli coast road between Haifa and Tel Aviv and had a murderous shoot-out with the Israeli armed forces in which some forty died early in 1978. So we give fighting women their full place in the sun here.'

A three-metre-high sand ramp marked their next halting place. Its base was held firm by sandbags, and there was a two-metre-high sandbag wall jutting at right angles from each end of the sand ramp; a shooting-range, for distance anywhere from 200 metres down to zero. Here they watched groups of twenty recruits on standard target practice with AK-47s and M1s. At an order, the twenty lying on the sand in the prone position stripped their automatic rifles right down, then reassembled them in about three minutes, and went back to rapid fire at the 100-metre targets.

At a smaller 25-metre range to one side, another group of twenty were training with Browning 9 mm automatic pistols and Colt .45s. There were ten black-painted man-size metal silhouettes standing on strong broad bases against the thick sand three-metre-high ramp. Ten of the men lined up first with Brownings to fire off their magazines of thirteen shots, then the next line of ten used the Colt .45s with their seven-shot magazines. They shot under orders from their instructors, single-shot, or two rapid together, or straight rapid. The instructors stopped the lines constantly, to examine results to advise, to improve. They corrected their pupils' postures all the time, stressing and re-stressing the ideal: the body square on to the target – like a sapling in the wind; this *wasn't* an exercise in fencing – with the feet say sixty centimetres apart with the weight nicely even on each and the knees slightly bent, and the firing-arm straight out, or, almost always better because steadier, the two-handed grip with the arms converging on the target like the two sides of an arrowhead, and the two eyes open sighting dead above them. And they ceaselessly repeated the true secret of good pistol-shooting: the pistol nested comfortably in the hinge of your hand, you tightened the tip of your forefinger – never the top joint – on the trigger as your foresight came in from the side in its tiny jumps onto the target, and you just maintained that pressure as you went past. As you came back on target from the other side you tightened delicately again, and so on, till finally the pistol shot itself, and generally the target too. Laborious to describe, the whole process could in fact take mere instants after a year or two's training, or three months' intensive like this. For intensive this was, and meticulously recorded; Blake saw how the instructors, after each line had finished firing its magazine, noted down the number of broad silver spots which marked the black metal targets, before that line painted its shots out from the small black pots next to each, to leave the targets virgin again for the next line.

'And perhaps our surprise shooting-maze may amuse you too,' said Salah Khalíl.

He took Blake and Feisal over to the far north-western corner of the firing-range. Here thin steel walls two metres high covered an area of some thirty metres square. Khalíl rang a bell, and a steel door opened to the limit of its ten-centimetre chain. A helmeted face peered out.

'*Marhába!*' said Khalíl. 'Anyone in the maze at the moment?'

'No,' said the militant face. 'The next one's due to go in five minutes.'

'That's just enough time to show my friends here round. Then we can watch your next live show too.'

The steel helmet grunted and opened the steel door all the way. Anticipating Blake's question, Khalíl said: 'You'll see why the door and walls are steel in a moment. It's to preserve the innocent bystanders outside.'

Within, Blake began to see what he meant. This was like a film-set of an Arab souk, a cardboard and plywood concentration of mean twisting alleys crowded by shops and coffee-restaurants and low houses. Here anything could spring at you from anywhere; particularly Man, the most cunning, deadly and cruel of all killers. Scattered among these treacherous bends and wicked shadows and behind these hooded door-ways and windows were black steel silhouettes of men, some crouching, some erect, all carrying mock lethal weapons. They were as mobile as true life mortal enemies, and the face in the steel helmet, whose name was Talal, could like a good general place them wherever he wanted, and make them spring up at the touch of a button. Men and women terrorists who already had excellent reports for their marksmanship for at least two months on the standard shooting ranges were put one by one through this specialized and far more realistic test – for no sane enemy, certainly no outstandingly well trained and equipped Israeli commando, just stood around and knowingly let you take shots at him at 25 or 200 metres. Instead he sneaked up on you as close and hidden as he could and struck murderously when you least expected it.

Talal got as near to that as he could, and he was very good. As the trainee skulked through the maze with his or her nerves at fever pitch, a black steel silhouette could snarl lethally to life at his very elbow, spring commandingly into menace from a shadowed doorway or window, or practically rise up his or her genitals from the ground in front. Feisal had told Blake the technique. The moment you knew the threat, you thrust your whole body directly at it with your left foot forward and your pistol in your two rigidly outstretched hands, and you always shot twice. That was the trick: to point at the threat immediately with your whole body – for even for the worst shot, if he pointed instinctively at a running cat, a flying bird, generally did so with extraordinary accuracy. If you shot twice, at least one usually hit. The British Singapore Police had developed the whole technique, with considerable success.

From the relative safety of Talal's command platform in one corner, lying prone, Blake and the others watched a young Palestinian Arab go through the test. Talal pulled five black steel silhouette threats on him, two from narrow alley-mouths just beside him, one from a window above and behind him, and two from masked doorways a few metres from him, to his right and to his left – one straight after the other. This was a Colt .45 man, so if he was going to fire his shot plus cover shot at each target as he had been taught, and need to fire at more than three targets, then he was going to have to change his seven-shot magazine straight after that. Indeed, Blake saw him switch magazines so fast on the tail of his third target that Talal had not been able to get the fourth and fifth targets up on him in time to catch him still unloaded. The four men and the youth looked together at his results. There were two small silver circles on the first and third black silhouettes and one on the second, all chest-high, and one on the fourth, high, and one on the last, rather low. But at this speed of action and reaction this was fair shooting, and he had hung at least one shot on every enemy. Feisal clapped the youth on the shoulder and the two beamed at each other.

It was as they left the shooting-range that Blake saw the five squads of guerillas, four of twenty and one of ten, running back through the opened front gate from the desert. There were some stragglers, but in general the blocks were holding pretty solidly together. All were wearing back-packs, and all, under the pitiless blazing sun, were sweating heavily, the men and the women, the fronts of their khaki overalls and the sides under the armpits blackened with it.

'In army boots too,' said Blake. 'And those packs are loaded?'

'Oh yes,' said Salah Khalíl. 'Fifteen kilos the men, ten the women. Some of the women won't accept that discrimination and volunteer for fifteen kilos too.'

'I admire their toughness and dedication,' said Blake. 'I'll bet they'd be a packet to take on in a real fight. However feminine they might look.'

Both Arabs laughed.

'They tend to play down their sexual charms pretty hard here, as I've mentioned,' said Salah Khalíl. 'To neutralize them puritanically so as to concentrate one hundred per cent on their guerrilla training. They're serious lasses. But if I ordered one formally to screw you to death, I've no doubt she'd do it, or die a willing martyr in the attempt.'

'I can think of no finer exit,' said Blake.

But he could about the next place they visited, which was the huge marquee in which the explosives and booby-trap training was being carried out. Here five groups of twenty and one of ten were been taken through all the basic steps of producing highly effective explosives from fairly easily obtainable household chemicals, of how to apply and detonate plastic explosives in all their forms, how to lay, and disarm, limpet mines, and how to leave deadly and demoralizing booby-traps behind them on their commando raids – one which Blake found particularly cruel was set in a loo bowl primed to go off when the next enemy sat on it. And it was after this visit that Blake saw Ahmed Feisal at his most powerful and impressive – and, he thought, most original; for this final and most vital segment of the instruction quite definitely bore Feisal's imprimatur of passion and total conviction on it.

To see it the three men went to the biggest marquee in the camp, the furthest back near to the western fence. The marquee was extremely well equipped with lecturing daises and lecterns and huge movable blackboards and cinema screens. It could be blacked out for film or slide shows, and it must have held a hundred plus seats. As they entered, the audience of some ninety young and fit men and women – the basic division of the four hundred and fifty then under instruction in the camp – got immediately and smartly to their feet. Their discipline looked total and eager, not at all forced; there was no doubt of their respect for Feisal and Khalíl.

'Please sit,' said Feisal, 'and go on as you were. We would just like to listen. We have with us a friend. He has been, he is, of very great help to us in our just cause – '

The ninety turned to Blake as one, as one face.

'*Ehlen wa Zehlen*! Welcome and Re-welcome!'

It was a huge, heavy roar, like a colossal wave breaking on a harsh night shore.

'Memorize his face well,' said Feisal. 'And, should he ever ask anything from you, you are please to do it for him *without limit*! For we are *all* under his orders, *taht amrihi* , and in his debt!'

The ninety-headed monster looked at him deliberately. It would know him next time, anywhere. Then it sat down.

The three newcomers sat in a side row.

'We were talking about the concept of the *Jihád*, the Holy War,' said the lecturer. He was a tall broadly built man with brilliant black curled hair under his cowl and a full lustrous black beard. His flowing full-sleeved white *jelabíah* reached right down to the ground, masking the carnal outlines of his body as was decently required of Islamic Fundamentalists, and Feisal advised Blake that that was exactly what he was – indeed, from that Militant Islamic group, *El Jihád el Jedíd*, The New Holy War, that had executed Anwar Sadat on October 6 1981 before the whole assembled might of the Egyptian army and air force. Happily, Feisal added, their lecturer had managed to escape that extremely violent and extensive search and repression that Mubárak had applied throughout Egypt immediately afterwards. Blake had been interested to note Feisal's use of the term 'executed' and not 'murdered' in describing the *Jihád*'s treatment of Sadat.

'Excellent,' said Feisal, replying to the lecturer's English in Arabic. 'Please go on.'

'Our guest would not prefer English? I think all my audience understands English.'

'Out guest speaks very tolerable Arabic,' said Feisal. 'I suggest you continue in that; it's what you normally do, and I can translate the few things our friend may not know as we go along.'

'*Hadhrítak*,' said the lecturer. 'Excellency. Then the *Jihád*. Now a Holy War can most morally and correctly be willed by even the most peace-loving Muslim if the affronts to Islam are sufficiently grave. Let's think of that practical saint, Hassan el Banna, who as we all know founded the great Muslim Brotherhood in Egypt in 1928, and whom the Political Police murdered in Cairo twenty years later. This martyr gave the *fellahin* and Egyptian labourers massive help and their first pride in themselves. Yet Banna, whose highest ideal was social justice in peace, still stressed that God gave the noble life in Paradise only to that nation "that knows how to die a noble death". He feared sadly that his great Muslim Brotherhood could not survive without a *Jihád*, and he quoted the Prophet: "He who dies and has not fought and has not resolved to fight has died a *Jahilíyya* death" – of that bleak pagan period before Muhammed. Banna knew that the Prophet explicitly forbids us to tolerate abominations. That is why –' the lecturer drew himself up to his full height, his hands curved as if holding a machinegun, his jet-black eyes glittering – 'The Militant Islamic Group to which I have the high honour to belong, the *Jihád el Jedíd*, New Holy War, two years ago *eliminated that abomination called Sadat!*'

The ninety in that great tent stood in one swift movement, their throats baying their approval, their hands clapping violently as a long roll of thunder. The lecturer raised his strong hands to them, open as the questing talons of a huge bird of prey.

'This *traitor* Arab,' he sang out, 'who sold his sacred Islamic heritage to the Americans, with his Open Door *Infitah* economic policy, letting in their evil pro-Zionist capital, and their godless materialism, immorality, sexual permissiveness, all to erode our finest Islamic values – just as did Iran's Shah. *And we served each his fatal and fully merited annihilation!*'

Again that deep back-of-the-throat, savage and bloodcurdling and marrow-melting roar, like that of a lion hunting; he held them hypnotized.

'– He even betrayed our sister Islamic national Iran blatantly, ignominiously by letting these atheist Americans use Egyptian territory as a staging-post for their abortive attempt to rescue by helicopter their fifty-two Tehran Embassy staff who Khomeini had held ever since his historic uprising in 1979. To such turgid moral depths could this dog Sadat descend! This *lackey*, sordid puppet of those *kuffár* infidel Americans who *alone* have kept Israel alive! Without their massive air-lift of aid to Israel in our glorious October 1973 War we Arabs would without any doubt finally have swept every single Israeli into the sea, so leaving free that beloved land of Palestine – home of the Aqsa Mosque and Dome of the Rock and other holy Islamic monuments – to those exiled and bitterly suffering Arabs to whom it truly belongs!'

This time the ninety-throated roar was like the bellow of as many cannon. Blake saw how the lecturer had skilfully led his audience with his images and rhythms and stresses to that key area of pain about all their hearts. Now he consolidated his bridgehead there.

'I remind you – you who need no reminder – that when a Muslim's land is stolen it is his duty before God to take it back. Take just the West Bank and Gaza alone. Will Israel ever really withdraw? Will they so much as tolerate free elections? How free, if Israel keeps military and civil control? How many Israeli voices cry out to proclaim in public that they wish to eat up the West Bank and Gaza forever? How many more in private? With how many Western governments secretly or openly behind them? And today, more than five years after the accursed Camp David Accords of September 1978, we still see no trace of political autonomy for the Arabs in these occupied territories, while the Israelis pour new settlements into the West Bank. Listen to the Accords' first document. Israel will eventually withdraw some armed forces, but "there will be redeployment of the remaining Israeli armed forces into specified security locations" . . .'

'That can only mean the Yigal Allon plan for guarding the West Bank by Israeli fortresses set along the Jordan River!' called a slim young woman from the third row, her face fine-featured, her skin light brown and her hair deep black – certainly a Palestinian Arab.

The lecturer beamed his approval. '*Exactly*, Sarah. The Camp David Accords actually have that dominant and continuing Israeli military presence on the West Bank *written in to them*.'

He lowered his eyes in contemplation of that atrocity. A long silence fell, and the audience stirred in discomfort. It was rescued by a voice pitched just at the threshold of hearing, in a tone of lyrical recall.

'And for this alone my great group, the New Holy War, would have judged Mohammed Anwar El Sadat a traitor. For this, and for so much more, my great friend First Lieutenant Khálid Islambouli and his three volunteer colleagues executed Sadat in front of the whole might of his armed hosts, knowing that they must be caught and killed themselves. Mubárak, succeeding Sadat, made that claim that all governments will – that the attack was the work of a few fanatics, desperate, rootless. How the facts mocked him! There were nine other New Holy War assault groups poised to act in Cairo that day to take all main police and army posts and arsenals and the TV and radio stations. The police found nineteen main arms and explosives caches in our Cairo houses. We acted just too late . . . '

'And there was Asyut!' The intervention came from a tall lean Bedu-like young man in the front row.

Again the lecturer beamed down confirmation on these bright pupils. 'Excellent, Zaid! Yes, in the religious city of Asyut, 370 kilometres upriver from Cairo. There we sent in fifty *Jihád* shock troops in police uniforms and Peugeot armoured cars fitted with machineguns, to attack the police station and security forces. We fought for thirty hours. They only stopped us by sending in massed helicopter-borne commandos. Our losses were nine, against seventy police and army dead. Altogether, Mubárak's police held 2,500 suspects for the rising. The Cairo police found long lists of assassination targets – cabinet ministers, armed forces officers, top businessmen, judges, the whole power élite. We were fully prepared, only *millimetres* from success.'

His voice throbbed louder.

'But the unbreakable will was there, and shall be again. We

287

should remember, carved deep in every mind, that vision of Khálid Islambouli, white-cowled, in his long white *jelabíah*, with his full black Islamic beard and his shining jet-black eyes, clutching the steel bars of his cage in that military court and shouting his contempt at the three generals even as they sentenced him and his three brothers and *Jihád*'s ideologue, Muhammed Abdel Salam Farag, to death in March of 1982. In April, after Mubárak had rejected their appeals, he had them killed at once, the military by firing-squad, the civilian by hanging. No publicity. Mubárak dared run no risk of a public martyrdom. So he wiped them out quietly – '

The lecturer stopped dead again, tense at his full height, his falcon hands curved, as if holding a huge dynamic charge, about to release it, in absolute silence, his dark eyes glittering.

As Islambouli's must have done, thought Blake. The lecturer was uncannily like him, perhaps *was* him, his Islamic resurrection. He had the same fantastic Messianic quality which Blake had felt acutely as he watched him close in upon Sadat, and which radiated even from the photos of the subsequent first trial. This lecturer held his audience as totally.

'But he can never wipe out that image!' shouted a squat dark girl from the back of the huge tent, perhaps Yemenite, and with more sheer force than grace. 'We can build such fighters, alone but not flinching before death, going straight by Islamic Law to destroy the Abomination, in the full calm knowledge that the act must bring his own death! That is the purest courage, of the true Islamic Militant!'

The lecturer drank this one in bliss, his face wreathed in smiles. Then he switched off that expression and froze tall again, curved hands commanding, building his suspense. The ninety throats of his audience muttered low, sullen, waiting in agony.

'Ah, yes, Fatima! My brothers and sisters! If we can indeed go on growing such men – and you must be the living proof of it – then – ' He hesitated, towered four metres above them, then surged on:

'*Then we can beat Israel*, my brothers, my sisters. *We can beat the world!*'

The ninety-throated monster was on its feet again, its roar this time almost lifting the marquee off the ground, the clapping near hysteria. Blake glanced at the lecturer, this master craftsman. He had the briefest coda to perform, the message that would focus the energies he evoked.

'It's a question of quality, my brothers, my sisters. In the end it so often is. My friend Islambouli and his fellow martyrs, they had it. Our *Jihád* fighters, they too. We are not anarchists, misfits, criminals!'

He looked down benignly from the papers on his lectern.

'I know that you here today have just such quality in common with those twenty-four gallant *Jihád* fighters held in steel cages like wild animals at that first military trial. I know that more than seventy of the ninety who listen to me now are graduates, and the rest of equal calibre. That's excellent. For essential though they are, physical strength and courage and endurance alone cannot win this war. For victory we must also have the sharpest intelligence, the most modern technical training and expertise, the greatest originality in our strategy and tactics, the cunning to use the most devastating weapons, the most lethal surprise attacks, against our very able enemy, strong in the deaths of their six million martyrs, the holocaust that we did not cause, did not commit. Our own morale must prevail. Today's Islamic Militant must have all-round excellence. He or she must have both skills and convictions as all-embracing as Islam itself. For Islam, we all know, is a total way of life. It is religion and state, spirit and deed, holy text and a sword.

'So it is total commitment, my brothers, my sisters, to the rebirth under the *Shari'a*, the one Islamic Law, of the great and indivisible Islamic Empire-State, even at the cost in martyrdom of our own lives – that highest honour that God can award us –'

His words died away, reverberating still in all their minds. Feisal got up, nodding his thanks swiftly to him and led his two companions out before the exodus.

'On his usual good form today,' said Salah Khalíl.

'Yes,' said Feisal, glancing at him.

'Would you gentlemen care to stay for lunch?'

'Thank you,' said Feisal, 'but I think we'd better get back. My friend here and I have other work to do.'

As they pulled away from the closed gate, the serried machineguns from the two watch-towers invigilating them just in case, Blake said:

'Well. I get the message.'

Feisal looked to his right at him from over the driving-wheel.

'You do?'

'Yes. It amplifies what you told me when I first came to work here six years ago. You're shooting far higher than Arafat and his official PLO line, which has always been strictly secular, driving exclusively for a single independent secular Palestinian-Arab nation-State. You want to suffuse the whole thing with the magic of Islamic Fundamentalism too. And you're shooting for a whole unified Islamic *Empire*, not just for one Palestinian mini-State.'

In profile to him, Feisal smiled.

'That's about right. As regards the ultimate aim, George Habash of the PLO splinter group, the Popular Front for the Liberation of Palestine, had it right from the very start. He always saw the enemies as Zionism and Imperialism, the target as a unified Arab Empire-State stretching from the Arabian Gulf to the Atlantic. For me, Arafat has always made the critical error of deliberately under-playing the Pan-Arab card.'

'But so much of the world has recognized Arafat as your leader, Ahmed. Russia, China, the UN.'

'Oh, sure, Yasser's always been a great propaganda success. Nasser first took him to Moscow in July 1968 where he met all the big shots, Podgorny, Brezhnev, Kosygin, who gave him half a million dollars' worth of arms. And Russia gave his PLO office in Moscow embassy status two years ago. Fatah's been close to Peking since 1964, and Arafat's been there personally in 1970 and 1981, meeting their leaders, getting arms. He gave his famous address to the UN in New York in November 1974 and got Resolution 3236 passed overwhelmingly, to reaffirm the Palestinian Arab rights to self-determination there, an independent sovereign State, even the right to return to their homes and property. That's when the UN, exceptionally, gave the PLO Observer Status there. Austria gave the PLO full diplomatic recognition in 1980 and so did Greece, last year. Sure.'

'Well,' said Blake, 'that's a hell of a performance.'

'Sure!' said Feisal again, but now savagely, so that Blake saw the wicked flash of his beautiful small white ferret-like teeth as he jerked his head round at him. 'And just how much goddamned good has it done us? Just how many tens of thousands of square kilometres of independent national Palestinian homeland has it won us back? In hard results, we've had a total failure. We've won back *nothing*!'

'Because your mixture's wrong? Something's lacking?'

Feisal beat the palms of his two hands down on the wheel in front of him.

'*Of course*! What you yourself so aptly called the *magic* of Islamic Fundamentalism! *That's* what's lacking! You saw how our speaker fired the whole mass of that audience! *That's* the magic we need! *That's* my secret weapon! Psychologically, I mean; I'll have a material secret weapon too, don't doubt it. But that's exactly what is wrong with the whole PLO-Fatah approach. It is shallow, lack-lustre – who can get lyrical about creating a resolutely secular State? It's like trying to write poetry about a dish-washing machine. Where's the bewitchment, the vision, the exaltation? Isn't life, isn't a great cause *worth* that? It just doesn't have that utter thrust and conviction that takes a man driving his explosives-filled car or truck right up to his enemy's headquarters, where he smiles gently at the guard, then blows them all sky-high.'

'Suicide with a smile!' said Blake. 'Bombs with a bow!'

Feisal half-smiled back, shrugged, and went on:

'This is a new world-hero figure, Philip: the Islamic suicide-martyr. Both the Israelis and the Americans will find it hard to stop him. He's the solitary man who used his van to bomb the US Embassy in Beirut this April 18 and killed sixty-three. He's the calm and smiling Shi'ite of the *Jihád el Islamí*, the Islamic Holy War, who drove his lethally loaded truck into the US Marine HQ at Beirut Airport six weeks ago on October 23 and killed two hundred and forty-one US marines and navy – and, of course, himself, in the US's worst single military disaster since Vietnam. And his brother, who drove his truck into the French command of the Peace-Keeping Force in Beirut the same day, killing another fifty-eight. And Terrorists like these, totally dedicated, and ready – indeed, *happy* – to die utterly consumed by their own final apocalyptic actions, are striking more and more now. Horace told me the other day at the US Embassy that his State Department estimates put this year of 1983 as the worst yet for international terrorism, with some five hundred attacks, two hundred against US people or property. And they'll see more. What can America expect, as the biggest and most passionate backer of our arch-enemy Israel?'

'And the PLO-Fatah don't have any of these ecstatic assassins?'

'No,' said Feisal. 'Though I like your metaphor. The Assassins, meaning the Takers of Hashish, were the guerrilla answer of Hassan ibn el Sabbáh, the Old Man of the Mountain, to the reigning Abbasid Caliphs in the eleventh century from his mountain fastnesses at Alamut in Iran, as you probably know. He used to dispatch his Assassins on suicide missions to kill the generals of the Abbasid armies sent against him. Kept high by hashish, the Assassins would be further sustained morally by Hassan's promise that if they were killed in action they would be wafted at once to a Paradise indistinguishable from Alamut – the exquisitely beautiful women which Hassan always kept there would be at their entire disposal from then till eternity to satisfy their every want. But no, the PLO-Fatah do not have ecstatic assassins like these. Arafat, I suppose you could say, doesn't believe in spiritual hashish. No magic for him. It's his greatest and gravest error.'

'But, evidently, not yours?'

'No, indeed,' said Feisal crisply. 'I'll use all the magic I can get. All the exultation I can evoke by pressing at all times for a great unified Islamic Empire-State from the Arabian Gulf to the Atlantic. And to achieve that I'll have my Islamic army all right, my ecstatic assassins. I have them already. You've just seen ninety of them at close quarters, receiving their skilled indoctrination. I've been training them in their hundreds now like that for many months. One great Islamic Empire-State under one *Shari'a*, one Islamic Law, and by our huge economic and financial power feared as is proper by all the world –'

Ahead through the jeep's windscreen Blake saw the great Arabian desert, clean and sheer as oblivion, pitilessly flat to the far horizons, void and arid under that murderous sun, its uniform tone an alien sharp light yellow, the oldest colour, like black, of death. This was the place of the wind, that clanging brassy sun, bleached bones, a falcon. Of humans, only the Bedu could survive long in it. He could see their tents again now, to his left, past Feisal, leaves scattered across twigs and blackened by that endless blazing orb. Would Feisal's Islamic Empire-State be like this, of this ageless huge cruelty, implacable silence? For he could have no doubt now, from what Feisal had said openly or hinted, that Feisal was striking out now for his own Empire. Not the PLO-Fatah's. Not Arafat's –

He suddenly felt Feisal's regard heavy upon him, with a shock. Feisal turned back over the driving-wheel as Blake looked round.

'I've always been most fully conscious,' said Feisal, as if replying stoutly to some explicit accusation, 'of the great help you've given me, us, by diverting that money to me. Without it my plan, to revive Islam's magnificence and to regain its true place in the world's sun, would never have been possible. And I try always to pay my moral debts.'

'Forget them, in this case,' said Blake. 'You're still getting your ten cents a barrel on Tulsa's seven hundred thousand barrels a day, because Tulsa renewed the contract this last November 1 for another five years on identical terms. But she may well kick at paying that ten cents over-ride at some time in the course of the contract – because I'm sure crude oil prices will start going down hard in a year or two. Because of that, had I been in Tulsa's shoes I'd no longer have agreed to pay that special secret fee over and above OPEC postings. So that useful income of yours of some twenty-six million dollars may dry up in a year or two.'

Blake had at least been consistent with what he now said. The preceding November 1, with Abdullah's prior agreement, he had turned back the secret 50,000 bd contract that Abdullah had first given him ten years before. He was sure he was *not* going to be able easily to on-sell that volume at ten or fifteen cents above postings when prices started dropping in the glut he foresaw. Besides after ten years, with the incoming Eurobond interest, and after deducting his fairly generous spending, he still had some $20 million in his Swiss bank account – plus his $200,000-a-year job with the Ministry of Oil. Enough, Blake had thought reasonably, was enough.

Feisal seemed to feel much the same way.

'It won't be too tragic if it does cut off after say another year,' he said. 'By then I'll have got some one hundred and sixty million from it, not counting interest and dividend income. That's already far and away beyond what I need for my plan.'

'Fine,' said Blake, restraining himself from asking what that plan was. Again Feisal must have heard his thoughts.

'I know you, Philip,' he said, 'after these ten years. I know your man-of-action syndrome, your mania for being part of your times, in step with the world's great political and economic movements, and half a jump ahead if you can. You're so fascinated by it that you're almost ascetic; gain's certainly not your first objective. It's a kind of power-puritanism.'

'In that regard,' said Blake, 'you're no amateur yourself, Ahmed.'

They were back on the coastal metalled road now, pointing south.

Feisal laughed.

'Well,' he said. 'I'm showing you the essential elements of my plan as we go along. I'm playing in with your manic interest in power structures, in great shifts of power which could change the face of the world. Plenty of magic here, Philip, and perhaps some of it a little black. What you saw this morning was of course a vital part of the plan. *The* vital part, psychologically. One day the whole thing will suddenly come together for you, you'll suddenly see the whole symphony in a second. It may shock you. But at least you'll see it. I'll take you with me, you see.'

'Fine,' said Blake.

Feisal jerked his head round onto him from above the wheel for a long moment. He sounded almost sad.

'As far as I can,' said Feisal.

He turned back. Blake looked at his exact, incisive profile, etched clear as a newly minted coin. Here, through this coolly passionate man, was Blake's own most certain way to the highest peaks of power. Feisal would, somehow, rule an empire, taking Blake with him, as far as he could. So Blake could, as Malraux said about T.E. Lawrence, leave his name on the map. Did it really matter so very much if, for that, men, women and children died? People died all the time, of flu or heart attacks or dope or falling under buses. What had the Swiss created after centuries of peace except Harry Lime's cuckoo-clock? Who now wept the many dead caused by

Alexander the Great, Tamburlaine, Napoleon? It was the great sweep of their actions on the world's history that mattered, the style of the victory. This was Blake's one slim route to immortality, through helping create the whole majestic revolutionary symphony, with its grave contours of tragedy. All greatness was somewhere tragic, its magnetism invincible. It called directly to that tiny racing flywheel in Blake, the core of his being, the lodestone to his destiny. Man's greatness lay too in his full consciousness of his fate, and, finally, his acceptance of it, of his own tragic contours.

29
Bombs for Khadaffi

'So what do you think of my friend Ronald Reagan's bombing of Khadaffi in Tripoli last week?' asked Horace B. Murgatroyd.

The three sat at one end of the magnificent walnut table in the dining-room of Horace's opulent residence in the US Embassy compound. Two portraits of exactly equal size surveyed them steadily, one was Abraham Lincoln, high behind Horace at the head of the table, the other facing him from the far end of the room. This was of Ronald Reagan. Horace had not demoted him from that lofty level even though Reagan, on his re-election in 1984, had evidently not thought to promote Horace to any higher ambassadorial position elsewhere. Though Horace, thought Blake, would probably anyway have preferred to stay here in the Kingdom of the Sun, where he had managed to become something of a minor king himself, certainly among the American and even indeed among the whole expatriate community; or perhaps you could think of him as a kind of Greek Oracle, his judgements sometimes impenetrable, but always formidable, and deliver-ed with utter conviction. Among these comments, though diplomatically toned down somewhat if the nature of his audience so dictated, were his bitingly puritanical criticisms of the often lavish personal spending habits of the royal family and indeed of the Kingdom's establishment as a whole, and his equally obvious and acerbic feudal antipathy towards those more sophisticated and uppity members of it, like Abdullah and Leila, who through no discernible merits of their own had received the highest benefits of Western education.

Horace's was unchallengeably the one American voice that really mattered back in the US in regard to anything concern-ing the Kingdom of the Sun. There were certainly other US embassies in the world where it was the CIA, who through the disguised Counsellor or First or Second Secretary really called the shots in the States through their headquarters in Langley and Foggy Bottom, or where the Military Attachés or Commanders of Military Missions dictated things through the Pentagon, but that did not happen under Horace. He had not risen to multi-millionaire stardom in the savage jungle in-fighting of US supermarket chains for nothing. People were often what they seemed. Horace's compactly muscled pre-historic rhino-bulk, wickedly armed and armoured, astound-ingly light and quick on its feet, that close-cropped and near-cubic head set menacingly still on its short bull neck, and those darting and astute slate-grey little eyes were simply his consolation. What Horace said went.

Which, Blake knew, was the main reason why Ahmed Feisal stayed this close to Horace. Feisal had a born politician's innate sense of where his true interests lay. Feisal always had good grounds for everything he did. He never wasted any slightest part of his considerable energies.

'I hold no particular brief for Khadaffi,' said Feisal elegantly, putting down his still half-filled glass of Montrachet, which Horace had selected for their main dish of Sole Meunière with what Blake recognized as great care; it was from the fine 1973 vintage from the Chassagne-Montrachet Grand Cru Vineyards, among the very best white burgundies, dry, yet powerfully rich. For their opening oysters, Horace had also scored high in Blake's book, with a 1978 Chablis Grand Cru from the Vaudésir Domaine.

Feisal looked up at the other two men. He was wearing a very lightweight pearl-grey suit that evening, of pure wool set off by a Giorgio Armani silk tie, tiny soft gold circles on pale blue, and there was a slash of gold on black from his left wrist, from the wrist-watch there. His beautifully chiselled film-star features and very small regular white teeth addressed them, so suavely that it sometimes cost an effort, thought Blake, to recall that this was a leader of what was still probably the most powerful terrorist organization in the world – even if, as was becoming increasingly apparent to Blake, he was diverging more and more critically all the time from the policies of that organization's top leadership.

'I think that even Muámmar Khadaffi's closest friends would have to admit him psychologically deranged. You might say mad. On the one hand you have the pious young Bedu-desert-bred Muslim, the twenty-seven-year-old and quite incredibly naïve Colonel who overthrows the monarchy in Libya in September 1969, then offers the country on a plate to Nasser, whom he has always hero-worshipped, to include in Nasser's marvellous new Arab Republic – which offer Nasser has the good practical political sense to refuse. Still, that gives a touchingly engaging picture of young Muámmar. And I, as an Arab, most fully sympathize with and support the passionate sincerity of his continuing ideal of Arab unity and Arab renaissance. But, on the other hand, in the practical business of international politics he can be a pain in the arse. I have to admit that. There are his exports of terrorism and revolution in bulk. He tried those takeover coups in Niger and Tunisia years ago. And in the Sudan. And Chad; he's still backing that. And the IRA. And he's sent out many hit-teams to kill off Libyan political opponents who have fled abroad. Exactly how much of the recent waves of international terrorism has been Khadaffi's direct responsibility we may never know. Some of it's certainly the work of Abu Nidal and his breakaway ex-PLO rejectionist faction – rejectionist because they reject *any* approach to Israel save by armed conflict. But it's at least probable that Khadaffi backed them too to some degree – with arms, money, intelligence, other help through Libyan embassies and diplomats – they're birds of a feather; Abu Nidal's Black June group are major exporters of murder and mayhem too, in their own right. *And* they've sworn to wipe out the present PLO leadership completely.'

'Yes, we've seen our fair share of terrorism in the Middle East and Mediterranean these last months,' said Blake. He turned to Horace. 'And your State Department must see Libya as having a hand in almost all of it?'

'Well, we certainly saw Khadaffi as sponsoring internal terrorism wholesale when it came to the murder of those twenty unfortunate people in Rome and Athens airports on December 27 last,' said Horace B. Murgatroyd, refilling Blake's glass and his own with the superb Chassagne-Montrachet. 'And the day after that double shock we began to plan our confrontation with Libya. On January 7 Reagan announced our trade embargo of Libya and ordered all Americans to get the hell out of there, or risk penalties from our side, as I expect you'll recall. Then we started to ready our reinforced Sixth Fleet near Libya for action. So when we crossed Khadaffi's so-called Line of Death in fully international waters in the Gulf of Sirte on March 24, just a month back now, and his gunners fired two Sam-5 missiles at our aircraft, we were all set to shoot back. We did. And, as I'm sure you know, we destroyed three Libyan gunboats and hit a fourth, and put in two strong attacks on one of his Sam-5 bases. After all, we can take just so much, friends. Five of the twenty civilians whom Abu Nidal's men massacred at Rome and Athens on December 27 were Americans.'

'And that's not been the end to the slaughter of Americans,' said Blake. 'There were those four killed when that bomb blew them out of the side of the TWA airliner that was getting set to land at Athens at the start of this month. But I don't think your people have claimed finding any really solid evidence linking that terrorist act to Khadaffi?'

'No, but by God we do in the case of that bombing of the West Berlin disco on Saturday April 5,' said Horace trenchantly. 'It only killed one American soldier and one Turkish woman, but it could have been in the forties or fifties. It wasn't for want of trying; our boys love that place. And our people tell me that they have *definite proof* that the Libyan People's Bureau in East Berlin planned and directed that explosion. That was the last goddamned straw. So we bombed the bastards in Tripoli, and I hope it hurt. I'm just sorry we didn't get him personally.'

'The world probably is too,' said Blake. 'Though it's not fashionable to say so. The only one openly on your side is Maggie Thatcher.'

'Thank God for that!' said Horace. '*That* woman's got balls. And a clear vision.'

'You wouldn't think so to hear Europe,' said Blake, 'or the rest of Britain. They've practically all united against you. Like the Arabs – '

He gestured towards Feisal, who shrugged slightly.

'Yes,' he said. 'That's true enough. In a case like this *all* Arabs will present a united front against you. All Muslims, probably. The moderate nations who might well approve or stay neutral daren't; they're too worried about the ground-swells under them in their own countries. So they go through the hallowed motions of Arab or Islamic Unity. I wish it *were* something more than just an act. About almost *anything*. Maybe some day we can make it genuine –

'But to return a moment to Muámmar Khadaffi, Horace,' Feisal went on. The three of them had been on a first-name basis for a long time now. 'I think the passionate puritanism and Pan-Arabism are perfectly sincere. In that sense he's a natural Fundamentalist. But the man's a mess, a mass of contradictions. This anarchic export of terror, for example. Now,' said Feisal, bravely leaving his glass of luscious Montrachet, then, his elbows on the table on either side of his plate, putting his fingertips delicately together in front of him, 'it's not that I'm *against* revolution per se. Indeed – ' and here his exquisitely-chiselled features, his fine light grey eyes, addressed the man in front of him, then the man to his left, inviting them like some infinitely graceful Lucifer to a chic conspiracy of their immortal souls, ' – I personally have a profound sympathy for the Islamic Revolution, as a movement to build a single pure and strong Arab Nation, rich in dignity and power, secure and wise in Islam. But I speak here of *one* Revolution, total, every facet most carefully prepared and polished, every human sinew and effort bent towards it; a lofty, exhaustive, and most exclusive enterprise. Against that Khadaffi appears as a mere very small boy, hurling his own excreta around all the walls of his nursery, just for the hell of it and as his fancy takes him – '

'Have another Montrachet,' said Horace, and filled his glass. Part of the glaze melted from Feisal's eyes, and he smiled slightly and went on:

'Also Khadaffi often seems manic, and he may be dangerously megalomaniac. The three volumes of his Green Book expound a kind of half-baked Rousseauist socialism, a poor man's Nasserism. He once advised the world in a speech that Libya was the kind of society where Messengers of God like Muhammed, Christ, and Moses were born, presumably thereby elevating himself to that category.'

'Jesus!' said Blake, and Feisal glanced at him. 'Yes,' he went on. 'As I said. But perhaps the greatest strike against Khadaffi in my book is his expressed hatred for the Muslim Brothers. It seems as fierce as Nasser's. Perhaps that's *why* he hates them, because Nasser, his Godlike hero in all things, hated them. The reasons he himself gives are his usual riddles; one sometimes has to ask if Khadaffi actually understands what words *mean*. For example, he's on record as stating publicly that, if I can get the quote about right: "The Muslim Brothers in the Arab countries work against Arab Unity, Socialism, and Arab Nationalism, because they believe these to be inconsistent with religion." That is nonsense. Hassan el Banna of Egypt's Muslim Brotherhood worked as hard for Arab Unity as he could. He fully supported the Arab struggle in Palestine with supplies, arms, and volunteers. And he was never against socialism; his network of branches, schools, clinics and welfare centres for the *fellahin* and labourers and their children across Egypt was the biggest piece of practical socialism the country had ever seen. And how the hell was he against Arab Nationalism? That *pride* in being an Arab was probably the finest thing he gave to Egypt's dispossessed; thanks to him, they learnt dignity and an identity for the first time in their lives – '

Feisal stopped suddenly, and looked at each of the other two men.

'Forgive me,' he said then, 'if I speak with this intensity, make this special pleading. You will have gathered that the *Ikhwan*, the Muslim Brotherhood, is a force very near to my heart – '

300

It was really beautifully timed and stated, thought Blake with respect, it was Ahmed Feisal brilliantly performing his bewitching Lucifer act again. It's even got to me, thought Blake.

And it had certainly got to Horace, teak-hard old Southern Baptist as he was or not –

'I find that truly impressive, Ahmed,' said Horace. 'I deeply appreciate your talking this frankly. I can only have admiration for these innermost feelings of yours. Why, I can recall being deeply impressed already at our first meeting here outside in this embassy, when I first met and talked to you at that Kingdom of the Sun National Day celebration just over five years ago now. You spoke then, right openly and honestly, of the extraordinary courage, discipline, and dedication shown by the Islamic Militants who forced through the revolution in Iran, in order, you said, to regain their own lost pride and identity in their own land, and the shining purity of Islam's first principles. The activists from *your* country of Palestine, you told us, were striving for just the same simple but profound truths. I said then that I liked that, Ahmed, and I'll say it again, by God. Courage, discipline, dedication; yes, I surely can appreciate those qualities. Pride and identity in your own land, a return to the purity of first principles. *Whatever* the State Department's official position on Iran and Palestine may happen to be. This inside story from one who's been right through it and is part of it, the way *you* tell it, kind of puts a new light on things – '

Blake could have sworn that there was even moisture now in Horace's eyes. It was as surprising as seeing an iguana weep. Horace really still was a Southern Baptist at base, a regular son of the Southern soil, brimming with hymns, big emotions and Puritanism, and dead sure of what he believed in; and God help you if you thought differently.

'So I think you can have Khadaffi as far as I'm concerned,' said Feisal.

Horace blinked at that. 'Oh,' he said. 'Well, thanks.'

He rang his little bell and his Pakistani butler came in promptly and removed their three ravaged soles. He came back with three raspberry fruit flans, tastefully accoutred with white cream and maraschino cherries. He went out again and reappeared reverently with a chilled bottle of 1975 Sauternes

301

from Château d'Yquem, sweet and golden and creamy to the taste. It was almost too good to be true. After savouring it, to get back to reality, Blake turned to Feisal and said:

'You mentioned, Ahmed, that Abu Nidal and his Black June splinter rejection group have sworn to wipe out the present PLO leadership. But is there still a present PLO leadership left to wipe out? Hasn't Yasser Arafat done a pretty good job of that already all by himself?'

Feisal beamed. He was really having a lovely evening.

'You mean the Larnaca affair, where Palestinian guerillas plus one British volunteer kill one Israeli woman and two Israeli men on a pleasure yacht in Cyprus?'

'That and everything else that Arafat's done or *hasn't* done over the last year or so. The murder of the woman was particularly brilliant propaganda for your cause because of the cold-blooded way your terrorists shot her in the back when she was trying to escape, then coolly shot the two tied-up men to death afterwards. The world was sufficiently disgusted by it not to give a damn when the Israelis sent in their aircraft with their usual precision and took out most of your new PLO Headquarters in Tunis, killing a hundred or so. Most people felt you got exactly what you deserved. Arafat's responsible either way. Either he directed the Larnaca operation, or a splinter group did that he knew nothing about. Then he's impotent. Either way you ought to change him.'

'Well – ' said Feisal, not exactly rushing into the breach to defend Arafat, but making a graceful and disarming sweep with his left hand.

'Not only that,' Blake went on pitilessly, 'but then your terrorists perpetrate that tragic farce of hijacking the Italian *Achille Lauro* luxury cruise liner in the Mediterranean in October last, then *of all things*! murdering an aged American invalid in his armchair and tossing his corpse overboard! What a marvellous sense of drama your people have! So when American fighter aircraft force the Egyptian airliner carrying the hijackers down in Italy, and Italy puts them all on trial save for the man who probably led them, the whole world cheers! Again, either Arafat planned that mad action or he couldn't control those who did. Either way he's not winning you many votes.'

Feisal raised his two hands eloquently, palms upwards,

matching the movement of his eyebrows.

'Then he really wins the leadership stakes in a canter,' said Horace, joining in the hazing, 'by going all the way along with that project, heavily backed by Reagan, King Hussein of Jordan, and Peres, for a tripartite deal, Jordan–Palestinian Arabs–Israel, linking the West Bank as a state federated with Jordan, so finally solving at last a major part of the infamous Palestinian Problem once and for all. So when Margaret Thatcher invites Arafat's two delegates to London for talks on the plan, and though Hussein swears that while they were with him in Jordan both of them had fully read and approved the agreement with its references to UN Resolution 242 – which implicitly recognizes Israel's right to exist – yet on arriving in London one of the two says piously that, well, no, real sorry, but he can't morally accept 242. Agreement out of the window. I guess you could call it a kind of anticlimax. A pity, because after London the Palestinian delegates were due to meet the President of the European Economic Community's Council of Ministers, and then Reagan, for the first time, would have sat down with them. Great stuff, great stuff.'

'Then King Hussein caps that a little over a month ago,' said Blake, 'by stating very publicly all over Jordan's and the world's TV that he can see no further point to negotiating with Arafat to solve the Palestinian question, nor to starting anything afresh, until, as he delicately puts it, Arafat learns to live up to his word – one of the worst insults one Arab can offer another. So an end, perhaps forever, to any hope of an independent Palestinian Arab State on the West Bank. Meanwhile the Israelis, unlike Arafat, have not just been marking time. The number of their settlers on the West Bank went up by almost twenty per cent last year – '

There was a pregnant silence. Feisal delivered it.

'Well, gentlemen,' he said smoothly; as smoothly, as creamily, thought Blake, as the 1975 Château d'Yquem Sauternes slipped down, 'I think you have almost convinced me that we Palestinian Arabs need a new leader.'

Horace, squat at the head of his walnut table, set his slate-grey eyes direct on him. 'Ahmed,' he said heavily, 'I can think of no one better. Why don't you pull out all the stops and go hard for it? Also, I can see no one better fitted to be the President of a new Palestinian Arab State – '

My God, Horace, thought Blake, if you only knew how central that was to the true thrust of Feisal's deepest ambitions –

'Moreover, forgetting our State Department worries for the moment,' Horace went on, 'your side; or your favourites, the Muslim Brothers, or what you call their spiritual heirs the Islamic Fundamentalists, seem to be winning the game all round the clock these days. Berri's fundamentalist Shi'ite group *Amal* seems to have evolved as the most powerful militia in Beirut today. The *Hizbollah*, Party of God, is not far behind it, at least in daring. The *Hizbollah* look about equal to that other Lebanese-based terrorist group, *El Jihád el Islamí*, Islamic Jihad, in their suicide-martyrs eager gloriously to meet their Gods – of which Iran must now have trained up many hundreds. You've a downright formidable new type of soldier there, Ahmed, your suicide-bomber, suicide-martyr – a kind of highly intelligent walking time-bomb; goddamned deadly, wouldn't you say?'

'Yes,' said Ahmed Feisal, still as silkily smooth as the Sauternes, 'I expect you're right, Horace.'

'And the home of your modern Islamic Fundamentalist Revolution sure as hell doesn't look as if it's losing out, despite the massive aid Iraq's been getting in cash and weapons from almost every other Arab State except Syria. Iran's still calling the shots in *that* war, to the terror of Kuwait and Saudi and the rest. Look at that bridgehead they made across the Shatt-el-Arab right into Iraqi territory to occupy the new razed port of Faw around February 10. They're still holding it, against everything the Iraqis have thrown against them in counter-attack. Not only that, but, by God, two weeks later Iran launches a second assault into Iraqi Kurdistan in the north, taking a major town and forty villages – if they can pierce through the ninety kilometres of hilly country to the oilfields round Kirkuk, they may really finally have Iraq by the throat. And now they even have the UN blaming Iraq for starting the war in the first place in 1980!'

'Khomeini won't lose,' said Feisal evenly. 'If you have that utter conviction, that total belief in your cause, the chances are you don't lose.'

'I know one character that I don't think has that utter conviction any more,' said Horace, 'and that's Egypt's Hosni

Mubárak. No one loves Murbárak much now. The standard of living's generally lousy. He hasn't stopped the population explosion. Without our US grants of two and a half billion dollars a year Egypt's dead. He daren't cut his four and a half billion of annual subsidies for food and fuel to help get his economy right. And for Hussein to throw out Arafat because of his screwing up the negotiations doesn't help Mubárak either; he was backing that hard. Now he's stuck with that nice little heritage from Sadat of an unsolved West Bank problem. That's a real load of dynamite. Meanwhile, as Philip says, the Jews keep on packing in new settlements there. Most Arabs, including your Fundamentalists, won't like Mubárak much for that either – '

Horace took a break, poured all three of them a generous last glass of the superb Château d'Yquem, and looked at his two guests expansively.

'You know, I wouldn't blame the Arabs, the Fundamentalists, too far for that. Look, I feel I know you two guys well enough by now to tell you this. I don't myself really *like* the Jews – '

He could have been a small boy back from school with a report in his pocket which did *not* show that he was the best in his class.

'I'm glad to hear that,' said Feisal.

Blake knew just how deeply Feisal meant that. Without moving a muscle of his face, Blake looked back at his host and said: 'I'd say it's a matter of taste, Horace.'

Horace's slate-grey eyes looked back at him shrewdly.

'Just that? No more than that? Not *good* taste? Or bad taste?'

Blake shrugged.

'I wouldn't qualify it. If you want the truth, I've no particular feelings about them one way or the other.'

The astute slate-grey eyes went on investigating him.

'You a Catholic or something?' asked Horace.

Blake laughed outright. 'No,' he said. 'I'm not a Catholic or anything, Horace. As I'm sure your highly efficient briefing services will have told you – that, and a lot more.'

But the eyes, slightly shocked, still watched him implacably, and the silence lengthened. Against it, Blake said: 'I'd say one thing, though. Thanks largely to this character facing me –' he nodded across at the exquisite Feisal. 'I've come to feel a great deal of empathy for the Palestinian Arabs. It's trite to remark that they've had a raw deal. They *have*, but I believe I'd go a bit further than just *talk*. I think I'd go a long way to try to set things right, to help them. To help this man Feisal – '

His tone was flippant, but the atmosphere was not that. It was suddenly extraordinarily charged, electric. It was not so much as if angels had walked over their graves, but as if those celestial beings, or their God, or perhaps devils, or the Devil, had in an instant struck those words into a pact, hammered it in gold, etched it eternally in bronze into the high heavens, or hell.

'I guess that's all right, then,' said Horace, evidently now letting Blake off whatever hook he had hung him on. 'Another thing,' he went on, turning now frankly and completely to the impeccable Feisal. 'Another reason why the winds of history seem to be shifting so hard in favour of your Fundamentalists, and *against* the conservative Arab Establishment, is the oil glut and the consequent vertical drop in the price of crude. The spot price is down to less than ten dollars a barrel these days. That's down to almost a quarter of what the OPEC posting was for Arab or Sun Light at thirty-four dollars a barrel only three years ago! So the Arab OPEC weapon for beating the shit out of the rest of the world has kind of lost its edge. Five years ago a scream by Khadaffi, with his near million barrels a day of oil exports, that all OPEC Arab countries should cut oil supplies to the US because we'd bombed Tripoli and Benghazi, would have scared the hell out of us. Now the crude oil spot price actually *dropped* at the news of the bombing. The big Arab OPEC nations just don't have us by the balls any more.'

Horace grinned, and his solid block of body leaned back a fraction on his chair.

'Because OPEC, and mainly the dominant Arab contingent in it, screwed us and the rest of the free world's oil consumers so goddamned hard and long while they could, we've all learned painfully to use that fuel much more sparingly and efficiently and to substitute it by others where possible. So now we just need less of the stuff. Also, Libya and the Arabs in OPEC just can't hurt us much in the States any more. Most of the lower oil volume we still import comes from non-OPEC countries like Mexico and Canada or from non-Arab OPEC lands like Venezuela, Indonesia, Nigeria. On top of that, we've now already built up our emergency strategic reserve of crude oil in Louisiana and Texan salt-domes to half a billion barrels – that's enough to cover our crude imports for a hundred days – and we're busy preparing another quarter-billion barrels of emergency storage space. I think the OPEC members themselves know that they've just been bleeding the rest of us too goddam greedily and too goddam long, forcing the free world into a major recession from which it's just *starting* to emerge – and here I include *this* particular well-heeled but still goddam voracious little country, the Kingdom of the Sun – and they're waking up to the ugly fact that their cosy little cartel's bust. In their latest crisis meeting at Geneva they're still a million miles from an effective production-sharing rationing agreement to stop the prices falling any *further*, and they'll get no nearer to it at their next meeting in June in the Adriatic island of Brioni. They *know* it. And its *hurting* them, but *bad*. And as for me,' Horace ended, his steely eyes still bracketing Feisal belligerently, 'I couldn't give a *damn*! I like that just *fine!*'

'You don't have to look at me like that, Horace,' said Feisal. 'I just mind the legal shop, remember? Tell them how much stamp tax they have to pay on their contracts, and how to hound any customer reckless enough not to pay his bill. I don't set any of their *policies*, you follow me? Fix any of these sales deals which have made this country one of the three richest in the world, per capita. I'm just a simple harmless back-room boy.'

'You have a point there, Ahmed,' said Horace, unplugging his gaze from him and sticking it balefully on Blake instead. 'It's the way the goddam little half-pint countries like this Kingdom have dictated to the good old USA that gets to me. My God, here we are, busting a gut to be the world's big policeman securing peace for one and all – unpaid, overworked, underloved – and these snotty little bastards have the goddam nerve to hold *us*, the USA, to ransom. And the rest of the free world's oil-consuming countries too, of course – '

They just got in under the wire, thought Blake.

'This Abdullah guy, for example,' Horace went on, his eyes still transfixing Blake beadily. 'This goddam *prince*, with his goddam Oxford education and that faggot accent he's so proud of – I mean he's fleeced some of our greatest and venerated multinationals like Tulsa just about out of their *skins*. And so, inevitably, the American consuming public too. So they cream all those many billions of good American dollars off us, and what do they do with it? Pack it into over-luxurious facilities for their working classes here. After buying all the most opulent cars and houses and furniture and modern gadgets for themselves, naturally. Meanwhile they've stuck forty or fifty billion of the dollars they took from us into stocks and shares in our and the Jap and the European markets. So what good does that do *us*, may I ask?'

'I know what I'd do with all those billions if I had them,' said Ahmed Feisal. 'If *I* were running this country. Like the Amir. The Crown Prince. Like Abdullah.'

'And what would *that* be?' said Horace, turning to him. 'As if we didn't know!'

'Yes, you probably do,' said Feisal. 'I'd certainly not invest it in new economic infrastructures for the underprivileged that aren't absolutely indispensable at this moment. Later, sure. Or in stocks and shares to produce five or six billion dollars a year of dividends and interest *again* just to come back to this small country for nothing more noble than their own improved physical comfort. I'd use it to achieve a great aim that should be nearest to every true Arab's heart – to free Palestine completely for its dispossessed and rightful Arab owners. Haven't they suffered long enough already for God's sake?'

'Well, that's a straight and honourable attitude at least,' said Horace. 'What do you say, Philip?'

He had turned his basilisk gaze back on Blake. He was insisting, wouldn't take no for an answer, thought Blake, a trifle grimly. For he knew without the faintest shadow of doubt that Horace, under that conveniently bluff, thug-like and gross exterior, the many goddams and occasional Yeahs and Southern slurs in his speech, was watching him as keenly as any investigating Jesuit, putting him up, indeed, with a Jesuit's beautiful and pitiless clarity, to this choice, and forcing him to see it as starkly. Horace knew what he was doing. Horace could play with souls too. Weren't Southern Baptists supposed to have pretty vivid and murderous Old Testament convictions about predestination and hellfire and eternal damnation? For this was a choice of that order of gravity. It was, thought Blake, perhaps man's oldest choice, and most tragic. It reverberated again and again across the vaulted voids of eternity. It was that between loyalty to a friend, and betrayal of him. Blake knew too that, despite his love and admiration for Abdullah, he would leave him and go with Feisal. As Horace had said, the winds of history were blowing in Feisal's favour now. In the end, that was Blake's way, to go with those winds. Even if that inexorably meant the saddest sin of all, betrayal.

'I'd say that Ahmed's was a perfectly understandable position too,' said Blake.

Horace gave a kind of sigh, and lifted his glass and drained the last of the Château d'Yquem from it.

'Now we've that cleared away,' he said, 'I've a question I'd like to ask you two gentlemen.'

'About the future?' asked Feisal, with interest.

Horace looked at him. 'Yes,' he said. 'I guess you could say about the future. About the shape the future may take.'

His two guests looked at Horace curiously.

'But perhaps,' said Horace, 'it would be more civilized to put it to you in the library, while you're at ease with your coffee and liqueur.'

They followed him through and sat in the deep leather armchairs. An entire wall was covered with bookshelves in which the leather bindings of the volumes, their titles picked out with shining delicate gold lettering, exactly matched the armchairs in colour; Blake wondered how many of the books Horace had read. The Pakistani butler served them coffee, and Rémy-Martin in warmed balloon glasses to the two guests, while Horace struck out on his own with a Benedictine. He and Feisal also each took one of the fat Dutch cigars from the proffered light brown wooden box. As they sat back, Horace said:

'Here's my question. Abdullah called on me officially yesterday here at the Embassy, on behalf of the Amir and Crown Prince. I guess they chose to send him as the emissary, and not the Defence or Interior ministers, although it's their bailiwick we're looking at here, either because they calculate Abdullah must impress me with all that princely title and Oxford education and fancy British accent – '

At this point Horace turned his head towards the purely decorative and never-used fireplace and spat curtly with remarkable accuracy at the cuspidor thoughtfully placed there; it was, Blake reckoned, at least an eight-foot shot.

' – Or because they think he represents that part of the Kingdom which we in the States are going to take most seriously, meaning the supply of crude oil, because we're always secretly scared shitless that they just might cut it off from us one bright day. Well – ' said Horace, turning his head and lining it massively up on Blake, 'from what we've been saying around that dinner-table in there just now, I'd see them as kinda out of date on that particular interpretation as of today, wouldn't you agree?'

Blake looked back at him and raised his eyebrows and ducked his head slightly to one side, but Horace was not buying any ambiguities this evening. Though a generous host, he liked to get his money's worth.

'Wouldn't you agree?' he said again, peremptorily.

'Look,' said Blake, 'I work for the man, remember? I work for their Ministry of Oil. So I ought to have *some* loyalty to them – '

As he said it the word hit him in the stomach. His loyalty to Abdullah was not the virtue that was going to come most shining and unsullied out of this evening, out of everything that was being said or forged subtly under the surface or decided explicitly here. Blake saw no way out of it. If you had two friends who diverged very sharply in key values of life and death, you could really only follow one. Your loyalty to one had to be expendable. All his instincts took him towards Feisal. Feisal, by some magic, was of the future. They said you couldn't serve God and Mammon, God and the Devil. Which friend did you drop? Blake had probably decided that irrevocably without even knowing it. When he had first diverted Tulsa's ten cents a barrel override to the needs of Feisal's shadowy works eight years before. When he had suffered the killing of Feisal's four hijackers with him nearly two and a half years before, or gone with him to his School for Death in the desert the next day or ten minutes before, at the dinner-table. It was anyway all set now, between these three men, here in Horace's library. It might have crystallized all on its own, like some fabulously harmonic shape precipitated out from a chemical solution. It was inevitable, less a conspiracy than a fatality.

' – But to answer your query, Horace,' Blake went on. 'Yes, I'd have to agree. No one could reasonably pretend that Tulsa's need of their 700,000 bd of Sun Light is anything like as critical today as they saw it say three years ago. If the Kingdom cut off supplies, Tulsa could replace them to-morrow, probably at a much lower price, from say Mexico, who'd be enchanted. No, I'm afraid Abdullah doesn't carry any invincible God-given thunderbolts in his hands these days.'

'It's what I thought,' said Horace, with some satisfaction. 'They've had us against a wall for years, but now their shot has no powder behind it. Now, the joke is that that's just what they want us to give them! Powder! And teach them how to use it!'

'Meaning?' asked Feisal politely.

Horace swung round to him over his cloud of cigar-smoke, like an old-fashioned galleon after firing a broadside.

'They want us to equip them with a fully-trained para-military Riot Police Force, pretty big stuff, ten thousand of their best men, equipped with every conceivable type of modern armament and all the latest Intelligence listening devices, helicopters, armoured cars, light field artillery, fast heavily armed patrol boats, the works. We'd need to send over a training corps of say two thousand of our best anti-terrorist specialists and Rangers for that full year, plus bring the élite of their leadership over to the States for further highly intensive instruction. It would require a really major effort from us, we'd have to dig deep – not just all that most modern equipment and the latest in armaments and helicopters and patrol boats; we could absorb that or they could pay for it – but much more in tying up our scarce and very valuable anti-terrorist specialists for a whole year. The cost of immobilizing so many of our finest tactical experts here for that long a time could be so goddam high – when Nicaragua could boil over, or if we have any more big crises around the world – that we simply couldn't put a price on it. Now what I want to know from you two gentlemen – ' said Horace, emitting another broadside of cigar-smoke, then piercing his flinty gaze through it at each of them in turn, ' – is what the hell's so special about the Kingdom of the Sun? Where's the fire, I mean to say? Where's the big threat around here? Can you gentlemen see one?'

His gaze came to rest pugnaciously on Blake. Blake's eyes locked a long moment with Feisal's. Then he looked back at Horace.

'I'm damned if I see one,' he said.

So far as a rhinoceros could look cheerful, a flash of lyricism illuminated Horace's bulk. He glanced at Feisal.

'And you, Ahmed?'

Feisal looked back at him and shrugged daintily.

'We're just on a thousand miles from Israel here, Horace. As the crow flies. And if it wanted to attack, it would have to be a pretty hardy crow. It's just about all waterless desert between them and us.'

'Just what I thought myself,' said Horace happily, removing his large cigar long enough from his mouth to get a shot of Benedictine through it. 'But I wanted to benefit from you two gentlemen's long experience, know what I mean? So, secondly, why must I put myself to one hell of a lot of extra trouble for Abdullah and the Kingdom of the Sun? What have they ever done for me and the US of A except screw the ass off us when crude oil was short? And I can't recall them laying it on the line for us when we went through our hostage crisis with Iran. They just kinda drew up the hems of their *jelabiahs* and said well, sure, we don't exactly *like* Khomeini, of course, but we *are* all Muslims, don't you know. And Abdullah and his Amir and Crown Prince friends are very happy to ask us this huge favour right after they've joined every other mother-fucking Arab State in the world in condemning us out of hand for our bombing that bastard mad dog Khadaffi last week. No, Abdullah and company didn't make any exceptions for us, though State tells me we have *absolute proof* Khadaffi was two hundred per cent behind that bombing of that La Belle disco in Western Berlin killing those two and wounding two hundred. And a pile of other recent terrorist killings and woundings beside. So I think we make no exceptions for Abdullah and company either. That's the way I'll put it to State, and they'll never go against my strong recommendation.'

There was a silence. Then Feisal said in it, silkily:

'Well, Horace, there's justice in that. I doubt that anyone could really deny that.'

Justice, thought Blake. For Feisal. Help for Feisal. For the Kingdom of the Sun's regular armed forces were small and very conservatively trained and pretty amateur. With that threat of a superbly equipped and highly trained paramilitary Riot Police Force out of the way, Feisal's would remain by far the most professional and effective fighting force in the land. Blake did not see that Feisal would have any objection to that.

'Glad to hear you see it that way,' said Horace, with a broad smile. 'Do help yourself to the Rémy-Martin. Justice. Yeah, I like that. I think I'll mention that point in my report. And you, Philip? How would you see it?'

The flinty eyes bracketed him, twin shotgun muzzles.

How would Abdullah see that?

'I don't think it's a word I'd have used,' he said, 'but all right, if you stretch it. A kind of justice, perhaps. Rough justice.'

Was there any record of how Pilate felt after he washed his hands? But he too had committed himself. And once committed, how could you change?

'*Rough* justice!' said Horace, sounding delighted through his broadside. 'I like that too! *Rough* justice is still justice too. Isn't it?'

30
A Fragile Last Stand

'It's rough justice indeed, said Philip Blake, three months later. 'We've simply pumped and supplied too great a volume of oil, at too high a price. We've semi-strangled, if not yet quite killed, the goose that lays the golden egg. The black gold egg.'

'That's how it looks,' said Sheikh Abdullah bin Ali bin Jibál, Minister of Oil of the Kingdom of the Sun. He sat with Blake and one other man, in Blake's suite with its magnificent view over Lake Geneva, at the top of the chromium and glass and concrete skyscraper of Geneva's Intercontinental Hotel, in the early evening of July 27 1986. In this tranquil sober city with its sparkling arches of floodlit fountains on the lake and the superb cathedral overlooking them from its hill, representatives of all the OPEC countries had gathered in yet another, and probably their gravest ever, crisis meeting.

'Consider that right up to 1979,' said Blake, 'only seven years ago, we in OPEC were producing and selling up to thirty-two million barrels a day of crude oil, and the world didn't even look as if it could ever get enough from us. Today we're lucky if we can place half that, around sixteen million bd. Why? Two reasons – by our high prices, we've forced the world to rationalize its energy consumption radically, and to move over sharply to alternative energy sources, notably nuclear and coal. Second, the *non*-OPEC oil-producers – strikingly, Britain and Norway with their North Sea production, and Mexico – have moved very rapidly and strongly into the picture, from producing some twenty million bd for the non-Communist world in 1979 to twenty-six million last year. Those two trends, that pincer-movement, has just about castrated us.'

'Yes,' said Abdullah, long and lithe in his armchair, elegant in his Gianfranco Ferre pearl-grey suit, his high-cheekboned olive face thrusting hawk-like at this world-shaking problem. 'And the near-vertical fall in price levels has compounded the gravity of our situation. Up to 1983, just three years back, the official OPEC posting for Arab Light crude – our Sun Light being virtually identical – was thirty-four dollars a barrel. Now we're seeing that go spot on say the Rotterdam market *at less than ten dollars*! The combined effect of the drops in the volumes we sell and in their sales prices is to cut OPEC's income by four hundred million dollars *a day*, or say seventeen million an hour! Moreover, my friend Philip Blake here calculates that, unless we at this meeting get out a really cast-iron cartel agreement to cut our OPEC-production by some 3.4 million bd from the twenty million bd we're trying to place now to not more than a total of 16.8 million, we'll see that already ruinous low price of nine to ten dollars per barrel drop by another third or half to five or six! The situation is *that* serious!'

Blake found it hard to tell if the third man realized that fully. Blake had picked him up on a sheer hunch in the hotel bar.

Blake knew that he was Iranian, part of their official delegation under Iran's Oil Minister Gholamreza Aqazadeh, for he had met the man at the OPEC Oil Ministers' prior emergency meeting in Yugoslavia on June 25 to which Abdullah, as usual, had taken him. The third man was slim, dark, about forty, and very astute; Khomeini might dominate Iran politically with his inflexibly orthodox Fundamentalism but there was nothing at all lacking in speed or suppleness of intellect about the Iranian oil delegation.

The third man's name was Albert Mazahéri, and he had his doctorate in economics from Paris; his French was as effortlessly perfect as his English. Khomeini had some very good men on his side. Mazahéri might be a very way-out chance, Blake knew, but then wildcatters were only genuine wildcatters if they went for the very long odds – and won. And there was one sound practical reason why Mazahéri *might* be the pivotal man. Because Iran almost certainly *was* the pivotal country. Iran, still full of vengeance against Iraq for the six-year war that Iraq had started, had always insisted in these production-limiting deals that she be allowed two barrels for every barrel on Iraq's quota – though in fact Iran had never recently managed to produce and sell that much more than Iraq; the current production levels were in fact nearer to Iran 2.3 billion bd and Iraq 1.9. If Iran could be influenced to accept Iraq going on producing at that level, while *not* insisting on markedly increasing its own – which, in view of Iraq's repeated bombing of Iran's terminals at Kharg and Sirri Islands, was probably unrealizable anyway – then the pass *might* just be held.

Albert Mazahéri smiled wryly.

'But you surely don't imagine,' he said, 'that we don't know all that perfectly well already? We have our own think-tanks too, you know. We've calculated that the total external accounts of only six Arabian Gulf oil producers – Saudi, Kuwait, Qatar, Bahrein, Oman and the Emirates – not even including your own Kingdom of the Sun – have been slashed between 1981 and last year because of these plunges in oil volumes sold and their prices levels by *ninety billion dollars*, from a surplus of seventy billion to a *deficit* of twenty billion. Surely we all know this sort of kindergarten facts?'

'Of course, of course!' said Abdullah soothingly, taking

Mazahéri's intellectual arrogance carefully in his stride; the stakes were too high for a big man like Abdullah to allow himself to be deflected by mere insults. Instead, he leant across courteously and poured some more Laphroaig ten-year straight Islay Malt Scotch whisky into Mazahéri's depleted glass, then topped up Blake's and his own. However heavily pan-Islamic a slant OPEC meetings might tend to have no one was taking this one to the extreme of barring hearty drinking in private. That created the right sort of convivial atmosphere in which reasonable men could make sensible deals, making meetings like this very similar to the *diwanías* by which most Arab rulers really ran their shops. But not quite yet as in this case. For Mazahéri simply took two large gulps from his Laphroaig and grunted:

'I get the point. So you want me to do a little gentle arm-twisting.'

'I wonder what could make you feel that?' said Abdullah, his tone and eyebrows shooting up. 'My friend here Philip Blake and I just saw you as an approachable and highly intelligent man!'

'An exaggeration. You're too kind,' said Mazahéri darkly, but beaming slightly despite himself; it was amazing what flattery could do. 'Still, you may just conceivably have a point. As things are now, we're *all* suffering.'

'Indeed,' said Abdullah. 'Only the highly industrialized West is benefiting.'

He omitted to mention, Blake noticed, that *whatever* happened now to OPEC oil volume sales or prices, the Kingdom of the Sun was going to ride things out very nicely thank you anyway, by virtue of that same highly industrialized West, in which the Kingdom now had over $50 billion expertly invested, yielding a cool $6 billion annually in dividends and interest.

'So you're asking me to influence my Minister,' said Mazahéri. It was a statement of fact, not a question, and he made it sound like high treason.

'I'm sure Gholamreza Aqazadeh's a reasonable man just like you,' replied Abdullah obliquely. Mazahéri chuckled suddenly and for the first time.

'You don't think he might have this sort of idea already himself?' he said. Then he finished his whisky with a quick swallow, got to his feet and bowed ironically to Abdullah and Blake, and left crisply.

Exactly ten days later Abdullah and Blake sat in the same armchairs at the same hour, with the same splendid view. The next morning they were due to fly back in Abdullah's Lear jet to the Kingdom of the Sun.

'It'll be no bad homecoming,' said Abdullah.

'It's fantastic,' said Blake. 'To think that, after five days of total deadlock, Aqazadeh suddenly goes into a huddle with Zaki Yamani in Zaki's suite here for a couple of hours. Then we learn he's come forward with a hell of a concession: for once Iran *isn't* going to insist that its quota be twice Iraq's. Instead, Iraq can go on producing as now at about full capacity of 1.9 million bd, and Iran will stay about where she is now, at 2.2 to 2.3 million bd. It'll involve the rest of us cutting back some, Saudi and Kuwait and the Emirates down from July's 8.9 million bd to 6.2 or by thirty per cent, and us by a bit less, from 1 million bd to 750,000. Then, to make the whole thing more credible, Aqazadeh astutely suggests we make the whole deal tentative and initially limited in time, for two months from September 1, extendable at our option, of course, and the whole OPEC production limited to the 16.7 million bd which we think the world can take without going into glut again. Aqazadeh's near genius for getting that deal through – and that first with Saudi, who've been putting up most of the money for Iraq's attacks on Iran. Why, even Iraq's Oil Minister, Qassim Taki, said that Aqazadeh's was a very good proposal.'

'Well,' said Abdullah, 'the effects on the market have been immediate and excellent. After we in OPEC announced our deal today, Brent crude, the most heavily traded North Sea oil, closed at $13.75, up *one third* on yesterday's closing level of $10.20. And the US's benchmark West Texas Intermediate jumped from $13.29 to 15.02. You've done another very good job, Philip!'

'We can't say it was me,' said Blake. 'Remember what Mazahéri insinuated – Aqazadeh already had the same idea himself. And the idea of making the deal credible by keeping it limited in time initially was absolutely his, without doubt.'

'Well, call it a team effort, if you like. We've *got* it, anyway, with those excellent prices I've quoted for September delivery. That success is in itself a pretty good reward.'

'Sure,' said Blake. 'It may be a little fragile, but we've still kept the world of black gold sailing. Or our small part of it anyway. You know, oil must be the most exhilarating game in the world. After all, it's genuinely vital – it still gives the world *half* of the entire energy it needs. So it's still, literally, a matter of life or death, making or breaking men and nations. And always fascinating. Oil's a kind of poetry, a poetic mathematics of power – '

'Well,' said Abdullah. 'Yes, I think we've changed the face of the world a fraction or two over the last ten days. Let's hope that change can last!'

PART FIVE

31
The Strike from the Sky

Philip Blake saw the beginnings of the outline of a really great change in the face of the world one morning though he did not then grasp that that was what they were, nor come anywhere near to understanding the whole lethal brilliance of Feisal's grand design. They had gone out again to Feisal's School of Death in the north, way past the Port of Peace and the glittering metal citadel of the Kingdom of the Sun's 200,000 bd refinery, with the mosque-like domes of its spheroid tanks and the high minarets of its fractionating-towers. A few flares burned a lurid red, like the open throats of Molochs awaiting their child sacrifices. Tall towers exhaled clouds of white vapour, mystic in shape, no doubt more deadly in content. They had turned left off the main coast road at the near-invisible rocky track, and driven due west again. Blake looked to his right from his seat in the jeep, but the Bedu were not there, the sun-charred leaves of their tents torn away from this harsh sweltering parched land.

In twenty-five minutes they came up upon the high-fenced encampment, reared there like a phantom city of the void. Efficient for its purpose, it had not changed. The .50 calibre Browning machineguns still lowered at them from the twin high hooded watchtowers, and the barbed gate was opened to them. Salah Khalíl still met them, and conducted them round the karate and judo training areas, and they watched a group of ninety, broken into sub-groups with stragglers stemming from them, pant in sweating copiously from their run in the desert. They inspected the firing-range and they saw the mock plywood city where man's worst enemy, himself, sprang wickedly up and out from improbable angles at indecent speeds. And they listened to the ideologist, tall on his dais curved forward above his lectern, gaunt in his grey full-length *jelabíah* and grey turban, in the great packed marquee tent with its rapt and reverberating audience, sometimes muttering with the sibilant sound of wind through corn, sometimes growling, sometimes roaring with the full force of their hearts and lungs; a different man, this, more majestic, older, his heavy black beard peppered with grey, his jet-black eyes scintillating and shimmering like a depthless midnight lake with the full moon on it, his voice like a scimitar piercing out to them their duty to die, need for redemption by the ultimate sacrifice if called upon for it – hardly an inequitable arrangement, he remarked sonorously; Allah had a fair name for holding to reasonably square deals, and by his death for Islam the martyr was after all guaranteed a short cut to Paradise.

The long sinewy man's tones rang powerfully out, many-layered, the brass cymbals of glory resounding in them, the slick inexorable key-in-oiled-lock clicks of predestination, the splendid epic poetry of doom. There was nothing fickle about Feisal, thought Blake. He had followed exactly the same training line throughout the time that Blake had known it, at both physical and ideological level, at both his camps. He was mass-producing, yet with beautiful individual precision, 3,600 a year of these highly intelligent and prepared, and totally dedicated walking time-bombs, every one of whom could drive an explosives-packed truck efficiently up to an enemy strong-point, nod politely to the guards, then blow all of them to smithereens. And more and more were proving it. That benign smile, before they pressed the plunger or pulled the trigger, was perhaps their most terrifying banner. In the long run, could even Israel stand that? Feisal had made himself master of a truly deadly specialized force.

And some, as Blake then saw, were being specialized in a new direction. For, after Salah Khalíl saw them courteously to their jeep, and helped shut the tall barbed gate behind them under the watchful black muzzles of the Browning .50 machineguns, Feisal drove *round* the camp and continued due west, again along a rocky track so faint that Blake could never have found it on his own. Fifteen minutes later he saw the aircraft; the jeep's motor drowned their sound. He could see three biplanes flying at the same time. They were doing circuits and bumps, landing on a hard airstrip which seemed just to have been levelled by bulldozers from the desert, still rocky in this area. There was no asphalted area or tarmac; the strip would have been invisible from the air, save to someone flying really low and looking for it. The big hangars too, which he made out as they got nearer to the airstrip, were carefully camouflaged the colour of the desert. Blake knew that Abdullah, and the rest of the Kingdom of the Sun's Establishment, were perfectly aware that Ahmed Feisal was head of the PLO-Fatah movement in the country and ran guerrilla training camps in its desert, but he doubted that they had the faintest idea how far Feisal now diverged from the official Arafat line, or that he was now apparently investing in an air force weapon too.

Not with his usual business acumen, thought Blake. For it was hard to see how these bumbling piston-engined aircraft were going to constitute much of a threat to the Israeli air force, whose pilots were probably the best in the world.

'What are they?' he asked Feisal, as the jeep drew up next to a low wooden shed, camouflaged like the hangars. A man came out and walked towards them, a submachinegun slung casually over one shoulder. 'They look like pre-World War Two vintage to me.'

Feisal glanced round at him and smiled. 'You're quite right,' he said. 'They're Stearmans. We bought them in the States from war surplus.'

'They won't win you many dog-fights against the Israeli F-16s.'

Feisal smiled again.

'Maybe we wouldn't point them quite that way,' he said. 'Careful! Remember the fable of the hare and the tortoise. In fact, an F-16 probably couldn't *catch* one of these. Not if it kept right down near the ground, which is what we're training them to do. And not because our Stearman flew too fast, but because it flew too *slow*. Say at comfortably down to 80 mph. At that speed an F-16's liable to stall itself to death.'

The man with the submachinegun had arrived. He was squat, with heavily muscled forearms, and wearing a short-sleeved open-necked shirt and light grey cotton pants, neatly pressed. His complexion was as light as Feisal's; another Palestinian. He looked as if he knew how to use that submachinegun.

'Meet Selim Kadi,' said Feisal, 'our Chief Flying Instructor.

And as good as they come. This,' he said to Kadi, 'is our friend Abu Jildah.'

Abu Jildah had been a notorious buccaneering Arab robber in the Jerusalem area in the 1930s. Blake liked his nom-de-guerre.

'Ah, yes,' said Kadi, giving him a firm dry handshake. 'We've heard of you, Abu Jildah, even out in this forsaken desert. One day we shall build you a statue in our regained land – '

Blake, somewhat surprised, looked at Feisal, but Feisal just smiled and shrugged slightly.

'Selim's right,' he said. 'We don't forget our friends. Even if we sometimes treat them roughly.'

'No complaints so far,' said Blake, also smiling.

'No,' said Feisal, considering him for rather a long few moments. Then he turned to Selim Kadi. 'So what progress, Selim? How many do you have fully trained now, ready to go?'

'Two hundred and twenty-five fixed-wing pilots,' said Selim Kadi promptly, 'and two hundred and thirty helicopters. I'll have the last batch of forty and thirty-five finished within ten days, to give your target of five hundred, plus a reserve of six per cent.'

'Fine,' said Feisal. 'That'll give the last lot just enough time to get into place and feel comfortable before their big day.'

'You mean you have helicopters in the act too?' asked Blake. 'I don't see any.'

'Look over there,' said Selim Kadi, pointing, 'straight across. See that blur near the ground? That's their rotors blowing up the sand. They've got their own sub-station and refuelling tanks and pumps to the north there. That's to leave our airstrip here free for the fixed-wing training. Helicopters can operate from any sort of land, of course.'

Straining his eyes, Blake could see them now, three pods and a criss-cross-girdered fuselage behind, like large locusts bumbling in a cloud of dust.

'My God, they're flying low!' he exclaimed. 'And I see your Stearmans are brushing the ground most of the time too.'

He half-noticed Feisal and Kadi exchanging glances.

'Remember what I said before,' said Feisal, smiling again. 'That way and flying that slow will have the F-16s piling into the ground trying to catch them. That's their safest way of going.'

'Also,' said Blake, 'I don't know what's in your hangars, but I can't see five hundred aircraft littering the place up to the far horizons.'

'No,' said Feisal. 'Well, you wouldn't, would you, if the action aircraft were all on site already, shipped by sea and assembled there? All we've got left here, in the air or in the hangars, are the training machines.'

'I see,' said Blake, and his heart gave a jump of excitement. Until now, Feisal had given no hint of his operational activities. Blake might have helped to charge the storm clouds but he had no idea how the lightning would strike. 'Already on site,' he echoed. 'Then it must be soon.'

'That's right,' said Feisal. 'In range of the F-16s, you might say.'

So the aim was Israel, of course. Blake had never really thought it would be anything else. The Return, freeing Palestine, had always been Feisal's first target.

As a step to ruling the whole Arab Middle East.

He had some idea of the demoniac range of Feisal's ambitions. If you were interested in moving up in the world's top power circuits, Feisal's was a good bandwagon to stay on.

The only question now was, how far would he get on this particular operation? This must be some kind of highly specialized commando raid. It might be on the top-secret F-16 bases, if Feisal's intelligence had managed to pinpoint them. That would make sense for the helicopters. They could land their commandos and pick them up afterwards anywhere. What survivors there were; casualties would be very heavy. But why the Stearmans? They could only take in a man or two, and probably crash-land them; they couldn't get any survivors out. But *that* of course could be the name of the game! They could be martyrs, suicide bombers. Feisal had after all been training them up at the rate of 3,600 a year for at least five years, his lean whipcord bearded and hooded mullahs rhythmically packing into them the fear of God and the reputed bliss of dying gloriously for him in little pieces.

What would make even more sense was the helicopters taking in the commandos and the Stearmans going in just with single pilots but packed to the teeth with explosives. You could stuff even a little aeroplane like a Stearman with, literally, quite a bomb of explosives if you really tried. That added up.

And Feisal had said 'in striking distance of the F-16s'. That strike could be launched from any of Jordan, the Lebanon, Syria, Egypt from around El Arish, even, marginally, Saudi, over Akaba. Hussein would probably shut his eyes; he might have been trying to make a deal with the Israelis over the West Bank for years, but it was unlikely that he actually loved them passionately.

Blake wished Feisal's helicopter commandos and suicide bombers the best of luck. The only other venture anything like as original that he could think of was the marvellously enterprising assaults launched after 1978 by Ahmed Jibril's splinter Arab Resistance group, the PFLPGC, or Popular Front for the Liberation of Palestine General Command. These consisted partly of trying to get highly armed guerrillas across the border from Lebanon into Israel by hot-air balloons and hang-gliders equipped with miniature motors. But, though highly spectacular, the plan had not succeeded notably. The only serious risk that the Israeli armed forces had run while confronting them was of collapsing with laughter as they waited for them to drift helplessly down to capture. Feisal's bunch ought to do better. Israel might have truly formidably effective armed forces, but she was, geographically, a tiny country. So Feisal's motley clutter of aircraft should easily have the range to hit virtually any target within Israel. If they got through. On their side they had their extraordinarily slow speeds and ability to fly very low, plus, in the case of the helicopters, extreme manoeuvrability; these should baffle and enrage the speedy Israeli air pursuit. Of course Israel's highly efficient radar would pick up some, and their own helicopter gunships and ground-fire down some, but Feisal's venture's second great advantage, surprise, should cut these losses. Suppose it totally lost *half* its attacking force. The remaining 250 aircraft, skilfully directed – and Feisal was most certainly no amateur – could still deliver one hell of a blow.

Enough to win a war?

Possibly, if well coordinated with other Arab attacks. Blake wondered what the score was there. He hesitated to ask. He was still a non-Arab *kafr* in this country, and in Feisal's cause, even if he had bought his way some distance into it with somebody else's money, Tulsa's ten cent per barrel override. Feisal anyway seemed to be letting him along into it as it developed, being very fair, paying him back meticulously. Feisal was a thorough man, thinking of everything.

'How's their skill in map-reading?' Feisal asked Selim Kadi, demonstrating that thoroughness.

'Pretty good now,' said Kadi. 'Every one of them knows his route to his target like the back of his hand. I've been testing them mercilessly.'

He turned to Blake.

'In that long shed there that I came out of we have a Link Trainer and a very up-to-date set of navigational teaching equipment. And a large-scale mock-up in relief of all our targets, the known airfields and anti-aircraft guns and missiles. Why not come in and take a look? I've a class in there now – '

Blake looked where he pointed. There were two young bearded faces watching them from the open window near the door with avid interest. After two or three months in a training-camp as tough as Feisal's, you probably looked at anything that came from the big city and its comforts with the sheerest envy. The two bearded faces disappeared abruptly.

'Many thanks, I think we'll give it a miss for now,' said Feisal. 'I just wanted to check with you and see how the training of the last batch was going. It sounds fine. And my friend Abu Jildah here and I have to get back and help run that Oil Ministry – '

'Of course,' said Selim Kadi. 'You must be a very busy man these days, Ahmed. That's clear.'

What was not so clear was Feisal's following remark.

'While it's under its present management,' he said.

'Sure,' said Selim Kadi, with a smile. Then he looked away swiftly towards the airstrip. One of the three Stearmans had not simply landed on its circuit and then taken promptly off again, but was taxiing towards them and the shed, its propeller whirling a pretty white disk and the multiple cylinders of the radial engine very black and oily through it. With its trim fixed undercarriage and neat black wheels and its twin wings exactly parallel to each other, it looked like a smart update from a World War One fighter. It stopped by the motor gasoline pump by the shed and cut its engine, the propeller materializing to the sight and stopping horizontal, wooden and polished. With these stocky little machines you really went flying, no question of being hurtled effortlessly at supersonic speeds through space by jets or rocket-power; here you worked hard for it. A man jumped down from the biplane to prove it. He was in khaki overalls and a black leather flying-helmet, the goggles pushed up on it. He took the muzzle of the pump's hose and stuck it in the side of his machine, then went behind the pump, waved at the group by the jeep, and started pumping by hand. That must be a very dedicated and very hot flying instructor, thought Blake. For the brass hand of the sun was pitiless that day. It hung in the shimmering pale blue sky like an outsize sacrificial gong.

The second man from the Stearman had moved differently. He was in an open-necked khaki shirt and khaki shorts so brief that they appeared South African, that is, with the underside of the scrotum just visible. He had taken his flying-helmet clean off. He too saluted the group at the jeep, but more formally, with his right hand. Then he walked to the door of the long low camouflaged shed and went in. An almost identical copy of him emerged and walked over to the Stearman, greeted the instructor, evidently offering to help him, then, rejected, climbed aboard. Nobody was wasting any time around here, thought Blake. The flying-instructor stopped his yo-heave-ho pumping, extracted the hose nozzle, hung it back on the pump, waved to the jeep group again, and got back into his machine. The propeller chugged and spun, caught, and spun, and the Stearman turned, blowing sand behind it past the shed. It taxied out. It looked pretty prehistoric. Blake supposed it inevitable that Feisal should have bought a fair amount of junk along with his mass purchases of aircraft from the States; some of it, he recalled Feisal had said, was war surplus. The stubby winged Stearman rolled out to the airstrip and turned, preened itself a few moments to its audience, then, ostentatiously, checked its ailerons by moving them up and down, did the same with its elevators, then waggled the rudder on its chubby fin a little pompously from side to side. It gunned and slowed its engine. Then, mollified, it began to taxi forward, lifted its tail primly, and took off. Blake looked round at Feisal.

'Pity, really. I'd have very much liked to see all the navigational kit and the class at work.'

'Well,' said Feisal, 'we can fit that in next time, no trouble. It's tomorrow you fly off to that meeting with your oil friends in Venezuela, isn't it? And seven days tomorrow you take your week's leave?'

'That's right,' said Blake. 'To my place in Hydra.'

'Some people have all the luck,' said Feisal. 'So that would get you back here two weeks tomorrow?'

'Exactly,' said Blake. 'I'm due back fairly early, at ten in the morning.'

'Fine,' said Feisal. 'I'll try to find time to bring you out here again briefly that day. Say early in the afternoon.'

'I'll be here,' said Selim Kadi. 'I might even give you a spin in one of the planes, maybe a helicopter.'

'I'd like that,' said Blake. 'Many thanks.'

'I've an idea Princess Leila bin Jibál's abroad too at the moment,' said Feisal, apropos of nothing in particular, and with his eyes scanning the horizon past the dust-enshrouded helicopters, just, so it seemed, for the sake of good order. Is there anything this bastard *doesn't* know about me? wondered Blake, somewhat needled, but still with some awe. But Feisal changed gear away from that delicate theme promptly.

'That all sounds neatly tied up,' he said. 'It'll leave us with our hands nice and free for the few days following – say for the Friday.'

Blake looked back at him suddenly, then away again, carefully. *That* was Feisal's D-Day, then. It made wickedly good sense. Feisal knew as well as he did that the Jewish Yom Kippur began in early October that year. The twenty-four hour fast started on a Saturday evening. It was the biggest feast in the Jewish calendar, and all Jews would tend to have their guards down a bit during it. Even the Israelis. After all, it was well over a decade now since anyone had hit them on it. Besides, Sadat had attacked then across the Suez Canal and through the Bar Lev Line into Israel on Saturday October 6, Yom Kippur itself. Certainly, Feisal was taking a leaf out of Sadat's book, but he was adding his own ironic twist to it. He would strike just one day *before* Yom Kippur.

'You've got a short trip yourself before then, haven't you, Ahmed?' asked Kadi.

'Yes, so I have,' said Feisal lightly. 'Just for a few days.'

'Where are you off to, Ahmed?' asked Blake innocently.

'Oh, Syria,' said Feisal. 'I have to see a sort of brother, in Damascus.'

Syria, thought Blake. *That* was where Feisal was going to launch his fragile but deadly little armada from. That looked sound too. From the villages like Halass and Harfa and Hadar just behind the Syrian front line which faced the Golan Heights it would be only some 110 air miles to Jerusalem and Tel Aviv and less than seventy to Haifa. Those were Israel's main cities and nerve-centres. The secret F-16 bases could be scattered anywhere between them. From simple airstrips or just hard roads near those villages the Stearmans could take off and be at their targets in an hour or less, and the helicopters could lift off from anywhere. *Some* must get through –

And the Sort of Brother Feisal had to see in Damascus probably also went by the name of Háfez el Assad, President of Syria. That choice was very shrewd too. Ever since he took power in Syria by a coup in November 1970, former Syrian Air Force Commander Assad had been Israel's most implacable enemy among all the Arab States. And almost certainly his was now the Arab State with the best equipped and trained armed-forces with the highest morale and dedication. Assad was thus an excellent bet for Feisal either to help him with his matchbox, incredibly valiant, and possibly lethal air assault of commandos and suicide-bombers, or to do that *and* to match it with an all-out Syrian surprise attack on Israel across the Golan Heights. A totally committed and ruthless assault of this order by Assad was quite on the cards, Blake knew; he had seen reports over the last two years of the Syrian armed forces, now equipped to the eyebrows with new Russian weapons, absolutely spoiling for another life-or-death go at the Israelis. Here was their chance.

'But you'll be back well before the Friday after next?' Kadi asked Feisal, his voice a shade anxious.

'Of course,' said Feisal.

'*Mumtáz!*' said Selim Kadi, his expression suitably relieved. 'So you'll have all the local forces ready too?'

'Without doubt,' said Feisal curtly, looking sharply at Kadi. Feisal had evidently been sitting still in the jeep under the broiling sun for long enough. 'Well,' he went on, 'congratulations. It all sounds fine. We must go.'

Kadi half-saluted him as he turned the ignition key and spun the jeep round on its tail and drove off eastward along the faint rocky track.

'Very efficient set-up, from the look of it,' said Blake.

'Yes,' said Feisal, glancing half round to his left at Blake. 'Well, we haven't wasted your money – the money you diverted to us.'

'No,' said Blake. 'It doesn't look as though you have.'

There was a silence. The desert peeled away on either side of them to the far horizons, flat and bleak as death. The huge bronze disc of the sun beat down. When Blake looked back after five minutes he could already see no hangars and no shed, not a plane or helicopter. They might never have existed. It could all have been a mirage.

'So you're going to a pretty powerful country,' he said to Feisal, wanting to get his feel back on reality. Feisal half glanced at him again.

'Syria?' he said. 'Yes. I think that, on their own, they're just about a match for Israel now. So with a little extra advantage they should win.'

'They're as strong as Israel in weapons?'

'Possibly stronger. In tanks, they've five thousand now, against Israel's four thousand, and a thousand of Syria's are those formidable T-72s, and another five hundred Russia's very latest T-80s. In combat aircraft they have six hundred against Israel's seven hundred, but a hundred of Syria's are the very latest Russian Mig-29s, which are probably more advanced than anything the Israelis have, even their F-16s. Also from about six months ago they've been getting Russia's Sam-10 anti-aircraft missiles with really advanced radar and other very modern electronic equipment. And some Sam-11s. In helicopters they've three hundred and fifty against Israel's two hundred, and in men under arms they've three hundred thousand, or *three times* Israel's strength. All right, Israel's armed forces have superb training and morale, but Syria's have been improved very impressively indeed over the last eighteen months. I think the two are about a match now. So we, if you like, may be able to put in the deciding vote – '

'In such a stand-off fight, you've no fear of Israeli nuclear reaction?' asked Blake. 'After all, they've that supposedly very advanced nuclear station at Dimona in the Negev desert. Western sources seem agreed that they've been making some ten nuclear weapons a year there for the last ten or fifteen years.'

'Yes, Dimona's certainly a major threat,' said Feisal. 'But I think we can take care of Dimona.'

'You've been thorough, I can see,' said Blake, and Feisal smiled again, his small neat white teeth flashing. 'Well,' he said, 'when it's life or death, you get no second chance.'

'And this time it really will be life and death?'

'Oh, yes,' said Ahmed Feisal, and this time he was staring straight over the driving-wheel, and there was no smile. 'This time it really will be life or death. And it will be we who are dealing the death.'

'Indeed?'

'You sound surprised,' said Feisal. 'And who can blame you for that? After we have failed so very many times in the past. But this time I think that the force of our air strike will surprise you very deeply, and with good reason.'

'Let us hope,' said Blake, 'that it will surprise the Israelis profoundly.'

Feisal's precisely modelled face contemplated him again from over the driving-wheel. Blake saw it with something of a shock. For there was no faintest hint of irony or lightness in it. It was that of a man staking his soul. Or of a man who had already irrevocably staked his soul, between good and evil, God and the Devil, for all eternity. It was entirely sober, deadly serious.

'If it goes through as we planned,' he said, 'it will astound and shatter and shiver the Israelis beyond belief.'

'Yes?'

'It will literally paralyse them,' said Ahmed Feisal. 'And it will shake the world.'

32
Capping a Gusher

'This agreement probably won't shake the world if we do push it through,' said Blake, 'but all of us oil-producers will almost certainly lose one hell of a lot of money unnecessarily if we don't!'

His eight male companions looked hard back at him. They were from Saudi Arabia, Kuwait, Iran, Iraq, Mexico, Norway and Nigeria, and from this meeting's host country, Venezuela. None of them was ministerial level, but from just below it, and between them they represented seventy per cent of OPEC's entire oil production and some thirty per cent of that of countries in the non-Communist world outside North America – the USA and Canada not being relevant in this exercise because North America was a heavy oil importer. That apart, there were still some conspicuous gaps in the picture. One, from the OPEC group, was Libya. She, producing almost 1,100,000 bd, made up 6.6 per cent of OPEC's total production, a significant volume. But all in this balcony-room knew that in the end Khadaffi always did what he liked, in regard to his country's oil production levels and policies, or international terrorism. There was nothing you could do about Khadaffi. He was just there. You had to put up with him, like a bad drought or a plague. And an even much more serious lack at this meeting was Britain. The UK's North Sea oil production was now hovering around 2.6 million bd. That put her up in the really top league of free-world oil producers like Saudi Arabia and Mexico, with double or almost double the output of famous traditional producers like Venezuela and Kuwait. The UK's absence from this meeting was, indeed, deafening. It was even the main reason for it.

'In August 1986,' said the man two away on Blake's left, 'my country showed that she could make an original production-limitation agreement to stabilize prices, for the benefit of all of us. And stick to it.'

He was slim, dark, astute, dressed in a smart dark blue suit. He wore too all the arrogance of his very old civilization, whether it was now Islamic Fundamentalist or not. There was the razor-edge of that pride in his voice. It was Albert Mazahéri again, one of Iranian Oil Minister Gholamreza Aqazadeh's trusted right-hand men.

'We should be profoundly grateful,' said Mr Smith sepulchrally, 'that so many of the *non*-OPEC oil producing countries came in right on the heels of the OPEC agreement announced following your minister's brave initiative, and themselves volunteered ten per cent cuts in their own production levels. As you know, my own minister, Rilwanu Lukman, then at once approached five non-OPEC producers – Mexico, Egypt, Angola, Malaysia and Oman – and the four he could reach immediately agreed to cut; the fifth's oil minister was ill and unavailable. I find that truly a most encouraging response – '

Mr Smith circled his gaze round the other eight men at the oval table, as if challenging them fair-mindedly to oppose him if they dared. But no one here seemed averse to the thesis of making the most money for their countries that they decently could, and to hell with the effect on the world's economy. That was hardly their responsibility, not in their terms of reference. They were neither God, Lord Keynes, nor the United Nations. They were simply amongst the most highly skilled and paid businessmen in the world, targeted to get the absolute maximum out of the market long-term that it would bear. Here the Iraqi delegate, a squat dark man with cropped silver-peppered hair and a toothbrush moustache, muscular and poured into his pinstriped gunmetal-toned suit so that he looked like an immovably dug-in army tank, and improbably named Abu Sulwan, Father of Solace, sat silently and with apparent total lack of concern right next to his supposed arch-enemy, the Iranian Albert Mazahéri. Neither of these two seemed in the least interested in the murderous continuing war between their countries. It was a question of focus. Business, after all, was business. Mr Smith, as if disappointed at the lack of any argumentative riposte, looked now instead out of the balcony window. Mr Smith was a large trim Ibo in a light grey Savile Row suit, a gold Rolex wrist-watch, and an Oxford accent which he had earned quite legitimately. The black of his skin was of that marvellous deep translucence that looks as if it has its own private and powerful electric generators buried within it.

Blake followed his gaze for a few moments. The men's balcony, in Caracas's opulent and stylish Tamanaco Hotel, looked directly down on the hotel's large and fine swimming pool. This was no bad place to look, for it was the habit of many of this rich oil capital's most fashionable and expensive ladies to come here and adorn it with their bikinied bodies. That mixture of their blood, of the Spanish and the local Indian, brought an extraordinary lucidity and impact to their complexions. It seemed to fine down their features, as if distilling them through the wrong end of a telescope. That concentration lent them an impression of extreme violence and passion, barely restrained just below the skin.

'Well,' said Ole Dreyer, three down on Blake's right, 'I think we in Norway have made our contribution. You'll know that, as soon as we saw that your production-limitation agreement initially for September and October 1986 was really working, we announced publicly on September 10 that Norway would be cutting her oil exports by ten per cent voluntarily from the start of November – naturally, to support your OPEC agreement. That cut equals around 80,000 bd, so is quite significant. And what is more – ' Dreyer glanced at Blake, the only Englishman present, ' – we announced that on the eve of the UK's Mrs Thatcher's first visit to our new prime minister in Norway, Mrs Brundtland, in an unmistakable signal to Mrs Thatcher that we did *not* agree with the UK's outdated free-market approach to this vital matter.' Dreyer, tall and whipcord-muscled and silver-blond, glanced in some triumph round the table.

'You were in good company,' said Arturo Sanchez, slick in a charcoal suit, olive-skinned and black-moustached, his pear-silhouette smoothly containing that groomed paunch that is the status-symbol for every arrived Venezuelan. 'For the Soviet Union, still the world's biggest oil producer at twelve million bd, though almost all of that stays within the Eastern Bloc, had also just pledged an export cut. As had Egypt and several other smaller non-OPEC producers.'

'And we here can all see why, very clearly,' said Sheikh Aqil bin Aziz, from Saudi Arabia, first on Blake's right. Aziz was deputy to the Saudi Oil Minister, Sheikh Hisham Nazer, appointed after the surprise sacking of Zaki Yamani in October 1986. He was a slight, quick man with a vivid high-cheekboned face, and eyes black and piercing as Abdullah's back in the Kingdom of the Sun. Both Aziz and his Kuwaiti colleague sitting on his right were dressed immaculately in their white full-length flowing dishdashas, their heads in white *khutras* crowned with the strict thin black lines of *ogals*; here were men who found and kept their dignity by wearing their graceful and traditional long robes – though that detracted no whit from the modernity and shrewdness of their commercial minds; their brilliant investment policies were adequate proof of that, Kuwait with $85 *billion* in the stock markets of the US, Europe and Japan, and Saudi with even more than that; these, despite their recent staggering losses, were still among the most powerful nations in the world.

'Because we here all know perfectly well,' Sheikh Aqil bin Aziz went on, 'that unlimited oil production according to the so-called laws of free competition *must* ruin us all. Indeed – ' the Sheikh waved his wide white-sleeved right arm elegantly to include his Kuwaiti colleague – 'as recently as 1981, the numerically small group of Kuwait, ourselves and the United Arab Emirates earned between us no less than one hundred and fifty *billion* dollars from our oil exports. By last year that fine sum had dropped *by eighty per cent*! Why?' The Sheikh brought his right fist smashing down into his open left palm, several at the table leaping in their seats at the pistol-shot effect. '*Overproduction!*' he said grimly. 'And overproduction means murderously reduced prices! That proposition is invariable and inevitable! And Mr Blake here of the Kingdom of the Sun was very right indeed to have pushed as hard and consistently as he has for this series of meetings!' The Sheikh beamed his falcon face full and flatteringly on Blake.

'I could have got nowhere without the full and unceasing backing of my minister,' said Blake, modestly and accurately.

'Yes, we all know Abdullah's strong and sane views!' said Sheikh Aziz benignly. 'He's a man of great common sense and moderation. *Not* a man of greed!'

Greed was the word, thought Blake. It was sheer greed in most cases that had thrust the oil-producing countries into pumping and selling more and more volumes of oil at almost any prices, as though once started they could not stop, as if this were some fatal drug addiction. It could have been a new sophisticated kind of death-wish. Man always seemed to keep death about him somewhere, even in the greatest opulence, comfort, modernity, the most total apparent safety and security.

As here. Blake gazed out at the lush urban landscape. Caracas must be one of the world's smartest cities, the capital of one of the world's oldest oil nations. Shell had made its first strikes here before World War One, in the steamy jungle-swamps of Lake Maracaibo. Venezuela was still in the top league today, with a production near 1.7 million barrels a day. Most of the money from that huge continuous flood of black gold had gone into developing the country itself, and much into its gleaming capital, whose lights shimmered and spangled at night like a million diamond necklaces. Blake looked out now across the Tamanaco's lissom-flesh-caparisoned swimming pool and the shallow valley dropping beyond it, and at the fashionable heights of Altamira on the far side. This part of the city was mainly fine soaring new skyscrapers of flats and offices, while to Blake's left were the great villas of the rich in San Román. These, and the city's luxuriously lawned clubs, were webbed together by ample curved roads, cut across by the racing arrogant lines of magnificent six-lane highways. This could have been a surrealist architect's lyric dream of perfection.

But death hunkered about this blithe city too, or its menace. For from the hilltops around it floods of *ranchitos* tumbled down, frozen abruptly just above the city's building-line. These tens of thousands of makeshift shacks, slung together from half-bricks and plywood and cardboard and corrugated iron, their walls often painted in garish light blues and sharp pinks, housed the many legions of the always exploding poor and desperate, those without work from Maracay and Valencia, Barquisimeto and Mérida, San Cristóbal and Puerto La Cruz and Maturín and Ciudad Bolívar and the Amazonas and the great cattle-farms of the *llanos*; or who had dropped perfectly good jobs and homes there to flock in faithfully, mesmerized by the magic lure of this resplendent city. But these were sad suburbs of it, almost without roads or water or electricity, without even the exuberant Carnival gaiety of the *favelas* around Rio. Here the myriad serried ranks of the *ranchitos* hung merely tragic above the splendid city, like paper shields against a steel-armoured enemy, yet ready always to engulf it in death at a given signal, which was never given. Not yet. But, if you listened carefully, if you looked, you could find that threat of death, of defeat, always there. In everything, even under the smoothest and most polished surface –

'If we here are all convinced then,' said Blake, 'we have still only one adversary. But that, let us not underestimate it, will be a formidable adversary – '

'Formidable indeed,' said Sheikh Aqil bin Aziz. 'Well, any fashion of thought set by the Iron Lady tends to be inflexible. Mrs Thatcher's oil policy was from the start absolutely consistent with her almost religious veneration for the principles of so-called free competition, and in the case of North Sea oil, the UK still pumps and sells every drop that it can place, at whatever price the market will bear. That practice *must* incline price levels downwards, for, as we all know, that market is still perilously near a situation of over-supply. And the UK's production of two and a half million barrels a day is one hell of a big volume to be overhanging it!'

'Sure,' said Philip Blake. 'And with no one in her cabinet tough enough to oppose that policy, her Energy Ministry just went ahead and implemented it. It became an entrenched attitude, like admiring motherhood. And it hasn't changed.'

A few round the table laughed. Aziz looked back at Blake. 'Perhaps we can still talk the British government round to adopting a position identical to ours,' he said. 'And to signing an explicit agreement to that effect. After all – ' He looked deliberately round the eight faces at the table, drawing them powerfully into his argument ' – The UK is now virtually the *only* oil producer of any substance which has *not* agreed to some form of sensible production-limitation pact so far. She's very much the Odd Man Out. And we have all the arguments of common sense and moderation on our side. Surely those must count strongly for us?'

Blake sincerely hoped that the UK would listen to that appeal. The welfare and development of all the oil-producing nations represented round this table, and many others, could hang on it. And Aziz's arguments were weighty enough, in all conscience. They were indeed common-sensical and moderate. Aziz, the Saudi rulers as a whole, had a touching faith in moderation. It would be sad to see that shattered yet again. The Saudis had demonstrated their belief in it often enough. As recently as 1982 their King Fahd had *nearly* succeeded with his moderate arguments in getting the rest of the Arab world to accept Israel as a fait accompli to be lived with in peace. Had he won, the Palestinian Arabs on the West Bank could probably have had some kind of independent state for some years now, and many thousands of lives and much agony and destruction have been spared. But the extremists, the fanatics, had annihilated that magnificent opportunity too.

'Our arguments are certainly well reasoned and moderate,' said Dr Juan Valdés, slim and dark and intense and trim, sitting four down to Blake's right, 'and we in Mexico back them without reservation. After the murderous earthquake that razed much of our cities to rubble in 1986 and killed thousands, we must earn everything we fairly can to rebuild. Today we produce just over three million barrels a day, and are thus a bigger producer than even Great Britain. So if we can subscribe totally to this production-limitation agreement, why can't they? We already showed our good will in this regard the very day you in OPEC announced your limitation pact. We in Mexico, though *not* a member of OPEC, and though still at the peak of our distress from the earthquake, at once publicly stated our plan to cut 150,000 barrels a day from our exports. I say this,' Valdés ended, 'not, I assure you, to vaunt the actions of my country, but so that we should feel all our moral strength, that we have reason and right on our side.'

The table thought about that, and clearly liked it. Sheikh Aqil bin Aziz turned back to Blake.

'What do you suggest as our best strategy, Mr Blake? I think we should all listen to you. It is, again, you and your Sheikh Abdullah who have pushed most consistently for this.'

Blake basked an instant in the table's regard. This was the centre of power, the highest and most sophisticated thrill of all: to have your hands, even if only momentarily, on the world's true levers of command. Somewhere, in the world's most secret and exclusive chart-room, he would be leaving his name on the map.

'I've taken the liberty of booking an appointment pro-visionally, Sheikh, at 10 am in the Iolanthe Suite in the Savoy

337

Hotel in London next Friday with the UK's Energy Secretary. That was the earliest appointment I could get. And I've reserved suites at the Savoy for your minister, Hisham Nazer, Sheikh El Sabah of Kuwait, Oil Minister Rilwanu Lukman from Nigeria – Britain is particularly likely to listen to him, for the UK still has huge investments in Nigeria – the Oil Minister of Mexico' (Blake ducked his head courteously towards Juan Valdés) '– as by far the most important non-OPEC oil producer in the free world outside North America. Of Norway, as Britain's partner in much of the North Sea development. Of Venezuela, as among the oldest and still a very important producer. Of Iran and Iraq. Then no more. That means eight men, from the eight most powerful free-world oil states outside North America. Eight Oil Ministers; the top men of these top oil nations. Thus *we* from the relatively small Kingdom of the Sun should not even appear. The English still have their public-school snobbery well ingrained,' Blake added, with an engaging smile, 'and we should play on that. With a deputation as select as this, we have the greatest chance of success. Of course, you will want to take your back-up staffs probably including most of you seated round this table. But I suggest only our top eight men actually go into the Iolanthe Suite negotiations with the British Energy Secretary – '

'The eight wise men!' said Sheikh Aziz, with a chuckle. 'Let's hope they succeed!'

'I think they will face one of the world's truly historic moments,' said Blake soberly. 'Perhaps a truly definitive change in the winds of history. A matter, even, of life and death, for many.'

'You're a modest man, Mr Blake,' said Sheikh Aziz. 'I admire you for holding yourself and your country back from the limelight here, for the good of all of us.'

'Modest?' said Blake, staring back at him with an expression of mild surprise.

It was not an idea that had struck him before. He found it quite novel.

33
A Return to Eden

It was the edge of the world again, a beauty between life and death. They had lunched at their favourite taverna in Vlichós, sitting in the sun above the ice-clear water of the tiny bay, bounded by its small stone jetty, at which a caique was moored, fat-bosomed, a broad red-painted line accentuating the bold upwards sweep of its deck, curved like a strung bow, and its naked mast telling the small beat of the sea, ticking off time against the clear blue sky and the grey-bronze run of the Peloponnese. She, smiling gently at Blake, had read this trim rhythm with delight. It was part of their known and beloved world, inviolate. The huge taciturn Greek had served them *kalamares* and a rich Greek salad, spiked with onions and white goat's cheese, and a kilo carafe of retsina, *tou varéliou*, draught, and still a little warm from the barrel. They drank miniature cups of biting Greek coffee, walked east across the pebbled beach between the spread spun gold nets, climbed the tufted hill to the stone-walled rampart, then launched themselves along the cliff-hanging path, the small jewelled blue bays vertically below them, locked between shattered rock. Offshore a small boat bumbled west, its Greek standing by its tiller. From round Dokos came the early afternoon hydrofoil, yellow-blue as a frozen caterpillar, vain on squat stilts. Blake walked just ahead of her. She saw his limp almost without noticing it. Part of love was the elision of defects, a warm blindness to them, without theatre. She watched him twist off left.

They crossed the tilled land, the coarse stone wall, trod in quick balance between the grey-white boulders and gorse, and down the steep faint path to the secret bay, backed by its near-vertical rock walls. Blake had his shirt and shorts off almost before he stopped walking. When they both stood naked, he smiled and turned and dived, and she saw his head pop up from the slick perfect sea, the water oiling his brown shoulders. She dived in too. The water was like an absolution. She cleft it smoothly, new-skinned as a snake. You would win a re-birth here every day, in this Eden before original sin. She swam out to Blake, fast. He smiled at her, and for a while they swam together. Under them the sea-bottom fell away almost vertically to dark ink-blue depths. Anything could pass silently down there, watching; great white sharks, Moby Dick. She swam back a little ahead of Blake, and climbed out onto the rocks. As she did so she saw her body, glistening olive-brown, unbroken. She turned and stood and watched Blake swimming in, the water about him aquamarine, submarine searchlights infusing it with luminosity.

He climbed out, shining drops cascading, and caught her eyes on him.

'My God, it's paradise! Why should we ever leave it?'

'It's we who decide,' said Leila. 'You could always stay.'

'No, I've had five perfect days,' said Blake. 'I'm booked back tomorrow, and I'll go back tomorrow. One shouldn't tempt fate.'

'No?'

'No,' he said. 'And there may still be great things waiting this week.'

'Ah? For example?'

But he deflected.

'But there's no reason why you shouldn't stay on for a week or two,' he said. '*Marhába biki*! Welcome!'

'Yes, I think I'll do that,' she agreed. 'For another week, anyway. I've nothing pressing to go back for. No great thing waiting.'

But he seemed not to have heard her banter, for he went over to the pool by the edge of the sea, constantly washed cool, and shadowed under an overhanging rock, where he had stowed the four half-litre bottles of Kourtaki Retsina from his little blue back-pack. He brought one over to their hot flat rocks, nipped its cap off with his Swiss army knife, and poured the two plastic cups full for them.

'*Yásu!*'

'*Yámas*! And may you have a good return tomorrow!'

She lifted her cup to him, and drank. The wine's piney bite purged her mouth. She lay with him on the hot flat rocks, drinking their retsina like lords. Their limbs still wet from the sea, they made love. Afterwards the cool blue sea redeemed them. They came back to the hot flat rocks, Blake with the second Kourtaki bottle. Filling her cup, he said:

'I'll be seeing Abdullah the day after tomorrow. We're going falconing, up north by the edge of the marshes.'

'That should be fun. You two always get on well together. Even in work, so he tells me.'

'Abdullah's been a very good friend,' said Blake, 'and a fine Oil Minister to work for. Wise, and a very fair man, very honest. Intelligent, very progressive, very human. He's a man of great worth.'

'He sees you as part of our family in the Kingdom,' said Leila.

'In the Kingdom, seen as a whole family, he would have meant?'

She blushed.

'Yes,' she answered, 'that's what he said. Though I've no doubt he'd be happy to accept you into our Jibál family too.'

Blake made no comment for a while. Then he said:

'Perhaps it's what I should do. I've been thinking of it more and more. After all, I think the Kingdom's interests are my interests now. I've no real home outside the Kingdom now. Except *this* – ' He gestured with his hand to the small bay. 'But I couldn't stay here all the time. As an unvarying diet, even paradise can pall.'

'And Feisal's interests are your interests too, these days?'

He looked at her sharply.

'I find him, and what he has done as the PLO-Fatah Leader there, quite fascinating. Certainly he interests me!'

Despite the hot sun, she shivered deeply.

'Philip, he terrifies me!'

But Blake simply glanced at her again in a good-tempered way and poured her some more retsina. She sighed, resigning herself. How could you convince someone you loved that a man whom he saw as a bosom friend was in fact a most deadly enemy – when you had no proof save that given you by your intuitions?

'Let's swim again!' said Blake heartily, in an obvious move to re-establish harmony, so that she smiled a little at the transparency of his motives. They dived in again, and hung tiny in that great bowl of sea, like hawks or falcons in the infinite blue inverted vault of the sky. They came back to their flat rocks, and lay in warm love under that sun. And when it dropped low near to the horizon, they dressed and climbed up out of the secret bay, worked through the rough rock and gorse and over the coarse wall and up the tilled land to the high narrow path, and went east along it. And round a sudden bend they came upon Kaminia, a frozen star-burst of sharp white cubes, spiked by the upwards penstrokes of cypresses. So they walked arms linked to that last curve which leads round to Hydra Port. She saw it then like an old and loyal friend. They stood as the lights glowed in all the shops and restaurants round the harbour and from the many lit pleasure-craft, with the buildings unlit above them, and the circling ranges of hills. So Hydra Port prepared for its evening trick of levitation. Leila watched that sweet sight with joy, and with only that one shadow in her soul, small as a man's fist, perhaps, yet insistently undeniable, not to be passed over, not to be forgotten.

34
The Cutting Edge of the Sword

'This is the machine we're most standardized on,' said Selim Kadi happily, secure in his profession, enchanted to talk about it, as they stood in the great camouflaged hangar by the desert airstrip that Thursday afternoon. Philip Blake and Ahmed Feisal stood with him and eyed the helicopter with respect. She was sleek, with a well-glassed cabin with what looked like five seats in it, and she narrowed then to an elegant boom to her tail, where a tiny fin jutted vertically up and down on the starboard side, a miniature helicopter blade echoing it to port. Her main rotor was still and she sat on twin light metal skids. She was painted desert camouflage and she looked very functional.

'Who makes her?' asked Blake.

'Bell,' said Kadi. 'She's a Jetranger 206, turbine-powered, you know.'

'What's that give her for speed and range?'

'Speed you can say 100 mph for ferrying to target. You'd spray at say 80 mph. Range? Well, her standard tank's 76 American gallons. She'll consume about 25 AG an hour. So say three hours safe flying, leaving a small reserve. Or three hundred miles. But look here – '

He stepped close to the side of the machine.

'See this here? It's the filling point for the fuel tank. Normally you can fill only to the lower edge. But Bell have added a funnel. Fit that, and you can add another 20 AG. And you can replace the rear seat with an extra fuel tank of 50 AG, at least. That doubles your range at 100 mph to six hundred miles, there and back. And you could still be carrying a load of 110 AG in your external tanks – '

Feisal coughed abruptly, and Kadi glanced at him and stopped. Before he went on, Blake broke in:

'So, starting at one end of Israel, say the north, you could cover virtually the whole country with a three hundred-mile range!'

'That's about it,' said Kadi. 'What's more, you could do it by night. So you could be ready on target at first morning light, when people are probably up and about, but not yet really very alert – '

'That's smart,' said Blake. 'And what's that tank under her cabin?'

'Oh, that's for chemicals, should you choose to spray,' said Kadi offhandedly.

'And what does a jewel like this cost?' asked Blake.

'They retail at four hundred and fifty thousand dollars in the States, which is where we bought them. That's not cheap, but they're first class for our purpose.'

'How many do you have?'

'About fifty,' said Kadi. 'Come and have a look at her smaller sister. *Older* sister, I should say; she's been around for some years; a regular work-horse, particularly in agriculture. That's why you see the spray boom fitted, sticking eighteen feet out either side, and why she has that 40 AG tank either side of her bubble. She's a Bell 47, single piston-engine, a three-seater – '

These were the models Blake had seen the week before, flying low well north of the airstrip in their own billowing clouds of sand. He gazed now at the model in the hangar, a generous bubble-cabin on twin metal skids under the rotor, light tubular metal girders going back to her tiny elevator and tail rotor. She looked like a dragonfly, busy and reasonably pugnacious.

'She's cheaper?'

'Much. You can't get her new now. Second-hand, we paid around fifty thousand dollars each for them; we've about a hundred. They're slower, with a shorter range, of course. They'll cruise or spray a little above 80 mph, and their full range there and back's about two hundred and twenty miles.'

'I see,' said Blake. 'So about Haifa and back, with half an hour over the target.'

There was a tiny silence. Then Ahmed Feisal said:

'Yes, you're right. That would be Haifa and around. And points further north, like Natanya.'

The Bell 206 took four passengers and the Bell 47 two. Blake wondered if bigger helicopters with higher troop capacity would not have been more efficient if they were to carry commandos. Still, Feisal and company would have done their sums. They would have planned all this to the finest detail.

'Come and look at the fixed-wing craft,' said Selim Kadi, evidently enthusiastic enough to want to go on. 'Here's the Ayres Turbo-Thrush S2R-T34. She's got a Pratt and Whitney PT6 turbine of 750 shaft horsepower. That gives her 140 mph on ferry and say 135 mph on spraying. I mention that because as you see she's got a spray boom too.'

Blake heard Feisal by him draw his breath in quickly in a saw-edged sigh. No doubt Feisal was bored stiff; he had seen it all before. But Blake looked at the Turbo-Thrush with great interest. She was neat, with two cockpits in line and glassed in, strikingly high and far back, and a single low wing. At its trailing edge was a short boom with what looked like four miniature ancillary motors on it. Each was a metal basket about six inches in diameter and eight in length, with metal blades six inches long sprouting fan-like from the front.

'She's got a healthy fuel tank of more than 190 AG too,' said

Kadi, his enthusiasm unabated, 'and that gives her four hours in the air, so a range of around five hundred and fifty miles. She can also deliver a 500 AG liquid load, carried in a hopper between the cockpit and the engine. And now the spray boom. Those four things on it are Micronairs, ULV or Ultra Low Volume pumps. When she's flying, the airflow turns those fans, which turn the hollow spindle inside those metal baskets. The chemical you spray goes through the hollow spindle and metal basket; it's a rotary atomizer. You can alter the angle of the fan blades. They push out a very fine spray indeed, much more efficiently than the traditional booms. We've a lot so fitted – '

'Selim!' said Feisal, a hint of steel whiplash in his voice.

'*Effendim?*'

'I'm not sure that we really need to burden our friend with *quite* so many technical details!'

'Pardon!' said Kadi, moving then very briskly to the last model of aircraft in the hangar before Feisal shut him up for good. 'Then let's have a quick look at the last aircraft type of which we have significant numbers – '

'You've a lot of the Turbo-Thrushes?' asked Blake, looking back at the trim craft with its high and generously glassed cockpit, which doubtless gave its crew optimum visibility, and its short spray boom. 'And how costly are they?'

'We've about fifty of them too. Oh, about five hundred and fifty thousand dollars in the US.'

'Was it a problem getting so many of each? I don't know what the factory production runs would be like – '

'Well, don't forget that we've been buying very carefully for the last four years, all over the States, and outside where it was worth while.'

Again, thought Blake, you couldn't fault Feisal's crowd on their long-term planning. Or their tenacity –

Kadi took them over another low-winged monoplane. Keeping a weather-eye on Feisal now, he went into his act again, but much more speedily and succinctly.

'The Piper Brave PA. She has a 375 hp eight-cylinder Lycoming piston engine. She's a great little craft. Cruises or sprays at 135–140 mph, with a range of five hundred and seventy miles and a delivery load of 220 AG.'

'You've a lot of those too? They'd be cheaper than the Turbo-Thrush?'

'Getting on for a hundred,' said Kadi. 'And you're right. You get very good value for what you buy. The last price figure I have is for 1983, in the States, at around one hundred and twenty thousand dollars ex factory. Add ten or twenty per cent to that.'

'And you have quite a lot of your fleet fitted out for night flying too?'

'A lot,' said Kadi. 'Pretty well all our Turbo-Thrushes, like the Bell Jetranger 206s. And quite a few of the others. So we can be on target nice and early in the morning, as the people come out of their houses to go to work.'

'You've identified some three hundred of your fleet,' said Blake. 'What are the others?'

'Everything under the sun' said Kadi. 'Like the Stearman biplane you saw here eight days ago, with its Pratt and Whitney 450 hp R985 radial engine. Or the excellent biplanes like the Grumman AgCat G-164B and the Turbo Cat G-164D. Their range is shorter, but we'll find a target for them, nearer the border. *Have* found already, of course. Then we have many of the very good Cessna '80 Ags.'

'Let's keep it moving,' said Feisal. 'I've got a lot to do back in the City of the Sun.'

'What about that helicopter ride I promised Abu Jildah?' said Kadi.

'Well, ten minutes or so – '

Kadi half ran to the small tractor just inside the hangar's entrance and jumped onto the seat. The engine caught and he manoeuvred the tug close to the bubble nose of the Bell 47. He hooked on the tow rope, got back into the tractor's seat, and pulled the helicopter very gently forward on its skids from the tarmac inside the hangar to the tarmac outside. The moment they were clear of the hangar, Kadi stopped, unhooked his tug, and drove it back to the hangar's entrance. He and Blake stood then by the side door.

'In you get. That seat, please. And buckle your safety belt.'

Kadi was inside seated swiftly too, clearly conscious of Feisal outside. He put on his crash-helmet with its built-in earphones and separate mike.

'Might as well put yours on too. You'll hear all right if I shout at you.'

'You don't need special flying overalls?' Blake asked.

'Well, on a thing like this protective clothing, of course.'

Kadi had switched on. The main rotor above their heads spun, caught, and spun faster. Kadi checked his elevator controls. The tail blade was already turning.

'All right? Then up we go!'

And so they did, vertically up as a fast lift in a hotel. Then Kadi eased her forward and opened the throttle.

'See? Eighty-five, ninety mph. And she can keep that steady – '

They were up a hundred feet or so now. Kadi banked suddenly, and Blake's stomach left him. The desert wheeled past him on its ear.

'Want to see what spraying's like?' asked Selim Kadi, eager as a small boy showing off his toy. 'Seeing that we've got that spray boom fitted.'

'Sure. Why not?'

They were now a mile or so from the hangar. Feisal, after watching them take off, seemed to have gone back inside it. He couldn't harangue them for taking up too much time from in there.

Kadi came down so low that Blake's entire stomach rebelled again. They would go clean into the sand. But Kadi levelled expertly between two and three metres above the surface. He pulled a switch. Looking down out sideways from the bubble, Blake saw the white spray projected out backwards from the thirty-two-foot boom. It billowed back, so smoothly and beautifully that it seemed impossible to believe that it could ever hurt anything, even agricultural pests.

'It's water, of course?' he shouted at Kadi.

Kadi's crash-helmet looked round at him like an astronaut's. Kadi beamed back at him.

'Of course. Just water. Quite harmless.'

35
Other Bolts from the Blue

'All set?' asked Sheikh Abdullah bin Ali bin Jibál, Minister of Oil in the Kingdom of the Sun, and a decent and honourable man in his own right.

'Your beaters are all ready to go,' said Philip Blake, his chief counsellor professionally, a multi-millionaire, a man who sought to be part of his times, and, by wildcatting, sometimes to be a jump ahead of them.

'Then give me time to get her to her striking height!'

'Of course.'

She was Saiqa, which meant Thunderbolt. It was also the title of that Arab guerrilla splinter group prominent in Lebanon and heavily backed by Syria. Abdullah would *not*, Blake knew, have named her after them. Abdullah had had Saiqa for years. She was a peregrine falcon about two pounds in weight and unquantifiable in courage and striking power. Abdullah had chosen a female because, like all birds of prey, she was bigger than her male counterpart. She had her stand now on the thick leather glove on Abdullah's left hand. She wore a fine black leather hood, a mixed design from Syria and Holland, with the Jibál crest of crossed scimitars stencilled in gold on the front, and the tapes at the back half loosened so that Abdullah could unhood her swiftly. There were flat leather jesses low round her legs for him to control her, and tiny metal bells made in Holland, which if she were loose in cover, would help her master find her. Her talons, three forward and one back on each foot were powerful and sharp yellow in colour, as was her great curved beak. But her eyes, now masked, were equally striking, dark, and focusing at once with absolute impact, leaving no blurred margin of error whatsoever, on the world and her prey. Her plumage was a mottled blend of horizontal light and dark greys; she could have been an exquisitely rendered poetic flying version of the Qaitbai Mausoleum in Cairo. Her wings, now vertically down each side of her body, were long and narrow. She looked what she was, the distilled perfection of a hunting machine, a most elegant projectile for killing.

With one swift fluid movement, Abdullah slipped Saiqa's hood and cast her off. With that marvellously efficient sensitivity she adapted her sight at once from the full night of the hood to the sharp grey light of the dawn. She showed no faintest trace of hesitation. Saiqa swung straightaway, curving round, gaining height with each circle, her long narrow wings outstretched to their full forty-five inches, nearly one and a half metres, and tapering finely to the tips. By full day when the brassy sun would be blazing onto that sand and bouncing hot thermal air-currents up off it, those slender sweetly drawn pinions, etched jet-black now against the grey-white glow of the sky, would delicately profit from every upthrust in them. But that Friday in early October Abdullah and Blake and their falconers had got up two hours before dawn, and left the City of the Sun an hour before it, so as to be here at this first light.

Now Saiqa had reached her pitch, her most effective striking height, about a hundred metres. She began to glide in tight circles, her slim wingtips springing pliantly, her head twisted to look down at her battlefield. This started at the erratic line of reeds fifty metres from which Abdullah and his chief falconer and Blake stood, the six so far scrupulously silent Bedu beaters being much nearer. After this clutter of reeds was a fairly open space of some 150 metres before the marshes began more seriously. This space was a perfect killing-ground for Saiqa.

'Now!' said Abdullah, and the chief falconer called to his beaters. They moved into the reeds at once, shouting and clapping their hands. Blake knew that it could easily be for nothing; game was scarce, even by water, in this land.

But the wild duck, all on his own, came out of the reeds like a rocket, his wings clacking, going dead low and straight as a bullet for the thicker marsh cover, his two-foot-long two-and-a-half pound body streamlined thrusting forward for life, his outstretched head and neck a brilliant dark glossy green, cut off by the white ring at the base of his neck from the brown of his mallard breast; he must have known Saiqa was above him, and rejected at once any thought of trying to outfly her in the open sky. By his route Saiqa had only seconds to catch him.

That was the measure of her speed. Her icy dark eye had

spied him instantly. She stooped immediately, her wings nearly closed by her sides. She hurtled down like a shell, reaching probably 250 mph. So still was that dawn that they below could hear the rush of wind through her feathers, and whistling faintly through the slits in her bells. She was almost on her target some thirty metres from the marsh.

But he, a seasoned cock made cunning by the cruelties of life, had banked and dropped abruptly, forcing her to throw up without a wingbeat. But she braked hard, turned at the top of her short curve, and dropped wing-sheathed on him again at once. This time she hit him full, ten metres from the marshes. They fell together to the sand, the drake's feathers scattering in soft explosion. If her strike had not already killed him, she would have snapped his neck with her beak.

'Efficient,' said Abdullah.

Blake looked round at him there, six foot three in height, lean and whipcord-muscled and olive-brown, the noble high-cheekboned and majestically beak-nosed face, with Leila's jet-black glittering eyes, under the flowing white *kefiyyah* crowned with its black rings of *ogals*. Abdullah was a friend who had not changed.

'Deadly efficient,' said Blake.

That slick killing was an omen. Falconry was part of mythology, mystery, the mystic. Falcons were given to the H'ia Dynasty princes in China in 2000 BC. India, Arabia, Persia knew falconry. Wales honoured falconers before the Norman Conquest. Abdullah's second falcon that day, which the chief falconer held now hooded on his gloved left wrist, was Lulu, meaning Pearl, and she was a Merlin falcon. The world, perhaps destiny itself, was a complex whole, intimately interrelated. This killing reflected another, probably at exactly this hour too, a little after first light. Blake knew that the other air strike must just have gone through by now, a thousand miles to their north-west. Just as lethally?

'*Íjlis, ya rájuln,*' said Abdullah, turning to his chief falconer. 'Stay.'

And he walked forward with Blake. Abdullah had picked up the lure. It was two duck wings bound onto a wire frame, with chunks of red meat stuck on the front. A cord five metres long held this to a short wooden handle. They walked through the ragged line of reeds and came up to Saiqa. She was tearing at the drake. Abdullah let her crop for a short while, then threw the lure for her. She, well-trained, came to it soon, her sharp beak going into the meat in it. In a minute Abdullah coaxed her again, and she flew up without delay, and took her stand on his leather-covered left wrist. He slipped the hood fluidly onto her head and tied it behind in one practised movement. She stood contented, the black hood on her like a royal helmet, then with a burst of pure white feather atop, with three jet-black single feathers jutting vertically up from it. Blake picked up the duck and put it in his game-bag.

'Great morning,' said Abdullah. 'We deserve some breakfast.'

The two of them walked back, Abdullah's slim length beating its customary rhythm against his full-length white dishdasha, and Blake, with his limp, just keeping pace with him.

'Yes,' said Blake, as they reached the chief falconer and Abdullah handed Saiqa and the lure over to him. 'A memorable morning, one to go down in history. You don't want to try again?'

'Oh, I think we've done pretty well,' said Abdullah. 'Once is enough, anyway for me. Once round the course. You won't see a better kill than that.'

They walked then the two hundred metres to the jeep, and Abdullah drove the three of them and the two falcons to the tent pitched half a kilometre away, and the Land Rover parked by it.

'It's good to come back into the desert like this from time to time,' said Abdullah cheerfully. 'Where all my forebears came from, of course.'

Blake knew and was mildly amused by the Kingdom's élite's romantic attachment to the desert, to which they would loudly repair on certain holidays. It sounded like an impressive re-tempering of their souls in suitable austere conditions, a discipline as ascetic and purifying as fasting in Ramadhan. But though the *Shemsi* élite did in fact go back into tents in the desert, they suffered in comfort. Fine Bokhara and Isfahan rugs were spread on the tent floors, small generators outside providing full power and electric lighting, refrigeration, TV and radio. Blake noticed that this time Abdullah had not brought his TV or radio, though the rest of the amenities were there. It was an omission that he was to look back upon afterwards in gratitude, for the world news that morning would have shattered an atmosphere which Blake would recall with love and agony. Abdullah's cook served them a splendid English breakfast, orange juice and corn flakes and twin eggs with tomatoes and beef sausages and kidneys, and toast and marmalade and coffee. This, and Saiqa's neat performance, left Abdullah mellow.

'That's a fine little peregrine falcon, Saiqa,' he said expansively, over his second cup of coffee.

'Yes, she is.'

'I'm using quite a few things I got from the British in my falconry, you know.'

'Oh? I thought you Arabs were among the top experts in the field?'

'Yes, but it's a passion that ignores frontiers. Like drugs or the Bedu. We all learn from one another. When I was at Oxford I was an honorary member of the British Falconers' Club. They offered a lot, beyond their Steak, Kidney, Lark and Oyster Pies.'

'They probably learnt from you too, Abdullah.'

'Well, from the Arabs; a bit, anyway. You British have your own long history in falconry. Richard the Lion-Heart brought falcons with him to Palestine when he came, unsuccessfully, to teach us a lesson in the Crusades. In return, the Crusaders brought the Syrian falcon's hood back to England with them. Then Queen Elizabeth had her Master Falconer, of course.'

'Yes. And Shakespeare's plays are full of falcons.'

Abdullah turned his head then, and looked levelly at Blake. Then he said, very warmly:

'Philip, if I've gained a great deal from England, from Oxford, even in falconry, perhaps we can repay that in part, through you.'

'Through me? How's that, Abdullah?'

'You like it with us here, don't you? After all, you've known us now for a long time. You've *lived* with us for ten years or more. So why don't you come over to us completely?'

Blake looked back at him in silence for some seconds.

'You mean, become a Muslim?'

'Among other things, become a Muslim. Look, I don't know how religiously orthodox a man you are; I'm not one particularly, as you'll have guessed. But you wouldn't have to take the whole thing too seriously, believe every single thing in the Muslim religion as the, if you like, gospel truth. It would just make you more certainly one of us. Your Arabic's already very good, and that already almost makes you a Muslim on its own; our language is very near to our soul, as you know. Then we'd give you *Shemsi* nationality, of course; you could keep your British passport as well; we wouldn't mind that; we don't see any conflict of political interest with Britain – '

'Why all the honour, Abdullah? I mean it; I'm not being satirical.'

Abdullah's strong very white teeth flashed in a quick smile in the dark olive face.

'You've been very loyal over the years, Philip. To me personally. To my Ministry of Oil. To the Kingdom of the Sun – '

Christ, thought Blake.

'Besides,' said Abdullah, 'certain key moves have been decided, and your being one of our rare adult recipients of *Shemsi* nationality, with full *Shemsi* rights and responsibilities, could prove very opportune for all concerned.'

'Oh?'

Abdullah's jet eyes, snapping back against the pure white of the corneas, pierced him again.

'No one outside the cabinet knows this. But the Amir's stepping down in a year. He's getting on, and he's led us through a difficult period to a position of almost invulnerable strength. The price of oil may have plummeted, but we now have fifty billion dollars in secure investments overseas netting us a twelve per cent return a year. With that, who can hurt us now? So the Amir'll take a well-merited and honourable retirement. Which puts the Crown Prince up into his place. And me into the Crown Prince's.'

'My God. Of course, you're of the royal family. Congratulations, Abdullah!'

'Which will also leave us short of a Minister of Oil.'

There was another reverberating silence.

'Come on, Abdullah!' said Blake. 'You can't mean it! You couldn't do that!'

'Not if you weren't *Shemsi*,' said Abdullah. 'But, if you were, why not? What about Sheikh Maher, now head of our

353

Research and Development Bank? He was an Iraqi till five years ago. No, you'd do excellently. I can't think of a better candidate.'

'I can,' said Blake. 'What about Feisal, for one?'

He saw Abdullah go absolutely rigid, in a split second. That shocked Blake icily, right to his guts. It could have been the Ice Maiden, indeed, grey and Old Testament, carved implacably still as a God, indicting him again mercilessly out of the mists of the past.

'Certainly *not* Feisal! He has already got too dangerously high! Were he not the official leader in the Kingdom of the PLO, an organization for which we as Arabs *must* show respect and support, whatever we might feel privately, I should have thrown him out years ago. Got him out of the country. Or *liquidated* him.'

'Indeed?' said Blake.

'Indeed,' said Abdullah. 'And, as Minister of Oil, if I were you, I should allow him no more powers.'

'Let me think about it, Abdullah,' said Blake. 'Your offer anyway shows me far more favour than I deserve.'

'Of course, please do think about it. It's still a vital job, remember. After all, oil still meets half of the world's total energy needs. We may have seen a glut of oil in the last few years and a consequent sharp drop in prices. But that could correct itself. Another leak or two from nuclear power stations, one more Chernobyl, and we'll see the world cutting back hard on their nuclear programmes, under public and environmentalist pressures. And it'll be many years yet before people stop depending critically on oil-fuelled motor cars and trucks and aircraft. No, we oil men can still be the superstars again one day.'

'That's a fair forecast,' said Blake.

'Let me know soon what you decide. We don't have too much time.'

'No. All right.'

'Ah, and another thing – I've talked of how you could move up our management tree in the Kingdom. As I shall. I should also be very happy to see you move into our family tree, Philip. Again, only should you so desire, of course; there's no obligation at all to either offer. I just wanted you to know.'

'Meaning Leila, naturally. You've known about us for a long time, of course?'

'Well,' said Abdullah. 'I'd have had to be blind not to. I've always been close to her. Again, I'm no fanatical Muslim. You've both always been discreet. One couldn't ask more. And you're both good people.'

'It's a hell of a generous offer, Abdullah. They both are.'

'Well, they'd give something. A dignity, perhaps. A very secure identity.'

'Indeed.'

'Perhaps not everyone has that these days,' said Abdullah.

36
Danse Macabre *on Dizengoff Street*

Two three-ton lorries heavily charged with young men and women with shattered national identities, and trained to be quite ready to die to regain them, passed Blake and Abdullah in their jeep on the coast road running south. Blake had no doubt at all that they came from Feisal's northern training camp. For the marshes where Abdullah and he had hunted were much further up along the coast, and they had already passed the turnoff west toward that camp. Moreover these young men and women, as well as being armed to the teeth with submachineguns and AK-47 automatic rifles and hand-grenades hanging from their belts, were dressed in the dark olive-green battledress overalls that Feisal's camp affected.

'On their way to Palestine?' said Abdullah. He would know, of course, about Feisal's northern and southern regular training camps, thought Blake. But *not*, he was sure, about the airstrip and the air training. Feisal's air strike must have gone in that morning. He wondered how successful the commando raids and suicide-bombers had been. Not very, he guessed. As so often before, it would really be little more than a pin-prick in the skin of a Juggernaut as armoured as Israel.

'I doubt that they'll be wresting power from anyone today,' he said, and he saw Abdullah beside him smile above the driving wheel.

The road block stopped them at the first northern outskirts of the City of the Sun. It was a three-ton lorry and, incongruously, a Cadillac, both parked effectively right across the road. Feisal's olive-green uniformed young men and girls were deployed about them, some lying prone between the wheels with their submachineguns or automatic rifles in the firing position, some kneeling, a small group standing. They did not look apt to be joked about at all. They looked sober and professional. They watched the jeep. No one was talking.

One of the group standing walked over to them, a sub-machinegun in his hands. Blake saw at once that it was Salah Khalíl, the commander of Feisal's northern camp. Now he was trim in his olive-green overall. He had the black holster of a pistol on the right of his belt and the crown and two stars of a colonel in canvas on his shoulders.

'Mr Blake!' he said, smiling slightly. 'A good morning to you!'

Then he turned to Abdullah.

'And your friend is – ' His eyes widened. 'Sheikh Abdullah bin Ali bin Jibál, isn't it? Minister of Oil, and member of the Amir's family?'

'That's right,' said Abdullah. 'And what the hell is this?'

But every trace of a smile had washed off Khalíl's face. He had brought the muzzle of his submachinegun up and was holding it very steady. Now Khalíl was not politely welcoming at all. He was just deadly.

'Sheikh Abdullah, please ask your Bedu in the back to get out. With his falcons.'

'What on earth for?'

'Because I and one of my men will be occupying the back seat.'

'What *is* this? Look, get those vehicles out of the way and let me pass, will you? You are dealing with a member of the cabinet!'

'What *was* the cabinet,' said Khalíl. 'Sheikh, my orders, the orders to all of us, are to bring you in at once. Wherever we find you. The rest of the cabinet are, ah, already accounted for.'

'Bring me *in*? Where to?'

'The Palace of Government,' said Khalíl.

Blake, his head twisted round, saw Abdullah's falconer get out and take Saiqa and Lulu, and saw Khalíl swing up into the back seat, and one of his young men beside him, with an AK-47. The muzzles of their two automatic weapons remained centimetres from the napes of the necks of the two men in front. Khalíl's troops disengaged themselves from under and about the Cadillac, and someone drove it a few paces forward and round to let the jeep through. They heard the sudden chattering run of a machinegun somewhere ahead, and crisp short runs of automatic fire coming back at it. The machine-gun went heavily into action again. This time there was no reply. That silence wrote someone's death.

'What goes on there?'

'Just mopping up, Sheikh. It's been going on for hours. The action started at dawn.'

'At *dawn*? We were through here an hour before dawn!'

'Then you must just have missed it,' said Khalíl. From the note of regret, genuine sadness, in his voice still hanging in the air, he might have been talking about some unique experience like the coronation of a king, or the Opening Night of some memorable musical extravaganza.

But they saw its effects, or some of them. Feisal's men must have massacred the Kingdom's small regular armed forces and police mainly in their beds, or while half asleep just having emerged from them. They passed two police stations with bodies in their forecourts and on the pavements before them. Almost all were police. They were tumbled every which way, like sawdust-filled dolls thrown down by bored gods. The Kingdom's men from its small regular army seemed to have died mainly at street corners, perhaps a logical final battle-ground for a war against guerrillas. At one such corner they saw a small regular army tank, burnt out though still smouldering, its main gun fully declined as though in the shame of defeat, some of its plates buckled by the intense heat, and one member of its crew, probably the tank commander, still hanging out from the top turret, his body half skeletal, half charred black.

So they reached the Palace of Government, in the centre of the City of the Sun. There was a giant courtyard before it, to which a huge immensely antique Arab door led. It was exquisite, of almost impenetrable black wood, heavily brass-studded; and the brass, polished reverently every day, shone like recently minted gold. One half of that monumental gate was almost always left open, day and night, so that passers-by in the main street outside it could easily see within to the courtyard's centre, decorated by a raised platform and two gallows, the looped black ropes hanging ever motionless and silently from their tops; the old Amir, a gentle but resolute man, had always felt that this sight edified the passing citizenry, helping them reasonably to crystallize out their true priorities in life; and far more psychologically than by live example, for these gallows had not been used in fact for the last fourteen years. But they knew death about them now. Blake and Abdullah saw that as Khalíl and his companion marched them across the courtyard. The bundles of flesh at the foot of the gallows, the cloth of their dishdashas rippling gently in the light breeze, were the Amir and Crown Prince and the other eight members of the cabinet.

Khalíl and his aide shepherded them past, their guns in the small of their backs. They went up the ornate marble flight of stairs to the first floor. The Cabinet Chamber was there. It was a square room, its floor, walls and ceiling filled with the most intricate mosaics. Round the walls on the floor were finely embroidered leather poufs. This was the shape of the classical *diwanía*, where the elders debated and wisely decided the tribe's policies and destiny.

Ahmed Feisal sat on the pouf on the slight master dais discreetly heading that room. He wore the olive-green battle-dress uniform of his own troops, the black holster of a pistol on the right of his belt like Khalíl's, but this time the crossed batons of a Field-Marshal's insignia on his shoulders; there had never, thought Blake, been anything small about Feisal. His exquisite features were glowing as they came in; from this cataclysmic victory, undoubtedly, and also from the flickering light of the television that he watched.

'Ah!' he said as they came to him. 'You come at a timely

358

moment. See what they say of our air strike early today!'

' . . . BBC World News,' said the TV. 'We warn our viewers that the scenes we are about to show are deeply disturbing. This film was shot just after first light this morning in Dizengoff Street, Tel Aviv, by our cameraman there, Harold Price. He died from the contamination he received in shooting it. The scene you will now see was echoed hundreds of times throughout Israel early this morning, in all main urban centres, army camps, naval ports and military airfields. Here you see the effects of what we now know was the chemical carbophenothion, sprayed down in the finest rain from the sky. Of the five hundred aircraft and helicopters which the new Arab terrorist group called the Scimitar of the Sun sent in from Syria before dawn this morning, the Israeli air force and ground fire shot down at least three hundred and fifty. But not before they had accomplished their mission, for their pilots were of that same atrocious mould as the suicide-bombers who in 1983 massacred the American Embassy and Marine headquarters and the French Peace-Keeping Force's Command Post in Beirut, killing some four hundred people and themselves. These are the world's new destroyers, the new and most deadly Angels of Death.'

Some three thousand miles to the north-west, an extremely distinguished gathering of nine men watched the identical programme. They sat at the superb round dark wooden table, glistening soberly from years of loving care and scrupulous polishing, which the hotel management had thoughtfully provided for this vital meeting in their magnificently furnished Iolanthe Private Room, beloved by Churchill for his wartime conclaves. There was place for fourteen of these blonde-pine chairs round this table, giving them a comfortable margin. The walls were a fine gold, and the floor carpeted in rich patterned reds and oranges and very dark blues. London's Savoy Hotel was adept at this kind of gathering. It had hundreds of years' experience of looking after crowned heads and lesser royalty and the world's great figures in politics, art, industry, commerce, the mass media. The Savoy had seen it all. It continued to gaze out imperturbably, one way at the great shopping and traffic artery of the Strand, and the other down over the Thames Embankment and the river, and across that at the South Bank complex of Royal Festival Hall and National and National Film Theatres and Hayward Gallery. Just to the right of that this side of Waterloo Station stood the high Tower Block of Shell Centre, one of the cores of that great international trader in the essential commodity under discussion in this elegant wide room today, that volatile yet indispensable lifeblood of every modern nation – oil, yet again in or near crisis. Well, the world would probably survive that, as it had survived all things so far. As the Savoy had survived. Cataclysms, wars, droughts, famines, even wartime rationing might come and they might go, but it seemed to go on forever, as unchangeable and inimitable as the famed Saddle of Lamb in its Grill. In a world shrill with disasters, the Savoy reassured, a bulwark of sanity and sound English breakfasts, its place probably as secure in British history as Canterbury Cathedral.

Not every one of those nine men who had come here for this 10 am meeting that morning had emulated that dignified calm. Some had arrived almost gibbering with excitement or strain. All the visitors to Britain had been constantly in contact with their embassies. All had heard the legion radio broadcasts about a terrible onslaught against Israel, by an unknown enemy, with an unknown but evidently lethal weapon – for the break in communications with Israel was total, arguing almost unimaginably high casualties. Later Radio Damascus had come across, to give the first but ominously detailed picture. The assault had been mounted shortly after first light by a Militant Islamic Group from the Kingdom of the Sun. They had used carbophenothion in the form of a very fine gas, fatal to the touch or if breathed. They had delivered it to every main city and town and armed forces centre and airfield, including those where Syrian Intelligence knew the Israelis had nuclear weapons stored. They gave a full description of the type of helicopters and small fixed-wing aircraft the attackers had used. Finally, Damascus said with relish, Syria had fully supported the assault, both morally and materially. It had been launched from Syrian soil. Its success appeared almost total.

The British Energy Secretary had rapidly become a near-expert in this horror. He had heard the first BBC radio broadcasts over his breakfast, and had got to the Savoy early, to field the many calls in from his visitors as to what news he had and whether the meeting was still on. He had reassured them that it was, and passed them his most magnetic news; the BBC would show a documentary film of the attack at 10.15 am. The Savoy had installed a TV for them in the Iolanthe Room.

So by 10 am the Energy Secretary had a full house of guests. As a much needed exercise in control (he felt that strongly), he got them to sit and, until the TV display, to discuss the critical theme which had brought them all here in the first place. The Secretary had opened the meeting by apologizing to Sheikh Ali el Khalifa el Sabah, as Kuwaiti Minister of Oil the doyen of those there, for bothering them this Friday, his first available day, since he knew of course that this was the Muslim day of rest. El Sabah had smiled his crisp dark face back at him a little sadly. 'I'm sure that Allah will forgive us for our diligence. Besides –' and he glanced round at the 24″ TV set – 'from what we're learning today, this gathering may prove to be concerned with a matter of life and death in more ways than one.'

As he had expected, the Energy Secretary found the arguments running along their usual ruts. The glut of oil was continuing. Only by sensible restriction of production could prices be kept up, in the interests of all concerned. The UK was the only major producer not concurring. They would produce what the market demanded. They had opted for absolutely free competition. Though admirable, this standing on principles was no longer practical. The UK was odd man out. She should join the club too.

The Secretary listened to them politely. Then, at 10.13 am, he said: 'Gentlemen, you may I fear find that, in a rather ghastly manner, the objective of your meeting may already have been achieved in part by the world's events today. You will now see the lethal nerve-gas attack on Israel which terrorists carried out by air after dawn today. You will see its impact on Dizengoff Street in Tel Aviv –'

The eight wise men tautened in their chairs, swinging them round when needed towards the set by the lavender-upholstered divan. The BBC announcer said, lucid and perfectly enunciated and unforgettable.

'These diagrams show how carbophenothion acts upon the human nervous system. It is manufactured as an organophosphorous insecticide, and as such is easily obtainable on the open market. It would appear that The Scimitar of the Sun had been buying it gradually, perhaps over several years, in many small lots so as not to provoke suspicion. Very heavily diluted, it is usually used to treat winter wheat seeds in order to control damage caused by the wheat bulb fly. In that role it is highly effective, although it has to be applied under strictly controlled conditions, and only to winter-sown wheat, never to spring wheat, where its residue – even so highly diluted – might be dangerous.

'The diagrams explain what happens when the concentrated liquid form of the chemical in which it is commercially available comes into contact with animal life. Carbophenothion is an organophosphorous compound, which means that it can function as a cholinesterase-inhibitor. It works on animals and humans exactly like the sarin nerve gas which the Germans invented during the Second World War. How do the body's muscles usually work? Electrochemical stimuli to motor nerves and muscles are set off by the chemical acetylcholine. The nerve fibres make that, and release it *here*, at the synapses, the ends of the nerve fibres. The adjacent end of the neighbouring nerve cell accepts it, and it is passed on to the muscle, to where the nerve and muscle meet. The message is delivered, the muscle contracts in response. But then the body has to *cancel* that message. So it makes exact amounts of the enzyme cholinesterase to do that, by breaking down the acetylcholine.

'Now, some substances can inhibit cholinesterase's action. The well-known poison curare is one. Organophosphorous insecticides and nerve gases are the others. The effect is that the muscles receive the order to contract *and no message to stop*! So they go into spasm. The muscles can stand that only for a short time. Then they relax totally. They are immobilized. The spasm causes convulsions in the victim, followed by paralysis, including that of the diaphram. The victim cannot breathe. He dies.

'How do you fatally deliver such a chemical? Sprayed from the air, as twenty years ago the Americans sprayed Agent Orange in Vietnam. The most effective way is ULV, Ultra Low Volume, by special pumps such as the Micronairs which the Scimitar of the Sun Group fitted to most of their helicopters and fixed-wing aircraft. They produce an absolutely lethal fine spray. The tiniest dose to a human being, inhaled, swallowed or merely placed on the bare skin will kill, painfully and very quickly.

'You are now about to see the effects of the ULV spraying of carbophenothion by the Scimitar of the Sun's aircraft early this morning on Dizengoff Street in Tel Aviv, just as people were going to their last day's work before the great Jewish fast and feast of Yom Kippur. This carefully – inhumanly – pre-meditated attack, whose degree of success is matched only by the totality of its horror, will probably have changed the entire balance of power in the Middle East. Perhaps in all the world. This is history in the making, in a malignant hideously painful form. Almost every world leader, including some Arabs, has already totally condemned it.'

The TV screen went completely white and silent for a few moments. In the Savoy's opulent Iolanthe Suite, Sheikh Ali El Khalifa el Sabah, chaste as a priest in his pure white dishdasha and *khutra*, looked round with staring black eyes at his eight companions, and said with deep shock in his voice:

'But this is the true *abomination*! We in my land would never countenance this! This is total cruelty! And political madness, which will set peace back in the Middle East for twenty or thirty years! Perhaps forever. For by this we could be now on the brink of World War III!'

Back in the Cabinet Room of the City of the Sun's Palace of Government, dominated by Ahmed Feisal in his olive-green battledress uniform and Field-Marshal's cross batons and black-holstered pistol, Philip Blake stared at the same blank white TV screen. He did not see the pitiless accuracy of that unintended symbolism until a minute later. For the shape of the agonizing death to come was of course white and silent. Then the whole TV frame came alive again, filled with the aggressive bustle and bursting colour, with the muscular angular Hebrew script above the shops and in the garish advertisements, of Tel Aviv's Dizengoff Street, one of the world's busiest commercial avenues.

The BBC cameraman who had died had done a vivid last job. There could be no doubt of the authenticity of his live sound; no one could have invented this cacophony. Cars rocketed about jauntily, the most popular being the Japanese Subarus. Israeli taxis with their green oval door-signs and eight-seater Mercedes-Benz *sheroots* competed lustily with them. A chunky blue Dan Tours bus bored an undeviating straight line through the lot of them. Shoppers shoved in and out of shops. Pedestrians marched purposefully along pavements, geared accurately to office opening hours under Dizengoff's sporadic bushy-topped trees. Mothers pushed beribboned babies in prams. Every walker waited for the lights to change at crossings, with a docility astounding in Israelis; the smartly uniformed and curvaceous policewomen would hit you on the spot with a fifty-shekel fine if you tried to cross against them. In short, here was the warp and woof of humanity, thrusting, voluble, gaudy and real.

The clatter of the Bell 206 Jetranger's rotar came identically with the sight of it as it flew along the length of Dizengoff towards the camera. It carried a short boom with the four tubular Micronairs fitted along it. At their fronts their fans whirred like delicate toy motors. They blew out fine pure white clouds unceasingly, like eternal and divinely swung censers in some heavenly church. Indeed, from that helicopter flying slowly just above roof-top level, that soft white swathe came down upon the street like a benediction, reaching everyone generously, even under the trees.

As such, it was oddly received. The whole picture suddenly went mad. It was like a puppet play on a stage that someone had abruptly yanked the master string from in a fit of bad temper. All at once the figures flung off totally uncoordinated in all directions, jerking their strawlike limbs. As if under a sudden evil spell, the long blue Dan bus swung completely to its right and charged straight across the street, bashing a careering Subaru on the way, half mounting it, then dragging it along to crash heavily into a kosher butcher's shop, penetrating it and exploding meat chops and gefüllte fish in all directions, and slamming finally to an inextricable stop with its blunt rear end still projecting, like a large hound stuck in a rabbit's hole. *Sheroots* seized the opportunity and sliced flatout into their lifelong trade rivals, the haughtier individual taxis. One copulating pair of Mercedes burst into flame and mounted the pavement to ram into the entrance of a glass and chronium-fronted office block. They burned sullenly. No one came out of them.

The dead cameraman's lens, catholic and democratic in its embrace, caught and immortalized the humbler pedestrians in their fate too. An elderly gentleman in close-up, smartly dressed in a light blue suit, and impressively hatted in a trilby, dived instantly into spasm, flung himself hooped forward into convulsion, as if under desperate fanatical command to do the toe-touching exercises he had weakly omitted before breakfast. But no sooner was he there, fallen now to the ground, than his muscles in spasm jerked him in cruel irony exactly the other way, his body whip-lashing and arching backwards, hurling his snappy trilby far off his head, snarling his lips wide open over irrevocably locked teeth, bulging his eyes, half-turned to the camera, into a dreadful fixed stare. That glazed. Everything relaxed, collapsed. He was dead. By him a young mother, screaming her discovery that the Apocalypse had come, grabbed forward at her prammed child to haul it free. As she straightened, that steel-sprung convulsion took her, jack-knifing her forward, so that she hurled her lace-edged baby downwards with terrible muscular force, braining it mercifully on the concrete. Like the trilbied elderly gentleman, she then obediently flung her whole body backwards in spasm, till she was arched rigidly in a swallow as sweet as any fine high diver's. And switched abruptly off, like a light; relaxed, collapsed, died.

The third close-up came right against the camera, the fingers of his left hand outstretched, as if they and his palm sought violently to block it off in human decency from this tragic sight of death and defeat. This was a slim and youngish man, blond and blue-eyed and thus unlike the supposed archetype of the Jew. He made up for that lack by the sheer ferocity of his defence; his people should at least be allowed to die there in peace, and privately, now that the fatal blow was irremediably struck. His mouth opened at the lens, his tongue whirred: '*Bekhaiyyái! Bekhaiyyái!* By my life! By my life!'

That was the last asset he had to swear by, and not for long. For the implacable gymnastic seized him too, arched him, hurled him convulsively forward, re-arched him like a strung bow, this time clenching the grotesque wide smile of his teeth rigidly down upon that tongue which had dared to protest, so that blood poured from his mouth as he collapsed and died. And all about him was terror, a world mad, evilly disjointed, a Goya scene of witches and witchery on a bald night mountain. So all fell and died, and the two *sheroots* burned in funeral pyre. Apart from the young mother's first scream, and the young blond man's By my life, there had been almost no human sound, save for grunts in the throat. Once locked in that deadly ballet, they could not scream out.

The BBC cameraman must have been a stoic, a dedicated professional. He had stood his ground as the frenzy jigged towards him, knowing that it must reach him too. And now it came. The picture blurred into a long lateral whirl, locked still again – focused, as it happened, on the cameraman's reflection in a shop window, tall in blue denim, only his cropped skull visible behind the camera, standing bolt upright, jerking in time with the harsh gasps picked up by the sound-track – then zoomed upwards, climbing the facade of the tall block above the shop, and jolted into final stillness, framing a square of sky.

The whole *danse macabre* had taken two minutes.

The TV screen remained focused on that pure blue sky, source of the soft white mist which had murdered the spectator along with all the dancers. Over it, the BBC announcer's Oxbridge accents said:

'One hundred and forty-nine of the five hundred aircraft that the Scimitar of the Sun sent in to the attack before first light this morning are reported to have regained their Syrian departure points. The Syrian authorities are at this moment giving them a heroes' welcome, an official parade through the streets of Damascus, where hundreds of thousands have gathered to acclaim them. We shall *not* be showing our viewers scenes of these celebrations . . . '

The Energy Secretary went over to the set and switched it off. As he sat down again, Hisham Nazer said to him, to all the room, to all the world:

'This is *not* how we choose to win our victories. This, as my colleague has said, is useless, and worse than useless. It is totally destructive. Because of it, we may now be at the end of the world. Of *a* world, at all events. Like this, the spirals of violence never end. It's a kind of Apocalypse.'

'Still,' said the Energy Secretary, 'it's as I said, isn't it? These events, whether we like them or not, have in effect largely achieved your objective for you?'

'How do you see that?' said Nazer narrowly, his clean-shaven chin pointing sceptically.

'Your objective has been to limit production so as to increase or at least stabilize oil prices. But *any* war in the Middle East must tend to force oil prices up. They always have in the past. And perhaps that is a further tragic irony in this barbaric act of mass murder – '

Two hours later Leila saw the same BBC programme relayed by Athens, as she sat in Blake's great high-ceilinged upstairs room on Hydra. She was horrified beyond words, and most of all when she learned that the authors of this second Holocaust came from the Kingdom of the Sun. Feisal's men, no doubt of it. But then where was Blake in this? Her family? Above all, her beloved brother, Abdullah?

In the almost equally blood-drenched Kingdom and City of the Sun, Ahmed Feisal used the remote-control switch to turn off his TV set.

'These were *your* men?' asked Abdullah, still standing.

'Of course,' said Feisal equably. 'Trained in this country, in the desert not far from our northern training camp. Your good friend Philip Blake here has even seen the airstrip. And had a flight in one of our helicopters – '

Abdullah looked round at Blake. Blake found it painful to meet his eyes.

'The Syrians helped too, of course,' said Feisal, being fair. 'They helped us assemble all the aircraft we shipped there, and gave us airfields and fuel. And helped store the carbo-phenothion which we gathered over the last four years. But all the planning came from here. The *inspiration*, you might say.'

'*Satanic* inspiration, I would say,' said Abdullah. 'This is the most diabolical act I have ever seen. You must be the Devil incarnate!'

Feisal's tiny and extraordinarily uniform small white teeth gleamed in a smile. He looked distinctly cheered at Abdullah's thought.

'Why not?' he replied. 'And I sold my soul to *Shaitaan* at the start of the deal? Again why not? It's perfectly logical. Unless someone was prepared to go to *literally any lengths*, we were never going to win Palestine back for its rightful Arab owners. Surely to God history has shown that? Were *you* here in your Kingdom of the Sun in your multi-billion-dollar comfort really ready to commit yourselves totally to achieve that aim? You paid only lip-service to that cause. Certainly, you permitted us to tax our Palestinian Arabs here, and to train our guerrillas in your deserts. You gave us some money, and you sent a small detachment of tanks to fight in the 1973 War, as a sop to your consciences. But that is all. In this we have done what no Arab nation has done.'

'Slaughtering your own Palestinian Arabs within Israel in the process?' asked Abdullah, mockingly.

Feisal shrugged.

'If they didn't listen to our message, yes. For we got the warning out most elaborately and extensively last evening, to all Arab communities in main centres – Eastern Jerusalem, Hebron, Nazareth, Bethlehem, Acre, the High Galil, everywhere – to get the hell out at once, leaving everything. Many hundred of thousands did, into Jordan, Lebanon, Syria through the Golan Heights, Egypt via the Sinai. If they didn't listen, that's too bad. People who won't face reality, who prefer to live fantasies, always suffer in the end.'

He looked somewhat pointedly from Abdullah to Blake.

'So the Syrians are in it with you,' said Abdullah.

'Yes. And about midday – in a mere hour or two – their forces will roll over the Golan into Israel. They'll meet very little opposition. We delivered our doses of carbophenothion to virtually every main Israeli army camp, military airfield and naval port. Their nuclear research centre at Dimona is a graveyard now. We naturally targeted it, as well as Lod International Airport and the main nerve-centre cities like Western Jerusalem, Tel Aviv and Haifa. Few Israelis are left capable of fighting. The Syrians will go in in protective clothing, and their main job will be simply to pull out the dead bodies and burn them or bury them in mass graves dug by bulldozers – '

'My God!' said Abdullah. 'It's another Holocaust! Will this heritage of killing never stop?'

Feisal shrugged again.

'We Palestinian Arabs have waited a very long time for our

revenge, Abdullah. You know the proverb that the Arab who complains when he has to wait forty years before he sees the body of his enemy being carried past his open tent-flap is showing a criminal impatience? Well, we've waited just on forty years, and, believe me, we savour this vengeance most richly.'

'If I could only tell the world outside about you!' said Abdullah.

Feisal looked at him levelly.

'Abdullah,' he said, 'you won't be going anywhere.'

'God damn you to hell!' said Abdullah. 'And what Devil's Cauldron have you left us with here?'

'A full Islamic State,' said Feisal. 'Which I shall head. The *Shari'a*, the full Islamic Law. We stand now, thus, with Iran. We are the first Arab purely Islamic State. The second will be our new Palestine, which I shall also lead. Now, with this long and deadly affront to our Arab dignity erased, others will join us, other Arab States in Islam.'

'You have fouled our Arab name for ever, worldwide,' said Abdullah.

Feisal smiled. 'On the contrary, our Islamic Fundamentalism will be honoured for having utterly destroyed your whole outmoded feudal Arab empire of oil, starting with your Kingdom of the Sun.'

'And to gain that honour,' said Abdullah, 'from what we saw in the courtyard below, you have murdered the Amir and the Crown Prince and all the members of the cabinet?'

'Also all hundred and thirty men of your officer corps,' said Feisal. 'We took a leaf out of Castro's book, when he deposed Batista in the Cuban civil war. Then, to get a clean slate, he lined up Batista's entire officer corps, and then shot them by firing squad. It's a great thing to start a new government clean, you know. Neat. That's one of the great advantages in using carbophenothion to retake Palestine, by the way. We don't even damage any buildings, as you inevitably do with conventional warfare, or nuclear. So we get our great Islamic monuments back intact – like the Aqsa Mosque in Jerusalem, the third most important shrine we have. And the Dome of the Rock. Not to speak of all the highly functional office buildings, flats and houses that the Israelis have built everywhere. We can just take them over too, as the Israelis, backed by their special legislation, occupied all the Arab dwellings left empty by our exodus in 1948. So we come full circle, see, Abdullah?'

'Where the hell did you get your aircraft?' said Abdullah. 'They and your carbophenothion and your flying training must have cost many millions. You couldn't have got that from your PLO taxes. I know how strictly you had to account to the PLO for those. And Arafat would never have let you use part of them for chemical warfare. That's not his style.'

'Your friend again there,' said Feisal with his ferrety smile. 'Philip Blake. He got a ten cents a barrel override from Tulsa and fed it to me. It was some twenty-six million dollars a year. We used that. You're right; Arafat knew nothing of it.'

Abdullah looked at Blake again. It did not seem likely that, given a free hand, Abdullah would be quite so enthusiastic about naming Blake as his substitute as the Kingdom's Oil Minister now.

'Abdullah!' Blake said desperately. 'It's true that I diverted money to Feisal. But exclusively for PLO-Fatah needs. Because I felt deeply sympathetic to the Palestinian Arab cause. And it cost the Kingdom nothing. You still got your full OPEC price from Tulsa. I had no idea at all that Feisal, striking off on his own, would use those funds for chemical warfare. Believe me!'

Abdullah observed him from his regal height of six foot three for some moments. Then he said, with an edge of contempt in his voice:

'These amateurs! These Western dabblers! They can sometimes do so much more damage than the professionals!'

'Perhaps,' said Feisal. 'He helped me. I won't forget that. Well, Sheikh Abdullah bin Ali bin Jibál, that's it. I thought you might like to have the full picture – '

'It's a courtesy,' said Abdullah. 'Before you take me out and shoot me as you shot the others.'

Feisal's piano-key-exact small white teeth fronted for him again.

'You know how it is. There's really no place for you now. One has to stay efficient.'

'Of course.'

They were like two leopards each straining to go for the other's throat.

'Colonel,' said Feisal.

'Yes?' said Salah Khalíl, ever present as an obedient shadow in the background, with his assistant and their battery of slick automatic weapons.

'Take him out and shoot him. As we did the others.'

'*For Christ's sake!*' shrieked Philip Blake. 'You want to kill *this* man? Who masterminded the whole massive infrastructure development for the poor and dispossessed here? Who gave them for the first time a dignity and identity, just as your goddamned Banna did in Egypt for the *fellahin*? This man has been your greatest *prophet*, your greatest practical everyday saint to bring the masses to a decent life, to true social justice, one of your highest ideals! Yet you want to kill *him*?'

The two others looked at him quite sympathetically, as if at a harmless lunatic. Of the two, Feisal had the least tolerance.

'Colonel,' he said, 'get on with it!'

' *Hather. Effendim.*'

It was at this point that Blake flung himself bodily at Feisal, grasping for the pistol in the holster, and Khalíl slashed him effectively across the back of his skull with his gun muzzle.

The room where he woke was small and locked, he guessed near Feisal's throne-room. His head ached outrageously. He went to the window. It looked down on the courtyard. There was a new bundle of flesh by the gallows, rather a long one. The light breeze rippled its white and bloodstained dishdasha, and those which held the other former members of the cabinet by him. Blake's heroic lunge at Feisal had achieved nothing at all.

A key turned in the small room's lock and Khalíl's aide came in, his AK-47 eloquent, No one had to say a thing. He took Philip back to Feisal. Another stood before him, heavy-shouldered, bull-necked; Horace B. Murgatroyd.

'I thought it would save time if I saw you both together,' said Ahmed Feisal. 'Well. We don't have to waste time on the preliminaries. You've both learned exactly how things stand. I've taken power completely here. Much more vital, we have destroyed Zionism in Palestine, and all but recovered our land for our people; the Syrians will be there in an hour to make the final clean-out. I shall then be President of *both* these Arab States, and both will be pure Islamic States. And our huge success now, after years of failure, will pull other Arab States inexorably to our Islamic fold.

'But what of the three of us here in this room? Old friends for many years now. And without you two I could never have succeeded. You, Horace, because had you approved the Establishment's request for your formation and training and full equipment of a totally modern paramilitary anti-terrorist force, I could never have made the utterly successful takeover I made this morning.

'And you, Philip Blake, perhaps the warmest personal friend I have ever had. Without the funds you diverted to be from the Tulsa contract, I could never have bought the aircraft we needed for our chemical warfare strike, nor trained their pilots, nor backed the research of the best chemists we could hire in the States to find the best agent with which finally to liquidate our Zionist foes, and which turned out to be, in highly concentrated form, an organophosphorous insecticide which almost anyone can buy. That, literally, has paralysed and killed our mortal enemies, and won us final victory.'

He's going now to announce some highest honour to Horace, thought Blake, and for me some éminence grise and incredibly powerful post in his new government, or governments. Which I reject.

Blake did not need to have concerned himself.

'I owe you both rewards,' said Feisal, with engaging frankness. 'And here mine is. I have shorn myself totally of anyone connected with this giant endeavour who has not been of my own armed forces. Liquidated them all. The Amir, Crown Prince, Abdullah and the rest of the cabinet. The entire one hundred and thirty men of the officer corps. But how could I decently have done the same to you? Of course, with my historic tasks, I cannot afford to have encumbrances impeding me. But how could I possibly wipe the two of you out too, after all you'd done for me, for my people. *Could* I, now? In all humanity? Though you *did* know too much!'

He sounded really pitious. He wanted their mature help. He needed their astute considered judgement.

'My God!' said Blake, appalled. 'That's all the recognition you'd give us? To save our *lives*?'

Feisal looked back at him with open contempt. 'What else do you want? Power? Money? Yet I've never done this for my material reward, but purely for the ideal. If you've not seen that you're a fool. I thought you more like me.'

'Sounds kinda right to me,' said Horace heavily, but quickly. 'Not to knock us off. I see what you mean. After what we've done.'

'That's exactly it!' Feisal exclaimed. 'I mean, what I feel morally. Practically, there would be problems too, of course. Particularly with you, Horace. I mean, an American Ambassador, after all. We'd have had to rig up some sort of accident. That can be tricky.'

'You have a good point there,' said Horace.

'But you can always beat these mere material things,' said Feisal largely. 'It's the *moral* side that really matters.'

'That's for sure,' said Horace.

'So I thought none of this liquidation for you two,' said Feisal grandly. 'No, none of that. I wouldn't take your lives. Instead, I'd give you twenty-four hours to quit the country.'

'Christ!' said Horace B. Murgatroyd. 'That's mighty generous of you, Mr President.'

Feisal nodded. 'I always like to be scrupulously fair,' he said.

'Sure,' said Horace. 'It's a credit to you. Field Marshal.'

Walking down the stairs past the slaughtered Cabinet, Horace asked. 'Like a lift?'

'Yes, I would,' said Blake. His head hurt.

They walked on to Horace's Cadillac.

'Kinda quick,' said Horace. 'Twenty-four hours. You got much packing?'

'Not so much,' said Blake. He half-turned to Horace. 'Can't we *stop* him somehow? Can't *you*? Can't the US?'

'Like how?' asked Horace. 'It's a fait accompli. He's a sovereign power already. *Two* sovereign powers! So we invade him? And get the whole damned Arab world at our throats again? No Sirree!'

Blake said nothing.

'So where do they send me next?' said Horace, resilient as an old saddle. 'After all, we still have enough money to live, right? And our health, haven't we? That's something!'

'Yes.'

'More than friend Abdullah has as of now. Poor bastard!'

'Yes, it's more than Abdullah has now.'

'I saw them shooting him while they brought me in across the courtyard, you know. I don't know if he saw *me*, mind. I think so. He *could* have. He refused the hood over his head. Just looked right at them. Listen, I never liked that guy's fancy British accent, you know that. But you have to admit that he surely had his guts.'

'He surely did.'

This spurious wake seemed to Blake so inane and inadequate, this whole anticlimax so mad and sad, that he knew that only a deep and agonizingly powerful belly-laugh could do it justice. Blake could not dig deep enough for that. He was weeping soundlessly as he walked.

'I helped cause that death,' he said. '*Those* deaths.'

And they were not the only deaths. His long and lovely love affair with Leila had just died too. After the killing of her brother, for which he was at least partly responsible, she would never take him back.

He felt Horace go into his rhino stance and swivel his slate-grey piggy eyes sideways at him without moving that formidable block of a close-cropped head on its squat neck and armoured shoulders.

'We both helped cause those deaths,' said Horace. 'That's what Feisal said. We made it all possible. I can't say that I knew what the hell it was all about before today, though.'

'No,' said Blake. He still wept mutely, like a window-pane minding its own business in the rain.

'It's a tough world,' said Horace. 'You just have to learn to roll with the punches. We both know that.'

'Fair enough,' said Blake.

'Right,' said Horace reasonably. 'After all, you can't strike oil every time, now can you?'

'No,' said Philip Blake.

'No,' said Horace. 'And I mean, even a wildcatter has to expect to kill a friend or two on his rigs some time, not so? That's the way it goes. Look on the bright side, okay?'

'Well,' said Blake.

'Sure,' said Horace. 'You just write it off to the overheads. You can't win them all.'